I0607609

LOVE BEAT

FLORA DAIN

Love Beat
ISBN # 978-1-78430-859-9
©Copyright Flora Dain 2015
Cover Art by Posh Gosh ©Copyright November 2015
Interior text design by Claire Siemaszkiewicz
Totally Bound Publishing

Published in 2015 by Totally Bound Publishing, Newland House, The Point, Weaver Road, Lincoln, LN6 3QN, United Kingdom.

Totally Bound Publishing is a subsidiary of Totally Entwined Group Limited.

LOVE BEAT

Dedication

To Coco, for all her help

Chapter One

"You want this?" His voice purrs close to my ear, part thrill and part threat.

Yes. Yes. You know I want it.

I can feel the heat from his powerful body at my back. A trickle of sweat starts under the blindfold, runs down my cheek and lands on one taut, exposed breast.

I nod.

"You're sure?"

Frantic, I nod again, jangling the chains that haul at my arms.

"How sure?"

I mewl helplessly against the gag as his breath burns into my shoulder. His deep murmur ripples through me as he runs a finger along the top of my thigh.

His lips hover close to my neck, fierce and hot. His hand circles my waist and slides softly over my hip and down my belly, infinitely gentle.

I grow still as he caresses my flank. His touch sparks tiny flames over my skin as his finger edges closer to the open peak of my splayed thighs.

The whip slithers over my skin, the snaking leather rough against the softness of my inner leg. I whimper as it trails *upward making me quiver, making me pulse, making me plead in silent despair.* Once more. Please, please, just once more...

My eyes open with a snap. The dream's tormented me all year but only ever at night. Now it's daytime.

My headphones crackle with sound. It cuts through the hum of the engine that lulled me into a doze. "And here we are, ladies and gentlemen. The Love Beat Corporation welcomes you to Beat Hall, your home for the next two weeks and the lavish setting for our themed media event where you'll meet and greet the stars, enjoy our unusual hospitality and taste some of the darker pleasures featured in our forthcoming movie. Enjoy your stay."

I shift in my seat as the pilot draws our attention to the lavish fairways, the extensive woods and the secluded parkland opening up beneath us in this large, privately owned chunk of Devon coastline. But the noise and the fabulous view seem tinny and unreal compared to the deep undertow of my dream. That voice, *his* voice, still pulses through me, making me wait, making me ache...

"Hey, Tunis, see that private jet over there? Do you think that's *him*?"

Mel, my co-presenter, taps my shoulder. She's leaning forward, her sharp eyes bright and alert.

He's here already? I feel a wave of panic.

Her eyes narrow. "Yep, that's the Love Beat logo. Wow, look at those suits. How many people does it take to feed the ego of a multi-millionaire? Hey, I might use that. Think I could slip it in at the end of an interview?"

"You wouldn't dare." I grin back, still shaky.

Mel Macallan is from Glasgow and proud of it. She loves a swipe at the super rich. In interviews her wit draws them in then her pale stare dazes them just long enough to put in a killer question.

Even Cade Fitzlean, CEO of the mighty Love Beat Corporation, might find her a tough nut.

Sooner her than me.

Ben, our producer, has a thing for Mel. He'll be only too pleased if I let her interview Cade Fitzlean. I make it a rule never to turn down work — we all do — but for him, I'll make an exception.

I'm the new one who asks the innocent questions, gets them talking. Sometimes that works too. I have my uses. We work well together.

While we're here, we'll have to. This is a tough assignment.

As we land, a rush of wind ruffles the branches around the clearing. I take off my headphones with a sigh. Dream time's over. From now on through the next two weeks we'll be hard at work here.

Within minutes we're clambering out of the helicopter and into the sunshine to shake hands with the pilot. In the soft, bright Devon air my demons fade.

The people around me are like family — Mel, with her craving to get into news, Ben Tyne-Follett, our producer, with his cut-glass accent, laid-back manner and a keen eye for a program opportunity, and Jake Simmons, whom I've known forever — floppy-haired, good-looking and an outstanding cameraman.

I owe him a lot. He got me this job. I used to think of him as an older brother until one evening when I found out he had other ideas, but no means no.

At least we're still friends.

"Are the others here yet?" I'm worried now.

So is Ben. He's muttering into his phone — a bad sign. The recording van with all our precious equipment and most of our luggage is coming by road.

At last he slips the phone into his pocket, his manner breezy. "It's okay. Hold-up on the M3, ETA one hour. Wow, this the welcoming committee? Big guns or what?"

I feel a lump in my throat. This is it.

And it's all because of *me*.

We're guests of the massive Love Beat Corporation with exclusive access to the cast and the production team of the new BDSM-themed movie, *Hit'n'MissTrix*, based on a recent bestselling book.

The movie's already in the can and out in a few weeks. We're here for the top-secret pre-launch party — invitation only, strict security. But, strictly speaking, we're not here to play. We're here to work. We're making a TV report on the party to air just before the premiere.

This place, once home to dukes, now hosts open-air concerts and an annual rock festival, so it's perfect for filming. While we're here, we'll mingle with visiting celebs, the stars of the movie and the super-rich, get five-star treatment and even red-carpet entry to the premiere. The whole bit.

But our report's got to be discreet enough — and *wholesome* enough — to soften up the movie launch, bearing in mind that most of the stars here will have to be shot in shadow, off camera, their voices disguised. It'll be a guessing game for the fans and a nightmare to edit. Plus they'll *freak* if we reveal too much.

It's a dream ticket but it'll be a close call. Headaches all around.

On the plus side, if it comes off, it'll be a terrific scoop. BDSM's still off limits, and the company hopes any fun spin we can put on it will soften the image, make it more acceptable.

And to make the TV doc, who better than Ben and his team, led by me, Tunis Vale, now a budding presenter, and—get this—the very person who destroyed the original launch? Perfect.

We're all really excited.

Correction—*they're* all really excited. I'm plain scared.

We walk across the tarmac, a vast golf course to one side of us, lush woodland to the other. Beyond loom the towers and pinnacles of the mansion. I feel small.

The others chatter happily. Their voices rise and fall on the breeze from the sea. I shiver.

Ahead of us a gleaming private jet crouches in the sunlight like a great white insect. Before it, a small group is waiting to meet us. Four are uniformed crew members with small enameled bows pinned to their lapels. There's a slim, neatly suited blonde with a notebook and a stony expression—I'm guessing a PA—and a chunky individual who has to be a bodyguard.

Next to him stands a sulky woman in tight black leather. She's got black hair and a slash of crimson lipstick for a mouth. A diamond-studded buckle at her waist spells *Nera*.

A Dominatrix.

Ben gasps and I see Mel's eyes narrow. Nera's a marked woman.

And standing in the center is Cade Fitzlean.

For an instant, the world stands still.

I did my research—not that he left much to find. Rich men cover their tracks. I found traces of a patchy past and some colorful connections. I even found photos.

They're nothing like the real thing.

Good-looking doesn't come close. This can't be a CEO. He looks too young, too mean—a sulky angel pushed into an Armani advert, all sculpted mouth and high cheekbones. And his eyes—dark, intense, burning into me like I'm wax.

And looking like he wishes I were somewhere else.

Me too.

In truth, we're all out of our comfort zone here. Ben misses his support team, his assistants and his rookies. Here he's on his own. Mel likes a constant stream of data and coffee. Jake likes an art director, lighting director, technicians and his camera firmly mounted on a tracking dolly. Here he's reduced to his beloved antique handheld.

And I've got Cade Fitzlean—but not for long. According to our notes, he's flying back to the States after lunch. And it's not really him that scares me. It's what he represents.

All at once I'm back on the rain-drenched sidewalk outside that scary private club a year ago, that terrible night when the bearers carried the woman on the stretcher right past me and the blanket slipped, revealing the bondage harness and the cruel spiked cuffs.

Later, the CEO issued a statement taking full responsibility, regretting the incident and attempting to reassure the public. The statement was signed Cade Fitzlean.

But we've never met.

Until now.

I clench my teeth. Now I'm different.

Back then I was a rookie runner on my first day, thrust in front of the cameras for the very first time. Now I'm a seasoned presenter, and I've got a job to do.

As we draw near, the blonde is murmuring at his shoulder, "And this is Tunis Vale, the presenter who will be—"

"I know." He steps forward and takes my hand. "Miss Vale. We meet at last."

He seems friendly. His hand's warm. I blink and remind myself that this man hates me.

I murmur something vague in greeting, but Ben's already crowding my elbow. I try to take my hand away but Fitzlean holds it fast.

His sudden glint of humor startles me into a smile. For a long moment we're alone, sharing some mysterious private joke, his touch sending urgent signals up my arm. At last he releases my hand and I step aside for Ben to push in.

"Mr. Fitzlean? Thank you so much for this opportunity to see you and your company at work."

To my relief, Ben gushes on for some time and I get a chance to recover while the others crowd round to meet him.

Fitzlean's easy, casual. He takes the trouble to say a few words to everybody but I sense tension in the air.

When he greets Mel, his eyes narrow slightly. Jake openly avoids his handshake, gesturing to his camera in excuse.

The PA touches Jake's arm. "Please stop filming, Mr. Simmons. I did warn your producer. We have to check all film in case of anything...commercially sensitive."

Jake glares down at her and lowers his camera with a scowl. "*Sensitive*? What? Here?"

It's an awkward moment. The PA recovers first and coolly ushers us into the great house, Fitzlean at her side.

I follow, lightheaded with relief. The worst is over. Meeting him was my biggest fear. It brings back that awful night in all its stomach-churning horror. Now I'm ready for anything.

Why did I react so violently that night? It could have been a lot of things. It was my first long, bewildering day out on location with the team and my first live encounter with the scary world of BDSM. I'd been as jumpy as a cat all day. I'd had hardly anything to eat. I'd been too busy.

The day I joined the team, they were putting together a report on the launch of a chain of *outré* private clubs under the Love Beat logo. Mel's heel caught on a paving stone and she sprained her ankle just before we went live.

Ben turned to me with a grin. "Ok, Tunis, here's your chance. Smile to camera, listen to what I tell you and, for fuck's sake, keep talking."

I stared at him, horrified. "What? *Me?*"

He thrust the mic into my hands and stepped aside for someone to tidy my hair while a technician fixed something behind my ear.

Through it Ben's panicky instruction hissed in my head. "Sure. *Now.* We're on air in two. *Go-go-go.*"

And I started talking. I trained with the ballet and I guess some instinctive sense of performance suddenly kicked in. From somewhere words came. I pretended I was talking to a friend. I explained what little I knew about the launch. To wind up I winked, playful. "So is bondage the new chic? Fetish the new normal? All bets are on, folks. We could be looking at a whole new — "

I broke off aghast as the stretcher appeared and the meaning of the flashing blue lights and the police cars sank in.

This was real.

"There's a Dom behind you. Ask him something." Once more Ben's nasal drawl hissed in my ear but all I could do was stare at the unconscious girl on the stretcher.

What had they done to her?

I had to keep talking. Obediently I spun round to find myself looking up into the glittering eyes of a dark, sinister figure, his face covered in a hood. He was naked to the waist, his powerful muscles gleaming in the flashing lights. His chest hair glittered with beads of rain.

I froze and everything slid sideways. As the wet pavement rose up to meet me, I felt strong hands catch me round the waist and heard a rich, deep voice close to my ear. "She's ill. Should she even be here?"

Then I threw up and everything went black.

I found out later he was a celebrity professional Dom known only as the Panther. And from that moment on, his hooded, muscled figure and his deep, stirring voice prowl my dreams, constantly replaying my fantasies of what he did to that girl to make her pass out and *what it must have felt like.*

And to my eternal shame, the dreams are deeply, gut-wrenchingly *hot...*

My one big chance and I blew it.

But then things happened fast.

Days later I was already looking for another job when out of the blue I became a runaway hit. Somehow my reaction clicked with the public and went viral.

It sparked a backlash. The launch of the Love Beat Corporation's private clubs was canceled and plans for the movie release put on hold. The Panther vanished. Even Fitzlean left the country.

Jake's unforgiving camera caught it all. It turned Love Beat, the Panther and everything they stand for into monsters.

But against all the odds, it made me a star.

And that's why he hates me.

As the others make their way into the vast luxury of Beat Hall, I trail behind. I'm sharing with Mel on the second floor. Our sumptuous room is all thick carpet and marble en suite, and it sends her into raptures.

As she hurls herself back onto the four-poster and sprawls across the crimson damask she grins up at me. "I could get used to this. Do you mind sharing, Tunis?"

I roll my eyes as I unpack and stow the few things I've brought onto jangling hangers. "I'm fine. I doubt we'll see much of each other anyway. There's too much to do."

Documentaries are hard work, especially on location. With security so tight here it's just us — no support team to advise, keep notes, fetch, carry or edit. The edit will be done back in London after we've finished filming so no chance of retakes. We'll need plenty of film to cut down to an acceptable length, and there are all the interviews to fit in.

Celebrities and their agents are picky about camera angles and lighting and with a topic like this we'll be treading on eggshells.

This is no holiday, more a marathon.

Mel senses my unease. "Hey, lighten up. It's a party. Think Halloween with whips. And look at these goodies." She's sorting through the gift basket and tips it out on the bed. "Not just shower gel... We've got condoms, blindfolds, three sorts of lube — and *nipple clamps*! Check out the kinky costumes. And look — invitations to receptions, a ball, the spa, salon treatments, swimming pools — *Oh.*"

I look up. "What's the matter?"

She's staring at two black cards, heavily embossed in silver. Each one has a whip-crossed heart etched at the top, the Love Beat logo.

She looks up with shining eyes. "We even get free S&M taster training. We fill them in, choose Dom or sub, and hand them in at reception. Ben and I are both training with Nera first thing tomorrow. Hey, you're listed too. You're with... Wow, look at this."

Her eyes widen with a glint of mischief. "You're booked in with the Panther, no less." She turns her pale eyes full on me. "And you know his specialty? I heard it's—"

"The bullwhip," I break in quickly. "I heard that too."

The Panther...*here*? My stomach shrivels.

I snatch the card out of Mel's hand, rip it in two and hurl it into the wastepaper basket. "And that's where he can put it. Lunch?"

* * * *

Lunch is more a glittering reception, all champagne and canapés. Stars and publicity people mingle with producers and moneymen—glamor and business, hard at work.

Cade Fitzlean is at the far end of the room, surrounded. As we walk in, he glances across and our eyes meet. Instantly he detaches himself from the group he's with and walks over.

I swallow.

"Tunis. Hello again. I suppose you'd like an interview."

I stare at him in panic. *No, no, ask Mel.* "Um, yes, thank you. If you can fit it in."

A glint of amusement flickers across his face. "If I can *fit it in*?"

Whoa. A faint lift of his eyebrow warns me not to go there but hints it might be fun if I do. Now I flounder.

17

"I mean—you have a tight schedule, Mr. Fitzlean. Your PA—"

The chilly blonde appears at his side but his eyes stay locked on mine. "Sonja, can I make time for an interview?"

She eyes me frostily. "Mr. Fitzlean flies out at three. There's no time—"

"Fine. We'll do it now." His gaze continues to hold mine. We might be alone in the room.

"I... Thank you. Yes. Now." My mind goes blank. Rescue comes as the team eagerly pushes forward.

Unexpectedly Fitzlean smiles around at them. "Interview, guys? Fire away."

Instantly they gather round while Jake's camera whirrs in the background. I try to compose myself while Ben snaps out questions from somewhere behind me.

I soon recover. "How did you come to write *Love Beat?*"

The jaunty single he wrote as a teenager was an instant hit and founded his fortune. It still earns him royalties.

Fitzlean grins. "Jotted it down after a chemistry exam. Took about ten minutes. Then a family friend offered to produce it. Took him three months. Worth every second."

"And the exam?" I smile at a sudden and rather appealing image of a sulky, beautiful teenager.

His eyebrow arches in surprise. *Am I the first person to ask him about chemistry?*

"I got an A."

"Are you dating anyone at present?" Ben takes a big risk. We were warned off his private life.

Fitzlean's expression chills. "Not at the moment."

"So—what gives you pleasure, Mr. Fitzlean?" I ask quietly.

Where did that come from?

He turns his gaze full on me and once more the earth spins away. "Watching business deals come together. Watching women come apart."

The others pitch in with a few final questions while I fall silent. He's good. I've done enough interviews to appreciate real skill when I see it.

After a moment he glances at his watch, murmurs something to his PA and strolls casually out of the room.

Sonja lingers, fixing me with her chilly blue stare. "Mr. Fitzlean would like to see you in his office for a few moments, Miss Vale."

Me? Why?

The others stare after me as I follow her out of the room.

Chapter Two

Cade Fitzlean's office gives few clues to his character. I'm in a lofty, elegant room, with tall windows, sparse but ornate pieces of furniture, priceless paintings and a striking central display of modern photos.

It's more imposing than I expected but somehow less personal.

He's standing over by the window and looks stunning. A shaft of sunlight slants across his face, etching shadows under his cheekbones and down one side of his jaw. He sweeps me with a practiced glance.

"Tunis. Thank you for giving me a few moments. I know your time's precious."

Mine *precious*? He's serious? He's got an empire to run.

As if his looks weren't enough, even his courtesy is alluring—and so is something else. Now that we're alone, I sense an air of power. It fills the room and surrounds him like a force field.

It's very disturbing.

"Please, take a seat."

I perch on one of a pair of low sofas near the window. He sits opposite, crossing his legs with one ankle over his knee, clearly at ease.

I draw my legs together at an angle in a dancer's natural pose. I aim for grace but feel prim. "Is there a problem, Mr. Fitzlean?"

"That depends. Is everything to your liking? Your room — and so on?"

Is that all? Relief floods through me. Foolishly I start to gush. "I have to agree with Ben. This is a terrific opportunity for us. And the rooms are spectacular. We can't thank you enough..."

I trail off under his steady gaze as he takes two jagged pieces of card out of his pocket and spreads them out on the low table between us.

I stiffen. *My training schedule...* An hour ago I hurled it into the wastepaper basket. How has he found it so fast? Does he have spies everywhere?

"I gather you plan to skip the training. Can I ask why?"

"Is it urgent, then?"

"It's part of your contract. Nera needs returns quickly. The sessions are individually tailored and she has to finalize dungeon bookings by the end of the day."

My insides shrink. "I thought it was just for fun. Do I have to?"

He frowns — a sulky angel cheated of a soul. "You're down for sessions with the Panther, our guest celebrity Dom. We're lucky to get him. We thought you'd be pleased."

My face starts to burn.

His flickers with irritation. "Setting aside the insult to his reputation and your ill-concealed contempt for our hospitality, I have to ask myself just how committed you are to this project."

I open my mouth to protest but he cuts me short. "Would you sooner leave?"

My stomach clenches. "If it's all the same to you, I'd sooner not do it with the Panther." That's putting it mildly. And I wish he'd stop looking at me like that.

This is complicated.

I crave this. I even *dream* about it. I should be thrilled. But somehow, faced with the reality of it, I'm terrified. Submission? Bullwhips? I should run a mile. So would anyone normal.

I make words flow for my living. I can talk without drawing breath on pretty well any topic you care to name in front of millions of people. Now no words come.

I try again. "I know it's only fun, a form of sex play."

His lips twitch.

I go on quickly, my words spilling out in a rush. "But to me it feels more important than that. And... Well — *private*. This all seems so...flippant."

He looks interested. "That's very touching." His low murmur flows over me like velvet. "I think so too. So that's easy. You can switch to Nera. She's good with vanillas. You'll be in safe hands with her."

I avoid his eye and carefully smooth the hem of my skirt where it skims my knee.

"What?"

"It's just... I'd sooner it was with a man."

He shrugs, unconcerned. "Most practitioners are female nowadays."

I frown as something snags in my brain. What did he mean — *he thinks so too*? Does *he* do this?

Somebody once said to me that it's easy to be a TV presenter. You just open your mouth and words come out.

Gee, thanks, Dad. But I know what he meant. I do it now.

"I read somewhere that you're a fully trained professional Dom."

It's totally untrue. I'm making it up. But the effect on him is electric.

For a few seconds he sits very still.

I wait for him to smile and lightly deny it. Nothing happens.

Bingo.

I take a split-second decision. "Forgive me for asking, but could *you* do it? My training?"

His eyes glimmer. "Me?"

What have I said? All at once words tumble out. "I know it's a crazy request. I know you're leaving soon. It's just... I get these dreams, and—" I break off, appalled at myself.

"*Dreams?*"

I swallow. "*Him.*" I can't even bring myself to say his name. "That man and a—whip. Ever since meeting him like that last year. It was such a shock. And I can't face him yet. It's too soon." A fleeting image of gleaming, oiled biceps and glittering, hooded eyes shrivels my stomach.

At the same time it sends a shaft of heat straight to my groin.

I press my lips together, furious that he's grinning.

"Maybe you should see a shrink—or simply talk to Nera. She'll take you through it step by step."

I fix my eyes on his face in one last, desperate appeal. "I'd feel safer with you. I feel I know you."

The grin fades, and I sense a sudden wave of anger.

"*Know me*? You know nothing about me." He rises abruptly and walks over to the window. He stands, looking out with his arms folded. "Seriously, don't you think that's a tad offensive—sexist even? Suppose I asked you such a thing? Strip for me, maybe, or give me a blow job—because I felt I *knew* you?"

I stare at him aghast, my cheeks burning. "I'm so sorry. It's just... I can't stop thinking about it. It's...confusing."

But he's absolutely right. What was I thinking? I get up and walk quickly to the door, fighting for calm.

Okay, that was stupid. Now move on.

At the door I glance back. "Please forgive what I said just now. I'm new to all this. I'll talk to Nera. But on behalf of the team, we're truly grateful for the faith you've shown in us. We're determined to make this a success. Have a safe trip."

I slip outside, close the door more firmly than I intended and let out a long, juddering breath. The ice-maiden is hovering just outside. Over her notepad, her pretty face is a mask of disapproval.

I grimace back. "He's all yours." *And you can have him.*

This is a disaster. I'm throwing away our dream ticket before we've even begun.

Why am I so rattled? It must be this place. Everything about it is disturbing. I should never have come.

I hurry away, trying to ignore the stinging feeling behind my eyes.

It's hard to take. Knocks are always hard. A rejected audition, a mistimed arabesque or even a spurned invitation to play kinky sex—they always hurt.

I've been a dancer. I know all about knocks.

Ginger Rogers had the only answer—pick yourself up. Start over.

So I do.

I find the others out on the terrace sprawling on sun loungers. Mel's stripped down to a T-shirt and briefs, her face covered by a large sun hat. Ben and Jake are blatantly feasting in a very un-PC way on the celebrity eye candy parading by the pool.

"Hard at work, everybody?" My tone drips acid as I pull up a canvas chair and throw myself into it.

Ben groans. "Don't rain on the parade, Tunis. We were, as a matter of fact. How was the job interview?"

I glare back. "The *what*?"

Ben yawns. "He wanted to see you alone in his office, didn't he? What else was it for? Or was the job on offer unrepeatable in polite company?"

Still rattled, I blush. "Ben, please."

The others look uneasy. A passing waiter offers a tempting tray of misted mint juleps. I take one gratefully and pass another to Mel. It disappears under her hat as she takes a long sip.

Jake fixes me with a scowl. "So what *did* he want?"

I sigh. "He's having second thoughts about me doing this. I gather I'm insufficiently dazzled by his halo."

Ben frowns. "That's odd. He was pretty keen when he offered us the deal."

"For fuck's sake, Ben." Jake sits up with a scowl.

There's an awkward pause. I look from one to the other. "What's that supposed to mean?"

"Nothing. It's the champagne talking. Ignore him." Jake looks sulky.

I hold my ground. "Something's going on. Tell me."

"He means you were the deal-breaker." Mel's sharp voice makes us all jump.

"Shut up, Mel." Ben kicks her ankle.

Mel kicks him back then stretches lazily. "Why don't you tell her everything? Tunis is the main reason we're here. She's got every right to know." She swivels to peer up at me, shading her eyes against the sun. "When his company offered us the chance to come here and film, it was on one condition — that you were the anchor. And when Ben asked why, all they'd say was the order came from the top."

* * * *

After another hour or so chasing agents round the pool and securing interview slots with celebs, I decide to slip away for a shower. It's getting late now. Time to change for the evening. And tonight we'll use the first of our embossed invitations — to the *Hit'n'MissTrix* Ball.

On the way up to our room I pause at a window to look out over the emerald sheen of the immaculate lawns, now streaked with late sunlight.

In the center of the lawn Cade Fitzlean and Miss Frosty are chatting to a couple of groundsmen.

I stand very still. *He's still here? I thought he was leaving?*

As I watch, Fitzlean claps one of the men on the back. I hear a gust of laughter then he and his PA turn and walk slowly back toward me.

He moves with fluid grace, talking earnestly. His PA is pale and slim, the breeze ruffling her silky hair. When her heels catch in the turf he pauses, smiles and waits for her to catch up.

They look easy together. She's very pretty.

I frown. His relations with his staff are no business of mine.

I warn myself sternly I should look away. Now.

Too late. He looks up and our eyes meet.

I step quickly away from the window, cross with myself. Now he's even caught me spying on him. *Can today get any worse?*

Right on cue it does. I feel a touch on my arm. Nera is standing at my elbow, the sunlight glancing off her glossy black hair and her hard, pale face.

"Tunis? May I call you that? We've just moved your things to another room. I'll take you up there now. On the way, we'll discuss your options for the week."

It's the last straw and I snap. "Why the move? Mel and I don't mind sharing."

As the elevator doors slide shut, Nera and I glare at each other. After a few seconds she manages a chilly smile. "Feel free to make use of our spa and beauty salon while you're here. We're very proud of our visiting stylists. You'll find them a far cry from the high street."

"Thanks, but I rarely visit the high street and I have my own stylist." My tone slices ice. I regret it instantly. It's her job to look scary and now she's offended. My heart sinks.

One more point against this place. "Anyway, why the upgrade?"

Now I sound rude. This is a private, if ultra-stately home, not a hotel. We're guests here.

The Dominatrix chooses to ignore my putdown as she shows me into a spacious apartment overlooking the park. "We hope you'll be comfortable here, Miss Vale. You've got the usual gift set" – she waves toward a basket brimming with lubes, condoms and naughty trinkets – "plus a few extras. You'll find costumes and some eveningwear in your dressing room. Your own things are already here. Ring if there's anything you need. I'll leave you to settle in."

"Wait. What about the others? Are they upgraded too?"

Her arched eyebrow tilts a fraction. "You'd better ask them. I never discuss other guests."

She steps back into the elevator. The doors close with a soft hiss, just as I remember I've forgotten to ask her about my training.

I'll do it later.

Left alone I explore. The suite's huge, the furniture elegant. The walls are covered with antique mirrors and works of art. The bedroom seems vast, the windows veiled in floating gauze. It has its own bathroom tiled with marble.

I find a separate dressing room with my clothes already stowed neatly on a rail.

On another rail hang the costumes. I flip through them, heart sinking.

Two or three elegant, full-length satin gowns look modest enough at first glance, but the necklines plunge to the waist and the slim, clinging skirts are slit to the hip. Near them a leather harness sports a jeweled slave collar. The same hanger holds a sleep mask and a vicious-looking leather riding crop.

At the end of the rail is an assortment of flimsy lace-edged lingerie, including a peekaboo bra and half a dozen thongs, designer labels still attached.

Beyond them are three lace-trimmed satin corsets, complete with suspenders, and below, in polished mahogany racks, expensive-looking shoes in matching colors, some glittering with brilliants.

In spite of myself I feel a quiver of excitement. I touch the scarlet lace trim on one of the corsets. It's made of silk and is whisper-soft.

These are no shoddy stage costumes. They're the real thing, *deluxe* designer. A small fortune's been spent here.

But why the move? Has Ben dropped a hint that I'm unhappy here? Does Mel want the room free so she can spend some quality time with him? She had only to ask…

A fond smile dies on my lips as a dreadful thought occurs to me.

It's an apology.

Cade Fitzlean is making up for my humiliation in his office with an upgrade. He'll have gone by now. Soon he'll be high over the Atlantic on his way back to the States. He probably gave the order before he left.

How crass.

For a full second I feel a mix of shame, fury and deep, biting resentment. Then I take a deep breath.

I've only myself to blame. I'm here to work, not to party. I've got a job to do and it's high time I got on with it.

Angrily I pluck a corset in scarlet satin off the rail and hold it up in the mirror.

It glows like flame against my skin. It looks distinctly *wicked.*

I feel a delicious, naughty thrill. Maybe I'll just try it on…

Some minutes later, showered, perfumed and made-up to perfection, I step into the corset, adjust the thigh-high black stockings and ease a saucy matching garter into place.

In the mirror I see a seductive fairy queen in sexy satin, breasts swelling against the scarlet lace ruffle, long legs elegant in sleek stockings, ending in tall scarlet heels.

Wow. I can do this…

At that moment my phone buzzes. I rummage for it in the untidy heap of clothes on the floor. The name on the caller display makes my heart leap. "Dad? How lovely —"

His voice is just what I need but as he talks on, my heart plummets. *Oh no.* Slowly I wander into the vast bedroom. I lean against the ornate gilt dressing table, legs straight out before me and take a deep breath. "So how long's this been going on? Yes, of course I'll talk to her. Janice? Are you okay? Dad said you've —"

I break off for a moment as my stepmother's familiar voice trills in my ear. From time to time I break in and try to sound patient. "No, we're staying in a secret location... It's a secret job. I'm not allowed to talk about it. It's not a holiday. It's for work... I *am* doing a real job. News is a different section —"

Her voice grows shrill and she cuts the call. Our old battle's reached new stress levels.

Why now? With a sigh I dial Ben's messaging service. "Ben — it's Tunis. I don't think I can do this —"

I freeze.

In the mirror opposite, a man is watching me.

Slowly I lower the phone. I wait for the tiny hairs prickling along the backs of my legs to lie down again before I spin around.

Cade Fitzlean is in my room. He's leaning on the frame of a doorway, elegant and stunningly handsome in black tie, tux and a dazzling white shirt.

I've no idea how long he's been there. I'd no idea there was even a *door* there.

"Quitting so soon, Miss Vale? Surely not."

My mouth feels dry. When I finally speak, I sound hoarse. "I thought you'd gone. What are you doing in here?"

He walks a little way into the room, completely at ease. Clearly in command. "I changed my mind about going. I had you moved up to the suite next to mine. I thought it would be more convenient for us both."

"More *convenient*?"

"For our little arrangement. You asked me to take you in hand."

I stare at him. "But…I thought you turned me down."

The shame of it still burns in my face.

He walks up close and runs a finger along the lace ruffle, following the swell of my breasts all the way down into my cleavage. His touch sparks tiny flames along my skin that tingle all through me.

He holds me with his eyes, his classic features composed and impassive, his chiseled mouth a work of art all by itself.

"Did I say that? I *said* your request might be thought offensive. If I'd asked it of you, you'd have gone ballistic."

I manage a rueful smile. "You're right. I would. I'm truly sorry."

"There are complicated reasons why I should turn you down. That was one of them. But there also complicated reasons which make your request…irresistible."

His intense look and the low, sensual note in his voice are doing strange things to me. I stand rooted to the spot like a rabbit in headlights.

With infinite care, like I'm some rare and exquisite object, he leans down and touches his lips to mine. It's barely a kiss, just the slightest brush of skin on skin, but for an instant the world falls away.

As he straightens up, I'm in a different universe, full of sudden doubts and nameless desires and they're about to collide.

Next second, they do collide.

His eyes narrow. "But I must warn you there are certain…conditions."

Chapter Three

Like leaves whirling in the wind, my thoughts are all confusion. It takes me a moment to regain control.

Cade Fitzlean just kissed me.

Dimly I realize he's said something. "Conditions?"

"I'm guessing it took courage to ask me to do this. It's something women almost never admit."

His angelic features split into a grin and now I see something new — the wicked glint of a demon.

All at once I'm treading water. "I wish I'd kept quiet."

His jaw stiffens. "So do I, but it's too late now. I still have problems with it. That's why there are conditions. One, I'll take you in hand for a week. I can't escape my commitments entirely — nor can you, I imagine. Nera's taster training takes an hour a day for just three days. But if you work with me, you'll get two sessions daily — one in the daytime and the other at night. All week."

"Two a day for a whole *week*? That sounds an awful lot. Are you sure — " I break off as he holds up his hand.

At the same time, excitement flares deep down. *Yes, yes...*

He's looking stern, his expression veiled. Mine is all quickening breath, parted lips and glowing cheeks. *He's noticed.*

"You need more than three hours to get anywhere with this." His eyes narrow. "And given your history, I think you should try something more intense than just a taster."

Wicked, forbidden thoughts race through my mind then a forest of questions. *Can I do this? Will I freak?*

Aloud I try to sound confident. "That's wonderful—"

"Let me finish. I'll work with you for a week on one condition—that you put yourself entirely at my disposal for the whole of the next. In other words, you agree to become my property."

My jaw drops. "Your...*property*? Are you kidding?"

"About property, Miss Vale? Never. Far too valuable." He looks amused but his eyes stay watchful. "You'll get routine training for seven days then you'll become my full-time sub for the next seven. Mine to do with as I please, when I please and where I please. You have a passport?"

"I'll need a passport?" What I really need right now is a stiff drink—or a fast getaway car. "Yes. Naturally."

"Good. Two. From now on, I want you to step back as presenter for your film report. Do some interviews, maybe a voiceover at the final edit. But I want you to distance yourself from your team."

Instantly a chill spreads through me. "But...I'm the anchor. It was your idea, they tell me, and we're a team. I can't just step aside."

In an instant he's switched from friendly host to brutally efficient CEO. For the first time, I feel a wisp of sympathy for the long-suffering Sonja.

"This is not a negotiation. It's what I want. If you agree, we'll discuss terms later, but only the detail—implements, equipment, timetables, all that."

Excitement flares again. *Implements? Ye gods.* I stare at him, helpless.

His eyes flicker as he resumes. "Three. No one must know. I insist you keep our arrangement a secret. I no longer practice professionally and I'm reluctant to give the impression that I do. My private life stays that way—private. I'd make you sign a non-disclosure agreement but I prefer to avoid a paper trail. Your contractual position here is, in any case, unchanged."

His smile carries a faint glimmer of triumph as he lowers his voice. "And I'm guessing you feel the same. You've got just as much—if not more—to lose, if our arrangement became public."

He's right. For me exposure would be a disaster. Presenters are public figures, some even household names. For me that's still some way off but to be linked to kinky sex? I'd never live it down, probably never work again. And at home...? I shudder.

"Those are my terms. You can think it over if you like. Sleep on it and tell me tomorrow."

It's wildly exciting but it's an awful shock. As questions bubble up, I seize one at random. "But the secrecy thing with the team... We're very close. That's how we work. I can't hope to keep a secret from them."

He looks unimpressed. "You'll just have to get creative. That's one of the reasons I moved you up here. At least you'll be out of range."

"But... Two whole weeks? Supposing they guess? Suppose somebody sees us...or *hears* us?" I try not to think of the awful noises they might hear...starting now. I feel like yelling already.

He smiles faintly, lifts my hand and touches his lips to my fingers. A whisper of sensation flashes all over me, making the down rise all along my arm. "Well, you'd better start praying. Because if that happens, you and your friends will immediately get the sack."

It takes a few seconds for this to sink in. "*What?* You can't do that."

I try to snatch away my hand but he holds it fast, turns it over and kisses my palm, his mouth hot and urgent. Signals flash all the way down and I begin to pulse.

He lowers my hand. "Oh yes I can. I own the network."

He does? He would. How typical.

I glare at him. "That's blackmail."

The sudden fury in his eyes throws me. "That's *justice*. You try canceling a launch. Employees had chosen homes, schools, prepared to settle here on the premise that the venture went ahead as planned. Now you can find out just what it's like to have other people's fate in your hands, even if it's on a smaller scale. It'll teach you a lesson."

A pit yawns in my stomach as his meaning sinks in. Did I really do all that? "But you can't just blame me. Maybe it was the wrong time. Maybe the public just wasn't ready."

"And maybe if you'd shown a little more self-control that evening, everything would have passed off smoothly, I'd have saved millions and all this would have been wrapped up months ago."

My mind races. *The order came straight from the top.* "So, why me? Ben said I was a deal-breaker. Why?" My words hang in the air. I've touched a nerve. "And now you want me to back off?"

35

"Partly that. What you want me to do won't be easy for me. I think you should have to struggle too. That's only fair."

Anger makes me bold. *"Struggle*? I thought you people did this for fun?"

His expression hardens. "We do. I did...until you came along. Suppose I told you that seeing you on screen that night shocked me almost as much as it shocked you? Suppose I told you I tried to change?" His expression clouds with some fierce emotion. "And suppose I told you that in my office this afternoon, you went one step too far? For you people, *most* people, this is sex play. Not for me. For me it's real. You play with me, you play with fire. If you want me to do this I'll do it, but only on my terms. Sleep on it. Tell me what you decide tomorrow. After that, we'll drop it for good."

He glances at his watch. "I must go. And you'd better dress. Keep that on. Put something over it. That black satin thing should do it." He gestures vaguely to the pile of gowns heaped on the chair then turns on his heel.

Outraged, I glare after him.

He glances back with a sudden grin. The effect is disarming. "Better get used to obeying orders if you're training with me. And pile up your hair. I like to see your neck."

* * * *

When I finally go downstairs, I'm relieved there's no sign of him. I need a breather.

Against my better judgment, I'd tried the black satin. It fits like skin and the scarlet lace trim of my corset makes a perfect ruffle along the plunging neckline. The slit in the skirt parts as I move to show the occasional flash of garter, the scarlet lace another perfect match.

The effect's sexy and surprisingly chic. *He even knows about clothes? Or was it a lucky guess?*

As I catch up with the others, the effect is instant and startling.

"Hey, Tunis — *wow*." Ben looks taken aback.

Jake's jaw drops.

I grin back. "Okay, you guys, chill. This place getting to you already? We've been here barely twelve hours."

But it's gratifying to see other heads turn. I should wear naughty lace more often. And it's a relief to see that most costumes here are far more daring than mine. I feel almost modest amongst all the bulging latex and oiled, naked flesh.

The glitterati on display like this will make terrific TV. Jake must be itching to get his camera rolling.

* * * *

As the evening wears on, I slowly relax. High living can be fun, even though we're only pretending and we're supposed to be at work. Dinner was excellent, the small tables in the dining room crowded and noisy. Afterward I spot four film stars, two sports personalities, an oil billionaire and an artist then lose count of the B- and C-listers before it occurs to me that I'm now almost one myself.

Many are with teams of people — stylists, publicists and agents — here to ensure we show their employer's best side and stay off sensitive topics. Setting up the interviews will be a nightmare.

There's still no sign of Cade. I firmly resist the temptation to ask where he is.

As couples begin to dance, Mel sashays over to the rhythm of a familiar, catchy tune.

"Love beat – had me in its spell,
Love beat – opened up your shell..."

It's Cade's original hit song.

"Don't say we're stuck with that damn tune all week." Jake morosely orders another daiquiri.

Mel grins. "I love it. I think it's a terrific song."

Ben leans forward and pushes his glass toward the barman. "Must have made him a fortune. His first hit single—in and out of the charts ever since. He used the money to finance all his other stuff. Nice little earner."

Mel raises her glass with a wry smile. "Here's to chemistry."

The song filters through to us, the words full of new meaning. *"Love Beat – open up for me..."* Couples are swaying to the familiar tune.

The song's so well known that before today, I'd almost forgotten Fitzlean's link to it. It's a simple ballad with a steady, catchy beat and a haunting melody that lies over the top like a lament. I never gave it much thought.

As a dancer, I'm more familiar with Prokofiev and Tchaikovsky, but looking around me now I see the effects of the money it makes and I understand a tiny glimmer of his power.

You can get this rich from something so simple. Astonishing.

And right on cue, he's standing in front of me.

"Saw you there and I knew you were sent,
Felt you here and I knew I was lost.
Love Beat..."

How can words so simple suddenly feel so apt?

I feel Jake crowding my elbow.

Cade casually greets the others but his gaze stays locked on me as he holds out his hand.

"Shall we dance?"

In his presence I feel like a rag doll. In his arms, I'm a princess.

Something about his touch on my arm, the feel of his body so close to mine, sparks instant energy. He moves beautifully, with an easy grace rare outside a dance studio.

Even more rare—we're perfectly in sync. His movements mirror mine. Not just from courtesy, from the soul. It's spooky.

Dancing's my first love. It comes to me as naturally as walking. He spins me round in an intricate flourish, and we share a smile—mine surprised, his triumphant. As he pulls me back into his arms I whisper close to his ear. "Is this wise? Won't people talk?"

"About one dance? Hardly. I saw you earlier from the lawn. You were admiring the view?"

So he did see me. I redden. "I was curious when I saw you talking to the groundskeepers. Are you that friendly with all your staff?" I try to sound cynical.

He performs another perfect turn and threads skillfully between the couples to lead me away from the tables to a place with fewer people. Now we're almost alone.

He ignores my sarcasm, his expression solemn. "His wife's just had their first baby. He's asked me to the christening. And yes, since you ask, I know most of the staff here by their first names. When it's not hosting festivals or themed weeks for sex-mad celebs, this place happens to be my home. Well, one of them."

"You *own* this place? Seriously?"

Smiling, he looks even younger, almost boyish. Is this how he wins loyalty from his staff? We know so little about him. None of his workforce would talk. It's unusual. Despite Ben's mania for research and Mel's nose for secrets, Cade Fitzlean is still a mystery. Apart from the one secret I accidentally pried out of him earlier today — and that has to stay secret.

Odd, for so colorful a character.

And he dances like he means it. But every touch, every move warns me that exactly *what* he means is way too personal for public view. He's lithe and responsive, like he feels the music and knows what it does. I rarely meet someone who so perfectly matches my own rhythm...

"You trained in Paris?"

Surprise almost throws me off beat. "For a while, yes. How did you know?" In his arms, I now sense power. I catch a faint scent from his neck, part cologne, part...*feral*. It acts on me like wine.

"I make it my business to know these things. You left suddenly."

I feel a prickle of unease. "Yes. Do you always grill your partners when you dance?"

He smiles slowly, like he's just settled a private bet. "You're a very private person, Tunis. Like me. Curious."

At that moment the music pauses, but instead of leading me back to the others, he guides me out of the ballroom and into the grounds. Silent security men eye us from the walls.

As if in a dream, I'm still in his arms. I'm looking up at the soft, scented night sky. A light breeze ruffles the leaves. The lawn beneath my feet feels chill on my toes. "Why are we out here?"

His eyes glint in the moonlight. Fear ripples through me, and something else, just as primitive...

"Is that cameraman your lover?"

What? I lift my chin, ready for battle. "Why?"

"I have to know."

Something in the universe shifts. *Did he really just say that?* "No, since you ask. I've known him a long time, that's all. And I owe him a lot."

His eyes narrow. "He's hot for you. And you seem very close."

I press my lips together. "I'm close to lots of people but not in *that* way. He's just a friend. What about Nera? Or your PA? Are they *your* lovers?"

He smiles slowly showing white, regular teeth — the smile of a movie star or a predator. A tremor runs through me. I get the feeling we're talking about something else.

"I rarely fuck the workforce, Tunis. Bad for business. Why are you so scared of me?"

Instinctively I step away. "I'm not scared. I'm just cautious when I dance on moonlit lawns with rich men who throw their weight about. If it comes to that, why are you so hostile?"

In an instant the magic disappears and the atmosphere chills. "You caused me problems last year. I have a duty to my employees. I want to make absolutely sure you're on board with all this. And, frankly, I'm getting mixed messages."

"*Mixed*? I thought I made things pretty clear this afternoon." It's impossible not to sound bitter but I stare at him in dismay. My job might be on the line here. This fun-filled fortnight is fast becoming a nightmare.

Is he doing this on purpose? Is this his revenge? "If it makes you any happier, I really, really want to make this work." I gaze up at him earnestly, willing him to believe me. "It's just... This is complicated for me. I'm in unknown territory here."

He runs a finger along my lower lip, his touch making me shudder. Am I dreaming it, or is there a flicker of pain behind his eyes?

"I know," he says softly. "Me too."

Before I can think this through, he dips his head and touches his lips to mine for the second time this evening.

Sensation rips through me like lightning. I react instantly, winding my arms up around his neck and responding eagerly as he parts my lips and invades my mouth, his tongue urgent, hungry, melting my will.

He pushes me back against a tree and pins me by the arms. Desire scorches through me as I kiss him back, reveling in his power and his heat as he presses against me, the rasp of rough tree bark rigid against my back.

As he pulls away, a startled bird shrieks in the branches overhead. Cade towers over and around me and once more I sense the streak of power that propels him through the business world and forged his millions.

"Have you decided yet?" Light from the ballroom filters through the moving leaves and plays over his face, making him mystical, beautiful, a demon from ancient legend. But the rippling muscles under his shirt and the hard lines of his arousal warn me he's a man, only too real, and his plans for me are less than romantic.

"Yes." My soft whisper sounds strange in the muffled stillness of the gardens. Close by I hear tiny rustling noises—nature on the prowl, just like him. "I've decided."

His eyes glint in the moonlight. "And?"

It's an effort but I manage a languid smile. "I told you... Yes, I accept. But I'm here to do a job, remember? I'll have to fit you in."

His face instantly tenses. "Either you accept or you don't. I warned you, I don't play at this. If you're expecting fluffy handcuffs and scented candles you'll be disappointed. I've got business commitments too. We'll both have to juggle our sessions with work. So is it yes or no?"

I smile at him calmly but excitement courses through me, fueled by the thought that he's taking so much trouble to be sure I'm on board with this, like he can hardly believe his luck.

Maybe it means something to him, too.

"Yes."

For an instant, some fierce emotion flickers in his eyes but it's gone before I can decipher it. At that moment he pauses to take a call and I seize the chance to slip away.

He calls after me. "We start tomorrow."

As I glance back, he's talking quietly into his phone but his eyes are still fixed on me, his gaze liquid heat. I hurry away across the lawn and into the comparative safety of the ballroom, my emotions in free-fall.

I wish he'd stop looking at me like that.

I wish I felt less idiotic when he does.

I wish it were tomorrow.

Chapter Four

"I warned you. I don't play at this." His voice is deep and
sexy, stirring and soothing. It flows over me, part growl, part
whisper.

The whip uncoils with a loud crack and I watch mesmerized
as the tip uncurls in slow motion and snaps along my thigh.
I give a long, juddering sigh as the jolt of it flares into heat
and settles in my groin in a low, burning ache.

Again. Please, please...

My arms are stretched high, my ankles cuffed wide apart.
I'm ready for him, poised for his pleasure, primed for my
own... But he's turning away, he's leaving me here, alone in
the dark.

No, no, come back. Please don't leave me... I can't do
this without you...

I scream over and over but no sound comes out.

I open my eyes and sit bolt upright in bed. A streak of
moonlight from the window splits the room into
patches of light and dark, making it hard to work out
shapes.

Something woke me. Slowly I make out someone
sitting opposite, watching.

For a split second, fear prickles all along my back. "*Cade*? Is that you?"

Instantly he crosses the room to sit beside me. Moonlight etches his face in silver and glitters in his eyes.

He looks beautiful. I'm still aroused, burning from my dream. I long to touch him.

"You cried out in your sleep. What was it?" His voice is low, husky with concern.

I gaze at him, drinking him in. He's wearing boxer shorts. Above the waist he's naked, the swell of his chest and the pads of muscle at his shoulders gleaming faintly. Below his neck his body hair fuses into a dark pathway leading down toward his waistband.

He smells all heat and skin and sleep, and from somewhere in the region of his neck, I catch a hint of citrus and spice. It's heady, unnerving. The burning sensation in my groin heats up. He's looking at me, waiting for an answer to something he said. What was it? Oh yes, what woke me... "It was — nothing."

My voice sounds muffled so close to his chest. I feel his hair bristle against my face.

"Tell me." He holds me close, his expression intent.

My thoughts take focus. He's asking about my dream. "You had a whip. You were going to... But you left me." Panic rises in my voice.

He touches my face. "Hey, easy. It was just a dream. Here, have some water." He pauses, one eyebrow arched in enquiry. "A *whip*?" He grins as he holds the glass to my lips. "What was I doing with it?"

Obediently I sip then dart him a look. "You're laughing at me."

He sets down the glass and pushes a stray tendril of damp hair away from my forehead. "*Would* I? I was curious. That's all."

I'm awake now, regaining control. "My lips are sealed." In that second, it flashes over me that I'm naked. I've brought a nightie—a flimsy white lace affair—but it's still in my case.

My breast tingles as his rough chest hair rasps against my nipple. I hear him inhale sharply.

"Did I wake you up? Crying out, I mean?" I shift again, this time on purpose, twisting a little in his arms. The roughness of his hair against my nipple sends a shaft of exquisite pleasure rocketing through me. It settles in my groin in a deep, pulsing ache as my nipple tenses, pressing against him. With a sigh I lean my head against him briefly. "I dream a lot. If it bothers you then you'd better leave the door shut."

"I'm in charge of you now. I need to know how you feel. If this is what happens when you sleep then it stays open."

I accept this in silence then shift again, thrilling to the feel of his hair on my sensitive skin. This time his hand folds round my breast. I shudder as his fingers find my hard, aroused nipple and give it a squeeze.

"I know what you're doing. And *this*"—he tweaks it again, making me gasp—"is doing most of it."

Close to my forehead, I feel his lips stretch into a smile.

Then his hand is moving up to my throat, along my neck, leaving a trail of sensation everywhere he touches. He catches my chin, tilting my head up to face him, and he touches his lips to mine.

Desire, raw and urgent, rockets through me. His kiss is light and teasing. It fans my flames, mocks my arousal. It's like he *knows*...

He pulls away. "It's nearly dawn. Go back to sleep. We'll talk later."

* * * *

"Hi. How's the upgrade? Mel's insanely jealous."

Ben and Jake grin up at me from their breakfast as I quietly join them. All around I hear the clatter of china, chink of cutlery and happy chatter. The air's rich with wholesome, everyday smells—bacon, eggs and hot rolls.

Sadly, I've already breakfasted from the lavish trolley in my room. On day one of my new servitude, Cade prowled through my room like a caged tiger, a restless bundle of energy, shaver in one hand, phone in the other. Between calls he directed me to eat and barked instructions.

We start for real this evening. Until then, he's got business. Keen to assert myself, I announced airily that I'm busy too. I've got linking shots and celebrity interviews to fit in. We agreed to part for the day.

I'm to text him where I'm going and with whom. When I gave him an arched look, his eyes narrowed. "I have to know. You're mine now."

I decided to avoid an argument so I accepted this in silence, showered quickly, got dressed and joined the others in the morning room.

But now my universe has subtly changed. My encounters with Cade are having an electrifying effect. Each one leaves me more confused, more aroused than ever. Desire rages.

I long for evening. It's hard to concentrate.

"And so we've got a problem."

Ben's been saying something. I tune in to see Jake nodding a yes.

Mel looks at me with a puzzled expression. "Are you all right, Tunis? You seem a bit vague this morning."

Dragging my thoughts back to work I remind myself sternly I've got a problem too. Somehow I've got to tell them I'm backing off.

I close my eyes briefly as Cade's hard, uncompromising words cut through my thoughts.

I want you to distance yourself from your team. He means it, no question.

I dread telling them but I must. If I don't, we're all out of a job.

Just then Nera appears and saves me the trouble. She looks exotic and deadly, her lipstick perfect, her expression more sultry than ever. Once again I sense a wave of dislike.

"Ah, Tunis. About time. What about your sub training? You're not on the list. I have to fix your sessions."

I feel myself color. The challenge in her eyes needles me, but I've got no choice. I must back down.

Be careful what you wish for. Now my dearest wish is coming true, and already I'm planning to let down the people closest to me without even telling them why.

"Sorry, Nera — everybody — but I'm not doing them. This whole thing's not really for me. I'll give your sessions a miss, Nera, if you don't mind. I'm sure the Panther will find someone else. I gather he's a big star, but I simply can't face him. Ben, would you let Mel take over most of my screen time? I'm sure she'll make a much better job of it. I'll stick to voiceovers."

I speak with airy confidence, but my heart shrivels as silence falls on the table.

"For crissake, Tunis." Ben looks really angry. "*Now* you tell me?"

Nera's lip curls. "Fine. Your call." Her tone is withering. She pats Ben on the head as she turns away. "See you later, babe."

Ben looks sheepish. Mel scowls.

"Anyway, what kind of problem?" With an effort, I haul us back to smoother waters.

Ben rolls his eyes and starts again. "For goodness' sake, Tunis, get a grip. I was saying Jake thinks his shots of you meeting Fitzlean yesterday aren't strong enough. He wants to retake them."

I frown. A shot of me looking scared is part of Ben's storyboard. He wants a repeat shot of my now famous reaction on that fateful night a year ago to give our report a dramatic opener, give his film a touch of symmetry.

No way. I brace myself for a fight.

Jake leans forward. "There's this great place I've found. It'll make a terrific backdrop."

Anything's better than meeting the Panther face to face. The very thought that he's here somewhere is making me twitch. Keen to make amends for my bombshell I agree. "Sure, anything. It sounds great."

Just then Sonja appears at Jake's elbow. "Mr. Simmons? Or can I call you Jake?"

The ice-maiden gatekeeper of the mighty Fitzlean Empire is actually smiling. This is a first. And she looks enchanting. "I've got a message for you from Mr. Fitzlean."

Jake glowers up at her. "And I've got one for him. Tell him to keep his hands off our presenter."

The PA blinks. "Excuse me?"

"Jake, for goodness' sake." Seriously alarmed, I smile kindly at Sonja. "Don't mind him. He improves with lunch. Have you worked for Mr. Fitzlean long?"

Sonja tears her eyes off Jake for a second, bewildered. "I... About a year."

I give her a friendly grin. "Never a dull minute?"

She smiles shyly and the ice thaws a fraction. She turns again to Jake, braver now. "We're arranging some classes to amuse the guests, Mr. Simmons. Mr. Fitzlean wondered if you'd give some master classes on photography. He's a great admirer of your work."

Jake stares sullenly at his plate. "No."

Sonja's cheeks turn the palest shell pink. For once she looks completely lost and remarkably pretty. I melt.

Under the table I kick his foot. "For crying out loud, Jake, you've seen what he's like. She'll probably lose her job. Just say yes."

Jake glances up impatiently. "Sorry, Sonja. Yes, then. And it's Jake. Please." He eyes her morosely while she beams back at him.

As she turns away, she gives me a grateful nod. "And you're due at the salon in five minutes, Miss Vale. Ask for anything. It's all on the house."

Jake glances at me and sighs heavily. "We'll do the shots when you're through. Text me, would you? We'll meet on the terrace."

Across the table Mel and Ben are deep in conversation, already drawing up their plan of attack on the A-listers and their agents, Ben on the golf course and Mel in the spa. I leave them to it and head for the salon.

* * * *

"Wow." Jake's pacing the terrace when I finally emerge, sleek and relaxed. Nera's right about the styling. It's surprisingly good.

My hair's lightly reshaped and a tender, loving manicure has settled my nerves. What helped even more was the friendly female chatter all around me.

Now I feel good. And hey, even Jake's noticed. From him, this is praise indeed. I smile a thank you and we set off at a brisk walk toward the woods.

Walking quickly soon undoes all the salon's patient work. Soon my hair's a mess from twigs and branches brushing past me and I'm growing uneasy. The woods are creepy. There are sinister rustles in the undergrowth, and I keep seeing black shapes among the trees.

At one point I jerk to a halt and Jake swears as his camera bag bumps into me from behind.

"What are you doing? Keep walking, Tunis. This stuff's heavy."

"But... I thought I saw somebody."

He gasps theatrically and lowers his voice to a stage whisper. "Maybe it's...*the Panther. Grr.*"

He lunges at me, teeth bared, hands clawing the air around my face. "*He's coming to get you...*"

"Stop it. That's not funny." I try to smile but I've broken out in a cold sweat.

He snorts. "Shapes? Just ignore them. Fitzlean's people are everywhere. The place is crawling with security. You mean you haven't noticed? We're Alcatraz central."

After that he goes quiet, but I'm even edgier. The farther we go, the more I sense his air of suppressed excitement.

Why?

Soon the path grows steeper and I start to hear a dull, roaring noise. It's getting steadily louder. A generator of some kind?

I stop to get my breath. "How much farther?"

"Nearly there. It's a terrific spot. You'll see."

At last he sets down his bag, takes out his bulky camera and starts to screw on a lens.

Now I see I'm truly honored. He's brought an early handheld camera, his beloved Éclair Cameflex, the French classic.

He holds it up proudly. "Look at that. What a beaut. You'd never guess it dates from the forties. If it was good enough for Orson Welles it's good enough for me."

I roll my eyes. Boys and toys. If Mel were here she'd tell him to shut up. I'm too soft on him.

Instead, I give him a wry smile. "So where's this view?" The noise is loud now, a dull roar. I see only trees.

"Right here." He steers me firmly down a short flight of wooden steps, through a wall of shrubs then gives me a sharp push so I stumble forward. "Now turn to face me."

I freeze.

I try to scream but nothing happens.

I seem to be suspended in space. In fact, I'm swinging on a narrow footbridge, a few feet away from a wall of solid rock with only rope rails between me and — nothing.

About fifty feet away I see a tall column of cascading water. That's what's making the noise. At the foot of the gorge, some hundred feet below me, an angry, frothing stream boils and swirls, flecked with foam as it snakes away from under my feet.

He's right. It's spectacular. To most people, it might even be beautiful.

But to me it's sheer terror, my worst nightmare.

I hate heights. He knows this.

Views are fine. I'm okay if there's a window or a barrier. But here there's just…rope.

I wheel round, my throat too tight even to cry out. At last I find a rasping, husky imitation of sound. "Jake, *no*. Get me off this."

Behind his camera, Jake's making soothing noises. "Brilliant. You look terrified. Again."

At that minute shadows erupt from the trees and figures race toward the footbridge. One lunges at Jake from the side in a full body tackle. Both men land in an untidy heap.

Another strides calmly onto the bridge toward me. *Cade.* He gathers me into his arms and pushes my head down against his chest. "Don't look."

The whole thing takes barely seconds. I bury my face against him and his heart beats close to my ear. Dimly I hear a scuffle on the path.

"Get rid of his camera." Cade's command reaches through his chest. A muffled shout from Jake tells me the camera's being wrestled from his grasp. There's a long pause then a distant crash.

"Now drive him back. We'll walk." Cade's voice echoes through his ribcage. He keeps my head pressed close against him.

From the muffled depths of Cade's tight embrace, I can hear Jake shouting.

"Get your fucking hands off me. That camera was a fucking antique, you moron."

Then his protests grow faint. After a moment I hear car doors slam, an engine start up then silence. Just the roar of the water.

Cade releases me and takes my face in his hands. "Look at me. Do you trust me, Tunis?" He holds me with a look of steel.

I take a deep breath. "Yes."

"Good. Now let's get you off this bridge."

Steadily, keeping his hands firmly on my face, he draws me back onto the path. Quickly he puts an arm around me and leads me up some steps to a car park with lookout points, telescopes and wooden benches.

We sit down on the nearest.

My breathing steadies but I still feel sick. Now that I'm out of danger, questions bubble up. "How did you get here so fast?"

He looks grim, his jaw rigid with suppressed fury. "Security spotted you. They told me you were heading for the gorge so I came after you. Lucky I did." He sounds gruff.

It dawns on me he's angry with *me*. So this is *my* fault?

He glares at me. "You were supposed to tell me. What were you doing in the woods?"

"Jake and Ben wanted shots of me looking scared."

His eyes blazed. "Looking *what*? Why?"

I swallow. "They thought the footage of us meeting yesterday wasn't strong enough." I sigh. "I don't know. Ask them."

"I will. I've seen the rushes. They looked fine to me." He sounds grim. "I did some checks. You've got a thing about heights. You had an accident on stage."

He knows? "Yes." I tense. "My fiancé and I were rehearsing for *Romeo and Juliet*. The balcony collapsed and I broke my foot." I allow myself a small, bitter smile. "So I lost the part then he broke off our engagement." My smile fades. "So I lost him too."

It used to hurt. Now it's sort of scarred over. I rarely talk about it, but I keep the phrase ready to roll off pat, just in case.

"And Simmons knows?"

"Yes." I swallow. *Please drop this.*

His jaw clenches briefly. "He tried to scare you witless for a *photo*?"

"He's a genius." From long habit, I spring to Jake's defense. "And he loved that camera."

"He'll get a replacement." Cade jabs at his phone and starts to issue a stream of instructions, his voice low and angry. "I want Simmons in my office *now*. I'll be back in ten."

He slips the phone back in his pocket, his mouth set and grim. "From now on you stay away from him."

I feel a spike of indignation. "That's unfair. He meant no harm. He gets — carried away."

Cade turns on me, his eyes blazing. "You don't get it, do you? We have an agreement. From today, you belong to me and I have a duty of care. I want to know whom you see, where you go and what you do. I don't trust him. You could have been killed."

He rises to his feet and looks at his watch. "We'd better get back. And as soon as we do you're scheduled for four hours in the spa, lunch included."

As I rise shakily to my feet I shiver.

Instantly he draws me into his arms, his eyes full of concern. "You've had a terrible shock. In the spa, try to relax. That's an order." He smiles but his eyes look worried.

Like a cloud passing away from the sun his mood changes in a second. He kisses my forehead. "I want you fit and rested for tonight."

Tonight. I feel a surge of heat so intense that I feel giddy.

His eyes cloud again. "What's the matter?"

I touch my cheek briefly to his. "Nothing. Excitement, that's all."

He leads me back along the path, holding me firmly by the hand. We talk little but as we emerge from the woods and cross the lawn, I feel I've known him forever.

Every look, every touch, sparks heat.

Once, where the path plunges into a dip in the trees, he pushes me up against a trunk and fastens his mouth on mine with a passion so intense, so sudden that my knees grow weak. As he explores me with his hands I respond, high on adrenaline, willing him to take me, control me, to dowse this furnace deep between my legs.

From his jagged breathing I know he feels it too. But he's mindful of security, wary of prying eyes. He pulls away, strokes my face gently and touches his lips to my eyelids and the tip of my nose.

"Later. Be patient."

Chapter Five

"At the start of a session, you kneel."

It's early evening and we're in Cade's apartment. It has spectacular views all over the park and it just doubled in size. With the communicating door thrown open, our suites become one vast complex.

I'm nervous. I've been nervous all afternoon, comforted only by a delicious lunch and a couple of hours of prime pampering in the spa. Now I'm standing before him in practice pose, as relaxed as my nerves and my excitement allow.

As instructed, I'm freshly showered and wearing slinky lingerie, stockings and high heels.

Cade, by contrast, is fully dressed in black jeans, loafers and a crisp white shirt, the cuffs loosened and folded back. He's reclining on a stylish leather sofa and looks stunning, like a male model between shoots. His legs are crossed, one ankle leaning casually on his knee.

He's flexing a slender cane.

The sight of it sends a shiver through me. But I've done my homework. I've got rights, even here.

Or have I? This is a verbal agreement, my reputation staked against his. It's a dangerous game—more like cold war.

And that's before we get to the caning part.

The air between us crackles with static. Every word, every move, is somehow charged with meaning, building the tension.

"And you call me Sir. It keeps a proper distance between us and helps the role-play. Creates respect and a feel for discipline. So kneel."

I do it, eyeing him warily. The breathtaking classical statue facing me is subtly different from the knight errant who rode to my rescue earlier this afternoon. He's darker, more severe, and looking at me like I'm his favorite meal.

And he's got a cane.

He rises, lithe as a cat, and walks slowly toward me, his gaze dark and penetrating. "Lose the bra."

Hurriedly I let it slip to the floor. With a twitch of the cane, he flicks it away.

I wince as the cane springs back. He touches the tip of it to one nipple then moves across to the other, drawing it slowly up between my breasts, along my throat and finally presses the point under my chin, forcing me to look up.

"We'll aim for two sessions a day, one in the afternoon or evening and one at night. Each session will last up to two hours. Is that acceptable?"

How do I know? I'm new at this. My only guide is the slow burn of arousal deep between my legs as my dream slowly morphs into reality. "Yes, Sir."

He, too, seems troubled, his breathing steady but noticeable. It surprises me.

"You must tell me when it gets too intense. I don't normally handle vanillas."

I close my eyes briefly as I begin to pulse.

When. He said *when* it gets too intense. Not *if,* or *it might…*

The cane swishes again and he's squatting in front of me, his face close to mine, his arms resting on his knees, his hands together. The cane trembles between us, balanced lightly in his fingers.

The end of it quivers a little.

"You flinched just then. That scares you, Tunis? Tell me."

My mouth's gone dry. "Everything about this scares me."

His face darkens.

The upward snap on my left breast is light but so sudden I jump.

"Scares you…*what?*"

My eyes widen.

He's hit me. With a cane.

It was barely a tap, but the fact of it rockets round my brain like a thunderbolt.

This is really happening.

My thoughts race. "It scares me…*Sir.*"

He smiles slowly. "Sure it does. Fear is part of the fun. Stimulates the senses, intensifies the pleasure. Being scared of the dark makes you like ghost stories. Being scared of pain makes you like this. You'll learn to manage it through ritual. And a simple way to start is to mind your manners. You just earned your second punishment, by the way."

"*Second?*" I feel a tremor go through me.

He arches an eyebrow. "You forgot to tell me you were going walkabout with your photographer friend today. I missed an important deal while I took time out to track you down and play Superman. It cost me upward of a million dollars. That earned you the first, so we'll do it now."

He rises to his feet and stands over me. "Keep your head down and your eyes on the floor until I tell you to move." He walks back to the sofa. I hear him sit.

"Now crawl over to me on all fours. Keep your eyes on my face."

Slowly I move toward him. Instead of shame, I feel rising anger. And at the same time this simple, primitive movement of my limbs is giving me a strange, feral power. As I reach him, I sense something new, something entirely unexpected.

This feels hot.

The gleam in his eyes tells me he *knows*.

He pats his knee. "Now climb up here and bend over. Legs straight, ass in the air."

He takes some time to get me into position. His touch is light, warm and thrilling. The thought of the cane, now lying across the cushion next to him, makes my stomach shrink. "What are you going to do?"

He runs his hands over my bottom and between my thighs, sighing deeply. "Wow. You're like peaches, Tunis. I'm going to spank you. Not with the cane this time. Maybe just a couple of taps at the end. We'll see. Ready?"

Without waiting for an answer, he eases one leg from underneath me and traps me with it, pinning me down, and at the same moment leans on my back with his elbow, forcing my shoulders down into the seat.

He fondles me again then his hand lands with a loud crack. I shriek, startled, as the sting fades to a hot glow. His hand lands again, this time lower down. With a supreme effort, I steel myself against the impact and grit my teeth as the blows rain down, again and again.

Once the initial shock wears off, the stings become simple flashes of heat and join up into a continuous, white-hot blaze. After a while he pauses. I feel like I'm on fire.

"How is it?"

What? "You expect analysis...*Sir?*"

I hear his breath hiss through his teeth. "Do I detect defiance? For that, you'll definitely get the cane."

He removes his leg, freeing my trapped knees, and pushes me roughly off his lap. He stands up, catching me as I slide sideways and he hauls me up at the hips.

"Put your fingertips on the floor and balance on your toes. Spread your legs wider."

My dancer's instinct arches me into position, but it's a tricky one to do well.

"Hold still."

He sounds angry. The thought sends a spiral of fear down to my toes, but not in time to prepare for the instant sting from a single swish of the cane as it lands across both cheeks of my fiery bottom. As I haul in a lungful of air to protest, it lands again at a different angle.

"The two promised strokes. Now maybe you'll think twice before answering back. Hold the position."

My legs tremble as I hold the pose, delayed reaction draining my muscles of strength. His hand once more sensuous and tender, he massages my burning backside with a gentle, loving caress. A sob wells in my throat as he leans over me and breathes close to my ear.

"You're so beautiful like this. You can have no idea." His fingers slide between my legs and explore my softest places, now swollen and slick with lust. I feel a trickle of moisture down the inside of my thigh as he lingers, his hand easing deep inside me.

"You're very close. You took that well, for your first time. Would you like a reward?"

How can I answer that? My throat's too full to speak.

My legs are stretched into an impossible position, my bottom is on fire, and to cap it all I feel—*I know*—that any second I'm going to explode in an orgasm. If he moves his fingers into me just once more...

He laughs quietly and his fingers move again. I give a shriek as I convulse in a shattering climax. It throws me off balance and I crash to the floor in a heap of spent, quivering limbs and burst into angry, emotional sobs.

Instantly he's on his knees beside me, gathering me up into his arms. "*Tunis.* I'm so sorry. We went too far. Hush. Don't cry, please, baby."

As my spasms die away, I lean against him, still trembling and fight for control. "I'm sorry. I'm fine. It's just... It's been so long..." I bury my face in his chest as tears well up again, and he strokes my hair, murmuring something I can't quite hear.

After a moment or two, I pull away and wipe my nose on the back of my hand. "I'm okay. *Sir.*"

He eyes me for a moment in silence. "That's for me to decide." He touches my face, his fingers surprisingly gentle. "And you should come more often. Maybe we'll work on that. Kneel again, hands behind your back."

Avoiding his eye, I assemble my limbs into a kneeling position. It's easier now. Amazingly, the sting on my bottom is already fading into bearable heat and my climax has left me glowing with content.

I smile up at him. Is this allowed?

I hardly care. I feel on top of the world, like I've just won a race. "Is that why you agreed to this? Simply to humiliate me? Aren't there easier and more public ways to do it? *Sir?*"

His eyes narrow. His tenderness vanishes and his face grows stern. "Plenty of ways. It's easy to humiliate a public figure like you. You might even enjoy it. Shame can be part of the thrill, as you just found out."

He touches my face, his hand cupping my jaw. His thumb moves gently along my lower lip. "I like to see you like that. It gives me unimaginable pleasure to do that to you. I knew it would. But that's not why I agreed to do this."

I stare at him. "No? Then why did you?"

He frowns. "That night you were caught on camera... You reacted so strongly that I wondered if it was really from distaste or if it was from something else."

"What do you mean?"

He leans closer, his lips almost touching my face. His breath feels hot on my skin. "I'm not sure, but I'm beginning to think..."

The rest of his thought is lost as he fastens his mouth on mine and claims me in a long, urgent kiss, forcing my head back and filling my mouth with his tongue. I react instantly, my own need building again as I respond to his, signals flaring all through my muscles, inflaming the glow from my tormented rear and fusing into hot, naked greed.

As he pulls away, he gazes into my eyes with a strange expression, like he's discovered something unexpected. He springs to his feet and helps me up, his breathing ragged.

Once again he's distant, severe. "That'll do for our first session. We'll join the others now and meet up again later. And don't forget... No one must know. If anyone so much as hints they've guessed about us, you and your friends are out on the street."

* * * *

As we dress for the evening, I can't shake off the feeling that he's watching me. He says little, striding about while he takes his calls, his look both intimate and arousing. Twice I drop my hairbrush under his steady gaze. I blush when I fumble with the zipper on my gown. Quietly he fastens it for me, his fingers lingering around my shoulders.

Is he enjoying this?

As he finally shrugs on his tuxedo and adjusts his tie, I'm smoothing my gown of shimmering peacock satin and stepping into matching, wickedly expensive heels. The sight of him — elegant, urbane, waiting for me at the door to our rooms — stops my breath.

How can he look so calm? I feel like I've been through a spin-dryer. As we walk to the elevator, he takes my hand. "You look sensational. Fucked, but sensational."

In a panic I glance at the mirrored wall opposite, and I see what he means. A mystical being stares back at me — part fairy, part enchantress, slim in brilliant satin, outwardly elegant but with that telltale glow that comes from only one thing.

He grins. "Except, of course, you're not fucked at all — at least, not yet." With a light laugh he lifts my free hand, turns it over and drops a playful kiss on the inside of my wrist. "After you. We don't want to come together."

I grin back at him, suddenly playful. "I guess not. At least...not yet."

I step quickly into the elevator and press the button for ground.

* * * *

"Jeez, Tunis, Jake got *caned.*" Mel fixes me with an accusing glare. Across the room I see Ben detach himself from the arm of an up-and-coming soap star to hurry over.

My cheeks burn for an instant as the glowing part of me that suffered the real thing reminds me of my ordeal. I start to throb. At that moment Cade emerges from the elevator and catches my eye.

I swallow and try to concentrate. "I'm truly sorry, guys. Jake tried for another scared shot but I felt faint. I gather we breached health and safety, or something."

My presenter's instinct finds words to smooth things over, while the rest of me strains to follow Cade as he moves around the room, meeting and greeting. I take particular note of the women, who cluster around him like flies.

As the others give me a blow-by-blow account of their short, sharp session in Cade's office I see Nera sidle up to him and give him a broad, full-on smile.

I answer Ben on autopilot, already aware of the gist of what Cade said.

Afterward, still angry, he told me about it at length.

Now, from the corner of my eye I watch Cade lean over and murmur something in Nera's ear. He pats her cheek, before moving away to join some film people.

I feel a spike of jealousy so acute it catches my breath. What, exactly, holds those two together? Every time I see Nera, I feel the same unease. They're evidently close, but for some reason they pretend they're unconnected.

Then it hits me. *That's how he treats all his women.*

He said the same thing to me. *No one must know. Pretend we're not together.*

Ignoring a burst of laughter from the group around me, I scan the room in a swift, furious sweep.

How many others? Are some of them here, his lovers — his *subs*? Are they all sworn to secrecy, like I am?

I've been such a fool. I've got no rights over a man like him. He's rich. He's beyond good-looking. He's got anything he wants, including any — possibly every — passing female.

What was I thinking?

* * * *

A few cocktails and a substantial buffet restore my self-esteem. I'm happily flirting with a minor porn star equipped with impressive pecs and a thing for TV presenters when the lights dim and the music changes to the *Love Beat* song.

Without warning, Cade steps between us and steers me onto the dance floor. "Enjoying yourself?"

I'm a little tipsy now. I give him a playful look. "As you see. Cade, where is he?"

He stiffens mid-beat. "Who?"

"The Panther. He's here. I know it. Which one is he?"

Jake's play-acting earlier this afternoon about the Panther lurking in the bushes reminds me that the mysterious celebrity Dom is an ever-present danger. He came here for me, and I've ducked out.

He may have been cheated of his prey but he's still here, camouflaged among the elegant guests as effectively as the real thing, prowling the jungle, watching me, waiting to spring.

I lick my lips. "He's one of these people. He's been here all the time, watching." The thought is terrifying.

"Sure he's here. So what? You're obsessed."

We're dancing close. As if by chance, his song's playing as a slow number. Our eyes lock as the words filter through to me. I never hear words in songs, only the music, but I notice them now.

"When will you wake me and make me behave...?
When will you take me and make me your slave...?"

Rattled, I try to keep on topic. "He still scares me."

His eyes flicker as his voice lowers to a private murmur. "Hey, relax. You're with me now, remember?" As the music dies away, he leans forward. "I want you upstairs in five minutes. I'll go first."

Casually he strolls away, leaving me shaky with arousal.

We're not even supposed to like each other.

Slowly I weave a path through the dancing and sidestep a couple near the elevator. With a shock, I recognize Jake and Sonja, deep in conversation.

She looks delicate in ice-blue satin but she's still at work, making notes on a pad.

Jake looks boyish and handsome in his tux but he's frowning. "Still one of the best in the business. Takes 16mm, 18mm or 35mm. You can even change the film while it's running. But they're all museum pieces. You'll never find one. Even if you did, you'd have to pay up to seven thousand dollars..."

Poor Sonja. Now she's got to find him a replacement camera for the one Cade's men smashed this morning.

What a life.

* * * *

In our rooms, Cade is waiting. He's in shirtsleeves and has a short, neatly folded satin garment slung over one shoulder.

He glances at his watch as I walk in, a little out of breath. "Past midnight. Time for our next session. Strip and kneel."

Slowly I do as I'm told, and he tosses me a flimsy pair of panties made of black lace. "Put these on. We'll do the rest when we get there."

"Where are we going?"

He takes the satin garment off his shoulder and shakes it out. It's a short black robe with a satin belt. I slip it on then kneel.

"We're going to the dungeon. It's fully booked all week, but it's always free after midnight. We've got sole use of it then."

His expression gives nothing away. "The paperwork you signed before coming here covers all this but we'll go over a couple of things. Your safeword, for instance. I'll try to be careful. If anything really hurts or gets too extreme just say *mercy*. Got that?"

"Can I just say stop?"

"If you like. But everybody says stop. All the time. If you do, I'll stop for sure, but if you say *mercy*, we'll call it a day. OK?"

Naturally the dungeon is in the basement. We travel down by service elevator. He explains it's been installed where the servants' back stairs used to be. When we arrive, he unlocks it with an ornate key and stands aside for me to enter.

I walk in and catch my breath as the lighting comes on, a soft glow from wall sconces shaped like regency candles. There seem to be several rooms. I guess they're the original cellars, used to store wine, maybe, or cheese.

All around I see a bewildering array of gleaming equipment. It reminds me of the tack room at the stables where I had a few riding lessons once. The walls hang with harnesses, whips and paddles. I can smell leather. I almost miss the rosettes from gymkhanas pinned on the wall.

But these rooms have a very different purpose.

"You mean... We're going to use some of this?" I sound husky.

Behind us the door closes with a soft click, a terrifying sound.

Dreams are one thing. This is reality. Ridged leather. Glittering steel.

Be careful what you dream about.

He's standing with his back to the door — arms folded, legs apart, very much in control. Every inch a Dominant.

"We're going to use all of it."

Chapter Six

"First time in a dungeon?"

The gleam in his eyes warns me that he knows the answer but he wants me to say it. He wants me to be a blank page for him, all wide-eyed and innocent. And so I am in his strange world of whips, chains and strict, scary women.

I nod, too wary to speak.

"Nervous?"

Excited, going on terrified, is closer. "Should I be?"

I raise my chin boldly but my quivering lip gives me away.

His nostrils flare slightly. Now he looks hungry.

He circles me slowly, holding me with his eyes. It's like we've started to dance and I'm unsure of the moves. All I know is it involves ritual, discipline—maybe pain.

This is his domain. He's at home here. I only know it from the dreams that wake me at night and make me *wet.*

He probably knows all this too. He knows what happens to women in here and what draws them in. And I thought I was special—more fool me.

He puts women through this all the time, maybe even men. *I don't normally handle vanillas.*

So I'll be a big disappointment.

I can see this place affects him deeply. His eyes seem darker, more intense, like he draws energy from these implements of torture. They give him a strange, feral power.

But I have power too. It pools between my legs as my arousal begins to pulse. It ensures his pleasure as well as mine, should it come to that...

He's considering my question. "Should you be nervous...? Let's see... You're due a punishment, so maybe you should be. Arms out straight. Spread your legs."

He fastens sturdy leather cuffs on my wrists and ankles. The cuffs are soft inside but they have business-like clips attached to them that jingle as he clamps them into place.

Instantly I feel trapped, like an animal. I grow wetter. I can almost *smell* myself. This is really going to happen...

He strolls over to a polished wooden rack and beckons me over. It holds gleaming canes in various thicknesses. He runs his hand lightly over them, his touch lingering with the reverence of an expert.

He selects one, lifts it out of its compartment and slashes it through the air with a sudden terrifying swish. It quivers to a halt as he brings it expertly to rest in front of him, its tip pressed against the floor between his feet.

I swallow.

"This is our toughest punishment cane. Pure Malacca, very painful, very extreme. For the true connoisseur." He slides it back and takes out another—a slimmer, whippier version of the cane in his room. He twirls it in his hands then runs the tip of it lightly down my breastbone to my navel.

The touch of it sends a flame straight to my groin. *And we haven't even started…*

"Turn around."

My mouth goes dry. Slowly I turn and brace myself.

"Open your legs. Wider. Put your hands behind your head."

Reluctantly I spread my legs, automatically assuming a dancer's pose, keeping my knees straight. Without warning, the cane lands on first one thigh then the other in quick succession.

I was expecting it, but I gasp as I measure the sting. The taps were light but I'm already tense as a bowstring. Sweat trickles down my left temple while heat glows between my legs.

He flexes the cane close to my face, his voice low, amused. "This is lighter than the Malacca but it can give you quite a sharp shock. And it makes pretty stripes if you like that kind of thing."

I glance at the mirrored wall opposite and see thin red marks appear on the backs of my thighs. I shiver as heat flares again.

His eyes gleam. "But you've tasted the cane already tonight, so now we'll try something else. You can stand up."

He leads me around the walls, casually pointing out the different sections like he's a tour guide. "These are the floggers." He runs his long fingers over the forest of leather strands that hang from the rail.

Some are long and fierce-looking, others very fine, with sharp little strands that whisper as he moves them. They smell of well-used leather.

One is short and bushy, with little metal tips at the ends and colored glass beads along the strands. He unhooks it and holds it up for me to touch. The strands are soft but surprisingly springy. It has a strong animal smell.

"Moroccan. Made of camel skin. Freshly cured, by the smell of it. Looks quite tame, would you think?"

I nod, wide-eyed.

"It's a scaled-down version of a flogger. Sometimes called a pussy-whip."

I dart him a look of alarm.

He smiles calmly. "We use it other places too. Floggers are perfectly safe."

He cups my breast with his hand, brushing my nipple with his thumb and two fingertips. "Look at me, Tunis."

As I meet his gaze, I feel a sudden rush of air and the whip lands on my bottom with a snap. It feels extraordinary as the stings from the little tips and beads blend with the sensual caress of the soft strands.

"Keep looking at me." His hand cradles my breast, his touch light and fiercely arousing. He lowers his voice with a smile. "I'm your Dom. I have to know how you feel."

I could look at him forever but right at this minute, I want to look away, to work all this out in private.

As if he knows this, his eyes lock onto mine, his pitiless gaze holding me in thrall as his fingertips continue to explore my nipple. It stiffens and swells, sending shafts of pleasure through me.

It tells him all he needs to know.

His eyes flicker as he leans forward and touches his lips to mine, tasting my lips with soft, light kisses and the whip lands again. As the tiny stings flare once more, I gasp and his tongue plunges into my mouth in a glorious thrust and slowly withdraws, lingering on my lower lip.

Heat consumes me as I kiss him back, panting now, eager for more.

His assessment complete, he gives my nipple a final, familiar squeeze and narrows his eyes. "Shall we continue?"

We pause before a long, flat bench, covered with a thin layer of padding. It bristles with fearsome straps and buckles.

"Spanking bench — where you'll spend some of your time. And on the far wall, the grown-up version." He gestures to a huge contraption like a polished wooden cross. It's fixed with strong-looking clips and restraints on each arm.

He smiles as I touch it then leans across me and gives it a shove. It rotates slowly then begins to tilt. "This can be fun for a change of scene. But tonight we'll try you on the trapeze. Lift up your arms."

With a swift movement he snatches at a rail suspended above where I'm standing. It's festooned with chains. They clatter and clink as he rapidly unwinds two of them and clips them to the leather cuffs on my wrists.

"Now spread your legs."

Delicately he lifts one of my feet, pulls it wide and clips my ankle cuff to a large steel ring bolted to the floor. "Stand on tiptoe."

It's hard to balance on my toes using only the chains for support. They swing and clank, making it awkward to stand still. He watches calmly while I strain to balance, tensing every muscle.

At last he reaches for my other ankle, pulls it wide and clips it to another ring. Arching my feet, I'm spread wide and helpless.

He walks slowly around me, eyeing me critically. "I think we'll spice this up a little."

He takes something out of his pocket—a soft black sleep mask. He slips it over my eyes, instantly blotting out the light. As my senses sharpen I become aware of the sounds of my own body, the rush of blood in my ears, the insistent private pulse of arousal deep between my legs that matches the drum of my heartbeat.

I'm making my own music. It's strangely soothing.

But if this is music I'm just the rhythm section. The melody is all him—the heavenly scent of his skin, whisper of his fingers on mine, the warm sigh of his breath as he runs his hands lightly over me, his electric touch making me shiver.

He leans close, his breath hot on my neck. It sends tremors all down my spine. "Have you any idea how beautiful you look at this moment?"

He finds me beautiful? Is this a good thing?

Moisture trickles down my back in a thin line. "Did you really try to give this up?"

He strokes my tense, quivering flank. "Yes." His low murmur caresses me like velvet. "When I saw you on the replays your reaction intrigued me. From that moment I've wanted to see you like this. So yes, I gave it up. At first it was easy. Once I'd got you into my head nobody else came close. And guess what? Now you're here of your own free will."

He kisses my thigh then pulls away and slaps me hard, making me yelp.

My mind races. "I suppose you want revenge?"

Of course he does. *How stupid I've been.* And now he's got me right where he wants me.

"Revenge? The dish best served cold? Oh no. I want something much more interesting. I want something *hot.*"

"What's that?"

He laughs softly. "If we do this right you'll find out soon enough. And by then you'll want it too."

At that instant there's a movement in the air around me, and I feel his head between my thighs, his breath on one leg and the faint brush of his hair against the other. His breath is hot on my skin as he leaves a trail of soft kisses along each side. Tiny flames sparkle all through me as he draws achingly close to my splayed slit.

The air around me cools like he's stepped away then, without warning, a flogger lands on the back of my leg.

It's not the springy beaded one. The strands of this are long and smooth. They curl lovingly around my leg before slithering away, their snap and their sensuous slide sounding the sweet, piercing top notes in the music we're making.

I cry out in surprise and it lands again, this time on my belly. It falls again and again, sometimes soft, occasionally harsh—excruciating and exquisite. Each new touch is a shock as my sensitive skin tries to decide if it stings or soothes.

Soon it hardly matters. I'm twitching all over, fizzing with arousal from both its sting and its caress. I begin to tremble.

His fingers slide into me, sending steady, pulsing bolts of arousal all through me. A trickle of juice, warm as honey, runs down the inside of my thigh and I hear him draw in a labored breath.

This affects him too.

"You're very wet and swollen now. Does this *arouse* you, Tunis? Tell me." He sounds husky with emotion, almost hoarse.

I gasp as the whip lands again, close to my nipple. It's barely a tap, but I jerk at the shock.

"I said *tell* me."

"Yes. Yes—it does."

It lands again, harder this time, on my still-tender bottom.

"It does—*what*?"

"It does—S*ir*."

It goes on, light, teasing—but relentless. Sometimes the blows whisper over my skin like silk, sometimes they sting. Each one sends a jolt of electricity straight to my groin, too sharp to ignore, too light to make me come.

I've no idea where it's going to land next. Soon I'm almost feverish, twitchy with arousal, aching for relief.

I grow weepy. When a precise blow lands squarely over first one tight, quivering breast then the other, I cry out without thinking, "*Stop.*"

Instantly the air around me stills. I hang limp in my chains for a moment, panting.

"Tunis? What's the matter? Too much?"

I nod in my private darkness. "Enough, please. I can't take any more right now. It's so..." To my horror I feel tears well up underneath the mask then, all at once, I'm being unfastened. He gathers me up in his arms and carries me a little way then I'm lying down.

He pulls away the blindfold and he's sitting over me, his expression troubled. I blink up at him, my skin on fire. A tear trickles into my hair.

"What's wrong? Tell me."

"It's just... It's so intense."

I close my eyes briefly and feel him stretch out at my side. We're lying on a wide, upholstered bed covered in satin. It feels silky and cool against my flaming skin.

At the corners are ornately carved bedposts in dark, polished wood. In place of drapes, they're festooned with chains and cables.

This is not a bed for sleeping in. The thought jerks me awake.

He's watching me lazily, like he's tracking my thoughts. "Feeling better?"

What a strange question. As his gaze burns into me, the tingles on my skin are blending everywhere into a hot, golden glow. To my surprise, I feel terrific—but strangely unfulfilled.

"I'm fine." I manage a shaky smile.

He frowns. "What? Tell me."

"I... It's just... I want something more." I stop, horrified at myself.

What am I saying? The walls are festooned with tools of torment. Goodness knows what he'll use next. "I can't explain it..." My eyes brim with tears. I feel like an idiot. "Cade, what's happening to me?"

He touches my cheek. "It's okay. It's normal. Some people get emotional their first time. People have been known to faint."

He pauses to let the meaning of his words sink in.

I sit up slowly. "You mean...that girl on the stretcher passed out from *emotion*?"

His eyes flicker. "Sure. It happens. Some run for the hills. Some pass out."

His eyes crinkle with amusement. "We'll finish here for now."

He takes off my cuffs, drapes the short robe around my shoulders and leads me back to the elevator. As it rises to the top floor, he looks me over critically.

He touches my breasts, my hips and my thighs with light, soothing fingers and the absorbed air of a craftsman surveying his handiwork. "The marks should be gone by morning. Ah, we're here."

He ushers me to the bathroom, gives me a few minutes then signals me to stand in the shower. He massages soothing shower gel all over my tingling body while I lean against him, sleep creeping up on me like honey.

He tests the spray on his fingers then hoses me down, holding me with his gaze as I alternately shiver and sigh under the teasing jet of water.

He makes me open my legs to allow the jet into my most private places, and holds me still when I wriggle. "Hey, easy."

He's enjoying this too, still playing my arousal like an instrument. At last he swathes me in a large, fluffy towel and pats me dry. I lean against him, content and grateful.

"Feel better now?"

Surprisingly, I do. I ache all over but I feel tingly and somehow gloriously *alive*. "I feel terrific."

He grins. "That'll be the endorphins kicking in. You get a real high after a good whipping—strange, but true." His voice lowers. "And now we come to your second punishment. Do you remember what it's for?"

I stare at him. "What? *Now*?"

"Certainly now. You earned two punishments tonight. You've had only one. Answer me."

I don't play at this. His face grows still. His smile has vanished. "I'm waiting."

Fear uncurls deep in my belly and with it, heat. My nipples tense then grow numb.

It's all part of the dance. But now the moves are clearer.

I can do this. "I forgot to say *Sir*?"

"Check. Stand facing the bed with your hands behind your back."

Slowly I do so, feeling my center throb and my muscles tense.

"Now, bend right over and put your cheek on the bed. Keep your knees straight and your legs apart."

Excitement mounts as I bend low, trying to appear graceful but keenly aware that my rear end is high in the air, leaving my slit wide and exposed.

He takes something out of his pocket and unfurls it in his hands. It's hard to see what it is from down here. It passes through his hand with a soft hissing sound. My stomach clenches.

"This is a leather strap. I'm going to belt you with it twice. One."

I yelp as the strap makes contact, so fierce it makes my eyes smart.

"Two." It lands again. This time I clench my teeth and take the blow in silence.

At once his hands are cool and firm on my punished rear as he massages me with his thumbs. The sudden tenderness of his touch succeeds where the slash of pain failed and makes the tears spring.

Now the sharpness of the sting is fading into fierce golden heat. It glows everywhere south and fuses into a heavy, insistent throb deep between my legs.

"Lie down."

He pushes me forward and I collapse onto the bed, spent and weepy. He flips me over then ties my wrists and my ankles to the bedposts. He uses the tasseled cords looping the drapes. When I'm tied fast, he tests the ties then holds my eyes with his as he eases his fingers into me, massaging gently.

Still pulsing with the rhythm of the blows, I shudder and let out a long sigh as my climax starts to build.

He pulls out his fingers and holds them over my face. "Lick them clean."

I stare at his command as another throb deep between my legs urges me to obey.

Do it. Do anything. But please, please make me come. I lick and suck his fingers eagerly, tasting my own saltiness, relishing this tiny act of submission.

His breath quickens as he gives a low growl deep in his throat. "You're good at this. I'm looking forward to you tasting the real thing." His mouth captures mine with a surge of his tongue that makes my heart leap.

Now. Please, please…

Gradually he loosens the kiss, ending it with provocative touches of his lips as he shifts position. In seconds he's kneeling beside me, his body curving over mine while he explores me with his mouth, his lips urgent, hungry, his tongue insistent. He fastens on one breast and sucks hard, sending lightning flashes through me as he draws away and licks my nipple with long sweeps of his tongue then fastens on my other breast with a muffled groan.

I arch to meet him as he travels lower, licking, nipping and sucking as he goes, lingering on my navel, along my belly, and finally arriving at my thighs with another low growl. I writhe as his mouth fastens between my legs and his hungry tongue punches at my center, the little stabs of its tip driving me to frenzy.

After the harshness of the blows and the emotion of my tears, it's all too much. I shriek as my climax surges up in an unstoppable tidal wave and crashes over me. Between my legs he laughs softly through his kiss and keeps his tongue firmly in place until the spasms die away, leaving me floating limp as a leaf in a sea of bliss.

I'm vaguely aware that he's unfastening my wrists. I feel the touch of his lips on my forehead as he stretches out beside me. His arms fold around me and in seconds, I'm drifting into sleep.

Chapter Seven

"Call them by midnight. If I'm busy, text me. I want the whole deal wrapped up by tomorrow."

Cade's deep voice murmurs through my brain, along with the heavenly aroma of coffee. I open my eyes in a shaft of bright sunlight and blink.

Through the open door of my room, I can see him striding about his sitting room in a shower robe, coffee in one hand, phone in the other, a tousled, preoccupied Greek god.

My heart turns over.

As he dials again, a woman's voice cuts in, too low for me to make out the words.

I stiffen. He's got company.

I slip out of bed, snatch up the thin satin robe and peek cautiously through the door. A small table is laid with silver, snowy porcelain and the remains of breakfast. Close by, notebook in hand, stands Sonja, businesslike today in a prim skirt and crisp white blouse, her face hidden by a curtain of soft, shining hair.

She's still murmuring something, but at that moment, Cade looks up and our eyes meet. He turns abruptly to

Sonja, his tone curt. "That's all for now. We'll go over a few things on the way. And don't forget the hat."

Sonja tosses back her hair. "Yes, sir. And I'll catch Mr. Simmons before he goes out."

I take a step back as Cade walks over, darts me a warning look and softly closes the door.

In the shower I still tingle all over. I feel a throb down below and close my eyes briefly as I relive some of last night's highlights. At last, when I'm sure Sonja's gone I knot the sash of my short robe tightly round my waist and head for the sound and smell of breakfast.

As I step into his room, Cade's pouring a fresh cup of coffee. He glances up with a smile, impish and appealing, designer ad made flesh.

He places the cup by my unused place and pulls out a chair for me to sit. "Morning. Sleep well?"

I smile a greeting as I take my seat and close my eyes briefly as he stoops to kiss my cheek. He smells heavenly—all damp, fresh-washed hair, bergamot aftershave and clean, wholesome *male*.

"Why does Sonja need a hat?" She'll need more than a hat to catch Jake. He's been in a mood ever since we got here.

Cade throws me a glance, his expression stern. "She needs a hat for the same reason you do. We're going out for the day, and you're both dressing up to the nines."

I pause, orange juice partway to my lips. "*We are*? But I don't have a hat."

He smiles airily as he sits opposite. "You'll find one somewhere among those costumes you fill so beautifully. And I must congratulate Sonja on her dress sense. The things I've seen on you so far look terrific."

So, Sonja bought them. I suppress a twinge of irritation. "They certainly fit well. So she could always find work as a personal shopper if she falls foul of you?"

I'm still drowsy and I speak without thinking. His face darkens slightly. Is he always this touchy first thing?

Light dances over his lean jaw and long, sculpted mouth. It strikes me that I've never seen anyone so handsome.

What is it about him? I work in TV. I meet good-looking men all the time. Even Jake's pretty fetching in his way. But Cade Fitzlean's the real deal, full-on, megawatt film-star. Something about him stops people in their tracks.

I must watch myself here. Charm's one thing—losing your head to it is quite another. That's unforgiveable—and naïve.

And, in his case, probably futile. I always seem to annoy him. Now he's looking at me coldly. "Sonja fall foul of *me*? That's pretty unlikely. I've no intention of letting her go. She's far too efficient. Did you enjoy last night?"

I tear my eyes and my thoughts away from his face and take a croissant from the fragrant pile heaped in a silver basket lined with fine linen. It's deliciously light and warm.

I try to sound neutral. "Thank you, yes. And I enjoyed sleeping it off. I'd had a long day."

His long mouth twists at the corner. "Well, today will be longer. We're going to a christening."

"The gardener's new baby?"

"Check. I've cleared my engagements for the day. I sent Sonja to drag out your boyfriend and put him in a suit. And he's bringing a camera."

"What about the one you smashed yesterday?" As yesterday's events rush back, I leap automatically to Jake's defense. "He loved that camera."

I falter and drop the croissant back on my plate as I recall those terrible seconds before I heard it smash.

That might have been me.

Jake went too far, but he meant no real harm. He never does.

The man sitting opposite me is a different matter. I know nothing about him—only that he wants to do strange things to me, things that for some unknown reason, I want too. But I'm not sure I should.

Hard to say which of the two is more dangerous.

I steady my nerves with a sip of juice.

He's frowning. "He'll get a replacement. We'll lend him another till then. Today's a private family occasion. I need a cameraman who's good with a handheld so he won't be too obtrusive. I've asked him to film everything."

"But…I thought you didn't trust him?"

Something flickers in his eyes and his jaw stiffens. "Around you? Definitely not. But his work's good. And, more to the point, he's available."

I down my orange juice and prepare for battle. "But he's working for us. We're on a tight schedule as it is, thanks to you."

The sulky satyr vanishes as the tough CEO snaps back at me. "He's taking a day out from the schedule. You too. And don't let him get you alone. I mean it."

Crossly I reach for the silver coffee pot and curse as some of it splashes on the tablecloth. My heart sinks. We're fighting already and the day's barely begun.

"Here. Let me do that."

I feel his hand on my wrist. His fingers are firm, his skin faintly bronzed. Fine hairs gleam along the edges of his expensive-looking watch. His touch sends a shimmer all along my arm.

I draw a long, calming breath. "So… Why me? Does it need all four of us, this private family occasion?"

Carefully he takes the coffee pot out of my grasp and fills my cup. Like the thin stream of dark liquid pouring from the spout, his wrist is steady and strong.

"I want you to be there."

Now he's deliberately messing up our schedule. I press my lips together as resentment builds. "Why? So I can see you playing at being the generous employer, barging into a private family event and turning it into a personal photo op? I suppose you'll be dazzling everybody with some extravagant christening gift as well?"

He leans back in his chair. "I will, as it happens. *You*."

"*Me?*"

He's grinning broadly now, like I'm missing the joke. "You. Martin the gardener asked me to get your autograph for his wife. She's a big fan of yours. I thought I'd go one better and take you with me. You can do it in person. Your boyfriend can film it all and Sonja can take notes. And mind you look stunning, because today you're the star of the show — so wear a hat."

* * * *

Luckily I've brought one or two cocktail dresses. I rummage quickly through my well-stocked dressing room and unearth some costly shoes, a couple of hats and a marabou fascinator squeezed in among the satin corsets, bondage harness and assorted fetish wear.

They've still got labels attached. The price tags make me catch my breath.

But now I've got a show to put on. Soon I'm in performance mode and in a surprisingly short time, I'm ready.

When I head downstairs to find the others, I'm sleek in bright turquoise Thai silk, my hair falling in a long, gleaming coil down one shoulder. My simple sheath dress is set off with gloves, high-heeled sandals and a tiny clutch bag. A wide-brimmed straw hat swings loosely from one hand.

This is Mrs. Martin's day, so I make a special effort.

It seems to work. I'm gratified to see heads turn as I cross the entrance hall and join the others on the steps looking out over the drive. The two men look a little taken aback.

Sonja's prettier than ever, a porcelain doll in pale shell pink with a matching hat trimmed with a white flower, the ice melting now. "Oh, Miss Vale, you look lovely."

Her warmth takes me by surprise. I smile back, genuinely pleased. "You too. And it's Tunis, please. Clever of you to get Jake into a suit. He hates dressing up in the daytime."

To complete my surprise, even Jake's mood has lifted. He seems distinctly upbeat this morning. He grins and makes a small bow. "Anything to please a lady."

Behind him Cade looks away and avoids my eye. I guess words have passed between them but I'm glad their spat has been patched up for today, at least.

* * * *

Soon we're all cushioned in the luxury of a swift, silent limo, Cade's regular driver a bulky presence at the front. The interior is roomy and quiet. As we leave the soft Devon parklands of Beat Hall and head north along the Severn estuary into Wiltshire, Cade and Sonja become absorbed in business. He dictates notes for meetings and conference calls while Sonja cuts in occasionally to check dates, times and numbers of people attending.

I lean over to whisper to Jake. "Sorry yesterday turned into such a big deal. Are you okay?" I keep my voice low so as not to disturb the others, but instantly I feel Cade's eyes burning into me. I resolutely ignore him.

Jake glowers at me and whispers, "The man's a megalomaniac. Someone should put a stop to it. I'll get my own back someday. Don't you worry."

He glances round to see we're being watched. In a louder voice he offers an apology. "My fault, Tunis. Should've warned you, I guess."

I distract him by asking how he feels about his coming task and he brightens up like he always does when he gets technical. "Today should be really interesting. I like doing family shots. You get some moving moments. Lighting might be tricky. Indoor locations can be a bit hit and miss." He leans forward to hiss in my ear in a loud stage whisper. "That's the trouble with these moguls — always throwing their weight around."

I grin back, relieved he's in such a good mood. "Watch you don't get trampled next time he heads an invasion."

He snorts. "If that's a veiled reference to Genghis Khan, it's Mongols, not moguls, airhead." Instantly we're teens again, sparring for fun.

As the car finally draws up at the pretty country church where the christening will take place, I've almost forgiven him for yesterday's ordeal. How can Cade possibly think that Jake, of all people, is a threat?

* * * *

By early evening I've signed my name dozens of times, posed with the beaming baby, posed without it and posed with beaming parents and small groups of beaming guests so often that I vow I'll never again be rude about movie stars or anybody else who has to do this for a living. I'm exhausted.

My face aches from smiling. My head reels with the names of people I'll never see again. It's very hard work.

Cade's everywhere, shaking hands, being the genial employer, making a point of keeping Jake in tow at all times. But most of all, I'm deeply touched when I meet the Martins.

"Mr. Fitzlean's paid for everything," Mrs. Martin whispers in her soft Wiltshire accent as I sign her autograph. "He's been so good. And I was thrilled when he said he'd bring you. It's like having royalty. Makes it a real day to remember."

The service is held in a pretty country church but the reception afterward is at a grand country hotel with a marquee set up on the grounds. As the sunlight turns to gold and the shadows lengthen into evening, the guests are invited to stay on for a buffet supper followed by dancing.

Cade appears at my elbow with Jake and Sonja in tow. "I think it's time we left these good people to party."

His look sweeps over me, drinking me in. Since stepping out of the car this morning, I've felt his eyes burning into me all day. We've barely spoken, but every time we've touched—during photos or talking casually with the guests—I've felt a tingle of electricity. Each time I've taken care to step out of range and focus on what I'm doing.

Each time the feeling has lingered, leaving a shimmer of excitement that's been building into a surge of heat.

As the others leave, I linger to make some final farewells. When I finally emerge at the entrance to the hotel, Cade is waiting alone. His eyes meet mine with a gleam that could melt rock. "I sent the others back on their own. We're staying for a while."

I take a slow, steady breath. "You want to dance?"

He smiles slowly. "Later, maybe."

* * * *

Our suite's on the top floor. It's smaller than the apartment at Beat Hall, with plainer furniture and homelier bedding, but I get no time to explore.

As we walk in, he seizes me by the waist, spins me round and fastens his mouth on mine like a man starved. I tear at his shirt and tie as he reaches behind me to slide down my zipper and unpeel my dress.

Soon we're standing in a pool of clothing. With an impatient thrust of his foot, he kicks it away and sweeps me into his arms. "I've wanted to do this all day. I couldn't take my eyes off you. I've never seen anyone light up a room like you can."

We land in a heap on the bed and his mouth descends again. I hear him growl low in his throat as I writhe luxuriously against his jutting erection, letting his heat scorch the cool, smooth skin of my belly.

His hands are everywhere — along my flanks, over my breasts, kneading my bottom with long, firm sweeps of his fingers. His touch is electrifying. It sends urgent signals all through me, fusing into a dull throb deep between my legs.

With a sudden lurch he rolls over onto his back. I sit across his hips as he holds me up by the ribs, his fingers gripping me firmly. His thumbs jut provocatively into my breasts. I survey him in triumph, his magnificent torso laid out before me like a banquet. I lean down and touch my lips to his breastbone to make a start.

He laughs softly. "Hey, not so fast. We've got things to do first."

I settle at either side of his chest and run my fingers lightly over his chest hair, thrilling as his tiny nipples sharpen into nubs under my searching, teasing fingertips. "What sort of things?"

I lean forward, letting my loosened hair flow over him. He runs his hand through it and holds a lock of it to his face. He breathes in with a deep sigh.

With a powerful thrust of his hips, he tips me onto the bed beside him. "Your training session. Forgotten so soon? You're not getting out of it just because we're off site." He sits up beside me, his face stern.

"*Now*?"

His smile has vanished. In a blink he's no longer the genial employer bestowing gifts all round, he's back in control and he's serious. "Now. Kneel."

"But... I need the bathroom. I've had a long afternoon, Cade. Please."

I need more than the bathroom. I need a few seconds to prepare.

He pauses, his expression opaque. "Okay. Take a few minutes then I want you back here."

He gets off the bed, finds his jacket in the heap of clothes he's just kicked across the floor and reaches for his phone. I watch mystified as he jabs at the keys then sets it carefully on a low table. "I've set a timer. Take five. Go."

I dart into the en suite, take a long drink of water from the tap and splash some on my face. With the door shut I look at myself in the mirror. I appear the same as usual, only with more makeup and glossier hair. My eyes look unnaturally bright.

But that's just excitement. I've brimmed with it all day.

As I walk slowly back into the main room he's leaning over a small bag on the floor. It gapes open as he takes out some items with exaggerated care, weighing each one as he lifts it out then eyeing it thoughtfully.

I kneel slowly by the bed, scooping back my hair, and watch him.

He seems remote, absorbed. He's naked, his erection jutting ominously into the air, large, luscious and purple. Along his back and shoulders, muscles ripple as he stoops to zip up the bag then stands up to push it away with his foot in a single, lithe movement.

He turns to face me, a perfectly honed, bronzed image of muscle, sinew and deep, carnal intent. His eyes lock on mine with a heat that sparks all through me.

"Put your hands behind your back."

He walks over to me with slow, measured grace and stands before me, his erection inches from my face. "Look at me. You're going to get a real spanking now. You're very beautiful. You've done everything I asked. You've been preening all day, the belle of the ball. But we have to get you back into submission mode for our second session to work. Agreed?"

His voice is low, his words so quiet I can barely hear them. His meaning sends a chill through me.

Do I want this? I can negotiate here. He's asking permission. All at once I have a choice.

I can smell his skin and the fierce earthy aroma of his private parts, so close to my face. I feel an answering signal from deep inside.

Yes, I do want it. And for some reason I've no wish to examine, I want it *now*.

"Yes, I agree."

He sinks back onto the bed and pats his knee. "Climb up here."

As I do so, I see the items from the bag set out neatly beside him. "What are they?"

He takes his time, arranging my legs into position, signaling I must keep my knees straight, and holds up the items one by one. "This is a duster, this is a wheel and this is a blindfold. These are for you. These four leather cuffs are also for you, and this" — he holds up a fearsome-looking bat made of carved wood — "is a paddle. This is for me."

A what? It looks like a table tennis bat but it's thinner and made of heavy, polished wood. It has an elaborate pattern carved into it that lets light shine through.

I see what it is, and I've already guessed what it does. I shiver as he fondles my bottom, his hands sweeping deep down between my thighs. A tell-tale trickle of juice runs down the inside of my leg. I'm already dripping with arousal, and we've not yet started.

"The paddle's for both of us — for one to give, the other to receive. Ready?"

I screw my eyes tight shut. *Be careful what you wish for...*

"Yes, Sir. I'm ready."

Chapter Eight

My spanking is harsh but mercifully brief.

After a slow warm-up with his hands that threatens to make me come every second, he switches to the paddle. Now I'm scared.

It looks ferocious. But I'm so hot already that the few sharp, stinging blows Cade delivers with it are nothing like as bad as I'd feared.

Now I'm really on fire.

He pauses to let me get my breath then slips the blindfold over my head.

As the stings fade into a hot glow and the light blots out, I feel his hands move over me again, firm but tender, hard and soothing both at the same time.

"Okay? How does that feel? Tell me."

It feels wonderful. *I* feel wonderful. But he knows this.

I take a long, shuddering breath as the heat fades on my bottom and burns somewhere else, with a fierce ache that throbs between my legs, but I have no choices here. I can only endure. "I'm fine. I feel... *Oh.*"

His fingers slip between my legs and deep inside me. He draws in a long, ragged breath as he encounters my wetness and my all-too-evident, shameful need.

"Okay. I can tell how it feels. You're dripping already. That should make the rest of our session pretty interesting."

In the soft, murky confines of the blindfold all my senses sharpen. As he gathers me in his arms, his touch is more electrifying than ever. I lean into his arms as he gets me into position on the bed, fixing my arms by clipping the cuffs to tethers looped round the bedposts then hauling me down to stretch them tight and securing my ankles.

It's thrilling and very scary to feel so vulnerable, to be so completely at his mercy, but this is taking a long time to arrange. "What are you going to do? This is making me nervous."

I sound husky. I realize I'm trembling.

I feel his breath close to my ear. It brings me up in goosebumps.

"Easy. Don't be frightened. Do you trust me, Tunis?"

"Do I have any choice?"

In answer Cade fastens his mouth on mine, his kiss long and deep, his tongue gentle but insistent. I reach along it with my own, shy at first then eager, as ripples of lust glow in my belly and spread out all over my body.

At last he pulls away and I shudder as he drops light, soft kisses on my throat and moves down to each nipple in turn, teasing each with a long, lascivious lick then moves further south, along my belly.

"You always have a choice, all the time."

His lips murmur against my skin, sending shivers all through me. "I try to guess how you're feeling but you must always tell me if it gets to be too much. Now we'll start."

I can hear music, but whether it's from the hotel or from somewhere in the room I can hardly tell. It makes a calm pattern in the background as a bewildering kaleidoscope of touch opens up in my world of darkness.

Each time I expect something painful, I feel only a soft, whisper-light feather or fingertip—or a kiss. Each time I start to relax I feel a harsh slap or a strange, metallic rasp as the spiked wheel runs over me, grazing a nipple or along the inside of my thigh.

It's delicious, fiercely arousing and acutely disturbing. Soon I'm panting, both dreading and craving the next touch, twitching and writhing at its contact, shaky and trembling as my tingling nerve endings try to work out which it is—sharp or soft, hard or gentle, pain or pleasure. After a while, it's impossible to tell.

All the time the deep throb between my legs is growing stronger, beating a steady drumbeat of its own as it stirs the strong, unmistakable glow of dawning orgasm. It threatens to explode inside me every time his eager, hungry lips brush along my cleft and nibble softly along my slit, swollen now and pulsing with need, every time his fingers brush my nipples into hard, jutting points, whenever his warm, firm hand lands with a slap on my rump, jolting me closer to the edge. It never quite arrives, leaving me poised on the brink of pleasure, aching for release.

At last he unfastens my ankles. I think my ordeal is over but he merely grips them firmly in both hands and flips me over.

I gasp as I cross my arms, tightening the tethers. I lean awkwardly on my elbows for support. "What's happening?"

I feel his mouth hot on my back then the hard muscles of his thighs as he kneels at either side of me. "Kneel up with your ass in the air. I want to see my handiwork."

I push my face hard into the mattress as he hauls me up by the hips. I gasp as he massages my punished ass, his thumbs rubbing painfully against my tender, twitching curves.

"You look sensational, Tunis—all rosy and beautiful." He drops hot, eager kisses all over my backside, lingering on each cheek then he pulls away. "Now we'll try an experiment."

I feel cool air on my tender skin as he reaches across the bed to pick something up then, without warning, the paddle lands again.

This time the blows are so hard I jerk at each one, but I'm thoroughly warmed up now and giddy for more. I hardly feel the sting as the jolts clutch at my aching belly and prod my arousal ever closer to the edge.

"Okay now?" He pauses just as I think the money shot is about to land. Writhing with frustration, I cry out through clenched teeth. "Yes, yes, it's fine. Again. Please, once more. Do it again."

I hear him laugh softly. I squirm as he caresses me again. Juice trickles down the inside of my leg, fueling my shame.

"You want *more*? Certainly. With pleasure. One, then."

It lands again, and again the jolt ricochets through me. But it's still not enough.

"Again?"

I give an incoherent grunt and it lands again, and this time he carries on, his arm setting up a steady beat. At the fourth he stops, pauses for a moment then gives me one last swat right across the base of both cheeks. This time I'm close, *really* close, and he slips his hand deep between my legs and reaches my aching bud with his fingers.

Without warning, my orgasm erupts.

I scream out loud with the glory of it, my spasms coming in waves, one after another as I convulse around his hand.

It's too much. I'm not used to this. Tears follow closely.

Instantly he unfastens me, tears off the blindfold and gathers me into his arms. I bury my head against his chest, wracked with sobs as my body eases back to normal and my pounding heart slows down.

"Wow, result. Easy now."

He seems to hold me for a long time, but I suppose it can only be minutes before he takes my face in his hands. "Tunis, look at me."

I do so, whisking away the last of my tears. I feel wonderful — soothed, content and ready for anything.

But his face is stern. "Now you must thank me. Kneel on the floor."

Languid, almost sleepy, I do so.

"Put your hands behind your back."

New excitement fizzles through me, jolting me fully awake. I do as I'm told. He looms before me, his erection impossibly large, impossibly hot. I can feel its heat on my face.

His eyes gleam briefly. "Take it in your mouth."

Automatically I bring my hands round to caress him but he shakes a finger. "No hands. Keep them behind you."

Really? He means it. Forbidden to stroke him, I burn even hotter. Slowly I extend my tongue to lick him, thrilling to the salty taste of his skin and his heat, then work him into my mouth and suck hard at the smooth, rounded crown.

This is a real challenge. He's very big and very erect. Positioning myself carefully so as to open my throat as wide as I can, I start to fellate him with slow thrusts. I work round him with my tongue, letting his flavor and his earthy, feral aroma fill up my senses. To my joy, I find my own arousal burns again deep below, where I'm still pulsing from his touch. As I work up a rhythm, I feel an extra throb of excitement as his breathing speeds up.

I push forward, yawning my throat open to take him fully, letting my weight propel me forward. I feel a surge of triumph as the tendons stand out on his neck. It's deeply moving to see this beautiful man react so intensely.

He growls low in his throat when I lunge forward to take his whole length, pausing to let the gag reflex ease off then lunging again and again.

With a sudden movement he grips the sides of my face to hold me still. I feel him quiver in my mouth then he gives a strangled cry and floods me with his warmth as he pumps into me over and over.

I relax around him, letting him soften slowly, careful not to make a sudden movement now that he's spent and tender. He holds my head in place, and I keep very still, unwilling to break the spell as his breathing slowly steadies.

At last he pulls away then leans down, seeks my lips with his and holds me fast in a long, lingering kiss.

When he finally releases me, he caresses my hair and slides his hand along my face to cup my chin. "That was sensational. *You're* sensational. Thank you, sub. You've earned yourself some fun. Let's go party."

* * * *

While I work miracles with a quick shower, a comb and my makeup bag, Cade strides about the suite, snarling into his phone and catching up on some of the business he's neglected during the day.

I look on in awe, like a star-struck teenager. Does he have any idea how compelling he looks as he paces the room? I could watch him all night.

And, surprisingly, I feel wonderful. My backside's tender, but I'm ready for anything. And I'm *hungry*.

As he finishes a call, I catch his eye. "Are we eating soon? I'm famished."

He eyes me from across the room, his gaze dark. "So you have other appetites. I must take care to satisfy them. Yes, we'll eat now, but not here."

I try to look unconcerned as we make our way down through the hotel to the main entrance. To my surprise he picks up some keys from the blushing receptionist at the main desk and leads me straight out to the front drive where a gleaming sports car is waiting.

The V-8 engine fires with a powerful, throaty roar and we pull away, heading into the shadows of the countryside and the scents and the warm, moist air of a lovely summer night.

"Where are we going?"

He flicks a button on the dashboard and I hear the plaintive tone of a solo jazz trumpet. It reminds me of empty New York streets in old black and white movies.

"To a restaurant I know. It's not far. Art Pepper suit you?"

"Mm, lovely. Why did you send Sonja back with Jake? Won't people talk?"

"About them? I doubt it."

"I meant about us." My voice is low.

"I said you were staying on with the Martins and I had business in Bristol. They don't know we're together. Or expect us back for a while."

As usual, he's thought of everything. In the soft glow from the dashboard, his classical features form a perfect profile.

I watch him, mesmerized. "You always have to be in control?"

He darts me a glance. "I like being in control. I feel safer that way."

Safer? How odd. I frown. "Is that why you like to beat women?"

His smile vanishes. "I don't beat women — not in that sense. Men who beat women have lost control, in my opinion. What I do is always consensual. I like it. They want it." In the faint light I see his lip curl. "*You* want it. That's why we're here."

"You're hedging. I'm talking about control. Why is it okay for Sonja to be alone with Jake and not me?"

The car screeches to a halt, and he turns to face me, eyes blazing. "They're with my driver, who also happens to be ex-army and one of my bodyguards. I told him to keep an eye on them. And I might remind you what Simmons nearly did to you on that footbridge. And he's still hot for you. I can tell."

His mood swing is startling. I fight to steady my breath, still uneven after the shock of the sudden halt. "But that's what I mean, Cade. With respect, my relationship with Jake is none of your business. We're old friends, end of story. And I can take care of myself."

His contented mood has vanished. "That I doubt. While you're in my care, I mean to look after you. So stay away from him. You could have been killed."

Angrily he jabs at the ignition, and we start off again. This time we drive in silence.

* * * *

We eat in a small restaurant over a quiet and very traditional country pub. The food is delicious — delicate scallops with fresh country herbs, roast fowl with new, crisp vegetables and a light, summery lemon tart. The wine is surprisingly good and comes in a dust-covered bottle with the compliments of the house.

Cade seems to be well known here, and the landlord and his wife — who is also the cook — both come to our table to greet us at the end of our meal.

I congratulate them on the food, and I'm promised a recipe to take away for the delicious lemon tart.

Luckily Cade seems to mellow with the food, and soon chats lightly about his big breaks in the entertainment business and his plans for the future. As we wave goodbye to our hosts and set off once again into the darkness, he rests a hand on my thigh and strokes gently, his fingers warm and meaningful. "Enjoy your meal?"

I run my fingers lightly over the back of his hand and his fingers move higher. "Among other things, yes. Thank you. It was delicious. How do you know so many people around here?"

I lean back in my seat and open my legs a little, inviting his insistent hand to move up a little farther.

I see him grin.

"We lived around here, for a short while, anyway. My father bought Beat Hall long before we moved in."

I see a sudden image of a younger Cade, the sulky teenager who penned his hit record after a chemistry exam, being a boy, exploring the grounds, making friends in pubs and climbing trees.

It's an intriguing picture.

Excitement builds as we drive through the imposing gateway to the Beat Hall Estate. But instead of driving up to the main house, we veer off to the left.

Soon we're driving along an unfamiliar narrow track lined with trees. I glance across at him, puzzled. "Where are we going? Do you have a favorite spot for making out, too?"

He looks at me and grins. "Something like that. Not that I've ever made out in it. I've never brought anybody else here before. But I thought you might like to see it. It's pretty at night."

He pulls off the narrow lane into a graveled space. In the headlights I can just make out a curved brick wall, with an elaborate doorway at the top of some wide stone steps. As he switches off the lights, I peer upward as a shaft of moonlight reveals a tall tower. I can just see its top, a sharp outline against the stars.

"This is the lookout tower. The third duke built it as a beacon during the Napoleonic wars when there was a threat of invasion. Spectacular views, especially at night. Come on. A climb will do you good."

It's a long way up. The steps curve upward in a seemingly endless spiral. Cade leads the way, apparently unfazed by the climb.

When we finally reach the top, I'm panting a little, my legs aching, but my breath soon steadies as I gaze out of the vast picture windows.

All around us the views over the park stretch away. Moonlight glances over the treetops, turning them into a billowing silver ocean. Far away, the towers of Beat Hall are etched against the deep midnight blue of the sky, its windows sparkling through the leaves like a magical palace.

In the distance a slim silver line marks the horizon.

"Is that the sea?"

"Yep. You can just see it from here on a clear night." He's close behind me, his voice oddly husky in the stillness.

"Why did you bring me here?"

His lips touch my shoulder with a whisper-light kiss. "I wanted you to see it. I used to come here when I was a boy — when times got tough."

I stiffen. "Was that often? After the crash?" I hold my breath. Is this the key to the mystery of who he is?

"Not often. But it got to me sometimes. Anyway, when you're growing up times are always tough at some point. I didn't do so badly."

Did it make him like he is? I must go carefully here, but I'm desperate to know. "Did... Did what happened to you turn you on to...BDSM?"

"Not especially. I was very happy on the whole. You don't have to be damaged to like BDSM. I just like it. I've always liked it. I like what it does, and I like where it takes you. I don't like women scared. I like them hungry. When I do it well, that's what happens."

He touches my face with his fingertip. "I want to see you like that — very much."

He kisses the other shoulder then turns me round to face him. In the moonlight his eyes glitter strangely, but his face is partly in shadow. "I suppose we've got to the point where we might as well face it. This is turning into something more than sub training, don't you think?"

For a long moment the world stands still, then I draw in a cautious breath. "Is it?"

His eyes glitter. "I think so, yes. But we'll hold the violins for a while. I'm on a mission here. I want to show you what BDSM's all about. It's a lot more than whipping the shit out of people. I want to show you what it does and why. And it'll take me more than a few days. And since you asked, there's another reason I brought you here tonight."

I gaze at him, spellbound. This feels unreal, like I'm in some fairy tale at the top of a magical tower where handsome princes say strange and wonderful things to princesses. "There is?"

He kisses me gently, his mouth touching mine with the lightest brush of his lips. "Yes. I brought you here because this is where I want to fuck you for the first time." He kisses me again. "But only if you want me to. And only if you promise we'll do it again—often."

Happiness flowers deep inside me. It comes with a shaft of something else, something even stronger but dark and urgent. It sends flames roaring through me, wetness pooling in the throbbing dip deep between my legs—*lust*.

I whisper against his neck, thrilling to the spicy, feral scent of his skin, the coiled power in his arms and the warm glow down near his hips. "Okay. I promise."

Chapter Nine

My happiness is brief. As Cade relaxes his arms, I see we're in an eight-sided space right at the top of the tower. It has huge windows with wide, cushioned seats underneath and spectacular views. Moonlight floods in, filling the space with silver light.

I stiffen. This is my least favorite kind of place.

He's staring down at me anxiously. "What's the matter? Too extreme for you?"

His jaw tenses, like my response is vital.

This really matters to him. I swallow, but I take the plunge. "I'm fine."

His fleeting smile expresses joy for a split second. With a swift movement, he unzips my dress and my fear melts in the heat of his look as I let the bright silk peel away. He fingers the plunge of my bra with a burning finger then runs his hands lightly down my flanks, lingering on the lace edge of my panties.

His touch is exquisite, his focus absolute.

"I could eat you whole. You're so beautiful..." He finds my mouth and finishes the thought with his tongue. Heat spirals through me as I lean into him, fired by the urgency of his hot, hungry mouth as the burning pressure glowing between our hips warns me of an invasion to come.

All at once I'm pinned beneath him along one of the seats, impaled on his hungry tongue while he tears at his clothes.

With a grunt he kicks them off then breaks the kiss to lean over in a lithe, athletic arc to search his trousers for a foil packet.

"Wait. Let me." I snatch it out of his hand, wriggle out from underneath him and leap to my feet. I wave it aloft, sashaying in the moonlight then I begin a slow dance, teasing and swaying my hips.

He leans back to watch, his gaze liquid heat as my bra straps slip slowly off one shoulder then the other. I turn and sway my rear seductively close to his face as I peel away my panties.

They get part-way down my thighs with my thumbs hooked in the lace before he gives a low growl and seizes me by the hips.

"Hey, you're cheating," I gasp. "You're not supposed to touch the stripper."

"I'll eat her then." His laugh is somewhere between a purr and a growl as his mouth covers me with hungry kisses, first one side then the other.

I lean into his grasp as his hot mouth works its magic, and I start to burn. After a few, luscious moments, I turn round and stoop to lick the head of his erection, jutting between us, glossy in the moonlight. With soft caresses I steady its angle, thrilling to its size and its silky heat.

I lick gently along the sides to make it moist, so the soft skin inside my lips will slide easily along its length then take it fully in my mouth. Meanwhile I tear open the packet and take out the small, rolled contents.

He groans as I pull away and deftly roll it into place, but I've woken a sleeping tiger. With a swift movement, he stands up and takes charge, spinning me round and leaning into my back, his erection jutting painfully against my tender bottom as he steadies me against him.

"You're sensational. Bend over."

He leans forward and I feel his chest hair rasp against my back as he gently nips the nape of my neck with his teeth. His breathing is ragged now like he's running a race and his voice purrs through me, deep and throaty.

"Put your feet apart. Wider. Keep your legs straight. Touch the floor to balance."

He sounds husky, impatient. I bend right over and steady myself on the floor with my fingertips, making a graceful arch, and with a lurch, he slams into me. I cry out at the suddenness of it then feel his hands slide over my body, one rolling and kneading my breasts and the other reaching between my legs, penetrating deep into my eager, swollen folds, now stretched tightly around him. He begins to move, gently at first then harder, each thrust tearing a grunt of pleasure from him that echoes through me, making my tense muscles quiver as I strain to balance and haul him in at the same time.

He feels wonderful, filling me deeply, his heat glowing inside me, his rhythm matching my heartbeat with utter precision, his own need for me so great I feel it burn through the condom. I've wanted this all evening, all day.

All week.

Maybe all year.

Soon my climax begins to build but to my amazement he slows, pulls me back on top of him as he collapses back onto one of the benches then eases me off him, holding me aloft with both hands.

"Turn over. We'll finish together. I want to kiss you while I do this."

He sounds harsh but as I sweep my leg high over him to shift position, he smiles with pure pleasure, the moonlight glinting on his regular teeth, and rolls me over so he's once more on top.

"Are you okay with this?"

I nod, breathless, marveling that he can sound so calm at such a charged moment. "You want a critique?"

My climax has been building, the pressure mounting, and now with all the upheaval of shifting position, I'm sure I'll explode. But this place is important to him and if I'm the first woman he's brought here, then this moment is important to me too. I want to make this special for him.

I look deep into his eyes, searching anxiously for clues to his progress so I can pace myself to match his thrusts, using every fiber of my technique to fend off my pleasure to coincide with his. He seems to know, maybe from the way my body reacts so sensitively to his every move.

In the moonlight I see a change in his eyes, a new intensity, an unexpected tenderness as he thrusts faster. My muscles contract round him as our bodies perform their own *pas de deux* and he fastens his mouth on mine, his tongue filling me as well. He thrusts again and again, each stroke a deep, hot pleasure until at last I can hold off no longer and my orgasm explodes inside me. My spasms rock through me and as I convulse around him, he jolts in my arms and erupts in his own.

He keeps his mouth locked on mine, loosening his kiss only to brush his lips softly against my mouth, the light, sensuous contact adding layers of sweetness to the waves of honeyed content that wash over me as I yield to his weight and his power.

At last he buries his head in my neck and heaves a long, contented sigh. "Hey, that was some critique — pretty impressive."

I smile against his ear and nibble at his earlobe with my teeth. "For a first fuck, that was pretty impressive too. You've set yourself a high standard. *Sir.*"

* * * *

It's nearly dawn when the powerful sports car purrs to a halt outside the massive entrance to Beat Hall. Despite the late hour, a footman instantly appears, opens the passenger door for me and accepts the keys from Cade.

In the elevator Cade holds me close. I lean against him, sleepy and sated, while he strokes my hair, his protective arm around my bare shoulders warm and comforting against the dawn chill we brought in with us from the park.

As we step out of the elevator into the hallway to our rooms, his phone buzzes. He glances at it idly then holds it to his ear. "Fitzlean."

We're almost inside the room. I can see my bed, invitingly made up, the smooth sheet folded back, waiting for my weary limbs to sink into it. It seems a long time since I slept.

His grip on my waist tightens, holding me fast, but he seems to have forgotten I'm here. Along my side I feel him tense as he listens in silence then slips the phone into his pocket.

When he looks at me, I see a stranger. My lover has disappeared and the magical tower is fading fast.

"What paperwork did you sign before coming here?"

I stare, my sluggish brain groping at his meaning. "*Paperwork?* I've no idea. There was so much of it. Why?"

There was a sheaf of forms to sign before we came. Non-disclosure agreements to protect the reputations of all the celebrities we're going to meet, consent forms and disclaimers, a simple but very scary dungeon contract. That was before the extremely thorough medical checks, declarations and insurance guarantees.

He's frowning. "The lawyers think there's a problem with the signatures from your team. Who was in charge of all that? You or your lawyers?"

I feel a twinge of alarm. "Ben would know. You'll have to ask him."

His eyes hold mine for a long moment, his glint of icy appraisal sweeping over me like cold steel. When he speaks, his voice is low and measured. "There are a great many famous people here. They're taking part in some very unusual activities. That's why we've gone to so much trouble to make this place secure and get signatures on everything. We can't afford any slip-ups."

A chill runs through me. Blackmailers, paparazzi, psychos — they'd all pay handsomely for a shot of just one of the film stars or celebrities sampling a taste of the whip. A lot of careers and reputations are at risk here, including mine. And so is our film and maybe even our future careers, if we've somehow fallen foul of his tight security arrangements.

I swallow. "Let me talk to the others before you do anything. Have you told them about this yet?"

"I'm starting with you." He glances at his watch. "They won't be up yet. Find them at breakfast and make a subtle enquiry. I want to know who gathered in the final signatures and if it was one of you. If so, we might be able to sort this out quietly. If not, I'll have to make you all sign afresh—or even expel the whole lot of you."

For a long moment I stare at him in dismay. The intense, passionate lover has vanished as completely as the magical tower and all the rest of the fairy tale. Once more he's the implacable man of business—curt, decisive, chilling.

And still in control.

"And don't forget our agreement. We have two sessions today. If you're still on the premises, I want you back here for the first at four this afternoon."

With despair comes real fatigue. A wave of weariness loosens my muscles and makes the room spin. Instantly his expression softens.

"What's the matter?"

I sway against him and somehow I'm swept up into his arms and he's carrying me into my room and murmuring into my hair. As if from a long way away, I hear him say my name and that he should have taken more care then he lays me gently down and I sink into soft, mellow darkness.

* * * *

Breakfast is a tense affair. My absence has caused a stir, but Jake's has sparked outrage.

Even Ben's tetchy. "You might have let me know. We looked all over for you. And Mel had a terrific interview lined up with Garth Delaney, of all people, and no one to film the thing. We got some of it on tape, but it's not the same." He stares gloomily into his cereal.

Mel takes a wider view. She's having the time of her life and the prospect of a repeat session with Garth

Delaney fills her with glee. "Don't be an ass, Ben. Tunis warned you she'd be unhappy here. And now she's got Fitzlean throwing his weight about and the Panther prowling all over the place."

My coffee cup clatters against the saucer and Mel leans across and pats my arm. "Sorry, Tunis. I forgot." She fixes Ben with an accusing stare. "You knew this would be an ordeal for her. Cut her some slack. She's doing her best."

It's a good time to change the subject. But my timid questions about paperwork bring snorts of derision and much eye rolling.

"Don't get me started." Ben groans. "It was a nightmare. But it's all fine, Tunis. Why do you ask? And by the way, when do we get invited up to see your super upgrade? Mel's dying to see how the other half lives."

At that moment Cade appears at his shoulder. I freeze, but Ben carries on talking, unaware of his presence. "Mel's got a theory that the boss man's fattening you up for some dark, murky scheme of his own."

"And what scheme would that be?"

Cade's deep voice is pitched low, barely audible beyond the range of our table, but Ben jumps so violently that his orange juice splashes all over the snowy tablecloth.

"I—ah... Hi, Cade. We were just saying..."

"That some mythical threat hangs over your star presenter? I gathered." He raises an enquiring eyebrow and looks directly at me.

He wants to know if I've traced the culprit.

I give him a barely perceptible shake of the head and see his lips tense slightly. The others look on, astonished.

I avoid their eye as I feel Cade's disapproval radiate like a wave of heat across the table.

"I want you all in my office. Now."

Sonja appears at his elbow, looking pale and tired. For once even Miss Frosty's subdued.

My heart sinks.

* * * *

In Cade's office, the atmosphere is tense as he outlines the problem. His words are few and terse, his tone sharp.

I daren't open my mouth. I've already raised this. Surely they'll make the connection and link us? If so, we're finished. Why, oh why couldn't he wait?

Our paperwork is spread out on his mahogany desk in a great pile.

"That's it, all of it. We all signed. I don't see the problem." Ben seems genuinely mystified.

Mel looks bored. Jake's openly yawning.

"Then we'll just glance through it." His voice low with menace, Cade starts handing out the papers

This is awful. I stare into space and my gaze strays to the group of stunning modern photos I noticed on the first day. They're high profile action shots from war zones, nuclear test sites, famine areas. Some of them I've seen before, often.

Jake leans over and whispers low, so as not to disturb the others. "You spotted them too? Genuine Gemmels. All signed. He's got a bunch of them. Must have cost him a fortune."

I lean forward, my interest spiked. That explains it— the savage lines, the raw, bleak emotion captured forever in the moment.

Jake's still whispering. "That one I don't recognize, though. See that one of the two kids on the bank? Same style—it must be one of his. But I've never seen it before. Have you?"

I peer again. The background's a blur of figures and patches. Maybe there's some momentous event taking place, or maybe it's just traffic. But the foreground is sharp and clear. It shows two young children, a boy and a girl, sitting on a mound. The boy's reaching out to the little girl, who seems to be crying.

Odd, I think, that with all the excitement going on in the background it's the children who caught the photographer's eye.

But the more I look, the more powerfully it strikes me, the extreme tenderness of the child—so protective so young. The shot hints at a private moment amid public activity—the classic essence of a great photo—yet they're probably nothing to do with the scene. In essence, it's just a couple of kids sitting on a bank.

I frown, sure I've seen it before somewhere. But the moment eludes me.

"And the signatures on the top copies are all fake."

Cade's voice echoes through the room. It's followed by a stunned silence. With a snap I drag my attention back to the problem of the paperwork and the photo is forgotten.

My subconscious patches up the conversation into a rough version of what was said. The paperwork appears to be in order, but the signatures on the top copies differ from those on our earlier disclaimers, so technically the top copies of the non-disclosure agreements are invalid.

In effect, it means that none of us has promised to keep quiet about what we see and do here. There's nothing to stop us from calling a reporter or gossiping on the Internet. And if we want to sell our story to the highest bidder, the Love Beat Corporation has no legal redress.

"So unless we find a solution right here and right now, we'll slap on a super injunction and you'll have to leave." He looks round at us with eyes of steel. I sense his fury and wonder briefly if the others have any idea how serious this is.

He leans forward, looking at each of us turn, his tone deadly quiet. "And what I have to know is, was it one of you? In which case, we just might be able to fix this. Or was it someone back in some office somewhere? Because if it was, you're all leaving as of now."

His eyes rest briefly on me but show no emotion as they pass on round the group. It's like being back at school, called to the principal's office about a broken window.

The silence lengthens. None of us look at the others.

I feel a stirring of alarm. Something's wrong here.

We're behaving as if we're guilty.

Surely we should be denying this? Protesting? Heaven knows there's enough at stake.

After a long moment, Ben clears his throat. "I—ah... I think it may have been me."

I hold my breath as the room slowly comes to life and the protests and clamor I've been waiting for suddenly drown out Ben's sheepish explanation.

When the final copies came through, he thought he'd save time by signing them all himself, one after the other. No, he'd no idea it was so important. Yes, of course he understands the significance now, but he hadn't at the time.

At last he stammers to a halt and looks down at his hands. I wait for him to apologize but he says nothing more. It makes me feel uneasy. He's usually so careful about paperwork.

Cade eyes him with distaste then for a second his eyes flick over to meet mine.

Oh no. He must think I'm part of this.

His gaze drifts back to the unhappy Ben. "Okay. So far no harm seems to have been done. Your emails and calls are being monitored, so I'll give you a second chance. Sonja's prepared duplicates of the top copies of all the relevant documents. You can sign them now. We'll witness them before you leave this room, unless you'd like to call in your lawyers and let them battle it out with mine."

We all sign. As the atmosphere eases, I breathe a sigh of relief as I follow the others down to lunch. Cade joins us, easy and relaxed. There's no trace in his manner of his earlier tension.

At one point Mel looks up with a grin. "Hey, Tunis, what about showing us your upgrade? We asked around, but no one seems to know where you are."

I feel Cade's eyes on me. I look up and smile brightly. "Well, I would, but there's an extra layer of security on that floor, so I wouldn't recommend it. You'll probably get a strip-search."

It's meant as a feeble joke—a play for time while I think of a way to put them off—but to my amazement, it works. After a moment's shocked silence, Mel changes the subject.

At that moment I remember where I've seen the photo before.

There's a huge copy of it hanging on the wall of Cade's sitting room.

Chapter Ten

I spend a shaky afternoon setting up interviews. It helps being almost famous myself, even if I'm only a humble TV presenter. It irritates me that for all her Glasgow bullishness, Mel is so coy with the stars.

She has a tough time explaining why she's in such awe. "I know. I know. I'm just a groupie at heart. Goes with the turf."

Garth Delaney, her catch of the week, is a case in point. Like millions of women all over the world, Mel blushes at the very suggestion that Jake should get him on film. She's still working out how to ask him when I lose patience, stroll casually past his sun lounger and murmur a lighthearted request. He simply turns over, raises his shades a fraction and sleepily agrees.

Easy-peasy.

Mel's jealous at first then ecstatic. She hauls Jake away from some distant part of the golf course where his hopes of completing an early round instantly nosedive into a bunker. Soon the second version of her interview with the great man is triumphantly captured on film with a blushing Mel gazing adoringly up into the eyes of her hero, unfazed by the scowls of his hovering agent.

As we walk back along the poolside, Mel runs through all the useful new tidbits of gossip she's gleaned from her session and gives me a hug. "Thanks, Tunis. You're a star."

I giggle from one too many spritzers, glad I'm forgiven for slipping off the radar yesterday. "Hey, he's the star. I'm just the presenter. Correction, *ex*-presenter," I add carefully, mindful of Cade's all-seeing, all-hearing security system.

He has spies everywhere.

* * * *

When I reach my room later that afternoon, I hurl my sun hat onto the bed, strip off my linen crops and head for the shower with a sigh of relief. We're on track.

Another long day, another successful chunk of film. The project's under control, even if my part in it — like my grip on things — is still uncertain.

With Cade Fitzlean around, it's impossible to tell whether things are going well or if some new crisis looms. All this week I'm inextricably linked to him while his life seems to lurch from one drama to another, dragging me with it.

As I wander out of the shower, swathed in a large fluffy towel and idly running my fingers through my wet hair, I pull up short.

He's sitting in my room, watching me. Once more he's stolen up on me but I feel it's me who's intruding.

I start to smile a greeting but something in his look stops me.

"You're late."

Instantly I panic.

My session.

I'd forgotten. Is it after four? A glance at his face warns me it probably is.

"Come here and kneel."

If his voice sends ice through me, his look sends pure flame. Clutching the towel tightly around me, I take a few steps toward him and sink to my knees.

"Lose the towel."

Arousal sets up a slow, steady beat between my legs as my skimpy towel slides from my shoulders and pools around me in a fluffy nest.

He's as elegant as ever and also recently showered. His short hair curls damply along his forehead and I catch the faint scent of his elusive aftershave with its heady hint of bergamot. He's wearing black jeans and shirt, the top three buttons undone, the cuffs folded back at his wrists.

He looks casual, stunningly beautiful — and angry.

"What did you know about that business this morning?"

I'm instantly wary. "Nothing. Why should I know anything about it? You heard what Ben said. It was a simple mistake. That's all."

But even as I say it, I feel there was more to it than that. Our project here is important, the biggest job we've ever taken on. It'll be a huge boost to our careers if all goes well. Ben would have been super careful to get things right. So why be careless about this?

Cade's eyeing me steadily. "What?"

My worried frown gives me away. Either that, or he has an uncanny knack of guessing my thoughts. "If you must know, I think it's out of character for Ben to make that kind of mistake. But I also think this would be a lot easier if you were less hostile. Why are you still so set against Jake, for instance? Are you jealous?"

"Yes."

"But that's ridiculous. I told you—"

"Not necessarily for you."

I stare at him in shock. He's jealous—for *someone else?*

This is a body blow. Instantly I sense how far I've traveled down this road. *I've got serious feelings for this man.*

And once more I've forgotten the simple fact that he may have other women, maybe even here, mingling with the guests, and maybe—in spite of what he says—they even work for him.

After all, I asked him to do this. And now I come to think of it, he took some persuading. And here I've been happily daydreaming about making love in magical towers.

What did he say? *Hold the violins...* I know nothing about him except he's rich and he's beyond good-looking. There must be other people in his life. How would I know?

My blood runs cold.

At that moment my eye falls on the photo. "What's the story behind that picture? Are you especially fond of it?"

It's a simple ruse to play for time, but for a few seconds, he sits very still.

"Ah, your friend the photographer again. I saw you whispering about it in my office. Yes, I like it. It reminds me of the need to stay in control. Did he tell you it's an original? Nathan Gemmel signed it for me shortly before he died."

"Jake thought so. We did a feature on Gemmel once. We tracked down most of his work, but this one's rare. I've never seen it before, nor has Jake. And he's even worked with him."

"I bought up all the negatives. It's the only copy, that and the smaller one in the group downstairs."

I catch my breath. How much did all that cost? It's like buying a Rembrandt. "But you should let other people see it. It belongs to the culture—"

"It belongs to me." He cuts in with an angry gesture and rises to his feet. "Our session's overdue and you've just earned another punishment for delaying tactics."

I make as if to rise, but he frowns. "Stay where you are. Since you asked, I've got more than one beef with your team. It's very high risk bringing you all here. I knew it would be tricky. Also, your photographer friend verges on a psycho, in my opinion."

"Oh? At least he doesn't whip people."

His eyes narrow in the icy silence. "Meaning what, exactly? That I'm a psycho because I do? At least I keep control, and I always get consent. Or did he ask your permission to throw you off that bridge? Maybe that was the bit I missed."

He paces the room, lithe and fierce. "And what does that make you? You're the one who wanted me to do this, if I remember."

He pauses in front of me, his expression opaque but his jaw tense. "Tyne-Follet and Mel Macallan are investigative reporters. In my book, that makes them dangerous. You know—and they probably know—that they're on a short leash, but I'm sure they're itching for a story. If we pull this off without a hitch, it'll be a terrific launch. If not, we're all in trouble—them too. I'll make sure of that. They don't know what they're getting into."

I open my mouth to speak but he puts a finger on my lips. "Uh-uh. No sound. From now until the end of this session, you stay silent unless I give you permission to speak. This is only your fourth day. You're doing well, but we'll have to speed things up if I'm to get you in shape by the end of the week. To be fair, it would normally take months, but I'll do my best."

I stare up at him in alarm. For me this week is unexpectedly searing. It's not only an emotional rollercoaster, but it's also physically hard work, even harder than dance. How much more of this can I take?

"From now on, you'd better start taking this a little more seriously. I'll make a point of correcting lapses in your manners." His face softens into a smile, and he reaches over to the table beside him. "And since you like dressing up and I particularly like the undressing part that comes afterward, we'll try out a little costume play. Today you're going to wear this."

He holds up a flimsy assortment of straps with gleaming buckles attached. I stare at it, my mind blank. "*Wear* it? How?"

His smile is calm, his voice low. I sense an edge in his tone that instantly puts me on my guard. At the same time I feel myself start to *burn*.

"It's a bondage harness but without the collar. You're going to try it for size. Stay on your knees."

His air of suppressed excitement sends a shaft of heat straight to my groin. This turns him on?

I'm instructed to hold out my arms and he slips it into place over my shoulders then buckles it tightly down the back. The straps are black leather and form a tight, strict rectangular grid, leaving my breasts sharply exposed and pinching in tightly at the waist. The arrangement of the straps also pulls my shoulders back, thrusting my breasts forward.

When he's buckled it tightly behind my back, he slips two of the straps between my legs. They pass underneath, exposing my slit, then widen out between the cheeks of my bottom to force me open.

"Stand up and turn around slowly then bend over and touch the floor. How does it feel? Point to anywhere that chafes or feels too tight."

I stretch and bend double, pointing toward the lowest strap around my ribcage, which pulls too tightly to breathe comfortably. He frowns and quickly refastens it, watching me intently as he does so.

At his direction I bend over again and stretch my arms wide. Movement is tightly constrained and newly disturbing. For one thing, it's humiliating, like I'm wearing an animal harness. I'm getting the same tiny thrill I get when he ties me up—a loss of control, the surrender of my will that somehow frees me to enjoy what comes next.

In this I can only receive and endure.

The thought is deeply satisfying and somehow startlingly, scarily hot.

But as I walk slowly across the room, I discover its other, darker secret. The straps pull so tightly that any movement presses into me, intimate and arousing, especially when I bend over.

The prospect of punishment just got interesting.

He orders me to stand facing him in the middle of the room and looks me over, his gaze nakedly hungry. For the first time I notice a riding crop lying on the cushion beside him. Absently he picks it up and flexes it between his hands.

"Today I want to see how flexible you are. You trained as a dancer. So I'd like you to show me some poses. We might use them later in the dungeon."

Quietly he directs me into some poses, tapping my limbs with the end of the crop to underline his instruction. I feel even more like an animal. The thought of the crop, more than the actual feel of it, is very frightening. It gives every pose an urgency I never got from simple *barre* exercises or the frown of the ballet master.

I try harder than ever to please him. The poses become exciting bordering on extreme. I lean right down, with my legs apart and my head touching the floor, or spread my legs wide and lean back, thrusting my breasts high in the air, or stoop low with my arms pulled back high over my head.

I'm instructed to stretch and bend to the limits of my ability then, when the pose is reached, to hold it for minutes at a time while he casually strolls about taking one or two shots with a small digital camera.

I soon become absorbed in the moves and the shapes, my body a willing and graceful tool. Up until now, some of his commands have been difficult to obey and hard to understand. But for me, this is as easy as breathing.

The whole exercise might be *barre* practice, but with one massive difference—the cruel straps. They constrain my lower body, pressing and pulling at my private places in astonishing ways, and soon I'm pulsing with heat, my belly on fire, the throb between my legs sending flaring arousal through me with every move.

My efforts seem to arouse him too. His breathing grows labored. As he moves around me, I see from the bulge in his jeans that he's becoming very erect.

At last I'm too tired to hold a pose for long. As my muscles quiver and I grow shaky, he stands in front of me and begins slowly to undo his zip. I glance up with alarm to see him smiling down at me, his eyes dark, his expression intent.

"You've done well. You're very beautiful."

The praise is brief. As his erection springs free, he guides it toward my face. "Take it in your mouth. Show me what you can do. Put your hands behind your back and spread your legs wide."

I'm already on my knees for an extreme pose on the floor, leaning on one knee with one leg pointing vertically high into the air.

Now I relax my thigh, kneel up and shuffle my legs apart.

"Farther."

He sounds stern, remote. *I don't play at this.*

I shuffle farther apart as heat flares between my legs. I've been burning down there for over an hour. If only he'd touch me, stroke me—anything to end this torment. Eagerly I lean up to reach him, thrilling to the salty taste of his erection. Forbidden to touch, I have a sudden urge to stroke it, squeeze its silky stiffness, make it swell and twitch.

Instead it's me who's twitchy. *Swelling too, maybe.* But I can't touch down there, either.

He thrusts lightly, shifting his angle so his cock tilts into my mouth. I swirl my tongue around the broad glans then lunge forward, letting it fill my mouth. I suck hard and lap gently, teasing him with my tongue.

As he hauls in a juddering breath, I lunge again and begin to fellate him, riding his length softly at first, taking just short journeys along his shaft before pulling back to lick the tip and tease the ridged, hot gristle with the soft inner edges of my lips.

Soon he begins to tense, the tendons in his neck standing out like rods, his breath coming in ragged bursts. I take him deeper, feeling the pressure build between my widely splayed thighs as the straps continue to work their magic.

It would be impossible, I think between thrusts, for me to come, surely, without his touch, without any stimulation...

"Harder. Faster." I hear him growl low in his throat then his hands grip my head, guiding me and speeding me up. I tense my body and stretch my neck, feeling the straps of my harness haul just a tiny bit tighter.

I'm so close...

At that moment he pulls free of my mouth and stands before me, his erection purple, gleaming and glossy with my saliva, only seconds from completion.

"Stand up and turn around."

Shakily I do it, my breath coming in shallow pants. Desire courses through me at the extra pressure of the straps from the sudden movement.

I hear the rip of foil and after a second's pause, he takes firm hold of my hips. "Now bend low. I want your head on the floor, your arms up. "

It's one of the most extreme positions. Normally I'd reach it easily, but my muscles are tired now and my shoulders ache. With an effort I obey, and as I achieve it, I feel the head of his erection push at my opening, teasing, probing, filling me with longing but infuriatingly poised.

As if from a long way away, I hear him speak, his voice husky. "Now I'm going to fuck you. While I do it, you can come. I can see you're close. You're very swollen. But you must do it in absolute silence."

At that moment he surges into me with a grunt and begins to thrust in long, heavy strokes that fill me with glorious heat, over and over. Again and again he pounds into me until I think I'll explode from the pressure. At each thrust, the straps tighten almost unbearably, their sweet strength pulling me closer and closer to the edge. And as he stills and judders I come at last, my belly convulsing with wave after wave of pleasure.

I clench my teeth, longing to cry out with the glory of it, but mindful of his stern command, I groan deep in my throat and fight for control.

My spasms overwhelm him, as I know they must, and with a mighty groan he comes too, holding me tightly against him, his flies and his hot, muscled abdomen hard against my tender, exposed bottom.

Time stands still as we stand locked together, and at last he releases me. Slowly I straighten up and feel him turn me round to face him. He takes me in his arms, his eyes bright with some deep emotion. He runs his hand over my forehead to wipe the damp hair away from my face.

His breathing's still unsteady, and I feel his heart thump close to mine as he draws me close and finds my lips. For a long time he holds me in a deep, searching kiss then draws away and gazes down into my eyes.

"Thank you, sub. That was magnificent. You've done well this afternoon. We'll run a bath now then our session will be done."

* * * *

"I'd sooner take it off." I lean back against him, letting the water swirl around me. Speech is a new luxury.

With twenty minutes of my session left, he insisted I keep my harness on in the bath. The upside is that I still feel the thrill of his control. The downside — or maybe it's an upside too, I've yet to decide — is that in the water, the straps tighten and my arousal's swiftly building again.

Does he know this? I daren't ask, but his amused expression hints that he's all too aware of the effect it's having.

I feel his lips on the back of my neck, light but hot. "Patience. It stays on till we finish."

He holds up a large towel for me as I step carefully out. As he pats me dry, I feel once more the link between us forged in the tower, before it was so brutally snapped apart by his fury over the paperwork.

I gaze up at him dreamily, lulled into contented, endorphin-led peace. "What about my punishment? Are we doing that now?"

He glances at me in surprise, a new gleam in his eyes a sudden warning that I might regret this. "Later, maybe. In the dungeon we could try out some whips."

His tone's calm, matter-of-fact, like we're discussing hairclips.

I suppress a shiver.

"For now, we'll try something else." He's eyeing me calmly, his eyes dark with lust.

I sense an air of excitement about him, but his next words baffle me.

"I think it's time I showed you some jewelry."

Chapter Eleven

"*Jewelry?*" I'm dumbfounded.

Cade throws open the tall doors of an ornate mahogany cabinet. From inside, small spotlights blaze into life. I blink, dazzled by the glare of silver and precious stones that spills out from the shelves.

I take a deep breath.

You don't see these in the high street.

Each piece is a finely wrought work of art. What's more, the brilliance of the stones tells me I'm looking at real gems. But they're not necklaces and earrings and they're not simply for adornment. They're lewd and they're cruel.

This jewelry has a purpose. There are nipple clamps, cock rings, dildos.

At the center of the display is a metal harness clasped around a dummy torso. Unlike the leather device I'm wearing with its strict rectangles and tight straps, this is graceful and elegant, a confection of silver leaves, the delicate fronds curved and clasping like living fingers. Some of the fronds curl upward to enhance the breasts and some slant down into the creases of the thighs, intimate, searching.

It glints seductively but I've been wearing the farm-hand version all day, and I get instantly what it's for and what it does. A tell-tale throb down below warns me another part of me gets it too.

He's watching my reaction closely, his eyes full of heat. "Restraint jewelry. Each piece is tailored for a certain body part. The fitting is crucial."

"It looks very uncomfortable."

"That's rather the point." He grins. "It has to be bent to fit. The points of the fronds can be angled to tease or torment the sub's most intimate places — at the direction of her Dom or to her own taste."

I swallow. This stuff's also meant to control. There are collars, cuffs, anklets, all with that little bit extra — a spike or two here, a carefully placed stud there.

Cruel jewels.

"Is it expensive?"

"Diamonds set in platinum and white gold or silver, so yes. The links, clasps and chains are made of steel. They start at about five hundred dollars for that adjustable cock ring, for instance. The largest piece here is around ten thousand."

I gasp. "Who pays that kind of money?"

He grins. "All kinds of people, with money to spare and quirky tastes. The harness is already sold. I'm arranging a fitting this week. My lawyer, Jo, wants it for her partner, Eileen. She's one of the stars in the film."

"The little redhead?"

He nods. "That's the one. She and Jo have been dating for a year now. But don't let on. It's still a secret. Jo's planning it for their anniversary."

I gaze at the cabinet, both fascinated and appalled. "But...where did you get them?"

"I design them."

I stare at him. "*You*? But they're...astonishing. You're an artist as well as a song-writer?"

His nostrils flare with a hint of disdain. "I'm no songwriter. I just jotted some ideas on a pad and somebody with real talent turned it into a hit. This is the same. I sketch an idea then a design team and a group of highly-skilled craftsmen turn it into a valuable work of art. Tonight I want to see the harness in action. So you can model it for me. Lose the towel."

I let it slide to the floor and shiver in the damp, taut straps of the harness. "Can I take this off now?"

His eyes darken. "Your fourth day of training and you still don't get it? I tell you what to wear, and when to wear it. I put it on you, and I take it off. And you don't ask. You wait to be told."

He leans down and kisses me on the lips, parting mine slightly with his tongue, sending a tremor all through me. He whispers, his lips brushing mine. "And we just agreed to new rules. So from now on, no talking. We're still in session. Got that?"

His fingers slide round my shoulders and unfasten the harness. As it peels away, I flex my body, relishing my sudden freedom. The straps were chafing a little, especially now that they're wet.

But he knows that. And it comes to me in a flash of understanding that he finds this idea arousing—*as arousing as I found it to wear.*

Restraint. The idea and the feeling are both new to me. They'll take some getting used to.

As if to underline my thought, I feel a trickle of moisture creep down the inside of my thigh. His eyes are burning into mine like he's guessed. He knows me so well. He's an expert at this...

"The harness first." He lifts the gleaming metal replacement away from its velvet-covered mount. The silver makes a faint tinkling sound as he flexes it in his fingers.

He passes it around my body. I shiver as the unforgiving metal fronds slip into place. The leaves press upward against my breasts—pushing them high—and curl in at the waist. The fronds penetrate deep between my legs and with a few tweaks of the leaves, he bends them into shape along my soft slit, forcing and opening me, leaving me exposed and needy. At my back, the silver leaves snake deep between the cheeks of my bottom, pulling me open.

I feel shamefully exposed. Heat burns deep in my belly.

As he curves the metal around me, he keeps his gaze fixed on my face, easing the metal when I wince, smoothing it when I relax, checking all the time for my reaction.

At last he stands back and eyes me with a gleam. "Look at yourself."

An exotic elfin figure stares back at me from the mirror. The silver has warmed up now and fits so well I'm only aware of it when I move, the taut, rigid leaves holding me in a firm, sensuous clasp. Every move teases and pinches, a persistent questing pressure that's impossible to escape.

He makes me walk a few steps then slips his fingers between my legs. Forbidden to speak, I mew in lustful distress as heat flares again.

He smiles slowly. "You're very wet. The thrill of restraint—interesting, no? You can speak now."

"How long must I wear this?"

He runs a finger along the rim of the silver frond where it clasps the swell of my right breast. "Tonight we're hosting a Fetish Pool Party. You're going in this. Is that okay for your image, or would you like to phone your agent?"

"And tell her I'm wearing this? No way. She'd freak."

He grins. "Okay, then we'll make some additions. You've got ten minutes to fix your makeup and do your hair. Then get back here."

* * * *

When I come back, he eyes me for a few moments then takes a matching breast piece off a velvet stand and tries it against me. It looks like a skimpy bra. Two large sliver flowers heavily encrusted with jewels are linked with a slender silver chain that clasps under the arms and over the shoulders.

The centers of the flowers are hollow. When he fixes it in place, my nipples bulge through the small holes, giving the flowers living, rosy centers.

He caresses them lovingly, teasing my nipples and pulling them a little to stretch them even farther.

I pant slightly as they stiffen almost to numbness.

Heat flares below and slowly fades to a dull ache between my legs.

Why is this so arousing?

He's watching me, his expression intent. "They're also nipple clamps if I screw them up a little—" He twists the flowers, making them even tighter. I gasp as my nipples grow hard as pebbles and darken. The throb comes again.

At this rate, I'll never get through the evening.

"Too much?" He eases the screws back just a fraction until my breathing steadies.

"Good girl," he says softly. "Now for some mystery. Try this."

He opens a drawer below the cabinet and takes out a length of scarlet chiffon. As he shakes it out, it flares around me, gossamer light. With swift movements he bunches it at one shoulder and drapes it front and back.

He fastens a thin, diamond-encrusted chain loosely around my waist, knotting it so it hangs modestly, covering the apex of my legs and loops a thin, matching chain of diamonds in my hair.

In the mirror, the elfin I'm staring at is transformed into some exotic Eastern princess. The colored silk floats around me but exposes my naked flanks. The jewelry glitters softly under the chiffon, hinting at splendor, showing my curves and my hollows in dazzling detail.

"Find some high-heeled sandals you can keep on in the pool."

In my dressing room, I quickly find a pair in glossy silver. Hoping they're pool-proof I slip them on and pirouette before him.

He smiles, his eyes narrow. "Perfect."

* * * *

The pool party sounds like fun but yet again, it's a glittering occasion. It's a warm summer evening and fairy lights twinkle in the trees and bushes. Waiters slide among the guests with trays of champagne as a dazzling array of stars and celebrities gather on the terrace, cluster in the shallow heated pool and spread out over the lawns.

Many of the costumes are truly shocking with straps, leather and studs exposing a great deal of pink, bronzed or milky flesh, some of it *striped*. Many people are wearing masks, some are in evening dress and a few in the pool are in kinky swimwear.

Everywhere, the newly trained subs and Doms are keen to show off their skills. Under the watchful eye of Nera and her assistants, one or two are already teasing each other with whips and floggers.

Among all these lewd and fantastical costumes, my chiffon is pretty and practical. The jewelry blazes underneath in a dramatic statement of veiled, erotic wealth. I draw envious looks.

In the pool I'm soon splashed from head to foot. When it's wet, the whisper-thin silk clings, shockingly transparent, but it quickly dries.

"You look amazing, Tunis, like a fairy princess. Are those real diamonds?" Mel and Ben look shocked as I joined them. Jake glowers from the other side of the pool then reaches for his camera.

As I greet the team, I fend off eager questions about my costume and my jewels.

Mel, stunning in skin-tight, bright blue latex, red hair flowing, fills me in on the team's activities.

It seems Ben's now deeply attracted to Nera—his training session Domme—much to Mel's fury. Jake's moodier than ever, while Mel's consoling herself over Ben's fling by attaching herself like a limpet to Garth Delaney, male lead in the coming movie and her all-time pin-up.

"And I'm going to extend that interview. But I'm not sure how to ask him." Just then Mel's jaw drops. "*Omigosh* — Tunis, don't look. It's *him*."

A ripple of excitement runs through the crowd and I spin round.

The Panther. He's on the terrace—a fearsome, terrifying gladiator with flowing black hair and a braided beard reaching halfway down his powerful, oiled chest. His feet are bare and he's wearing only his trademark hood and a black leather loincloth. A coiled bullwhip hangs casually over one shoulder.

I freeze as he scans the crowd and his gaze falls on me.

And I thought I was safe.

Mel puts an arm around me. "Hey, it's okay. We won't let him get you."

Then a strange thing happens. From all around us, women are leaving their partners and moving forward. Soon he's mobbed and starts signing autographs. Nera fights her way through to murmur something to him and he glances up with a grin. Or is it a snarl? The crowd backs off a little.

Nera turns to the crowd and makes an announcement. *He's going to give a display.*

I stare spellbound as a space opens up on the terrace and at Nera's direction, two of the women haul a third forward and hold her by the arms. It's Eileen, the pretty little redhead, the other star of the movie and the intended occupant of the harness I'm wearing.

The crowd surges closer. Mel's grip on my arm tightens. "Tunis? Don't look."

I have to look. It's my dream made flesh.

The Panther waits, poised and still. Women scurry around him and the crowd grows quiet then he slowly unfurls the whip. It looks enormous. The tail end alone seems several feet long, the business end near the handle, powerful and thick.

Yards away the quivering Eileen is being tightly held. She has her back to him. Her arms and legs are spread wide, firmly clasped by willing helpers, her plump little rear fully exposed. Her pretty face is a picture—a mixture of fear, hunger *and excitement.*

I know the feeling.

The Panther takes a step forward and, in one lithe move, his body uncoils. The whip follows his arm with a sudden crack, its whole length unfurling in a single, fluid movement. The thin tip lands on Eileen with a force that makes her jerk, even though the fist gripping the whip handle, sole source of the blow, is yards away.

I see instantly how the Panther got his name. His single flash of uncoiled power is unleashed in a move so graceful that I feel a lump in my throat.

He lands two more blows then turns to the crowd with a smile, coiling the whip with a flourish and slinging it over one shoulder. The crowd roars applause. He bows to Eileen, now blushing and restored to the protective arm of her lover, Jo. The fans crowd back for more autographs and cell phone photos.

But before they close in, he holds them at bay with an upraised hand. His eyes glitter through the gaps in his hood as he touches the coiled whip to his forehead, and he looks straight at me in a final salute.

I turn away, shaking. *He knows I'm here.* He knows who I am.

And he's just like my dreams...

I swallow.

"Hey, this is Tunis, right?"

I spin round as Garth Delaney holds out his hand.

"So glad to meet you at last, Tunis. Saw you by the pool. Hey, how about a dance?"

Mel looks on in disbelief as the star leads me to the center of the pool. Others follow and soon we're surrounded as Jake's camera whirrs away in the background.

As we dance, I slip in some questions and find he's surprisingly normal for a star. "It's a lotta fun here, honey, but I miss the kids. And back home the wife's getting, you know, *edgy*. So I'm leaving tomorrow."

I accept another cocktail from the tray of a passing waiter. As I open my mouth to reply, a rich male voice cuts in from somewhere just behind me.

"Shame. The party won't be the same without you." Cade steps smoothly between us and lifts the drink out of my hand. He takes a sip, eyeing me over the rim. "You've had enough." He touches my arm and arches an eyebrow. Startled, I nod a brief farewell to the star and turn away with a quickening heartbeat.

Cade's eyes scorch briefly into mine.

What?

I feel heat flare between my thighs as my arousal rebels against the torment of his fabulous jewelry, reminding me of its dark purpose—to make me ready for him, eager to submit.

He looks ahead, as if our leaving the pool together is mere coincidence. He speaks too low for others to hear, but his low growl is already making me pulse and ache.

"I've watched you flirting with other men for long enough. Now it's my turn. Get upstairs, now. I'll follow in a few minutes. Wait in the middle of the room, eyes down, hands clasped behind your back. And don't touch anything. I want to undress you myself."

* * * *

When he walks in, I'm standing as commanded. When I'd come in, I'd taken a few minutes to freshen up, but I'd hardly needed to. In the mirrors I'd looked bright-eyed, pink-lipped, *eager*.

I had lacked only one thing—and he's on his way up.

The instant his eyes fall on me I can tell *he knows*. He'll always know. He plays me like a violin.

The chiffon comes away first. He simply rips it off. It floats down to the floor like scarlet smoke. He runs his hand lightly over my belly and down to the apex of my thighs, his fingers slipping inside me, intimate, searching. "You're so wet I can *smell* you. Delicious."

I groan as he quests higher, his hand brushing agonizingly close to my center. A shaft of pleasure shoots all through me, setting up ripples of excitement but leaving me aching, unfulfilled, endlessly denied.

"And the jewelry? How is it? Tell me." He's being serious now, an artist testing his materials, the scent of my juices simply a measure of his success, like the smell of paint on a canvas. "You found it arousing?"

"Partly. And so was something else." I arch my neck as he gently cups my breasts, teasing my stiff, swollen nipples.

He frowns. "What else?"

"You, watching."

His jewelry's designed to torment me, but the real torture was his steady gaze while I tried to move and talk normally as I wore it. His hungry eyes have burned into me all evening, underlining the signals shooting all through me from his disturbing design.

He's eyeing me now with satisfaction, like I've passed some kind of test. "I think we can safely say this piece does the business." He unfastens the harness and the breast pieces and replaces them in the glass case, closing the doors on their splendor and turns to me with a stern, remote expression. "Keep your hands behind your back and your head down. You are required to be graceful, humble and obedient at all times during submission. Understood?"

His voice is quiet, slightly sinister. This is new. I'm unsure what to think of this but my body has already decided. Down below I start to pulse with excitement.

He leads me to the service elevator at the far end of the apartment and jabs at the buttons. Once more the journey is swift, far faster than the elevator in use at the front of the house.

As the door opens, I see the dungeon laid out ahead of me in all its harsh detail, the racks of canes, the rails of whips and straps, the glitter of chains and the gleam of cable. The flat surface of the spanking bench yawns, an invitation and a threat, and at the center looms the circular platform with the loops of chain, the trapeze and the evil snaking ropes.

Within minutes, my wrists and ankles are cuffed and secured to wide, sturdy loops of chain from the ceiling and fastened to two stout rings on the floor. He angles the lighting so that it falls directly on me. In the mirrored far wall I see myself suspended like a butterfly caught in a web, displayed for his pleasure.

But he's in no hurry to begin.

He's still barefoot from the pool, his ankles glistening and wet. Now he slowly removes his shirt and strolls over for a leisurely inspection of the whips. He touches them with loving fingers, letting the strands of one slide over his hand, running a finger over the braided leather handle of another, his expression absorbed and thoughtful.

He knows them well. He handles them with the reverence of a master craftsman for his tools.

At last he makes his choice and unhooks it from the rail, turning toward me with a gleam.

Excitement and sheer naked hunger clutch at my insides.

All at once it's no longer a dream. It's about to get vividly, painfully real.

Chapter Twelve

In the dungeon, Cade seems to change. He's more commanding, more powerful—but absorbed and focused, an artist at work. My body is his palette, the implements around us his tools. The final result— pleasure, pain and maybe release—is his art.

But maybe I change too.

He trails the whip along the inside of my leg, letting it slither over my sensitive breasts and along my taut, aching arms.

"This is a fairly mild whip, used on livestock. More direct than the flogger, more accurate than a horsewhip, more sensual than a crop."

With a sudden flick of his wrist it uncoils and the end of it snaps on my bottom, making me cry out.

It's more in surprise than pain. It stings, but not too badly. I relax a little as he slides it over me again. "Hush. You're very tense. Relax. This takes time. I want you to enjoy it."

Enjoy it? Is he mad? The whip snaps again. This time it taps the back of my thighs, leaving a thin streak of heat. With an effort, I control the urge to cry out as it trails once more over my belly and my nipples.

"How does it feel? Tell me. I have to know."

"It feels… It stings. *Ow.*" It snaps again, the sting on my breasts and my tender nipples, harder this time. It occurs to me he's keeping his touch light. Heaven help me if he ever applies full strength.

"It stings — *what?*"

I fight for breath as it lands again. "It stings – *Sir.*" I jerk as it tingles over my belly.

The blows keep coming, now teasing, now harsh. I give up trying to guess which. Each one sends a spike of arousal straight to my groin. I lean into its touch, the feel of the slithering leather doing strange things to me, blending with the roll of his wrist and his soft, deep voice in my ear.

The blows rain down, light now, sinuous and sensual, but I'm growing tired. He frowns as a tear strays down my face. He tracks it with his finger.

I see his jaw clench as he steps back to take a swing.

Surely not…*there?*

With heart-stopping accuracy, the whip lands with one sharp crack then another. The sting is far softer than the sound, but to my dismay, the ends are snaking up into my groin. With sickening certainty they land again and again along first one then the other side of my wide, splayed slit.

I've been clinging to a cliff-edge all evening as first his jewelry then his burning, hungry look inflamed me. Now this teasing pressure, its energy flowing directly from his wrist, tips me over the edge. With a shriek I convulse with a massive orgasm, my body jolting in my bonds.

The whip clatters to the floor as he flings it away and holds me close, his arms folding around me. He captures my mouth, his kiss robbing me of breath, and I'm being carried. I've no idea how far. I land on some soft, flat surface and almost instantly I sink into sleep.

* * * *

Some time later my eyes snap open. It's still dark but I wake instantly, my body limp and content, my belly still aglow.

He's sitting on the bed, naked to the waist. He looks angry. "I have to know. Are you okay? You passed out. I left you as long as I dared. Tunis? Talk to me."

I smile lazily up at him. "I'm fine, thanks. You?"

His eyes glitter. "Are you serious? I was worried sick."

Eyes wide, I sit up. I feel wonderful, ready for anything. He looks drawn and hollow, his hair all mussed.

"I'm fine, truly."

His eyes narrow. "Glad to hear it. Now get up."

I blink. "Why?"

He smiles briefly. "You're forgetting your manners. Passing out is one thing. Turning in for the night while your Dom is still high and dry is quite another. Bend over."

My senses now on high alert, I notice just two things before he takes the back of my head in a firm grasp and bends me forcibly down to the edge of the bed. I'm already burning with arousal — *and he's holding a riding crop.*

With impatient taps of the whip he takes a few moments to get me in position, indicating I should spread my legs wide and keep my knees straight.

"Put your arms behind your back."

I shiver as my wrists are swiftly encased in cold, hard metal. The handcuffs press into the small of my back as I stretch and tense to his instruction.

At last the instructions cease. I feel a cold rush of air as the whip descends. The flash of pain is so sudden that I gasp and rock against the bed.

Only minutes before I was fast asleep...

He steadies me with one hand under my pelvis. "Easy. Don't cry out or you'll get an extra. You'll get two more."

I clench my jaw tight and screw up my eyes as the whip lands again, then again. Each time he waits for the pain to flower fully before taking aim. After the third blow, there's a long pause as the fierce heat blooms, spreads and settles into a hot, burning glow.

I feel his breath on my skin, then his lips as he kisses the searing places with a loving sweep of his tongue. Heat burns between my legs as my arousal flares. It burns brightly as the sting of the whip fades to golden heat. His hands move gently over my strained, aching thighs with a fond, loving caress.

"Another?"

I close my eyes. The punishment's done, I counted the strokes. But now he's asking me something else. Do I want *another*?

This is for pleasure. But for his, or mine?

I have to find out. "Yes. Please, Sir. Another."

It lands again, on my legs this time. Again the pain flowers, blooms and fades. The glow between my legs burns hotter.

"And again?" He sounds husky. His breath comes in long, shuddering spasms.

"Yes, again. Please. *Sir.*"

It lands again. Once more the pain flares. I let out a long, shuddering sigh, savoring the ache between my legs, letting that bloom too until I'm pulsing with excitement.

I'd never have believed it. I'm *enjoying* this.

He hauls me upright and turns me round to face him. His eyes rake my face, his expression awed. "Did that really just happen? You really wanted me to do that?"

"Yes."

His eyes narrow. "Now you can thank me for your punishment, sub, and for your session. Kneel."

As he says it, I know instantly what he wants. To my surprise it seems only natural, in fact essential, that I should kneel and return his courtesy.

I sink slowly to my knees. Without being asked, I lean forward to drop a reverent kiss on his fly.

I hear another sharp intake of breath then with a few swift movements of his fingers, his erection springs free. He's huge—as I knew he would be, very hot and glowing darkly purple. With my hands still cruelly cuffed behind my back, it's impossible to feel his silky skin with my fingers, to caress his heat. Instead I roll my tongue over the broad, gleaming crown, brushing with the soft inner skin behind my lips before licking eagerly along his length to moisten him fully before taking him into my mouth.

"In your own time, sub. But be warned... If I come before I reach your throat, I'll whip you again."

His tone's harsh. I pause, quivering, as I weigh up my chances.

He's very erect. A throb from below spurs me on. He's throwing me a challenge. He's clearly close, but I'm in no hurry to finish. I want to enjoy this.

And for the first time in my life, the thought of another whipping is *exciting*. Only hours before I'd have shrunk in terror.

Game on.

I smile around his erection, letting it fill my mouth to stretching point. Slowly I take him deeper and ease into a steady, pulsing rhythm as I get into my stroke. His breathing's ragged now. As I lunge forward to swallow him deep, I yawn open my throat to ease the gagging, hardly waiting for each spasm to die away before lunging again.

Soon the reflex eases and I take him fully, savoring his salty taste. Low, appreciative growls from somewhere deep in his chest stir my arousal like music.

All at once he stills and I felt a thrill of achievement as his creamy honey flows over my tongue. I swallow triumphantly, letting my mouth ease round his shaft, careful not to suck too hard while he's still tender.

He towers over me, his breath easing like he wants this to last.

So do I.

He's so beautiful—perfectly honed, powerful, dominant. A golden glow spreads all over me as I kneel before him to perform this simple and ancient act of female submission.

It feels right and just, a courtesy and a homage, and doing it in the still small hours just before dawn gives me a total, all-consuming thrill.

What's happening to me?

* * * *

Morning comes in a blaze of sunlight. I wake to the deep, thrilling murmur of Cade's voice as he strides about taking one call after another. In the background I hear the rarefied strains of a Bach Cantata. The rhythms of the singing match his pace while his low murmur makes a stirring ground bass to the familiar, soaring anthem.

As he catches my eye, he ends a call and comes quickly over, tucking in his shirt. His look sends my heartbeat into overdrive as he sits on the edge of the bed and tenderly pushes some strands of hair away from my face.

"Are you okay? Things got pretty intense last night."

I shuffle up the pillows and stretch. "I'm fine. Truly. I feel wonderful."

He smiles back briefly then switches off his phone as it buzzes again. Without looking at it, he slips it into his pocket and pulls back the cover.

"Let me look at you."

"Now? You're insatiable."

He meets my playful grin with a grave stare. "I'm your Dom." His eyes darken as he lowers his voice. "It's my job to take care of you and make sure we don't...overdo things."

"*We?*"

His eyes gleam. "We. I go only as far as you let me. Turn over. I want to check your beautiful backside."

I sigh as his hands move over me in a slow, sensuous caress. One or two places are still tender, where the whip landed with unexpected force. He traces the marks with his finger, making them burn, making me shiver. "Does this feel *good*? Or not?"

In the mirror on the far wall I can see some faint marks, but very few — just one or two thin red lines and a patch of rosy skin where I still feel *used*. Moisture pools between my legs as I recall how I earned them — the long, slow burn and the pleasure that followed.

I feel my cheeks redden and hear his sharp intake of breath.

He tilts my chin to face him. "Tunis?"

I swallow, my face burning. I never thought I'd say this. "Yes," I whisper. "It feels good."

His mouth curls, a slow smile of triumph. "Good. Then we're getting somewhere."

He touches his lips to my neck, my shoulder, then my lower back just above my tailbone. "Mm, delicious. I could eat you for breakfast. Maybe I will one day."

He sits up and slaps my bottom hard. I yelp in surprise as he laughs and springs to his feet. "But not today. Get up. Nera just called to say you're due at the salon in five minutes. You're getting a massage, pedicure and a medical. I'll see you back here at" — he glances at his watch — "three. We'll start our session early today. Dinner might take longer than usual. I've got some investors flying in for a meeting."

As he strolls back to his room to fetch his jacket, he closes the door behind him. I stare at it, puzzled.

Salon appointment? First I've heard of it.

* * * *

In the salon, it's clear I'm expected. I'm led to a small room, brought a coffee and asked to strip and lie on a table to await the masseuse. But the first person to arrive is Nera.

She sweeps me with an icy look then quietly locks the door.

I sit up in alarm. "Where's the masseuse?"

Nera looks down at me with open dislike. "Waiting outside. I want to talk to you."

I clutch the sheet over myself. Somehow the thought of this hard-edged woman seeing me naked makes me queasy.

At the same moment an image of Mel's tense, thin face crosses my mind. I strike first. "What's this about you and Ben?"

Nera blinks. "What about him?"

"I hear he's a little too keen."

For a second she looks wary. "Meeting a Domme for the first time can be a very powerful experience. You should know."

What? I ignore this and lean forward. "He's taken, Nera. You're treading on someone's toes. Back off."

She presses her crimson-painted lips together in a thin, spiteful line. "Some people get emotional. It usually passes off in a few days." Her eyes flicker with something unpleasantly like triumph. "And I know all about Cade's little arrangement." Her lip curls. "And don't think it'll get you anywhere. He's just doing you a favor. And, frankly, I think you had a lot of nerve asking him."

She knows everything. I glare at her. "And this is your business *why*, exactly?"

"Because I know what's good for him, that's why. And you're anything but. You'll ruin his career. We booked you the Panther. You'd have been far better off with him. A lily-livered vanilla in need of a good thrashing would have suited him just fine. Cade's the last person you should have asked."

Fury consumes me. I get that she's cross about me messing up her bookings, but inwardly I rage. *She knows*, while I'm sworn to secrecy.

At that moment there's a discreet tap at the door.

With a scowl she unlocks it and Sonja looks in, her pretty face white and strained. She's about to speak when she sees me and stops. She and Nera exchange a look then Nera glances back.

"Gotta go. And believe me, I wish *you* would. You're not doing any of us any favors."

She slips past the masseuse, who enters with a bright, professional smile and closes the door.

Despite all the pampering that follows, I stay tense. *Nera knows.* But how much does she know? And who else knows?

He's taken me over. I've thought so much about pleasing him and accepting the pleasures he gives me that my brain's shut down and I've forgotten to think.

I've been such a fool. I'm simply playing into his hands. He's a hard-edged businessman with an empire to run, money to make and a grudge against me.

Last year was a fiasco for him and his business. It was all my fault. Now he wants payback. And if I fall for him, lose my job and ruin my friends' chances in the process, his revenge will be all the sweeter.

Leaving the salon, I walk straight into Mel.

"Tunis. They said you'd be here." Mel's clearly fresh from a training session. Slightly flushed, she looks chic in tight latex and tall boots, a perfect budding Domme — sure of herself, in control.

Unlike me.

She lowers her voice to a friendly stage whisper. "Can't stop, I'm doing another session in a few minutes with Ben. And guess what? We're planning a little diversion in the next day or so. Just thought I'd let you know. I'm getting mighty sick of Nera and Mr. Media Mogul bossing us all about."

"*Diversion*?" I stare at her, instantly alarmed. "What kind of diversion? Mel, please don't—"

"Not now. No time. We'll talk over lunch."

With a conspiratorial wink and a wave of her thin fingers, she's gone.

At that moment my phone vibrates.

Oh no.

I stare at it, my heart sinking. After a long moment I take a deep breath and dial. "Mel? I've just had a message from home. Yes, it's—the usual. I have to go.

I'm so sorry." I stare at the phone as emotion wells up, making it impossible to speak for a moment.

I don't need this. Not now.

I take a deep breath and lift the phone again. "Mel? Still there? Yes, I'll be fine. Can you explain to the others? Thanks. You're an angel. And please, *please*, don't do anything until I get back — about the diversion, I mean."

It's the best I can do.

Now life has to go on hold.

* * * *

Ten minutes later, I've ransacked my room for my bag and jacket, and I'm headed for the main door. Luckily there's no sign of Cade. An encounter with him at this point would make things far too complicated.

But how to get out of here? Security's everywhere, the gates kept locked. The place bristles with hidden cameras, tracking every doorway, every exit. What keeps the paparazzi firmly out keeps all the rest of us firmly in.

Cade will be alerted instantly if I try to leave. But if I slip out now, there's an outside chance I can get back before he finds out I've been away

It's a long shot, but I'll have to try.

At that moment I hear a commotion in the entrance area. Garth Delaney is leaving. A fleet of cars has drawn up to the entrance to convey him and his entourage of agents, spokespeople and image consultants away to the capital.

Inspiration strikes.

"Mr. Delaney?" I approach him with a bright smile. "Any chance I could ride with you as far as the main road? I need to go over a couple of things from Mel's interview…"

* * * *

Some hours later I'm staring at my phone, my heart close to breaking, as yet another text from Cade lights up on the display. He's been calling and texting constantly.

Where are you? CALL ME.

I lean back with a weary sigh as the taxi winds deep into the country lanes and I switch off my phone. It's cruel, but it can't be helped…

"This as far as you want to go, lady?" As the cab driver eyes me in the driving mirror, I snap back to the present with a jerk. For the last hour or so I was happily lost in memories of last night. Now dream time's over.

I'm back in real life. *My* life.

It's been a long, fraught journey and it's a while since I've made it. Long ago I promised always to heed the call whatever time of day or night and to make the journey as fast as I could.

I've never regretted it once — until today.

It comes at the worst possible time. I'm right in the middle of an important job, I'm leaving my friends in danger of losing theirs and, worst of all, I'm turning my back on something new in my life, something entirely unexpected.

Maybe my strange relationship with Cade Fitzlean will never come to anything. Maybe to him I'm nothing special, just one of a thousand women, one in a million pleasures that his looks and his wealth can buy.

Now I'll never know.

I never thought this promise, made with so little thought so long ago, would cost me so much.

In the back of the taxi I close my eyes and take a deep breath. I'm here now. I know what's waiting and I dread what I'll find. But it has to be done.

Life's a bitch.

"Thanks. This is fine. How much do I owe you?"

Chapter Thirteen

An hour or so later, there's a loud banging at the door. In the chaotic kitchen, the two people I've come to see look pale and drawn in the glare from the overhead lighting.

The knock startles us all. For an instant, I see them in freeze-frame. One is my father, his old familiar self, apart from a new and unfamiliar patch of wet all down his shirt.

The other is Janice, my stepmother. She's distraught, her hair, normally smooth and elegant, a spiky mess. Her face is tearstained and distorted.

We've got potato peelings in our hair.

She's screaming.

I look at my father, willing him to stay where he is. "Don't answer the door, Dad, please."

He shuffles past me. In a sudden dash, I get there before him.

As I open it just a crack, it's suddenly wrenched from my grasp and flung wide. I clap my hand to my mouth. "*Cade*? How did you get here?"

He's staring at me, his eyes wild. Behind him I see the headlights of more than one car and figures on the path. One is his driver. Another is silhouetted in the blaze of the headlights.

"What's going on?"

"Go away. You can't come in." I might as well push back a hurricane. He's already striding into the kitchen.

My parents stare as he enters — over six feet of rugged, masculine willpower — and glares at them. The screams stop mid-flow.

In the sudden silence, his deep voice rings out, making us all jump. "Where's her medication? Somebody fetch it."

It's like watching something happen in slow motion. He takes charge with quiet command, taking the pills from my father's shaking hands and passing them to the white-coated figure he's brought with him. As I shrink back against the wall, bewildered, a paramedic drapes a blanket round the distraught Janice and gently leads her out to an ambulance. Dad follows. Cade gives a quiet instruction to the driver to take them both to their regular clinic.

It's all happened so fast and so smoothly that I can barely register he's here.

Now we're alone.

He turns to me, his face gaunt, takes me over to the sink and gently picks the peelings out of my hair. "Did she attack you?"

At last I find my voice. "She objected to the way I cut up the potatoes. But...how did you know? And how did you find us?"

He sighs wearily and sinks into a chair. "Jake Simmons, your so-called boyfriend. He told me everything."

Flora Dain

He passes a hand over his eyes. "Any chance of a coffee?"

"*Jake* told you?" I stare at him. I've known Jake for years. I trust him. It's impossible.

But then, so is the sight of Cade Fitzlean — handsome multimillionaire, legend — actually sitting *here*, in my parents' kitchen.

He looks weary but he's wrought magic. My parents are safe, my stepmother calm. All because he turned up when he did.

But to accuse *Jake*... "He'd never do that."

Cade stiffens. "So I'm a liar now? Thanks." His voice is dangerously soft, his look pure steel. "Why did you switch off your cell phone?"

"Don't change the subject. We're talking about Jake."

"No. We'll talk about you." For a second the steel flashes white-hot. "We had an agreement. Today you broke it several times over. You should have said you had commitments. You should have told me where you were going. And you should at the very least have answered my calls."

He glares at me. "You will never, *ever*, do that again. Understand? Anything might have happened. Paparazzi, kidnapping — reporters are desperate to know what's going on at the Hall. Why do you think we went to town on security?"

His rage fuels mine. I resist the urge to shout back. "Cade, with respect, this is a private matter."

His eyes blaze. "So is our arrangement. While you're my sub, you're in my care. I have to know everything — where you go, who you see, when you eat."

I give a weary sigh. "When she's really bad, I have to get here fast. The others are used to it. I just did what I always do. I hadn't told you because her attacks are quite rare now. I didn't expect one this particular week.

I'm sorry. Does that satisfy you? Now, please go away and leave me in peace."

"*No.*" The cups on the draining board rattle. "I'm staying here, and I'm taking you back. Where's that coffee?"

* * * *

"So what did Jake tell you?" I glare at him.

It's late now and we're eyeing each other over empty coffee mugs, two empty glasses and a half-finished bottle of wine. We've been talking so long that I've lost track of time.

But it's only a lull in the storm. I want answers. "What did he say *exactly*?"

His jaw stiffens. "When I heard you'd gone, I tried to call you. Then I sent security after you. Nobody saw you leave. Nera saw you with Macallan but when I asked, she denied it point blank. Then Simmons told me where you'd be. He said—and I quote—'I should know just what sort of people I was mixing with'."

"He said *what*?"

"His exact words. So you've told him about us?" His tone slices through me.

"No. I told no one. I hardly see them, remember? You've done everything you can to keep us apart." I sound sharper than I mean to.

My mind races. *Have* I given something away? "Maybe he guessed after that business at the gorge. Or maybe…"

"What? Tell me." His voice is low, his tone sharp.

I feel myself color. "I was just thinking… Anyone who'd seen us dance together might…guess."

When we dance, I simply melt into his arms. We move together as one. At least, that's how it feels. Maybe that's how it looks.

I start to clear away the things, avoiding his eye.

As I lean over to pick up his cup and his wine glass, he grips my wrist. "So why did you tell him and not me?"

"I've told no one." I pause and lean against the sink. "He's always known about Janice. His family lives nearby. We're practically neighbors."

He eyes me steadily. "He's hot for you. And he seems to know a lot about her condition. Is he unstable too?"

Poor Jake. I take his part, as always. "He's…creative. He just gets excited. That's all."

To my relief, Cade changes tack.

"Your stepmother's always been like this?"

"Only when she forgets her pills." I unclench my fingers. "Very few people know. Look, I'd sooner keep this private. I don't want my parents pestered by reporters. Dad has a tough enough time as it is."

"But your colleagues know?"

"They cover for me when I have to come home. But I can't believe Jake said that." I put my head in my hands. It's been a long day.

He frowns, his voice gentle. "Hey, easy. Maybe he was just worried about you. I sure as hell was."

For a fleeting moment I feel a surge of joy at the thought that he's missed me then it instantly fades.

I'm just an investment. He wants me back on track. Our documentary's going to be one massive promotional ad for his launch, and I'm the main theme.

He needs me commercially. That's all. I feel bitterness well up. "Yeah. Sure you were."

I glance round at the untidy room, avoiding his dark, steady gaze. I'm too tired to argue. "Shall I fix you some food?"

With a glance at his watch, he gets to his feet. "My driver's booked us into a local hotel. He's waiting outside. I'll bring you back here in the morning. Unless you want join your parents at the clinic right away?"

I let out a slow breath. "Thanks, but Dad likes to settle her in quietly. I'll call them tomorrow. I'll stay here. I'm fine on my own. You don't have to…"

I look down at my hands. They're shaking, and I feel a sudden urge to cry.

There's a movement in the air around me and all at once I'm in his arms, my head pressed against the soft leather of his jacket, his hand warm against my hair. "Hey, you're exhausted. When did you eat last?" He tilts up my chin with one hand and scans my face, his eyes hot with concern.

"I don't know. Last night, I think." Something inside me begins to melt and the tears prickle again. This time there's no stopping them.

"You're coming with me. My driver will come back here to keep an eye on the place tonight and take any messages." He releases my chin and, after a second, passes me a spotless, neatly folded handkerchief. "Dry your eyes. Let's wrap ourselves round a stiff drink. I know I could do with one. Then we'll get some food into you."

* * * *

The hotel is on the outskirts of the town, set some way back from the road in woodland. As the car purrs to a halt, spotlights gleam on old wooden timbers, pitched roofs and hanging baskets full of flowers.

As we check in, I remember someone might recognize me and rummage quickly in my bag for a ponytail band and sunglasses.

But the receptionist has eyes only for Cade and seems to lose all coordination, turning bright red as she passes him the register to sign. "You're booked into our best suite, Mr." — she glances at the register — "Mr. Mason. I'll take you up myself. This way."

Our suite's much smaller than our lavish quarters at the Hall but bright and comfortable. There's a sitting room, a traditional four-poster in the bedroom, flowers in bowls and a modern, gleaming bathroom.

While I freshen up, I hear Cade on the phone to reception ordering food. As I emerge, he's peeling off his jacket and unbuttoning his shirt. As he catches sight of me, he flings himself back on the bed and holds out his arms.

"Come here."

I frown as I join him. "You ordered already? Do I get to choose what to eat?"

He pushes a stray tendril of hair away from my forehead. "No. I'll choose. And if you don't like it, you can go without. You've been enough trouble for one day."

He touches his lips to my face. "And here's that drink." He passes me a gin and tonic from the minibar, and we touch glasses and sip.

Just then a thought strikes me. "Wait — there's Nera. She knows. She had a go at me this morning."

He sits bolt upright, his drink forgotten. "She *what*?"

"She tried to warn me off you. So why is it so wrong for Jake to know and okay for Nera? What is it between you two?"

"It's okay for Nera because I trust her."

"And not me?"

His jaw tenses. "What do you think?" At that moment our meal arrives. The waiters clatter about for a few moments setting up crystal and silverware. They leave the food under domed silver covers, along with a large bowl of cherries and a bucket of ice, cradling a bottle of champagne, and silently withdraw.

As the door closes behind them, I glare at him. "Nera? You were saying?"

"She knows because she's in charge of the dungeon rota. But that's all. Your boyfriend can only know because you've told him, dancing or no dancing."

I spring to my feet. "I've told him nothing. How could I? I spend most of my time with you — being tied up."

He grins. "So you do," he says softly. "Most enjoyable."

I turn away angrily. The thought of the unbearable pleasure he gives me seems wicked at a time like this. But now I'm tired. All at once the room begins to spin.

In a bound he's at my side. "You're pale. Let's get you out of these."

Slowly, gently, he begins to undress me, peeling my clothes away, lifting my top over my arms and rolling my jeans down to the floor. Like a weary doll, I surrender to him, winding my arms round his neck and kicking off my trainers when he scoops me up in his arms and carries me into the bathroom.

"Stand in the shower." He reaches over me to detach the faucet from the holder and turns on the taps. "Put your arms up and take hold of the fitting with both hands."

Wearily I obey, stretching my arms up high while he douses me with warm water then lays the showerhead down at my feet. The water hisses and gurgles around my toes as he ransacks the shower gels, tearing off tiny caps and squirting the little tubes into his hands.

While I cling on, facing the tiles, he begins to smear the gel all over me in long, firm sweeps of his hands, lingering on my tense shoulders and my taut waist, easing over the curves of my bottom.

It's soothing and deeply, achingly arousing as he murmurs in my ear, his hands never losing contact. "Keep hold. Don't let go or I'll tie you up."

He turns me to face him and begins to massage my breasts and my tense ribcage. I arch my neck and groan as his hands slide farther down, easing into my groin, the gel sending flashes of electricity from his fingertips all through me as he fondles me lovingly.

"Now close your eyes. Keep them closed."

A thrill ripples through me as he bends to pick up the jet and begins to dowse me with it in short, fierce bursts of the warm, pounding water. He massages me all over as he does so, switching from hot to cold to warm to hot again without warning and aiming now close, now from high up, so the jet switches from soft rain to fierce, searing force with bewildering suddenness.

I moan and gasp as he torments and soothes me, and soon my arms begin to ache. At last the water stops. In the sudden silence, I feel a soft towel being wrapped around me. His warm, firm fingers tuck it in under my arm.

"You can let go now. And you can look."

He's wearing a toweling robe and as I blink drops of water off my eyelashes, he scoops me up and carries me back to the table, keeping firm hold of me as he pulls out a chair.

"Now you're going to eat. And just to make sure you do, I'll feed you myself."

I giggle as he gathers me into his lap. "I can lift a fork. I'm not that far gone."

His damp, tousled hair makes him look impish, irresistible—a hungry satyr. He gives me a superior look. "Not this time. My treat."

I nestle in his arms as he samples the dishes, cold chicken and salad in one, strawberries and a bowl of whipped cream in another. He takes mouthfuls himself then feeds me small morsels with his fingers, smiling when I lick his fingertips and suck them clean.

As he drinks his wine, he allows me small sips from his glass then kisses some into my mouth. I begin to feel as drowsy as a rescued kitten. Finally I refuse one more strawberry and feel my head droop onto his chest.

* * * *

"What did you say to her? Tell me?"

I open my eyes and blink. Cade is pacing at the far end of our hotel room, his phone to his ear. He's still in his bathrobe.

"Enough. I'll deal with it. Leave her alone."

I have the impression he's been talking for a while—about me.

As I shift on the bed he looks up, tosses down the phone and sits beside me.

"How are you?"

"Mm, wonderful, thanks to you. What time is it?"

"No idea. Why? Are you late for something?" His sardonic grin makes me smile. Suddenly I feel light, happy. "Are you coming to bed?"

He leans over me, pinning my arms over my head, pressing my wrists into the pillows. "Not yet. We have an appointment."

I stare up at him. "We do?"

His slow smile warns me instantly what's going to happen.

"Your midnight session is two hours late. There's no dungeon here, so we'll have to get creative."

I'm lifted off the bed and told to kneel and look down while he walks slowly around me, his bare feet denting the deep pile of the carpet as he peels away my towel.

"Time's short and we're both tired, so I'm going to tie you then we'll fuck. But first you deserve a light spanking for today's indiscretion. Agreed?"

Heat flares in my groin as I watch his legs, fine dark hairs springing out of the bronzed skin, his calf muscles tense and perfect. "Yes, Sir."

"Good. Now climb back onto the bed and lie face down."

I hear him unzip his soft leather overnight bag, our only luggage. He comes back holding a coil of soft rope in one hand. He keeps the other behind his back.

I gasp as he grasps my ankles and ties them loosely together.

"Now stretch your arms behind your back." He grabs both my wrists and hauls them behind me, tying them together then looping them to my ankles. With a few jerks, the rope is secure and I'm tied fast.

I hear his robe slither to the floor and feel his erection brush my legs as he leans over me. "Now you're in a perfect hogtie. Anything too tight?"

What a question. But I have to admit that the knots, though firm, allow some movement. "I'm fine."

He grins. "Good. Now for your punishment. A few swats of the paddle should do it." With a jolt he hauls at the rope and my feet and arms are pulled high as the paddle lands on my bunched bare bottom with a loud snap.

"One."

The pain's instant, fierce and hot, then fades to a hot glow.

"Two."

He slaps me again and again, leaving just enough time between blows to let the pain flower and fade and for me to get my breath.

It feels extraordinary—humiliating, shaming—and yet fiercely, desperately *hot*. I'm helpless tied up like this. He can pull and roll me every which way. My groin begins to burn and throb as the simple but effective restraint puts me completely in his control. Each jolt of the paddle, equally simple and just as effective, jolts my arousal, fueling my flames.

At last he pauses. He massages my burning bottom with loving hands, making me glow. My arousal burns even hotter.

"You look amazing like this. I could eat you alive." He breathes in my ear as he fastens his lips on my neck, his mouth hot and urgent. "Now we fuck."

With a wrench he flips me over onto my back. With my legs and arms bent underneath me I arch in front of him, my breasts thrust upward, my thighs and knees splayed wide. He leans over me, his face solemn but his eyes pools of liquid lust. "Beautiful. And now *you're* going to get creative."

With a grin he kneels up over me, his erection looming over my face. I can feel heat from his thighs at either side of my head. Slowly, deliberately, he rips open a foil packet and extracts the rolled condom. "Put it on."

"Me? But—" I gnaw at my lip. My arms are beginning to ache from the unnatural position, fueling my arousal even further. He shows no inclination to untie me. "How?"

He smiles slowly, a new gleam in his eyes. Above my face his erection twitches in anticipation. Way above it, I see his eyes narrow. "You've got just two minutes to work out a way," he says softly, "or I may have to whip your breasts."

Chapter Fourteen

"What did you expect? Commands are to be obeyed."
Cade runs his fingertip over my nipple. At his touch, it
hardens into a tight, aching nub.

He'll whip my breasts? *Yikes.* I hope he's kidding.

I gaze up at him, wide-eyed. Arched beneath him in
the unforgiving hog-tie, I'm bound — exposed, and
vulnerable. With my wrists and ankles tethered, my
breasts jut upwards, thrusting toward his face, inviting
his every whim. *Would he really go that far?*

And how can I possibly put on a condom without
hands?

Does he seriously expect me to use my mouth?

Playing for time, I reach out to lick him, running the
tip of my tongue over the hot, silky head of his erection.
It jerks vigorously over my face. Way above it, I see him
smile.

Of course he does.

"Good girl, you're getting the idea. Keep going. Make
it wetter."

All at once it's a challenge — *and it's fun.*

He shifts position so I can reach. I lick him eagerly, relishing his hot, salty taste, and spurred on by a new sense of power as his breathing quickens.

When I've licked and kissed all along his length, I finish with a long, loving suck at the wide, glossy head. He leans back taking deep, uneven breaths, and dangles the rolled condom over my face with finger and thumb, his eyes amused, his eyebrow raised in sardonic enquiry, waiting to see how I'll perform.

But I've been forming a plan. I arch my neck and hook the condom confidently onto my tongue, sliding it into my mouth with a flex of my lips.

I roll it round in my mouth to get it into position on the tip of my tongue and open my mouth to show him I'm ready.

He laughs softly. "Very good. Now let's see if you get it on."

I reach out with my tongue again, but this time I get my teeth behind the rolled edge and push and tease the condom onto his shaft, tweaking the taut roll carefully with my teeth to snap it into place.

It's hard going. He's so big the rubber's stretched tight as it gets close to his root.

The thought of my vulnerable breasts, mercilessly exposed and now under threat, makes me nervous. I dread nicking him with my teeth, or worse, tearing the thin film of the condom, but at last it's in place.

I feel a thrill of triumph as he grins then plunges his head between my legs and fastens his mouth greedily onto my pulsing, aching center, hauling and sucking on my tiny bud till I cry out from sheer pleasure.

It's made even more intense because I'm still fixed, immobile, my bent legs splayed wide, all my muscles aching from this unnatural position. This way up there's no way I can flex or writhe. I can only yield and endure, helpless in his thrall.

Just as I think I can bear no more, he lifts his head.

"You want more? Or shall I come in now?"

I close my eyes briefly, astonished at his power of control. I can barely breathe. I reply through gritted teeth. "You choose. *Sir.*"

With a light laugh he surges up over my curved, arched body and plunges inside me. He takes me in long thrusts while he fastens his mouth on mine, his tongue invading me with its own matching rhythm, a double assault that fills me at both ends in a deluge of pleasure. His tongue works its own magic while the pounding beat of his loins as he thrusts hard against my splayed apex quickly brings my excitement to a head.

I quiver beneath him, rigid in my bonds, my taut muscles braced to absorb every plunging ounce of the impact as he slams into me, his erection propelled by six feet of pumping, triumphant male animal. As he pauses, poised on the point of rapture, my own climax explodes around him, rippling through me in spasms of bliss, its waves like the endless swell of the sea, and we sink together as I pull him down with me to drown in our pleasure.

* * * *

Next morning I wake limp as a doll. The sun's high. I can smell the heavenly aromas of breakfast. Cade's pacing the room, half dressed. He looks handsome and toned in boxers and a crisp white shirt as he murmurs urgently into his phone.

As one call ends, he takes another, absently munching on mouthfuls of toast washed down with impatient swigs of orange juice from a tall glass, endlessly snatched up then set down again.

As I yawn and stretch, he cuts off in mid-call, discards his toast and sits next to me. "How are you?"

I wince as I haul myself up against the pillows. "Terrific. A bit stiff."

He grins. "And you a dancer? You're out of condition. Be sure to eat some breakfast. I need to get back but we'll call at the clinic first."

Janice. I'd almost forgotten. A twinge of guilt is followed instantly by a wave of gratitude.

My orgasm still glows deep inside. Everywhere south is at peace, golden and content. It's a delicious start to the day ahead, even if it might be just a distant memory by the end of it.

These trips home are always hard, but just this once, I've had help. Usually I'm on my own, and that can be tough.

But now guilt creeps in. He's given up a lot of his time to my problems. "Are you sure you don't want to leave straight away? I can call a cab."

He gives me a dark look as he fastens his trousers. "I'm coming too."

I stare for a moment then pour some juice and reach for some toast as I carefully detach myself from the thought that he's doing this to please me.

He's back in control. That's all it is.

* * * *

In the car he leans back in the corner, his expression brooding and watchful. His gaze is disturbing and I still burn from the afterglow of his passion.

I try to find words to describe how I feel. "Thank you for last night. It was…indescribable."

His reaction surprises me.

"For me too." He looks away for a moment as his hand steals along the seat and fastens over mine.

Bolder now, I try again. "Do let me know what I owe you. I'll pay you back…"

Abruptly he lets go of my hand. "Forget it. All I want is for this launch to succeed."

As we head for the clinic, the countryside around us grows familiar and I spot landmarks from our trip to the christening a few days ago. But today our smooth trip in the upholstered luxury of his car is a far cry from my fretful journey yesterday.

It must be fun to be rich.

"I did some checking on you during the night."

His voice breaks into my thoughts and instantly I'm on my guard. "You did *what?*"

He's eyeing me calmly. "Normal procedure. Came across some interesting things we'd missed."

I frown, alarmed. "Such as?"

"Such as…when that balcony collapsed, putting paid to your engagement and your career, Simmons was there."

His expression is stony.

I dart him an indignant look. "So? He was filming."

He lifts a cynical eyebrow. "Coincidence?"

I decide to ignore this. "I told you… He's creative. And if you're trying to scare me off him you're wasting your time. I keep telling you that there's nothing between us. He'd never hurt me."

His jaw tenses. "He might have."

I glare at him, indignant. "Well, I'm still here. He's a good guy and he's good at his job. Leave him alone."

* * * *

My indignation lasts right up to the moment I walk in through my parents' front door. I stand in the hallway and stare. The chaos of the night before — the muddy smears from the scattered potatoes, the broken dishes — has all been cleaned away.

The house is spotless, surfaces gleaming. A bowl of fresh flowers is in the hall. Beyond it, I see another on the kitchen table.

"What's happened?" I turn in a daze as Cade comes slowly up behind me.

"Mason, my driver, stayed overnight. He brought his girlfriend. She's one of the housekeepers at the Hall. I asked them to tidy up for you."

I swallow. "I don't know what to say. Thank you."

He smiles briefly then takes my arm. "I have to get back. If there's nothing else you want to do here, I'll take you to the clinic."

After gushing my thanks to a bashful Mason, we arrive at the clinic where we're ushered into a sitting room and I fling my arms around my father.

As I make the introductions, he shakes Cade warmly by the hand. "Can't thank you enough, young man. Lucky you came when you did — the longer these attacks go on, the longer it takes her to recover. They're keeping her in for another day for observation."

After a reunion with a subdued but cheerful Janice, I have a brief word with the doctor while Cade and my father discuss the finer points of the Grand Prix.

When I get back, they look easy together but Cade's time is valuable, so I cut in. "Do you want me to stay on for a few days, Dad? The house will be lonely till she gets back."

"No, sweetheart, I'll be fine." He winks. "Wouldn't want to keep you and your young man apart for that long. I'll manage."

My cheeks burn as I avoid Cade's eye.

I hear a smile in his voice as he takes my arm. "Fine. Then if it's okay with your father, *darling*, we'd better get back."

* * * *

The drive back is peaceful, but it's been an emotional thirty-six hours. As the reaction sets in, I sit in silence, uneasy and close to tears. Janice's attacks are a private part of my life. I've always fought to keep them that way.

Cade glances across once or twice, his look dark and unreadable. As we speed through the fields and country towns of Wiltshire and head back into the rugged red earth of Devon, he leans across and touches my hand. "Hey, you're not the only person in the world with a weird family. Try mine. My dad's a corrupt politician-turned-playboy. My mom was a hippy and her lover was a maniac. That was before she died in a car crash. Then the two guys raised me and my sister between them, half the year with one, half with the other."

I forget my troubles as he talks, interested in spite of my woes. He gives an impression of a fun-filled, easy-going youth but under his light tone, I sense real tension.

Clearly he's got issues. He says nothing else about his mother and gives only sketchy details about the others, leaving me no clear idea of them as people.

I burn to know more. "You've got a *sister*? What's she like?"

He stares at me. "*Like*? I don't know. Sisters aren't *like* anything. Fran's pretty, I guess. Younger than me."

"Is she in business too?"

"Yep."

I smile at his hint of pride, and I'm touched that he's so fond of his family. It's kind of him to try to make me feel better. "Is she good at it?"

"She's very successful. Ah, we're here."

I give his hand a grateful squeeze, but he's already back on his phone.

* * * *

We're back in time for lunch, but quietly join separate tables. I find Ben and Mel and quickly reassure them that my home life's back on track. "And thank you so much for taking over. I don't know how I'd cope if you—"

Mel grins at me across the table. "Don't mention it. And thanks again for giving me the chance to anchor this thing. I'm getting really excited—and hey, look who's here."

Jake has arrived, his handsome face beaming with excitement. "Guess what? My replacement camera's arrived, and it's even better than the old one. It's another antique, a Cameflex just like the other one, but in better condition. Sonja tracked it down in a museum in Geneva. It's got six lenses instead of three, and a reverse winding mechanism that—"

He continues for some minutes while Mel rolls her eyes and Ben drums his fingers on the table. I smile at Jake, glad he's pleased with his new toy and feeling bad about letting Cade accuse him behind his back.

At his elbow, Sonja gives me a weary smile. I'm shocked at how pale she looks. Her pretty face is almost hollow, and she has dark circles under her eyes.

Cade is spending all his time with me. It must make a lot of extra work for her.

Jake ignores her but after a few minutes, she leans close to me to whisper, "Glad you're back, Miss Vale. I do hope he won't break this one. It took an age to find."

She slips away quickly. I watch her go, thoughtful. Yet another of Cade's victims, as are we all. But poor Sonja's in the front line. She actually has to work for him. Our servitude only lasts until the coming premiere.

Poor kid.

* * * *

The team's full of news about how things are going. By the time I make it back to the suite, I realize I've forgotten to ask Mel about the mysterious diversion she mentioned.

Maybe she's given up the idea. I'll ask her at dinner.

As I walk in, I give a deep sigh and kick off my shoes before I notice the communicating door between our rooms is already open. I can hear music, a piercingly sweet air by Handel. Then I hear something else, the unmistakable sound of a door closing softly and the click of a key in a lock.

Cade is standing behind me, elegant, completely at ease, once more in control, like he's just stepped out of a movie.

He's my lover. The thought takes my breath away.

He's also my Dom. *That* thought makes me throb.

I move toward him, my heart full. "Thank you so much for yesterday. Dad's more comfortable than I've ever seen him. And Janice…"

I trail off.

Something's wrong.

He's looking at me like we've just met and he's already regretting it.

With an impatient gesture, he flicks the remote and the Handel is replaced by a hissing sound then a woman's voice. *Mel's voice.*

He speeds through some surface noise then some words sound clearly. *"I'm getting mighty sick of Nera and Mr. Media Mogul bossing us all about..."*

I feel my stomach clench.

In the sudden silence, my heart beat drums in my ears. Over it, his voice is quiet and measured.

"Security caught this on a routine check. So maybe you can explain... What's Macallan's beef with Nera?"

I breathe again as relief flows through me. Thank goodness they missed the bit that came before it — *We're staging a little diversion...*

But I've still no idea what Mel plans. I press my lips together in frustration. Why, oh why, haven't I pinned her down and made her talk? This could be serious.

I manage a carefree smile. "It's really quite simple. For ages Mel's had a crush on Ben. Now Ben's clearly bowled over by Nera. I gather Mel's less than pleased."

I keep my tone light, glad I've got a ready explanation. Our jobs might be on the line here.

Cade's frowning. "Security thinks there's more. They've picked up other things — the odd phrase, stray encounters." He stops.

I glare at him. "What is this, a Soviet state?"

Something in his eyes snaps. "No, this is a carefully choreographed event for some very expensive people with even more expensive lawyers to safeguard their image and sponsorship deals. We can't afford any leaks."

"Cade, we're making a film. We're just doing our job. Anyway, you brought us here."

"And I'll send you away again unless you're very careful. Now it's time for your midnight session. I've brought it forward this evening. Sonja's set up a call to Japan later. Get yourself ready."

* * * *

"Bend over."

We're in the dungeon. I'm standing in front of the spanking bench. On the wall beside me hangs the scary assortment of whips. He leans across and selects one — a long, thin, snake-like length of evil-looking leather. With a flick of his wrist, it cracks loudly over his head and rattles an assortment of chains dangling a few feet away.

I watch, mesmerized, as he replaces it on the bench and unhooks a riding crop. It's made of braided black leather and smells new.

My hands are clasped obediently behind my back and I'm naked, except for wrist and ankle cuffs and a tight leather harness that pulls back my shoulders. It's clipped at the back to a tightly buckled leather belt.

I feel a sting on my thighs as the crop snaps just below my bottom. I gasp and bend instantly.

"Keep your legs straight."

I sigh as he massages my buttocks with both hands, molding and kneading my soft curves, dropping kisses along the small of my back. "Delicious. But they've had more than enough action over the last few days. Stand up."

He spins me around, takes both my arms and shackles them high up over my head to a wide trapeze hung from the ceiling. It's on a track and he pulls me into the center of the room and angles the spots so I hang in a pool of light.

With swift, efficient moves, he fastens my ankles wide apart with a spreader bar and pushes me forward a little, making me arch. I feel my breasts swing free. He walks slowly around me, his expression solemn and intent. With one hand he caresses my nipple again, smiling as it swells and hardens to his expert touch. In his other hand, he holds the crop.

From time to time he flicks it upward, so the soft flap at the end snaps on my quivering muscles where I strain to keep position. When I cry out, more from surprise than pain, he flicks it upward with a sharper snap and it lands squarely between my legs.

"Quiet, or I'll gag you as well. I think it's high time we paid some attention to these."

He taps each nipple with the crop. The touch is light, but by now I'm so nervous that I whimper.

"Jumpy?" He taps again, and this time I close my eyes and let the sting join the slow bloom of heat flowering in my groin.

At that moment everything goes black.

As the lights come on again, I see a stark image of the dungeon around me, the gleaming equipment on the walls, the instruments of torment he's laid out on the bench ready for our session — a spiked wheel, a soft, multi-stranded flogger and the evil-looking whip — then the room goes black again.

As the lights come back on for the second time, he's rapidly unfastening my wrists and ankles. His jaw is tense, his voice a hoarse whisper. "Get back upstairs. Now."

"Why?" Raw fear pins me to the spot as I hear a rattle at the door and voices outside.

He stands very still, his eyes dark, his expression tense. "There's some kind of emergency. That's Nera's signal for a raid. You mustn't be found here. Go, now. I'll hold them off."

"No. I want to stay here with you."

Something glitters in his eyes then abruptly he spins me round. I yelp as a sharp slap lands on my backside, propelling me toward the service elevator.

"Do as you're told for once. Scoot."

Chapter Fifteen

The great reception rooms at Beat Hall are all confusion. Uniformed police are everywhere. Through the tall windows blue lights flash on the convoy of cars and vans out in the driveway turning the scene into an action movie.

Police—just what no one here wants, me included. They ask questions, bring reporters with them. Draw the tabloids.

I speed up to my room and slip into a cocktail dress. It covers the harness but the leather cuffs are still fixed on my wrists and ankles. Cade's got the key.

Now I watch aghast as the police stride about, peering into doorways and prowling through the ballroom.

Stars scuttle to their rooms, covering their faces with menus. White-faced staff plead for calm. Phones ring incessantly.

An action movie… And still no sign of the team. That's odd. Where's Jake with his camera in all this excitement?

We're arranging a little diversion…

As people rush past me on the grand staircase I stand very still. Is this what Mel meant? Come to think of it, why would police *raid* Beat Hall? This is a private house party—no licensing is involved, and there's plenty of security on hand.

Surely they'd call beforehand...

At that moment boot heels ring out on the marble floor as Nera strides into the reception area. Under the heavy makeup she looks scared.

I spring to life and catch her up. "Nera, wait."

"Not now, Tunis. I'm busy." Her crimson mouth snaps into a tight, thin line.

I catch her arm as she turns away. "Wait. Are you sure it's not a hoax?"

Nera blinks. For a few seconds she looks almost vulnerable, like a small child. Then it passes. "That's ridiculous."

"Is it?" I lower my voice to a murmur. "Have you checked their IDs? Call the local station. Check they've sent someone out here."

Nera stands very still, her eyes wide then snaps into action. Within minutes, one of the women at reception gets through to the local police. Another is calling the dining room to summon the waiters. The footmen form a cordon to prevent the invading officers from leaving.

Nera barks out a stream of instructions then takes charge of the phone. Through gritted teeth and with furious looks at the rest of us she relays the gist of the polite murmurs coming from the other end.

Ten minutes later the panic starts to subside. It turns into gales of laughter and much backslapping.

The local force has no record of a call. The duty officer is confused. Is it urgent? There's an important athletics event north of here and he's short of officers but he can send someone along later.

"Thank you, Officer, no need. Sorry to trouble you." Nera slams down the phone and fixes the nearest policemen with a gimlet stare. After a few moments he confesses, sweating slightly.

They're all from the film crew. They're wearing uniforms from the studio wardrobe. Now they're loud and hearty, congratulating themselves on a job well done.

Just then Mel and Ben appear at the head of the staircase and walk slowly down, to a chorus of cheers. It seems they've promised drinks all round if the hoax works.

Mel takes one look at me, spots the cuffs on my ankles and wrists, and raises an eyebrow. "Well, well, what have we here? What have you been up to, might I ask?"

I grin back, scouring my mind frantically for some possible explanation, when there's a sudden silence.

At the head of the stairs leading down to the cellars a small group of policemen have just appeared. They look triumphant. Handcuffed to one of them is Cade, ashen-faced, his eyes dark with fury.

Nera quickly takes charge and has him released, but not before his eyes rake the crowd and finally fall on me, half turned away from Mel, who has a small smile still frozen on her lips.

As our eyes lock I see his face darken even further as Nera murmurs something in his ear, recounting the real cause of all the excitement.

I feel my stomach shrivel.

He's furious.

There is no way I can save my friends now. Keeping his eyes firmly fixed on me, he holds one hand aloft, still in handcuffs. The arm of the fake officer who has just captured him shoots up with his.

Cade ignores him.

I stare as his face relaxes into a broad grin. *How does he do this?* He's taking this remarkably well. Either that or he's a brilliant actor.

"Well done, everybody. Remarkably like the real thing. The excitement's over, folks. You can all go back to what you were doing before our mock raid. Drinks on the house. Thanks to the documentary team. Thanks, again—and congratulations."

Guests flush with relief and break out into excited, adrenaline-fueled chatter mingling with the actors who are proud of their show. Music starts playing again as everyone heads for the ballroom and the bar.

From the look of things, it's going to be a long night.

But Cade's grin fades abruptly as his hands are freed. He raises his voice once more. "And I'd like to see Mel Macallan, Ben Tyne-Follet and Tunis Vale in my office—*now*."

* * * *

"And guess what? We're planning a little diversion in the next day or so. Just thought I'd let you know. I'm getting mighty sick of Nera and Mr. Media Mogul bossing us all about."

"Diversion? What kind of diversion?"

We're in Cade's office. I cringe as I hear the security tape replay for the second time. I'm standing a little apart from the others. For them, it's one big joke. They've taken Cade's reaction at face value.

I feel sick.

Cade leans on the imposing desk, arms folded. Next to him stands a furious, quivering Nera.

The only other people in the room are a thin man with a crew cut and the lean look of an ex-Para who is introduced as Alford, head of security, and the burly figure of Mason, Cade's driver – also, it turns out, his bodyguard.

It's the same tape he played me, but this time he plays all of it. The hiss has been erased and it's very clear what's being said – and who's saying it.

I'm furious with myself. This is deeply humiliating and dangerous. I should have stepped in at the first hint from Mel that something was in the air. What do they think they're playing at? At this rate we'll all be kicked out – not just from Beat Hall but from our careers as well.

And all because I was called home. This is my fault. Everyone else behaved beautifully, even Cade. And this is how I repay everybody...

Mel and Ben are relentlessly upbeat about their ruse, blithely unaware of the danger they're in. "Lighten up. It's just a bit of fun. And what were *you* doing down in the dungeon, Cade? I think we should be told." Mel sounds playful.

I wince as I see Cade's jaw stiffen.

"Me?" Cade directs a glint of fury at me as he turns his attention back to Mel, his expression cool. "Just checking on a few things. One of the whips was reported missing. We like to keep the equipment fully stocked and ready for use. I hear you're a star pupil."

Mel is instantly distracted and launches into a glowing account of her training. She's proud of her success as a budding Domme. She glances pointedly at Ben a few times. He looks sheepish but pleased. Nera soon visibly relaxes and even joins in with a few sharp comments of her own.

Cade's eyes lock on me. "There, Miss Vale, see what you're missing? You should have joined in. Why not ask Mel here for some instruction? I gather she's quite proficient." His sarcastic tone could slice lemons.

"But hey, she's been busy too, by the look of it." Mel turns to me with a grin. "Why the slave cuffs, Tunis? Suddenly got a taste for the dark side?"

The cuffs. I've forgotten all about them. My stomach churns. With an effort, I match her playful smile. "They were in my dressing room. Now I can't get them off. Maybe I should ask a policeman." As a joke it's pretty feeble, but it snaps the tension. Ben laughs out loud and even Nera smiles.

Within minutes, the room empties and I'm alone with Cade.

This is not over yet, not by a long way.

"You knew about this?" His tone is quiet, heavy with menace.

My cheeks burn as the air between us turns to ice. "No. I told you."

"I find that hard to believe. Within minutes of Macallan telling you they're up to something, you jump into Garth Delaney's car and make a getaway. Looks to me like you jumped ship."

"I can't help how it looks. You know why I left. You were there."

"All I know is your relative had some sort of attack and the next morning she was fine. So I'll ask you again, did you know what they were going to do?"

"No. Mel never got a chance to explain. I'd no idea it would be a stunt like this. If so, I'd have stopped it—or at least tried to."

He watches me for a moment then sighs. "Okay. But if something like this happens again, I'm pulling the plug."

I let out a long breath. "Thank you." I turn away and make for the door.

"Where are you going?" His tone is low, barely a murmur. I pull up short and tense all over.

A tremor runs through me. "Down to the bar to talk to the others. Why?"

All at once he's behind me. I feel his breath on my neck. He reaches around me, his face close to my cheek, deliberately pushes the door shut then turns the key in the lock.

Slowly he scoops the hair away from my neck and kisses me just under the ear, his mouth hotter this time. "Not so fast. You're not going anywhere. You're staying right here. And you're going to bend over that desk." Slowly he turns me round to face him. "You defied me, Tunis. That was a clear breach of the rules. So now you'll get punished."

Heat burns deep inside me as my mouth goes dry. "Why? Why are you doing this?"

"Because you deserve it. And because I feel like it."

He captures my mouth, his tongue invading my lips in a thrilling surge, eager and hungry. I press against him, my will dissolving as his erection presses into my belly, hot and painfully hard through the thin silk of my tight sheath dress.

And all at once I feel like it too. We were torn away from each other mid-session, and now I realize how intense these sessions have become. We'd hardly started but the heat of it still burns deep inside both of us.

There's only one way to relieve it.

This is less a punishment—more a gut-wrenching *need.*

We've been doing this just six days. In fact, it's barely a week since we met.

I can hardly believe it.

I mew deep in my throat as he presses deliberately against me. He knows what I want. I deliberately reach down and spread my hand wide to fondle the hard bulk swelling in his fly, stroking, pressing as I moan into his kiss, imploring him to free himself.

I want him. Every time I see him I want to feel his warm hands on my backside, his hard, silky heat thrusting into my belly — but now I'm desperate. I want to feel him too — right here, right now — and there's no better place for it than over his desk.

He growls low in his throat in answer and he's clawing at my gown, pulling it up, sliding it higher and higher up my thighs until it sits around my waist in a tight ring of rumpled silk. Below it I'm naked and shamefully exposed, my slit pooling with moisture, my folds already pulsing with lust, aching and ready for him.

His hands search between my legs, his fingers questing deep into my swollen, lustful creases. His lips stretch against mine in a sardonic smile as I moan into his kiss, my sex throbbing instantly at his expert touch. The faint growl deep in his throat tells me he knows I'm ready and that I want this, badly.

"Over the desk. *Now.*"

Swiftly he gets me into position, making me reach out sideways across the desk. I cling on to the beaded mahogany edges with my fingertips. With my cheek pressed hard against the leather top, I peer into the depths of the heavy antique chair he was sitting in. It smells of leather and spice and warm, disturbing *male*.

The aroma sends another pulse to my groin as he starts to massage my bare skin, firm and caressing, preparing me for what's to come.

His voice is low and deadly. "This is a punishment. It will hurt. There's no soundproofing in here so you'll have to keep quiet. If you cry out, I'll give you extra."

At that moment the massage stops and I feel a thunderous slap on my bottom. I jerk painfully against the desk, and it stings hard.

I need this...

I grit my teeth and screw up my eyes in an effort not to cry out but the blows fall so hard and fast it's almost impossible. After a few minutes there's a pause, and he reaches round the desk to open one of the drawers.

What I see lying there makes me gasp. As he lifts it out, I know the worst is still to come. His hand brushes past my head, the object traveling close to my face. I smell new leather and recognize the strong, braided curve of a coiled belt.

The deep throb between my legs grows worse. Each blow of his hands jolts me against the polished mahogany, firing extra spurts of heat into my mounting climax. As the sting of the blows fades to a hot glow, he gets into position and my arousal flares to white heat.

Just one or two blows should do it... Am I really looking *forward* to this?

"Now the belt. Hold still."

I screw my eyes tight shut and wait, holding my breath. *Yes, yes, please...*

Without warning the strap lands across the very top edge of my thighs, where they're the most sensitive. I shriek, and it lands again.

No, this is wrong... "No, stop, stop. *Mercy.*"

I gasp for breath as the safeword explodes from my lips. I lie across the desk, panting as the room starts to spin.

"*What?*"

I hear the strap clatter to the floor. I stand up stiffly, my lower regions on fire. I turn to face him, pulling awkwardly at the hem of my dress. "You heard. This feels wrong — different. You're angry."

He takes a step forward, his expression curiously rapt, a new gleam in his eyes. "You mean you can *tell*? Well, hallelujah."

With a lithe movement he leans over and scoops up the strap, coiling it expertly in his long fingers and dropping it back into the drawer, his breathing still uneven. "This calls for a celebration. How about that drink?"

* * * *

The ballroom's quiet. The team has vanished and most of the guests seem to be out in the grounds where the pool's back in use and a live rock band is echoing through the soft summer night.

I glance round to check that there's no one close enough to hear us. "Why did you lose your temper?"

I feel rumpled and shaky and deeply resentful that Cade can lean casually on a bar stool and look so elegant, so in control.

He signals to the barman. "Two Sidecars."

The drinks arrive quickly, a rich tawny color, smelling of spirits. He passes me one.

I look at it doubtfully. "What's in it?" I've never got the hang of cocktails.

"It's like a daiquiri, but with brandy."

As he reaches for his drink I lay a hand on his wrist. "Cade?"

He glances up. Something in my face catches his attention. "What?"

I lick my lips. "I'm causing you problems?"

His nostrils flare. "You *are* the problem, damn it."

He makes for his glass again but I grip his wrist harder. After a second I let one finger move gently on the back of his hand. He looks up with a frown.

I hold his gaze and lick my lips. "I thought you people never drank before a — scene?" I hold my breath as I keep my hand in place, my finger still moving. I see him swallow.

Between us time seems to stand still.

His gaze locked on mine, he signals the barman. "I changed my mind. Bring me two mineral waters. Sparkling. Ice. Twist of lime." He sounds husky.

I slide my hand discreetly away so the barman won't see but Cade captures it out of sight. He keeps his eyes locked on mine.

"You sure about this?" Below the rail his grip on my hand tightens. "You mean you want to...?"

I nod. As the drinks arrive he passes me one. Something flickers in his eyes. Triumph? Relief?

He waits for the barman to move away then murmurs low. "Look, Tunis, I'm running a tight operation here. I can't have you and your team going off at tangents."

I take a long sip, barely listening. I've just invited him to finish what he started. The gleam in his eyes tells me he's back on track while I'm in free fall.

But I've made my decision. *This is what he likes. Stay with it.* And for once I've called the shots. His shots, granted, but still... One small step.

So now I'm a little bit in control too. "That's no reason to lose your temper. Maybe you should loosen up a little."

He downs his drink and spreads his hands on the counter. "Okay. I'm sorry it was too hard. I forget you're new to this. If you must know, I was afraid. You scared the living shit out of me, going off like that."

Cade Fitzlean *afraid?* I take a gulp of my drink.

"And now, if you'll drink up, we have to get back upstairs." He smiles slowly, his hand stealing round to my back and slipping downward. I wince as he gives my left buttock a squeeze, and his smile fades. "Lively down there? Serve you right. You're still in session. We'll go back up now and finish it."

As if in a dream, I follow him into the elevator and feel his arms close around me. His knee presses between my legs as the doors slide shut.

He kisses me hard, ramming my head back against the wall and releases my lips only when it arrives at our floor with a loud *ping*. He pulls me out with him, striding along with his hand gripping mine in an iron clasp. He wrenches open the door and pushes me inside, slamming it shut behind him.

"Did anybody ever tell you" — he advances slowly, his eyes raking over me — "just how sexy you look in that dress?" He reaches around me with a swift lunge and jerks down the top half of the zipper, baring my breasts and trapping my upper arms as he peels it down toward my waist.

He stoops and fastens his mouth on first one breast then the other, hauling at my nipples with his mouth, sending the blood rushing to my head. "And did anybody ever tell you" — his murmur reaches me as his lips move against my breast, his low growl sending a tremor through me — "how damn sexy you look *without* it?"

With a violent jolt he jerks the zipper all the way down and peels off the dress in a single, flowing movement. I sigh with pleasure as he runs his hands over my flanks, catching my breath when he fondles my tender backside.

"Turn around. I want to see." He swivels me round by the shoulders and in the mirrored wall opposite I see the trace of his hands on my punished rear glow in crimson, glowing patches, the marks on my thighs two angry red stripes. He caresses them gently, running his finger along the lines, making me shiver.

The sight of them is strangely arousing, glowing against my skin, cruel reminders of a contact so fierce it left stains but so violently arousing I'm still weak from the force of it.

He buries his face in the dip where my neck meets my shoulder. "Tunis, Tunis… I want to fuck. You?"

"Mm." Too overcome to speak, I breathe against his ear, feeling his erection spring free as he swiftly unfastens his trousers.

Just then his phone signals. He snatches it out of his pocket and glances at it with a frown. "*Shit.* That call from Japan. Forgive me, Tunis, I have to take this. Back in five."

Chapter Sixteen

I curl up on the quilt as five minutes drag by then another five. Still no sign of Cade. I sigh. It's too late to call home.

I use the time to freshen up, check my makeup and slip into a thin satin robe.

Maybe the dungeon will be free. Is that what he wants? I shiver, part scared, part thrilled at the thought of what he might do.

Or maybe we'll just make love...

His call's taking an age. Or is it just me? I'm getting impatient. Needy. Starting to resent the many other claims on his time.

At last I lean back on the pillows with a sigh and relax. He has a lot of demands on his time this week. I'm lucky he's given me so much of it. Business has to come first. That's how he makes money.

All at once the door crashes open. He's standing in the doorway glaring at me.

I sit up, rigid with alarm.

He's whey-faced, his hair tousled like he's repeatedly run his hands through it. For a second I wonder if he's been drinking.

"Where are they?"

I spring off the bed as he advances slowly into the room, his eyes burning into mine. This time there's no warmth. His look could snap steel.

"Who?"

"Don't play with me. So this was the point of the little diversion, was it?"

I clutch my satin robe together. Faced with his fury, it's a flimsy protection. "Cade, stop this. What's the matter?"

For a long moment he looks at me then closes his eyes briefly and takes a deep breath. "Okay, we'll take it slow."

I decide to start with what I know. "There was a problem with the call from Japan?"

"What call? There was no call." His eyes bore into mine. "Sonja's message said she'd set one up but the call was a hoax, and now she's disappeared. And Alford tells me your boyfriend's missing too. We think he's got her. Look at this."

He flicks a remote at the wide TV screen in his sitting room and scrolls through some channels until the screen becomes grainy. We're looking at security footage from a camera downstairs. There are various random shots of guests in corridors, in the dining room and the grounds.

He pauses the film to enlarge a frame.

"This is from the past three days." His voice is low, clipped, his profile rigid.

The image is fuzzy but I make out Sonja and Jake at the end of a corridor. They seem to be arguing. He lunges at her, and she darts out of sight. He appears to follow.

"There's more." He scrolls through more film and it pauses again. This time, Sonja's walking slowly through the entrance hall. Jake's following, his expression set, and he appears to call after her. She glances back over her shoulder then hurries out of shot. She looks scared.

In another shot they're together, but all at once he snatches at her arm and she tries to break free.

I frown. "But you've kept Sonja pretty busy lately. Maybe she was just in a hurry. There were other people around. There could be any number of reasons—"

"Always trying to defend him. *What is it between you?*" His tone is deliberately sarcastic, mimicking me asking him about Nera.

"Just because you dislike him doesn't make him a psycho—or a kidnapper. Maybe it was all about his camera."

He gives me a strange look. "Then we found these in his room."

He takes an envelope from his jacket and tips the contents onto the bed.

It's a set of contact strips of tiny black and white film. I peer at the images, trying to make sense of them. They look like shots of a glamour model, but slowly I realize they're all of Sonja. In some, she's in flimsy lingerie—in others she's nude. She looks natural, happy, meltingly pretty—and entirely unaware she's being watched.

Jake—a voyeur? I look up, appalled and speechless.

"He must have used a long lens. And he's doing it to get back at me." He gives me a simmering look. "Mason told me you were whispering in the car on the way to the christening. Simmons was saying he wanted his own back. What do you know about all this, Tunis?"

"Nothing. Truly. And I can't believe…" I stop mid-flow as I recall his exact words.

I'll get my own back someday. Don't you worry…

My stomach turns to ice. Back then I thought he was joking. Now the photos take on a new and terrifying significance. I stare at them, horrified. "But I've known him for years. He'd never harm anyone…"

How sure *am* I? He has mood swings. He gets fixated on things. For years I've put it down to his talent. Could it hint at something more sinister?

Is it this place? Beat Hall's affecting all of us. I should know. My arrangement with Cade is only days old and it's taking over my life. When he's in a room, I can hardly take my eyes off him.

Ben and Mel are changing fast — and becoming deeply involved. But we've all forgotten about Jake. Creative, moody — maybe it affects him too.

"What about Sonja? Did you pick up any clues from her? She's been looking very run-down the last day or so."

"Has she?" Cade's cramming shaving things and a couple of shirts into a small case. He snaps it shut and pauses as he catches my eye. "How should I know? I'm her employer, not her doctor. Maybe it's her period."

"*Cade.* That's a dreadful thing to say. Surely you notice when your staff are ill?"

He gives me a withering look. "I pay her well. She's good at her job, and she keeps personal stuff to herself. She's one in a million. And if he's done anything to her, I'll kill him."

He means what he says. I feel a shaft of fear. "But Jake would never hurt her."

He glares at me. "No? He tried to kill you. And there are other ways — ransom, torture… Fuck knows. If he wants to get his own back on me, she's a good place to start." He glances at his watch. "I must go. Alford's got a fix on Sonja's phone. We think they're in London. It's only an hour by helicopter if we get a move on. We might even get there in time to find them and put a stop to this."

"Have you called the police?"

"Are you joking? I don't want police involved. I'll let my security people handle it. And I've got contacts in Interpol. We'll know if he tries to leave the country."

"Wait—I'm coming with you."

He's already halfway to the door. He glances back, exasperated. "That's crazy. You stay here. You'll just be in the way."

I dart in front of him, barring his way. "No, I mean it. Let me come too. I can talk to him. I know Jake better than anybody. If he's…ill, then maybe I can make him see sense. Strangers might only make things—worse."

I break off, as the fleeting image of Sonja's pale, shell-like face swims before me. *Suppose something happens to her?*

"Please, Cade. Take me with you."

* * * *

Ten minutes later, in jeans, trainers and a borrowed jacket, I'm following him out onto the helipad. Alford, Mason and a grim-faced pilot are waiting for us. The helicopter looms like a menacing insect, its metal flanks gleaming in the spotlights, the propellers already in slow spin.

This time it's not a celebration. Faces are grim. Words are curt. Their terse exchange means little to me, muted references to wind-speeds and direction and mention of clearance to fly over Green Park. In minutes we clamber up into the helicopter, strap ourselves in and are rapidly airborne.

As the roar of the engines fills the cabin, Cade leans across and shouts in my ear, "It's definite. They're in the capital. We'll try there. Once she's safe, we'll worry about Simmons. Here, put these on."

He hands me a pair of ear defenders and puts them over my head, his face very close to mine. "And if anything's happened to her, I'll never forgive you."

The helicopter makes short work of the distance back to London. In the dark it's hard to make any sense of the landscape. I peer in despair at the network of streetlights far below us, stretching in glittering strings across the black countryside, thinning out along the motorways and blazing into full glory in the towns.

In the cabin the men look tense, their profiles etched in the glow from the controls. Next to me Cade looks set and grim, his jaw rigid, his elegant profile etched in soft light, his eyes in shadow. From time to time he glances at me, the glitter in his eyes far from friendly.

In the window all I can see is my reflection, white-faced and terrified.

Soon we reach the capital and the view clears. I see a giant H sketched below us and realize we're coming in to land on the roof of a tall building near a dark swell of trees.

Cade leans over and shouts into my ear again. "Alford thinks her signal comes from here. If not, we'll try the other hotels in Park Lane. It's round here somewhere."

As we land I see a reception committee lined up, their hair blowing in the rush of air from the propellers. The deputy manager and a couple of security guards greet Cade respectfully and lead us down into the hushed sanctuary of the hotel corridors.

The manager is a small, round man with a thin mustache and frightened eyes. I get the impression he and Cade have met before. Cade's leaning toward him, his voice low. "And they checked in when?"

I strain to make out the words, but they're walking too quickly for me to keep up easily. After descending two floors, they pause outside a bland, anonymous-looking door.

"This is their suite. And I've no need to remind you, Mr. Fitzlean, we'd be glad if you could resolve this quickly. Needless to say, a police intrusion—" His voice drops to an anxious whisper. Cade silences him with a faint lift of his hand.

I touch Cade's arm. "Are they in there?"

He nods. "Keep your voice down. Alford wants to break in."

"No." Four startled faces fix on me. "Let me try first. Anything sudden might be—dangerous."

Cade's eyes flicker and he gives a brief nod.

I step forward and knock gently on the door. After a few seconds I hear a faint scuffle from inside. I knock again. "Sonja? Are you in there? It's me, Tunis."

After a long, agonizing pause, the door opens a sliver. Around me there's an instant quiver of movement, as four testosterone-fueled, angry males prepare to attack.

I hold them at bay with an up-raised hand, and they grow still. "Sonja?"

The door opens a little wider, and I see Sonja, pale and tousled. She looks terrified. She's clutching a toweling bathrobe tightly under her chin.

I scan her anxiously for any signs of blood, injury or bruises. Apart from her white face and wild hair, she looks normal. "Can I come in?"

* * * *

After a few minutes I open the door again and slip back out, pulling it to behind me without closing it. The men are tense, still poised to spring. I glance round at them and keep my voice low. "I'd like a moment with Cade."

I pull him inside and close the door. We're standing in a slim corridor leading into a small but elegant suite.

Cade glares down at me, consumed with rage and anxiety. "Where is she? What's going on?"

I lean up and whisper close to his ear. "This has to be the most embarrassing few minutes of my life. We're in a hotel room. What do you *think's* going on?" I press my lips together, take hold of his arm and lead him forward.

As the room opens up before him, he stands stock-still then takes a deep breath. "Okay. Just tell me you're all right, Sonja."

The bedroom's vast, the lighting low. There are other rooms beyond but here we're surrounded by chaos. Bedding is piled on the floor, clothes strewn in all directions, draped over furniture, rumpled in heaps on the thick, pale carpet. On the bed, looking very pink and exceptionally pretty, Sonja is curled up, her face a mask of fear. She's nestling against the protective arm of a furious Jake, clearly naked under the corner of sheet he's grabbed from the floor to cover himself.

He leans forward, his blue eyes ablaze, and glares at Cade and me. "What the hell do you think's going on, Fitzlean? Nothing much, thanks to you. Now fuck off and leave us alone."

"And Sonja? You're all right?" Cade refuses to leave until he's sure, and Sonja's too scared to say so. But slowly her shy blushes convince him.

Cade glances at me, and I blush too.

We're back in the corridor and we're preparing to go. The two lovers are clearly enchanted with each other. I find the sight of them together, their snatched encounter so cruelly interrupted, poignant and touching. As they clutch each other and steal yet another kiss, it's also becoming painfully clear that Cade and I are very much *de trop*.

I'm glad to see that Cade senses this too. Luckily he's so relieved to find Sonja safe that he seems willing to forgive her moonlight flit and the considerable trouble she's put him through. And thank goodness — a crinkle at the corner of his eyes tells me he's even starting to see the funny side.

With luck, Jake will never know how close he came to sudden, violent death.

Cade tears his eyes away from mine and turns his attention back to the lovers. "Look, Sonja, take the rest of the week off. Stay here if you like. It's on me. I'll have a word with the manager. Anything else you need, just use the corporate card."

Sonja leans up and kisses him on the cheek, her eyes shining. "Thank you so much, Mr. Fitzlean. I'm really sorry about the fake call. And — everything."

Cade smiles briefly then glances at Jake. "Not as sorry as I am. We'll miss you, Simmons. I was counting on you for tomorrow at least."

"*Shit*, sorry. I forgot." For the first time, Jake looks sheepish.

I frown, puzzled. *Tomorrow?* What's going on?

When Cade speaks again, the mystery deepens. "We'll manage. The film crew is still on site. I'll ask them to do it. We'll split the footage with your team. Have fun."

Now he's keen to get away. The mystery is solved, the danger past.

The lovers tell us everything—how Mel and Ben planned the diversion to cover their escape at Jake's urgent request, because Sonja was scared of offending her stern employer. She knew he was too busy to spare her and dreaded being caught on camera. Flight seemed the only option.

The risk of getting fired, she proclaims hotly, is well worth it. She'd do it all over again.

When I think how easily Cade manages our own encounters, I feel deeply sorry for Sonja and Jake. I make a note to tackle Cade about his attitude to his staff the first chance I get. I'm also deeply relieved everything's turned out well.

The flight back, after the high drama of our trip out, is relaxed and calm. I even doze for a while in the dull hum of the engines and the soft darkness of the cabin. Cade's hand steals to my thigh and stays there, a warm, stirring reminder that our own lovemaking was also brutally interrupted.

He's clearly impatient to get back to Beat Hall, even turning down the tempting offer of a suite for the night from the grateful manager.

My heart leaps. In the darkness of the cabin, I lean into his touch. We exchange a look from time to time, his heat fueling mine.

* * * *

When we arrive back at Beat Hall, the eastern horizon is already flushed with the new dawn. He mutters hasty thanks to his security team and the crew then hauls me down to our rooms, his hand clasping mine in a firm grip.

Does all his staff know about us? I suppose they must. The thought makes me tingle.

In our rooms he kicks the door shut and pulls me into his arms, fastening his mouth on mine like a man starved.

All at once we're tearing off our clothes, ripping at zips, peeling off trousers and somehow I'm pinned down on the bed, my arms hauled over my head and lashed to the bedposts with soft cotton rope which appears as if by magic from a slim drawer in the side table.

He straddles me, leaning back on his thighs. In the low lighting his eyes glitter, black with lust.

"If you had anything to do with that episode, you're going to be extremely sorry."

I open my mouth to laugh a protest but he surprises me by fastening a hand over my lips. "Quiet. I need your mouth."

He leans over me, shifting slightly from time to time to adjust his angle. He watches breathless as I fellate him gently, deeply touched that he wants this so much.

As I lick him, yawning open my throat to swallow him then pulling back to lick along his length, tasting his silky, salty heat with lustful sweeps of my tongue, I marvel that such a simple caress can arouse him so far and so fast.

It arouses me, too. My excitement builds as I suck, at the thought of how it will feel—how it always feels—when he finally plunges inside me. He leans back to tease my splayed cleft with his fingers.

"Your mouth's good. But your tail's better."

He grasps me by the ankles and flips me over, pushing me up onto my knees. With my arms still tethered, I lean on my elbows as my hands cross over and hear him growl low in his throat as I rear up with my backside high in the air. I felt his breath on my skin, hot and fierce on my tender patches, where his paddle and his whip have made their mark.

"You're so beautiful, Tunis. Your ass is fantastic like this — marked as *mine*. Open your legs. Wider."

I hear the rip of foil then with a grunt he slides inside, hardly giving me time to brace as he thrusts again and again. He fondles my breasts then squeezes hard, first one then the other, gripping my nipples painfully. I gasp and instantly he murmurs close to my ear. "No noise, or we'll finish this in the dungeon."

He squeezes again and I shriek as he gives both my nipples a playful tweak with his fingers and thumbs. Instantly he pulls free and stretches out next to me, a slow smile spreading over his face. His erection, high and proud and still sheathed in the condom, beats against my hip. "What did I just say?"

I stare at him, dumbfounded.

Surely he can't mean… "Not…the dungeon? *Now*?"

He smiles, fondling my breasts with his hand, and tweaks me again, making me cry out. With a swift movement he wrenches the condom away, hurls it across the room then reaches up to unfasten my wrists. "Check. Get up."

Chapter Seventeen

He wants me in the dungeon at this hour? What happened to sleep?

As I kneel beside the bed, he drapes a towel over my shoulders. "Our week's nearly over and we've still got some ground to cover. You asked for training, and you're going to get it. We'll cut the formalities that normally start your session. Just kiss the tip."

This is scary. He was surely only seconds from orgasm. How can he hold off like this? His erection's still fierce and purple, glossy with my saliva. I swirl my tongue eagerly around the head then touch my lips to its tiny opening in a loving, reverent kiss.

I know how much he loves this. Maybe it'll lure him back to bed.

No such luck. He draws in a deep, ragged breath then signals me to get to my feet and follow him downstairs.

As the events of the past few hours flash through my mind, I feel distinctly jaded. I could really use a nice cozy orgasm followed by sleep, the deeper the better.

But Cade Fitzlean doesn't do nice and cozy.

Or sleep, apparently.

I bleat a feeble protest. "It's nearly dawn already. Can't we just go to bed? *Ow.*" I get a sharp slap on my rump.

"You forget your manners, sub. You speak when I give you permission."

The dungeon is just as we left it, the rails of gleaming equipment still undisturbed. The items he'd selected before the hoax raid hours ago are still laid out in a neat row on the bench. The sight of them makes me shiver.

This time he ignores them and positions me in the central beam of the main spotlight, pulling a rack of chains fixed to the ceiling down to head level. "I'm going to suspend you by the arms and one foot. As a former dancer, you should be able to hold a position with one leg high in the air. Safeword if you have to. After that, I'll gag you and you'll have to signal. Remember what it is?"

I lift two crossed fingers, my agreed safe signal for when I'm gagged. I thought he was kidding when he told me I'd need one. Silly me.

He clamps the cuffs on my wrists and fastens them to the chains, hauling them high over my head with a tug on the ropes at the wall.

"Now your foot. Go on tiptoe." He catches my arched foot as I raise my leg, running his fingers lovingly over my instep and my neatly pointed toes. He lifts my foot to his lips in a fond kiss before stretching my leg at the angle he wants, my arched foot pointing upward.

In dance this pose is simply a dramatic peak in a graceful sequence but here I'm chained into it, exposed and vulnerable, poised in the air like an insect trapped in amber.

He tests the cuffs and anxiously scans my face. "Okay?"

I nod, eyes wide. Heat sparked by dread burns again. *What's he going to do?* Deep down I can think of only one possible answer, one possible reason he wants me splayed wide like this.

He frowns. "What's wrong? Are you afraid?"

I nod again, glad I'm forbidden to speak. I might give too much away. It's not just fear. *It's excitement.*

He runs his hand up the inside of my leg, closing his fingers lovingly over my slit. I hold my breath as he slides his fingers up inside me, lingering in my soft, moist creases, now slick at his touch.

I see his eyes gleam. "Wet already? We haven't started yet." He kisses my cheek, his expression unbearably tender. "Don't be afraid. Sex happens down here" — he flexes his fingers inside me, making me moan — "and up here." He kisses my forehead. He gestures to the rails, bristling with implements. "All the rest is just theater. Maybe that's why you find it so affecting." He eyes me hungrily. "Ready?" He works his fingers deeper.

I'm forbidden to speak, but an eloquent trickle runs down the inside of one tense, quivering thigh.

His eyes flicker as his voice lowers to a velvety murmur. "I thought so. Now the gag. Open."

He holds it up in front of my face, a fearsome studded strap in black leather, with a soft plastic ball about halfway along. Like a pet collar, it has a sturdy buckle at one end. He slips the soft ball behind my teeth where it springs back into shape in my mouth.

It looked small but it feels huge.

His calm smile is making me nervous. Like some trapped animal, I'm intensely aware of his mood. I can sense his growing excitement. It's very disturbing, and on some deeply primitive level, *hot.*

"Delicious. If I were feeling especially strict, I might tweak your lip and make you drool—intensely humiliating. But since you're pretty wet already somewhere else, I'll spare your blushes for now." He buckles the strap at the back of my head then stands back to admire the effect. "Beautiful. You look hot enough to eat."

He starts to drop kisses on my straining muscles. He soothes my quivering skin with soft touches of his lips and long, sensuous sweeps of his hands along my waist, down my wide, splayed thighs and over my breasts. He smiles fondly as I mew helplessly into the gag.

I watch with growing alarm as he strolls over to the rail of bushy floggers hanging by the wall and slowly runs his long fingers over them, a master craftsman assessing his tools, weighing up the possibilities for maximum pleasure.

He finally makes his choice and unhooks a large black flogger, the long strands evil and businesslike.

"Now let's see how fast you can come."

He gives the whip a few expert flicks of his wrist as he turns back toward me. The strands swish through the air in a brisk figure of eight and make a terrifying hiss before he moves around behind me, out of sight.

A trickle of sweat crawls down my back as I close my eyes. I feel a rush of air as the strands swish around me again then land on my back with a muffled slap. They slide sensuously off my skin, agonizingly slow, snaking round my legs and my quivering arms.

The whip falls again and again, on my breasts, my arms, my back and my legs.

I wait for the sting, the awful pain that a whip that size must surely have, but it never comes. Either his touch is deliberately light—I've taken a lot of punishment this week — or the whip is *soft*. It must be suede.

At each blow I flinch, but I receive only endless shocks of sensual pleasure. Soon I'm tingling all over, the softness unbearably repeated, the strokes never ending. The blows grow harsher, but now the hissing strands have lost any power to sting as my skin glows all over, craving each new contact, tingling and burning from the constant stimulation.

But the blows speed up along my inner thighs and now I guess what's coming. Why else would he want my legs forced open into a tempting, vertical line?

Each new blow lands a fraction closer to my aching, burning center. The soft strands hiss along my skin, higher and higher. At last, with terrifying precision, the whip lands right across my splayed slit.

I've been teased and aroused for hours, perilously close to the peak again and again, continually denied. I've been dreading and craving this moment and now it's here.

Helpless against his onslaught, I surrender to his will as the whip lands again and again, his aim precise and merciless, stoking my excitement to agonizing heights. Finally I explode, the spasms erupting through me in waves of pleasure. I quiver in my bonds, too tightly held to writhe and thrash like I want, as tears of relief course down my face.

With a shout he throws down the whip and folds his arms around me. Impatient fingers tear at the buckle of the gag. Gently he eases it out of my mouth, flings it away then captures my lips. His eager tongue surges into me, warm and thrillingly alive after the unfeeling plastic.

As my spasms die away, he releases my lips and gently unhooks the chains, holding me fast as I sway against him, weary now and trembling with relief.

"You're so beautiful. I could watch you for hours." After a few moments he gently pushes me down. "Now me."

His erection is huge now, a touching reminder that he's held off for so long. As it leaps before my face, I take him gently in my mouth, eager for him to share the rapture still coursing through me. Above me his chest heaves as I take him deep, swallowing lustily.

At last he pauses, quivers and comes over my tongue, filling my mouth with his stinging, fizzing essence. I'm almost relieved for him. It seems a small thank you for such an intense experience.

At last his breathing slows and he raises me gently to my feet. "You amaze me, as ever." He kisses me gently on the forehead and enfolds me in his arms. "And now to bed. We've had a long day."

I smile up at him. "And an even longer night."

It's already growing light as we reach our rooms. He makes me kneel beside him while he runs a bath, swirls in some foam then climbs in, signaling for me to join him. He massages my aching shoulders with scented gel.

"Today's our last day. I can hardly believe it." I lie back in his arms with a sigh. It's been a turbulent week, but it's been heaven.

"Have you enjoyed it?"

I feel his breath on my ear as he clasps his arms around me, pulling me to him. The suds swirl over my breasts. Below the surface I feel his erection rise again and press into my back, pulsing a little as I flex against it.

"Yes. Very much." Am I giving myself away? I hope I won't regret this.

Next week I'll be his twenty-four seven. That was the agreement. Goodness only knows what he plans to do to me then.

"It might be your last day of training but up to midnight, you're still in my care." His voice is soft but his tone is stern. The water swishes around us as he pushes me forward, rises to his feet and raises me up to face him.

As I open my mouth to protest, he smiles, places a finger on my lips and reaches for a towel. "Hush. Save your strength for your last day. You're going to need it."

He climbs out of the bath, sweeps me up in his arms and carries me over to the bed. I nuzzle into his neck, limp with content as he lays me down then curls around me, pulling his toweling robe over us both. He buries his face in my hair, murmuring his last command of the day in a soft baritone.

"Sleep. Now."

* * * *

I wake late in the morning in a shaft of noon sun. Cade is standing over me with a glass of orange juice. A trolley heaped with good things is standing by the door.

"Here, try this. Then come and eat. You must be famished after yesterday."

The juice is fresh and sweet.

He glances up as I join him at the small table and help myself to a croissant. "Leave the coffee. I've ordered fresh."

As I eat, I gaze at him, drinking in the sight of his firm, regular features gilded by the sun.

He glances up, his dark eyes alight with mischief. "Looking forward to your last day?"

When the waiter's gone, I sip the fresh coffee. "You make it sound very mysterious."

At that moment he takes a call, listening for a while and issuing the occasional terse instruction. As he puts down the phone, he smiles. "It's meant to be. I've lined up some surprises for you. I'd hoped Simmons would be here to film everything. No matter, we'll manage."

"Film what?" Do Mel and Ben know about this? I'd better check with them as soon as I get downstairs.

"Nera's arranged a couple of events to finish off the week. The Beat Fair takes place in the grounds all afternoon. The trainees will get a chance to show off their new skills and the professional Doms will stage some displays. Naturally we'll be taking part. So I want you up here fit and ready by two at the latest."

"We'll *what*?" I set down my cup with a clatter. Coffee splashes a sticky brown puddle all over the spotless linen. "But we can't—"

He eyes me calmly. "Oh yes, we can. You're still in my service and you'll fit in with my plans. Nera's gone to a lot of trouble for you and your crazy friends. It's the least you can do."

"But—" My mind races with awful, terrifying images. I try again. "But if people see us together—"

His mouth gives an impatient twitch. "They'll see us, sure. That's rather the point of a display. But we'll be fully masked. And we're going out on a high. We'll combine it with your last daytime session. We're going to do a caning display."

For a second the room seems to spin. I close my eyes briefly, indignation rising.

"I bet this is Nera's idea. What exactly *is* her hold over you, Cade?"

His smile instantly fades. "We're just helping out. And if you remember, *you* asked me to do this. I was all set to fly home." Abruptly he rises to his feet. "I've got calls waiting. Get back here by two. Eat now. Skip lunch in case you throw up. And don't be late."

His tone is icy. Once more I've overstepped some mark drawn in imaginary sand. And I'm going to be publicly *caned*.

* * * *

Today it's gloriously hot. Sunlight shimmers over the park. The pool's already crowded.

I slip into a pale linen shift and matching sandals and set off to find the others. I need to check how much of this Jake's going to miss so we can reclaim missing footage from Cade's people.

Everywhere seems strange, transformed. Nera plans to go out with a bang.

In the great reception rooms and hallways, decorations are speedily going up and some of the guests are in costume already, fantastical creations of straps and feathers, latex and studs. Many are already partying, and outside in the grounds a huge marquee has been put up, its walls scrolled up to reveal the rock band already setting up equipment and testing sound levels.

The tables inside are being laid out for the Midnight Fetish Feast announced on billboards at the entrance.

Nearby on the lawns a stage has been erected for the Beat Fair, and whipping posts, stocks and a spanking bench are already in place. Chairs are being placed in rows for the eager spectators, already crowding forward.

Flora Dain

Across the lawns a giant screen partly hides the trees. Technicians in shorts and T-shirts are everywhere, hammering planks, laying cable. Excited guests are clustered round the pool and the lunch tables, mostly in masks.

Nera, her expression even sourer than usual, prowls about with a clipboard.

I spin round at a familiar voice.

"Tunis, hi. Hear about Jake? He's run off with Sonja. He won't be back for a week. What'll we do?" Mel, startling in scarlet latex hot pants and thigh-high boots peers at me through thick black eye makeup. Her nails are painted a savage black, and a slender whip swings at her waist.

I sigh. "It's under control, no thanks to you. I suppose you thought it was funny helping them bunk off. You might have got us all the sack with a stunt like that."

I pause as Ben joins us. He's strapped into in a black leather harness and loincloth.

He gives me a small, sheepish smile. "Heard about Jake?"

"Hi, Ben. Yes, I heard." I smile in spite of myself. He looks so happy, such a change from his usual gloomy self. "And you're a disgrace, both of you. But Jake's not a problem. We've been offered some of the footage from the film crew you called in to stage the phony raid, including their star cameraman."

"You fixed all that? That's terrific." Mel eyes me with new respect. "See, Ben? She also serves who merely stays in bed." She winks at me. "Ben thinks you're lazy. And we've already heard from Jake, by the way. They're having a great time." She rolls her eyes. "Jake and Sonja... Who knew?"

I grin. "You two, clearly. And hey, I love the costumes. So you're both really into all this?"

"You *think*?" Mel eyes Ben hungrily. "We've had a fantastic week. Girl power's taken on a whole new dimension. Come on, slave, I'm going to treat you to some lunch." She moves away with Ben in tow and calls out to me over her shoulder. "We're on after two. Cock and ball torture. Don't miss it."

* * * *

As I watch, the Beat Fair starts. A hapless sub is led onto the stage and tethered to a whipping post by a fearsome Domme who sets about her pert little bottom with a tawse.

The crowd gathers to watch, many bringing their lunch in handfuls from the loaded tables under the marquee. They cheer loudly when the sub is finally released.

She turns to face the crowd, blushing almost as brightly as her crimson rear. She takes a shy bow and is led away as another display is set up, this time with three participants, each taking turns to spank the other two.

I ought to go up. It must be nearly two, but it's impossible to tear myself away. To my shame, the sight of the eager, pink subs, their submissive poses belied by their gleaming eyes and eager expressions, is as fascinating as the breathtaking skill of their tormentors.

I watch spellbound, feeling almost as guilty as I did during the Panther's stunning display. I feel every blow.

After a week with Cade, I know just what the panting subs are going through. But it's the first time I've *seen* it.

"Enjoying the show?" Cade's deep voice, so close to my ear, makes me jump.

Flora Dain

I clutch the rail in front of me, my knuckles white for a moment, then turn to look up at him. How long has he been standing there? I sense a distinct air of suppressed excitement. It fires my own. "Yes," I whisper. "I'd no idea."

I feel his hand on my back, moving slowly around my waist. I glance round nervously but everyone's looking at the stage. "Good. I hoped you'd say something like that."

I feel his touch on my hair, and his hand squeezes my left flank in an intimate, private gesture.

I lean back and murmur low so no one can hear. "Cade, why do I feel like this? Is there something wrong with me?"

He squeezes again, pressing against me like the crowd is accidentally pushing us up close. I can feel his erection through our clothes, hot against my back. "You're just exploring your dark side. We rarely get the chance. How is that wrong? Some people would call it healthy. Me for one."

For a few blissful seconds we're clasped in a subtle but powerful embrace as I lean against him, reveling in his heat.

The three people on stage draw their act to a close and take a triumphant bow to a loud ripple of applause.

He murmurs against my ear, "Time to go. Ready to face your public?"

Chapter Eighteen

"We're driving somewhere? I thought we had to go up to change?" I pause on the top step at the entrance to the Hall as the sleek car waits in the driveway below.

There's no one around, only Mason, bulky and respectful, standing by the rear passenger door.

"We are. But not here. We're going to the tower. Quick, get in before someone sees." Cade hustles me down to the car and nods to Mason, who climbs into the driver's seat and fires the engine. Cade pulls the door shut as the large car sets off, silent and swift.

I sit rigid. We've climbed the tower only once but that was at night. I had no clear view of the ground. It's already a special place. He made love to me there for the first time. Echoes from our passionate encounter still pulse through me every time I think of it.

But now it's different. It's daytime.

I shudder. My dread of high places seems silly at times. At others it's terribly real. He knows this. I hiss back at him, keeping my voice low so Mason won't hear. "Why are you doing this? Just to get even?"

He eyes me sternly, one eyebrow faintly raised. "This is your last day. I warned you it held some surprises. You're doing well, but you've tasted only mild submission—kneeling before sessions, routine restraint play. I need to test your commitment before you go on to the next stage. Maybe the quickest way is to make you face your fears."

The next stage? He means next week. *I'll be his.*

I feel a surge of excitement. His fee for my week's training was just a form of words on my first day here. I consented lightly, with no idea what to expect. But now…

He's strict, harsh even. I'm swept off my feet by his energy, his passion—and his utter dedication to detail. And he's probably been going easy on me.

Suppose he lets rip?

He's smiling. "Nervous?"

I swallow. "Like I'm on a cliff. I'm more scared of next week than I am of the next few hours."

He takes my hand, a mysterious smile playing over his beautiful, sculpted mouth. "Very natural. It'll be a big step for you. That's why I have to make sure you're ready."

He lifts my hand and kisses my palm. His touch sends shimmers along my arm.

"Do you trust me, Tunis? I'd never knowingly hurt you. You must know that. Tell me honestly, have I ever taken you further than you really wanted to go?"

The car's drawing to a halt at the foot of the tower. Before I can reply, Mason springs out of his seat and is already opening my door.

Cade smiles again and releases my hand. "Here we are. After you."

The climb up the spiral stairs is long, and I try not to look out of the tiny windows that show the ground getting smaller the higher we go. As we reach the viewing chamber, my heart's racing, not entirely from the climb.

And I'm still puzzled. "So we change up here then go back down to the stage?"

He strides about the room, shrugging off his jacket. He flings it onto one of the flat seats under the broad windows.

In the distance Beat Hall looks festive and cheerful, colored pennants flying from all the turrets. Far below, the guests are milling in the grounds, bright dots among the endless green. From up here the stage looks like a toy, with tiny marionette figures on it.

I turn away from the windows, feeling sick. Instantly he turns me round to face a large screen set up in one of the octagonal bays. It shows Mel and Ben performing their act.

Cade puts an arm round my shoulders and holds me close. "Don't look down. Keep your eyes on the screen."

I stare spellbound at Ben, hooded and masked, twitching as Mel lays about him with a riding crop. The expression on her face is one of intense concentration. The expression on his is of utter, blissful content.

As I watch, gauze screens behind me lower to cover the windows, dimming the light and blurring the terrifying views. Now the strongest light in here comes from spotlights trained on what looks like a corner of a film set. It has a camera set up on a tripod, a white umbrella to diffuse the light and a wide patch of bright, rumpled satin heaped with a pile of matching cushions.

Cade lowers the sound. "This is our communications tower. We can pick up satellite signals and radio frequencies. And the security TV cover's based here too."

"Making you the ultimate control freak?"

"Making us the most secure venue for rock festivals in the country. That's how we keep ahead of the market. Today we're going to perform up here. Our every move will be relayed to the giant screen down there in the grounds."

He gestures to the large screen, where Mel and Ben, their routine over, are now taking a bow. "At the same time it'll play in here, so you can watch as we do it."

I shudder. "Cade, I'm not sure I can do this."

He takes me in his arms, his expression unreadable. "Hey, you're a performer. We're just putting on a show. Do you trust me, Tunis? Tell me."

I gaze into his eyes as images from the past week flash through my mind—his fury on the footbridge when he thought I was in danger, taking charge of Janice, shifting heaven and earth to trace Sonja when he thought her life was threatened.

Do I feel safe with him? I kiss him gently on the jaw. "Yes," I whisper.

"And you'll perform for me?"

I gaze up at him, my heart full. He's done so much— everything I've asked of him and far, far more. I nod, my throat too tight to speak.

I can do this. I owe him.

It's as if I lit a fuse. Instantly his expression changes and he becomes purposeful, focused, issuing instructions, outlining precisely what he wants. "You'll make a sequence of moves, positions, poses. While you do it, I'll move around you and tap you with the cane—lightly while you hold position, then sharply when I want you to shift. You can pose any way you want but I want you to create a kind of—ballet."

How exciting. We've had no rehearsal time so this will be entirely off the cuff. My mind fills instantly with ideas, movements and shaped sequences. He orders me to strip and do some warm-ups while he watches.

"We'll both wear masks—and you can try out some jewelry. It'll be an interesting workout for some of the new pieces."

* * * *

In half an hour we're ready to start. I'm limbered up now, eager and glowing. He fastens me into the silver harness, the salacious leaves twisting and curling around me. The wicked pointed fronds press into my groin. Every move makes me pulse and throb.

I step into a pair of high heels in turquoise snakeskin, the color sharp and vibrant against my skin, and when I put on a bright, jeweled mask, crowned with brilliant turquoise feathers, he adds a twist of matching chiffon to cover my hair.

My costume's completed with elaborate silver nipple clamps designed as clusters of leaves to match the harness. He pinches and teases my nipples a few times, smiling as I wince, then screws them in place.

"I'll leave them looser than normal. We'll be performing for nearly an hour. Clamps that really do the business have to be pulled off after about twenty minutes, and I'm guessing we'll have our minds on other things so we may forget. I'll just slip into costume and we'll make a start."

The camera's running now and I catch sight of myself on screen. I perform a few simple moves to test out the jewelry. It's very constricting, and the constant pull down below makes my every move an agony of arousal. My breasts look huge, glittering in their jeweled cages, my nipples rosy and swollen among the finery.

He covers my modesty with another surprise—a silver fig leaf. This one hangs from a thin silver chain that loops over my hips in a graceful drape. It's held in place by a ridged stem that fits directly *into my sex*. I have to clutch it in place. Instantly it sets up a maddening pressure — and I'm already pulsing with need.

I look like some exotic bird, glittering and graceful, my face masked in bejeweled splendor, my hair veiled in chiffon, my body all a-glow — and deep down I'm on fire.

This will be fun.

At that moment he comes back in and I gasp. "You look sensational."

He's naked to the waist and wearing black leather jeans and a menacing black mask. He's flexing a slim, whippy cane.

His low growl raises the soft down along my back. "You too."

He moves up close, his long mouth stretched in a wide grin. Behind the mask his eyes glitter. "Ready?"

I drop a kiss on his breastbone, at a point right between his pectorals. I move my thumbs over his tiny nipples and thrill as they sharpen into hard little nubs. "I can only hope so."

He smiles briefly. "Me too. Just one more thing before we start. I want you to wear this."

He holds up a flimsy, glittering spider's web of diamonds, with a soft, silver-colored ball about halfway along. The brilliants catch the light and spray rainbows all over the ceiling.

It's beautiful but I know instantly what it is.

"A gag?" *On no.*

He frowns at my evident dismay. "We'll work to a sound track, but I don't want you crying out. You might give us away. Just think of it as jewelry."

He slips it into place. Once more the ball, smaller this time, fits behind my teeth. The diamond web arches away from my lips in a graceful network. It looks like spun sugar, but the piece in my mouth feels as rigid as a horse's bit.

With a light, cynical smile he adds some flashy earrings and touches me lightly under the chin. "Perfect."

In the mirror I sparkle in the spotlights. The effect is spectacular. He looms at my side, a menacing, leather-clad Captain Hook to my jeweled, naked and very vulnerable Tinkerbell.

The cane in his hand quivers ominously.

As the music begins, I ease into position on the circle marked out on the floor and begin to dance. After a few experimental stretches, he moves up close and silently indicates I must kneel then tilts up my chin with the tip of the cane. I look up at him and shiver, as a shimmer runs over me — part dread, part arousal — and partly the thrill of performance.

The music is Ravel's *Bolero*, used often for display dance. It's a classic sound picture of macho man at his most controlling — the toreador twirling his cloak. As the rhythm pounds through my brain, I lose my fear and I'm consumed by the music, my limbs finding patterns and shapes in the space around me and blending them into sequence to create dance.

I recall seeing this ballet in Paris, and I set up a deliberate pulse, catching the beat.

Soon it matches my own heartbeat, my rhythm perfectly in sync. And as I move, the cane begins to fall. At first the touches are light, teasing, the cane swishing in the air around me, its fearsome hiss sending shivers through me.

I tease it and seduce it, offered first one breast then another, turning this way and that, using the power of the music to control the urge to flinch as it lands, remembering to hold position when it taps, shifting into a new pose when it stings.

At the start, I focus on it and my dance turns into a duel, a battle of wits between the cane and me as I lure its snap then twist away. But soon I sense impatience in its master — the sinister, shadowy figure wielding it. Slowly he draws closer and his parted legs tower over me as I twist and writhe, laughing softly behind my gag each time I outwit him.

The music's on a loop, but at last it swells toward its frenzied climax. I hear his breath hiss through his clenched teeth and with a final swish, he lands a double tap at each side of my slit as the cane lands twice in rapid succession.

It feels extraordinary. I'm so aroused now that I have to steel myself not to come, keenly aware we have an audience.

I scream against the gag and suddenly the music is over. As he passes between me and the camera he eases the ball out of my mouth and lets it slip down onto my neck, where it nestles at the base of my throat. The diamonds either side loop into a graceful necklace.

In the silence he murmurs low, as if to himself. "We're done. Stay on your knees then swivel round to face the camera and smile. Put your hands behind your back and take a bow. Keep smiling."

I obey in a daze, seeing myself smiling on screen like I'm somebody else. He looms behind me, his face in shadow. He stands with his legs astride, arms folded, the cane dangling from one wrist.

"That's it. We're off air."

The shot pans out to show the audience far below are cheering and shouting at the giant screen in the park where Cade and I are posed in freeze frame, taking our final bow.

I hear him give a low chuckle. "I offered our set as a simple filler between acts. But from the look of it, you're the star of the show."

I spin round to gaze up at him. He tilts up my head and stoops to kiss me on the lips. When he pulls away I see his face crease into a frown.

"Does that always happen when you dance?"

"Does what happen?"

His frown darkens. "I'm not sure. You…changed."

I dart him a playful look from under my lashes. "You too. You look very scary in that."

His eyes narrow and his voice drops to a sinister murmur. "You were defiant. Definitely a breach of the rules."

I start to rise to my feet but I feel his foot on my shoulder, pressing me down.

He's smiling at me strangely, his eyes glittering behind the mask. "Oh no, you're not going anywhere. That was just a demo. Now for the real thing."

But our display's over. Surely he can't mean — ?

Some instinct tells me he does. All at once the tower room seems silent and still.

Cade looks down at me, his eyes full of heat. "I'm guessing you enjoyed that." His rich, dark voice flows around me.

His skill created the display but it was mine that made it art, turning it into ballet and an unexpected triumph. Now he switches off the camera and gently removes my jeweled gag. He stands over me, his chest heaving.

I tingle all over where the tip of the cane teased and snapped on my skin. My nerve endings fizz like champagne. I feel almost as heady as if I'd drunk some. I beam at him. "Was that the surprise you meant—that I'd *enjoy* it?"

"So—did you?"

I feel my cheeks burn. "Maybe." My husky whisper hides a torrent of feelings, some of them entirely unexpected. I'm on top of the world—and oddly emotional. I want to laugh and cry all at the same time. With an effort I manage a bright smile. "Quite a surprise."

"I think you surprised us all. But now playtime's over."

My smile slowly dies away.

"Lose the mask."

His voice is low and quiet, his expression stern.

Alarm clutches my belly. "What are you going to do?"

Behind the mask his eyes glitter dangerously. "You broke the rules. Defiance earns a correction. You might have been on camera, but you were still under instruction. Did you think I'd forgotten? You'll get six strokes on your thighs, three a side. And we'll try out a new position for this."

He instructs me to lie down at the center of the circle and hoist my body and my legs upright into the air like I'm doing exercise cycling. He takes his time tapping me into position. When he's satisfied that my toes arch far enough and my knees are straight, he makes me splay my legs.

"Wider. I want full access."

He really means it. Indignation burns. This is so *unfair*, only minutes after such a triumph.

Then I stop myself. It's all my fault. Maybe the caning display aroused him. It sure aroused me.

He tried to give this up. He told me so.

Tease the tiger, you risk a bite. And now, against all reason, I'm so jumpy and excitable and deeply, hotly aroused that I'm looking forward to it.

Our caning display was a triumph — and a prelude. Like he said, just the warm-up. Now I want more.

"*One.*" The first blow lands with a snap, stinging on my sensitive skin like fire. The sound lingers far longer than the sting. I close my eyes, savoring the sensation.

I open them to see him watching me, trying to gage my reaction, to see how I'm doing. Not just for his pleasure — he has to. He's my Dom.

But it's an effort to meet his gaze. Oddly, I'm ashamed of him seeing my reaction. *I'm ashamed of my pleasure?*

"Two." The cane lands again. As I tense the gleaming silver ivy leaf jolts in my groin. The metal's warm now, the silver so smooth I'd have forgotten it but for its precise, unmistakable pressure.

I'm building to a climax.

Even the sight of him doing this turns me on. Can I really be *enjoying* this?

As the third blow lands, he draws away and starts to trace patterns on my skin with the very tip of the cane. "How does this feel? Good?"

I stare at him, my eyes filling as emotion and endorphins rage together.

"Answer me." The cane taps briskly at my upraised rump, making me twitch. The next second it lands with a sharper tap across my nipples.

I gasp, then moan a little as the sting warms my groin to a pulsing, throbbing ache. "Good, Sir. It feels good."

Please, again — just there — once more…

Chapter Nineteen

The cane trails again. This time it teases between my legs and along the curves of the silverware that press my folds modestly together. It travels farther, the tip slipping inside me, circling in my moist, hidden dip and easing out again, lingering along my slit.

I whimper as heat flares between my legs.

"You've made the cane wet. You'd better lick it clean." Cade smiles beneath the mask as the tip quivers close to my lips.

Slowly I extend my tongue and lick, then fellate it gently, tasting the salty flavor of my own juices, stirred and ashamed.

After a few moments he slowly pulls the cane away. It swishes through the air with a terrifying hiss. "Four."

The sting's lighter now. The pressure and the heat in my groin fuse into a dull ache as each blow takes me closer. He circles around me, tracing my silver harness with the tip of the cane. It snaps again.

"Five."

I gaze up at him from the floor, admiring his firm, muscled thighs so close to my face and the distinct bulge at his fly where the tight leather jeans stretch over his swelling erection. The sight of his arousal fuels mine. Now I'm getting agonizingly close.

One more, please, please...

"Six."

The last stroke is the sharpest, but now it hardly matters. The wicked jewelry takes over and does the rest. My orgasm flashes through me like lightning, swallowing up the effect of the blow in the violence of the convulsion that seizes me.

Instantly he knows.

"Hold the position." He stands over me, directing my pleasure as sternly as he directed my limbs.

I writhe and twitch, desperate to balance, intensely aware of his gaze as my orgasm consumes me, the storm of it raging through my splayed legs and my tense supporting arms.

As the heat fades, the force of it leaves me drained and limp, my thighs on fire. He watches in silence as I fight for control and to stay in position.

"Now relax. Curl up into a ball then kneel up, hands behind your back."

Shakily I do it. I hear the telltale rasp of his zipper as he unfastens his jeans. This can only end one way.

Menacing and stern, he towers over me as his huge erection leaps free and jerks in my face. He stays silent, his stance alone expressing his desire.

As my climax still ripples through me, I lick gently at his hot, swollen tip then surge forward, my rhythm swiftly matching the rise and fall of his heaving chest.

"Easy." He sounds surprised.

Smiling around him, I slow a little, thrilling to his hard, ridged length as it fills my mouth.

Gently he withdraws. "You're too good at this." He lays a hand along the side of my face, his gaze warm.

I close my eyes and lean into his touch. His tenderness, so soon after the torment of the caning, is deeply unsettling. The aftershocks from my climax still rage inside me. I think I'm close to tears.

He tilts up my face, scanning me anxiously. "What?"

I swallowed. "Are you — turning me away?"

He drops a kiss on my hair, his voice barely a whisper. "Never. But — I need more of your mouth."

Startled, I scan his face. I can see he does. He looks huge and ready — and good enough to eat. But for once he seems unsure.

I feel a rush of tenderness at the thought that at a moment like this he can hesitate. What is it he wants? Is he scared to ask? Scared of hurting me? Or of going too far?

With a flash of inspiration I slip onto the leather-clad seat under the window and lie back along it with my legs splayed, my breasts thrust upward and my head hanging off the end. "Try now."

Do subs take charge like this? If not, I'm in big trouble. But taking charge gives me the confidence to smile up at him, touched at his look of surprise. He crouches down by my shoulders, his grateful gleam telling me he understands.

I shiver as he strokes the side of my face, his touch loving and gentle, then kneels up to prod my lips with the head of his swollen erection, now glossy with my saliva. Instantly I open wide to draw him in. With a sigh he slides deep into my throat.

This angle is a revelation. He slides right in to his full length. For once I've no need to fight the reflex or pause to swallow. It's glorious.

He thrusts again and again. I accept him eagerly, letting him possess me, fill me, glide through my mouth with the lithe ease of the conqueror.

It seems to be just what he wants — and right now, it's everything I need.

At last he pauses, quivers, then comes with a shout of triumph, his hands clasping my head. Slowly, almost reluctantly, he withdraws. He hauls me down onto the floor and takes me in his arms, burying his face in my hair, murmuring my name over and over.

Sated with pleasure, I close my eyes, leaning back in the rare luxury of his embrace. When I open them again, he's smiling, his dark eyes as deep and blue as the sea.

"Today I'd planned a day of surprises for you. So far, they're all on me."

At the end of our session he carefully lifts away all my cruel finery, the silver body harness, the naughty nipple flowers and finally the wicked ivy leaf, suspended by the glittering diamond chain that loops from my hips.

It fits so neatly over my most private place that it looks modest and beautiful, while its hidden secret, the deep ridge at its underside, makes it anything but. I'm still aglow from the orgasm it gave me.

I feel vaguely disappointed when he frees me from my elegant silver restraints. Without the teasing pressure on my nipples and the tight, provocative pinch of the silver at my waist and between my legs, life seems tame and flat.

But as we get dressed, I feel light and happy. He seems different too. He catches my eye like he's seeing me for the first time.

It reminds me fleetingly of Jake, unable to tear his eyes away from Sonja, the now-not-so-chilly ice maiden. "How's Sonja?"

"We only talk about work." Cade shrugs. "Like when she called me from the hotel this morning. How should I know how she is?"

"Maybe you should ask." I glare at him, exasperated. "You treat all your staff like this? No wonder she ran off. And it's her week off, by the way."

"So? She's still on the payroll." He's pulling up his trousers. Now he pauses midway. They hang temptingly at his hips as his eyes narrow. "That hoax raid's all my fault now, is it?"

I press my lips together. "She's a human being, Cade. You could ask her how she feels occasionally, that's all. If you scared her less, maybe she'd have asked you for some time off."

With impatient fingers he swiftly fastens his trousers and reaches for his shirt. "And since when did you become such an expert on handling staff? The fact that your team is completely out of your control hasn't quite sunk in yet? Even I can guess their plans before you do."

With an angry jab at the button he summons the elevator to take us down to the ground floor of the tower. As the doors close, he turns to me with a look of steel. "I'm not finished with your friends yet. I still think they're up to something. Maybe you should ask them how it feels to kick a gift horse in the teeth."

On the ground floor he strides away the second the doors slide open. "Mason's driving you back. I'll walk."

* * * *

Back in my room I head for the shower. Outside in the park, the sun's already going down. As the sky darkens to soft mauves and purples, the fairy lights strung in the trees around the stage start to sparkle. Soon it'll be time for the auction and I promised Mel I'll be there to watch.

As I put the finishing touches to my makeup and pile up my hair, my phone rings. "Dad? How are things?"

For the next ten minutes I listen intently then put the phone down with a sigh of relief. For once he sounds pleased. The new medication's doing wonders. For a few seconds I'm almost weepy.

"How is she? Your stepmother?" Cade's leaning in the doorway, stunning in black tux and tie. Once again I've no idea how long he's been there.

"Much better, thanks. Dad was just saying how grateful they are to you for the private nurse. She's made a big difference—"

Cade's done so much. I break off and turn away, suddenly overcome.

"What's the matter?" Instantly he's at my side.

"I'm okay. I still feel a bit...weird."

He frowns, his jaw tense. "I've asked a lot of you this week. It takes time to adjust to this. Are you sure you want to come down tonight? I only came in to ask what you're wearing."

"I'm fine. Really. Wait. *Wearing*?"

What an odd question. I'm instantly on my guard. "Why? What do you suggest?"

"Our Slave Auction's going to be Nera's grand finale. It's a formal occasion. Your dress sense is immaculate, so I leave it to you, but something simple, stunning..." He scans the rail absently and picks out a bright satin gown in rich kingfisher blue. "This?"

I hold it up in the mirror. The deep jewel color turns my skin to honey, my hair to gold. *How does he know so much about clothes?* "Sure. But if I don't get a dance partner, I'll blame you."

He grins. My heart turns over. How boyish he looks — a long way from the stern man of business or the capricious, time-fixated Dom.

He takes me in his arms, his expression solemn. "You've worked hard this week. The first stage of our arrangement ends tonight, and there's a surprise still to come. But whatever happens, I want you to have this. You've earned it."

He produces a small velvet-covered box and flips open the lid.

"*Cade...* It's beautiful." Inside I see the flash and sparkle of diamonds on a small silver key. It nestles in the coil of a fine, diamond-studded chain.

He lifts it out and fastens it around my neck, his fingers warm on my skin. His lips touch my face in a soft, lingering kiss. "I guess you know what it opens." His soft murmur is oddly husky.

I glance up in surprise.

"You've had the key to my heart since the moment you fainted in the rain on national television. Call it a memento." He kisses me gently on the forehead, his lips lingering. "And a heartfelt thank you for a wonderful week. Enjoy your evening."

I look up at him in dismay. "You're not coming down?"

"I'll be around. But I've got calls to make and people to see. Enjoy yourself."

And all at once, he's gone.

I dress quickly, trying to swallow my disappointment.

When I try it, the gown he picked out so casually looks stunning.

The diamond-studded key glitters in the valley of my breasts. Tonight I look like a princess.

Sadly, my prince forever eludes me...

* * * *

"Tunis? Where've you been? You missed all the fun." Mel greets me with a squeal of pleasure as I make my way through the crowd to the seats near the stage. The final act has just finished to rapturous applause, a group of female subs whirling around a single fearsome Domme. They might be dancing around a maypole except they move only at the flick of a whip. They end up on their knees in a rosy ring, foreheads pressed to the floor facing her, their pink, punished bottoms high in the air.

Ben looks at me anxiously. He's still in harness, smiling idiotically and flushed with endorphins. "You look pale, Tunis. You okay? Not really your thing?"

Mel instantly looks contrite. "Poor Tunis. But did you see us?"

Their excitement's infectious. I nod. "I saw you both on the screen. It was…really moving. Congratulations." I feel a sudden wave of emotion.

I've got my own endorphins to deal with, plus I always cave in after a performance. Now the afternoon's catching up with me big-time.

"Hey, that's really sweet of you. Don't cry, Tunis. We loved doing it, truly. Ben, have you got a tissue?"

I perch gingerly on the edge of a seat as Mel puts her arm around my shoulders. She looks anxiously at Ben but he's staring wide-eyed over her shoulder as a shadow falls between us.

"What's the matter with her?" Cade's voice breaks into the sudden silence.

Mel's eyes narrow. "Tunis is a bit shaky. That's all."

"She is? Why?" He sounds harsh.

Mel glares at him, tightening her grip. "You should know."

Alarmed, I sit upright.

Mel's eyes are blazing. "She's edgy about all this. It upsets her. *Remember*?"

I breathe again. "Mel, I'm fine, truly."

Cade is standing behind me, his face creased into a worried frown.

Mel gives him a fierce look. "You heard her. She's fine. And she'll feel a whole lot finer if you're not crowding her." Mel's getting into her stride now.

Desperate to break this up I rise quickly and turn to face him. People are beginning to stare.

He ignores them, his eyes fixed on my face. "You're okay? Are you sure?"

I whisk away another tear. "I'm always weepy after... I'm fine, truly."

He turns away. "Keep an eye on her, you two. We can't have guests taken ill during the finale."

He strides casually away, the image of a polite, concerned host. Mel glares after him as the onlookers drift away in search of cocktails.

I stay close to Mel and Ben during the buffet supper and learn that a host of new celebrities have turned up during the afternoon. Now there's a real buzz in the air.

Some of the *Hit'n'MissTrix* stars have evidently given enthusiastic whipping displays. Many faces are flushed and excited as the afterglow sets in.

"Look, that's Izzy Bash, the pop promoter. He flew in from L.A. this afternoon and came straight here. Cool or what?" Mel digs me in the ribs as a gangly, wrinkled figure appears at the edge of the crowd and gives a wave as a cheer goes up.

Izaak Bashnikov, the self-styled Bad Old Man of Rock for over forty years, is causing quite a stir. A startling figure in white leathers and flashy scarlet boots, his dyed scarlet hair sculpted into a blow-wave, he flashes his trademark lopsided grin over the crowd.

He's surrounded by some of the Bash Babes, part of his original stage act, dancers who double as session singers and bodyguards and accompany him at all times. As I watch, he greets Cade with a slap on the back. He takes him aside to talk for a few minutes before the crowd, herded into line by the Babes, push forward for autographs.

"And Garth Delaney's back, too. Isn't it terrific? They've come for the grand finale. It's starting in a few minutes. Come on, Tunis. Even you mustn't miss this. I only wish Jake was here to cover the Slave Auction."

As I follow Mel back toward the stage, I feel a hand on my arm as the crowd surges around me.

"Are you really okay?" Cade holds my arm in a fierce grip, his eyes blazing. "When you left earlier, you said you were fine." His low growl draws curious looks.

I try to pull away but he holds me fast.

"I was, then. It came later." I glance round but no one's paying much attention as they push past, crowding to fill the seats closest to the stage, where Nera's introducing Garth Delaney as the on-stage co-host.

Cade glares down at me. "You should have warned me. You've taken a lot this afternoon. I'd never forgive myself if—"

At that moment his name comes over the loudspeakers. Nera's just announced him as the chief sponsor and all at once we're flooded in dazzling light as spotlights sweep the crowd and pick him out.

It shines on me as well.

"Catch up with you later." He abruptly lets go of my arm and steps in front of me, shielding me from the glare as he smiles round to acknowledge the applause.

I slip back into the shadows and make my way quickly to where Mel and Ben are sitting.

"You will stay for the auction, Tunis? All the trainees are up for sale for slots of an hour. The money's going to the Wannabe Fund." Mel's sparkling eyes hint she's still flushed with her success in the Beat Fair.

"*Wannabe*?" At my puzzled expression, Ben leans over. "Izzy's charity. Gets young hopefuls into the music business. That'll be why he's here. It's his pet project."

The Bad Old Man of Rock is up on stage now, beaming his trademark wrinkly grin as Nera starts the bidding and the Babes look on.

The bidding's brisk. A blushing extra is offered as the first lot. Her dainty French maid's costume proclaims her a sub. As she parades around the stage showing off her pert little rear and her plunging neckline, the bidding becomes frenzied, not all of it from men.

"Two hundred? Who'll give me two hundred pounds for an hour with this cheeky little sub? Come, ladies and gentlemen, think of all the naughty things you can do with Lina in a whole hour."

Nera's in her element. She taps Lina briskly on the rump, making her trot and giggle. Soon a pink, excitable businessman near the back of the crowd carries the bidding at six hundred. He beams as Lina trots over to him and bobs him a curtsey.

Mel winks at me as the next lot clambers up onto the stage, a pale, bearded technician. He's tightly trussed into a bondage harness and a loincloth. He flinches as Nera taps her riding crop absently against one boot.

At my side, Ben stiffens.

He catches my eye, his expression pained, and hisses in my ear. "He trained with me. There's nothing he can take that I can't. It's so unfair."

The auction's clearly going well but I lean back and try to shut out the sickening excitement building all around me. I want no part in this. It's unnerving to see how eagerly the trainees parade themselves, hoping to get an offer from the highest bidder. I know it's all in fun and for charity, but still…

I look anywhere but at the stage and think instead of my emotional afternoon. Maybe after all I'm not so very different…

"It's me! It's me!" At my side, Mel leaps to her feet as her name is called. She pushes eagerly up to the stage.

Startled out of my reverie, I give Ben a reassuring smile and lean forward to watch.

Nera welcomes Mel up on to the stage with a rare smile. "And this is Mel, famous from TV and the media. She'll give you a spanking good time, guaranteed — as I'm sure you all saw during her spectacular display this afternoon. What am I bid for an hour with the lovely Mel?"

"One hundred pounds." Ben's arm shoots up, and Mel blows him a kiss.

But bids pop up from all over the crowd. She's clearly an even bigger hit than we thought.

"Seven hundred."

"Seven fifty."

"Eight hundred."

By now Ben's slumped back in his chair with a sullen frown. I reach over and pat his hand. "Bad luck, Ben. Don't let it get to you. It's only for an hour. And hey, you get it for free, right?"

"Five thousand, for a whole night."

The marquee suddenly goes very quiet. Mel's jaw drops as Garth Delaney strolls confidently up to the stage. Nera glances round at the crowd, now stunned to silence, waits a moment and bangs her gavel. "Sold, for one whole night, to the star of our movie."

To wild applause, Mel, eyes shining, slowly walks down the steps and takes the hand of her heartthrob. She's led away blushing and triumphant while I try to console Ben.

I fail spectacularly. With a bitter smile, he jolts to his feet and blunders away through the crowd, leaving me sitting on my own.

I get up and follow slowly, sad for him, glad for Mel. She's always had a thing for Garth Delaney. She'll dine out on this for years. Ben will come round eventually.

But my evening's not quite over. As I reach the edge of the crowd Nera's voice rings out behind me. "And our final star lot this evening, ladies and gentlemen, is a delightful former dancer, now a rising star in the world of TV and the arts. What am I bid for one whole week with the lovely Tunis?"

Chapter Twenty

I turn slowly, blank with shock as the onlookers cheer and clap.

There's a surprise still to come. Is this it?

I'll panic later. Right now, I'm faced with an audience. Instantly I beam round at the crowd like I knew about this all along and I walk confidently up on stage.

Nera gives me a chilly smile but her eyes look wary, like she's unsure how I'll react, telling me instantly that this must be someone else's idea.

Cade. It has to be.

She leans away from the mic to whisper a greeting. "Hope this is okay, Tunis. You looked scared there for a second."

The whispered words, like her tight, crimson smile, are meant to be friendly but I sense something held back. There can be only one reason. *She's jealous.*

I give her a brief, non-committal smile as if I'm up for auction every day of the week and at that moment, I see Cade at the fringes of the crowd talking to some Japanese businessmen.

He glances up with a smile and a half-wave and instantly I relax.

He's here. He's in control.

Everything will be fine.

While I compose myself, Nera's been pitching my charms to the crowd. Now she pauses for bids. "So, what am I bid for a whole week with the lovely Tunis? That's one hundred and sixty-eight hours, ladies and gentlemen. Who'll start us off at the bargain price of ten thousand pounds?"

How much?

The bidding starts well, the first for eleven thousand shouted out by one of the movie producers. My head spins as more bids fly, even one from Cade's group. He stays noticeably silent.

But soon the bids thin out as the sums rise to crazy levels. The crowd grows quiet.

"Any advance on thirty thousand for this lovely celebrity presenter? Going, going –"

"Thirty-one." The crowd gasps as Cade coolly steps forward. The businessmen with him exchange worried looks as the bidder in their midst weighs his options, fearful of offending his host.

They're now in close discussion and one of them raises his hand. "Thirty-two."

I shiver.

Maybe this is a group bid. Are the men planning a *share*? All at once this is no party game. I face a week with a group of strange men, doing goodness knows what...

How could he? If this is Cade's idea of a joke...

At this point Nera holds up her hand for silence. One of her assistants is walking quickly across the stage toward her, waving his phone. He whispers something in her ear.

I freeze as a murmur runs through the crowd.

Now what?

"Ladies and gentlemen, at this point I have to tell you that a new bidder has joined us and is bidding by phone. I have a bid of thirty-three thousand pounds from none other than our guest celebrity Dom, the Panther."

What? I stand very still.

The audience is equally stunned. After a few seconds, a buzz of excitement ripples through the crowd and the onlookers break into loud applause.

This is my worst nightmare.

Minutes ago I'd no idea I was even on sale. I was heading for bed.

Cade's steady gaze keeps me calm. I let out a deep breath as he steps forward.

"Thirty-four." His bid silences the crowd as they sense a real contest.

I can hear my heart thumping against my ribs in the agonizing wait as I scan Nera's face, creased into a frown as she listens once more to her assistant.

It seems an eternity before she looks up. "The Panther bids thirty-five thousand."

"Thirty-six." Cade bids again, his tone casual, his voice low in the tense silence all around us.

But Nera's frowning at her assistant. This time she makes him repeat what he said.

My mouth goes dry.

"The Panther bids fifty thousand pounds."

There is a gasp from the crowd as Cade smiles lazily at me.

I'm safe.

But I rejoice too soon. His smile slides over to Nera and he gives a slight shake of his head.

He's pulling out? He's handing me to the Panther on a plate.

I feel the universe spin.

I've known him a week. I feel like I've loved him a lifetime.

In just seven days we've scorched through all the emotions from lust to fear, ecstasy to despair. Now he's turning away…?

There's an agonizing silence as Nera scans the crowd for any further advance but the sullen looks from the handful of stunned competitors warn us they're far outrun.

I feel like I'm turned to stone. So this is his surprise — and his revenge.

I agree to be his, and he sells me on to the highest bidder, a complete stranger. And not just to any stranger but to the Panther, no less.

All week he's made my dream come true. Now he's turned it into my worst nightmare.

How did I not see this coming?

I know the answer in a flash. He kept me deliberately out of the loop, split off from my team. It was all part of his trap.

And like a fool, I walked right in…

I close my eyes briefly. When I open them again, the universe is still the same. The faces in the crowd are jubilant. They've just seen an execution, the mighty Cade Fitzlean taking his revenge on the silly little TV presenter who dared to challenge the march of his empire.

"Are there any more bids?" Even Nera looks dazed. I get a twinge of satisfaction to think that she's surprised too.

The seconds tick by while I scan the crowd for any sign that Cade's changed his mind. Maybe he'll step in at the last minute…

But as Nera triumphantly bangs her gavel, there's no sign of him.

My fate is sealed.

I lean close to her to whisper. "I'll be…tied up this coming week." I try not to think how true this is. "I can make another date for the Panther, right?"

Maybe I'll skip the country before then.

"Too bad." Her eyes glitter as she hisses rapidly into my ear. "Our sponsors come first. Your contract's very specific on that point. And these sessions are also covered by the legally binding confidentiality agreements. So the prizes take place right away. Technically you're with the Panther from midnight tonight."

I swallow. "But I'm already booked for next week. Cade said —"

Her eyes glint with triumph. "He's fine with it. His idea, actually."

Stunned, I turn and leave the stage, my smile fixed firmly in place.

I'm still on show. I have to make the best of this, nightmare or not. I'm a professional, and I'm here on a job.

The auction is followed by a massive firework display. It's starting already. Rockets explode into the sky as I make my way through the crowd, thinning now as people hurry past, spilling out onto the lawns to get a better view.

Their faces light up in the glitter from the sky overhead but for me, the party's over.

Nera's final announcements are ringing in my ears. "And our finale tonight raised the staggering sum of one and a half million pounds for the Beat Hall Wannabe Fund for Young Musicians. And here to collect it is none other than the Bad Old Man of Rock himself, the infamous Izzy Bash..."

I have a sudden, desperate need to be alone. It's been a weird day full of shocks, its climax the worst of all. I walk quickly, dreading an encounter with Ben or Mel. Tears are close. It'll be too embarrassing.

As I finally make it to my room, I hear music, a stirring Bach Chorale. The door between our rooms is open, and the melody is coming from Cade's sitting room — soothing, measured. After my emotional day, it feels likes like warm, flowing water.

To my horror the tears, held back for so long, threaten to squeeze out. I sit on the bed for a moment and will them away as a familiar, elegant figure leans in the doorway.

He looks debonair as ever, seemingly unaware that my universe has just fallen apart. "Enjoy your evening?"

I pull myself together and rise quickly to my feet. "No. Is *this* your idea of a surprise?"

"One of them. What's the matter? Not to your taste?"

I look away. "I thought we had an agreement." My voice sounds hoarse.

He walks toward me, his expression unreadable. "We do. You agreed to be mine for a week. I made no promises about how you'd spend it. As my sub, you agree to accept what I choose to give. If I choose to hand you over to another Dom, that's entirely my right. If it's in a good cause, that's even better. You accepted my terms willingly enough, I seem to remember."

So I did. Silly me. "But I thought I'd be spending the second week with you. I'd no idea I needed a team of lawyers to check the small print. I assumed you meant—"

It occurs to me in a flash of bitter clarity that I'm making an awful lot of assumptions here. One is that I'm worth anything like fifty grand to anybody. Another is that Cade Fitzlean, of all people, would want to waste another week on me, after giving up a whole week of his busy life already.

Why should he? I'm new at this, not one of his trained-to-be-perfect, delectable subs.

I've no right to feel angry. I should be grateful.

He's done everything I asked and more. He's been the perfect gentleman.

I'm just a selfish, conceited bitch.

But now my intensive training takes on a whole new, utterly sinister meaning.

He was preparing me for somebody else. And like a fool I thought he was doing it because something had sparked between us.

I've been so stupid.

He's smiling now. "Please, let's not spoil your last two hours of training with a fight over detail. We've still got one final session in the dungeon. I intend to make it…interesting." He catches my hand and kisses my fingers then deliberately turns over my hand to kiss my palm, his tongue hot, his mouth urgent.

I shiver as the familiar shimmer shoots up my arm and tingles all over me, raising all my tiny hairs. The idea's alarming. I've been caned once today. I'm still shaky. How much more can I take?

And from midnight tonight, I'm in entirely new hands. I have to face a whole week with the Panther. My worst ever nightmare. I swallow. "What are we going to do there?"

"You'll see."

"Cade, why did you put me on sale? Were you really so keen to punish me? Or do you just want to get rid of me?"

His face splits into a delighted grin. He's clearly enjoying this.

"You mean you haven't *guessed*? Then that's another surprise. All will be revealed in due course. Now we must get you out of this delectable gown and into the shower. The dungeon beckons, and I'm getting twitchy."

* * * *

The shower takes a while. As he unfastens my gown, his hands run lovingly over my breasts, my curves, my thighs, dropping kisses where he touches until I glow all over.

It's like he's committing every part of me to memory.

I'd better do the same. This may be the last time. I decide to forget about tomorrow and lose myself in the moment.

In the shower he holds my hands high over my head and massages me first with the gel then with the warm jet, until I laugh and squeal in protest. As he towels me dry with my hands still held high, he forbids me to lower them.

"No touching. I want to do that. Keep your hands away." To make sure, he lowers my hands, slips handcuffs behind my back and clicks them onto my wrists.

I shudder as the cold, hard metal presses into my skin. I stare at him in alarm. "What are you doing?"

He kisses me gently on the tip of my nose. "Cuffing you until we get down to the basement. Feel good?"

It's an odd question but I consider it carefully. I know now that the answer's never simple. Once more I feel vulnerable, subject to his will, and yet oddly, now he has me in his control, *safe*. And already I'm starting to guess what he has in mind. Even as I think it I'm growing excited, aroused — and *curious*.

What's happening to me? How does he make me want this so badly?

"Okay, it feels good. But I'm scared."

He looks genuinely interested. "Of me?" His voice drops to a velvety murmur, sending a throb straight down to my groin.

"Of what you'll do."

"Sure you're scared." Slowly, deliberately, he runs a thumb over my left nipple then tweaks it gently. "Like I said, that makes it fun. Do you trust me, Tunis?"

"Yes." *In spite of everything.*

A slow smile spreads over his stunning features and tears at my heart. Will I ever tire of being a plaything to this beautiful man?

He tweaks my other nipple, watching my reaction intently. With a supreme effort, I suppress a wince and smile up at him instead.

He kisses me again. "Good girl," he says softly. "You're getting the idea."

In spite of the fabulous firework display, many guests are still partying. Against a background roar of bangs, fizzes and explosions, music and laughter echoes all through Beat Hall as he leads me down to the dungeon. But as the padded wooden door closes behind us, we're engulfed in silence, the soundproofed room shutting us in with our own sinister noises — the creak of leather, the rattle of chains, the soft intake of breath and the wild, regular pounding of my heartbeat.

Without being told, I kneel on the central dais, my cuffed hands resting at the small of my back and wait.

This is the last time he'll bring me here. The thought brings a surge of emotion so strong that I feel the room spin.

Instantly he raises my face up to his. "What's the matter?"

"Where will you be this time tomorrow?" My quiet question surprises him, but his answer comes at once.

"On a small island in the Western Isles watching seals in the moonlight."

"And me? Where will I be?" My question sounds bitter. It was half to myself but he answers that too.

"That will depend on where you're taken. Ready?"

He's impatient to begin.

I bow my head to signal a yes. I'm impatient too.

I'm only sad it all has to end.

For a few long moments he moves around at the far end of the room, out of my line of sight. Increasingly nervous, my stomach tight with excitement, I try to work out what he's doing. The sounds of a drawer opening and closing and the clatter of metal objects raise my excitement to fever heat but give me no clues.

At last he walks back toward me and stands before me with his legs apart. "You can look up now." As I do so, he unzips his fly and frees his erection, already frighteningly large.

"Take it in your mouth. Just as a courtesy, not to completion."

I do so, soothed by the ritual, relishing the familiar taste and girth of his arousal, pleased when I hear him draw in a sharp breath.

"Enough." He cups my cheek in his hand, loving and tender then fastens his fly and raises me to my feet. "I'll undo the cuffs, but you must keep your hands behind your back. Tonight you're going to be fixed on the saltire for a whipping. And no blindfold—I want you to watch this."

The saltire? What's that?

Then I remember. It's the strange contraption on the far wall in the shape of a lazy cross, each arm fixed with various gleaming leather cuffs and buckles.

"It rotates, so we can have some fun with the angles. But we have to go easy. You've taken a lot this week. I don't want to hurt you."

"You've got a funny way of showing it."

He glances at me with a frown. "What's the matter? Too much for you?"

I hold his gaze, bewildered at his sudden change of tone. I'm still tingling all over from our caning display and the sight of this place is working its magic already. I'm *wet*, tense with excitement, but something needs to be said. I'm too wound up to keep the bitterness out of my voice. "You just want to scare me, beat the crap out of me. That's what this is all about. Be honest."

He eyes me for a moment in silence. When he finally speaks, his voice is low, measured, like he's talking to a child. "A week ago you asked me to take you on a journey. I'm trying to show you where it leads. Sure, it gives me pleasure. I enjoy this, very much, especially with you. But I want you to enjoy it too."

He sounds so reasonable. And the plea in his eyes is unmistakable. It touches something deep inside me. But still…

I look up at him, troubled. "I feel guilty. Doing this makes me feel so—primitive."

His expression softens. He runs a finger down my cheek and folds his hand along the side of my neck. As I lean into his touch, he rubs my earlobe gently with his thumb. "Don't bring too much baggage to this. It's really very simple. Dominance raises male hormones, submission raises female. Together they take sex to a new level. What happens next isn't wrong if you both consent and if you both enjoy it. It's just sex—only deeper, more primal. Maybe unexpected. That's all I wanted to show you."

He leans forward and touches his lips to mine, his kiss soft, lingering, infinitely tender. "Do you still trust me?"

I nod.

He kisses me again. "Good. So—shall we make a start?"

The saltire opens up a whole new world. He fastens me so I lie face up. He takes his time to check my wrists and ankles are secure and supported, pausing to touch and caress my rigid, quivering limbs.

"You're very tense. Loosen up. You'll enjoy it more. I'm going to rotate it slowly. Safeword if anything feels too extreme. No gags or blindfolds for this. I want you fully aware."

Slowly the dungeon starts to rotate. I begin to feel weightless, detached, my splayed legs and up-thrust breasts moving gently through the air like I'm floating. I feel almost drowsy as his voice hangs in the air around me, now close, now farther away.

"The whip I'm using is called a quirt. It's used to encourage teams of horses. We don't use it much. It's too unpredictable."

As I rotate slowly past him, I see he's running two long strands of leather through his fingers. As I come round again, they're still moving, slightly thinner this time.

"It's very long, and has two thin strands, designed to make a loud noise over their heads. So if one happens to land on you, you'll get the occasional surprise. It makes a very satisfying crack, like this—"

I jump in my bonds as a deafening thunderclap sounds close to my ear. I feel the air whistle as one of the lashes flicks past my arm.

It sounds terrifying. *What would it feel like?*

He moves to a point some feet away and lets fly. As I move slowly, the lashes crack and snap around me, terrifyingly close. I feel the ends of the leather flicker across my skin on my thighs, my breasts, over my belly. Once one of the lashes spirals around my lower leg, gripping with a vivid, scorching sting then slithering softly away like a snake.

Deep between my legs, heat begins to glow then burn, the flames leaping higher and higher as the thin ends of the whip whistle past or make vivid, stinging contact.

At last he gives a final flick and a leather snake coils round my thigh and slithers horribly close to my wide, gaping slit.

It's too much. "*Mercy.*"

The sudden silence falls around me like a blanket. As the saltire slows to a halt, he's instantly at my side, unfastening the cuffs, gathering my sweating, twitching body up into his arms. "That was sensational, Tunis. Hush, don't cry."

Weak, aroused, overwrought, I feel the tears flow as soon as his arms curl around me.

I sob against his chest as he carries me to the elevator. I have a confused feeling of movement, of lights changing, of elevator doors opening and closing then the soft, familiar sound and smell of our rooms, music and laughter still echoing through the great house from the dance floor and the moonlit grounds.

Without letting go, he pulls me down into the bed, still entwined as I fold my legs around his waist, burying my face in his neck,

I hear the rip of foil and suddenly, gloriously, I feel him surge inside, thrusting again and again, murmuring into my hair until he quivers and stills. And with miraculous timing, the ripple of muscle through his abdomen rasps against my splayed dip and I erupt in my own surge of pleasure.

My orgasm is so intense and so long awaited that I think I'm going to faint. Instead I'm held fast in his arms as I drift on a sea of content, with his soft murmurs still in my ear and his face buried in my hair.

Chapter Twenty-One

It's morning. I feel wonderful. I blink through a dazzling ray of sunshine at the sumptuous decadence of the cherubs painted on the ceiling and glance across the bed. I half expect to see Cade stretched out next to me, tousled and beautiful, a work of art all on his own.

He's not here.

I can hear voices from his room. I stretch and yawn and tumble out of bed. Winding a bath towel around myself, I catch it over one breast, open his door a crack and take a cautious peek.

The maids are stripping down his bed and cleaning the shower. The cupboards are empty, hangers clinking on the rail. One of the women is cleaning them with a can of spray and a cloth. I step back quickly and shut the door, leaning against it for a moment as reality floods back.

He's gone.

Tonight he'll be watching seals then he'll fly home.

I'm yesterday's news.

And this morning I've got a date with the Panther.

After some coffee and a quick shower, I snatch my clothes off the rail and pack quickly. When my things are neatly stowed, I consider the Beat Hall costumes. Will I have to dress up this week?

Probably. I'm now a sex-slave, albeit a costly one.

I decide to play it safe and seize a couple of gowns and lace-trimmed corsets, rummage for toning accessories and hope for the best.

Then I pause. Better do this properly.

I make a further selection from the rail. I strip off and wriggle into some sexy underwear and slip back into my own things.

If Nera wants the costumes back, I'll ditch them in the hall. Anyway, maybe clothes won't be needed…

As I leave, I glance round at the vast suite, with its elegant furniture and tall, gilded mirrors. I've been here only a week. Already it feels like home.

With a lump in my throat I think of all that's happened in here — the battles and the victories, the rapture and the despair. It's been some journey.

I take a last look round, grab my purse and head for the elevator.

* * * *

Down in the entrance hall Nera is whip-smart in tight latex and thigh boots as she supervises departing guests and welcomes new arrivals. A rock festival is planned for next month and technicians and producers are already arriving to assess the site.

She hails me with a tight-lipped smile. "Ah, there you are, Tunis. The Panther's flying out this morning. You're to meet on the plane. Izzy's waiting for you. He'll drive you to the airfield."

I glance across to see the Bad Man of Rock flanked by two of the Bash Babes. He gives me a half-wave, and I look away quickly.

Nera leans close. "I take it you've had breakfast?"

Food's the last thing on my mind. I just want this over with. "Thanks, Nera. I had coffee in my room. Terrific news about the Wannabe Fund. I'm glad you made so much money." She looks pleased, so I take a deep breath. "Can I ask you a favor?"

Her glance flickers to her watch but her smile stays in place. "Ask away."

"Can I borrow a couple of costumes for the week from my room? I'm not sure what I'll need...." I tail off, feeling awkward.

"I'll have them packed up for you." She lowers her eyelids. "And they look terrific on, by the way. You've made quite an impression. I'm sure he'll have the time of his life. So, enjoy your week."

She turns away to greet a group of technicians, and I feel a touch on my arm. It's Mel, dazzling in tight latex and high heels. She's also awaiting her purchaser but with a lot more enthusiasm than I am. Her blazing hair's been streaked gold and bronze in the salon and springs round her shoulders in a tawny halo, making her pale eyes sparkle.

"Gosh, Tunis, a week with *the Panther*, of all people — who'd have thought? If only you'd done some training, you silly girl. Anyway, if you get back alive, you must do a special on him. Mind you, get some quotes." She gives me a wink. "And wish me luck. Garth's driver's just fetching the car."

I grin and kiss her on the cheek. "Have a terrific time, Mel. And don't worry about Ben. He'll come round, especially if you get an exclusive on the back of it."

I sound braver than I feel.

Mel looks at me in surprise then leans forward and lowers her voice to a hiss. "You sure you're okay? Izzy's tapping his watch but I just wanted to let you know we're on to something about Fitzlean. You know that business outside the club last year, that night you passed out on camera?"

I freeze. "*What*?"

"Jake's been in touch. Remember how Fitzlean said he was in charge all that night? Jake's found out there's some security footage that proves Fitzlean wasn't anywhere near the club that night. Even the Panther came late. He got there after we did. Jake's back tomorrow. We'll find out more then."

My blood runs cold. "Mel, please, *please* don't do anything just yet. We don't know the full story — "

"Ah, but that's just what we're going to find out. Don't you see? Fitzlean's story doesn't add up. Maybe somebody else was there that night. Maybe that's why things went wrong and he's covering up for them. And now he's gone we've got a good chance of finding out more. By the time you get back, we might even have enough to work it into the end of our report. It'll be terrific — a news scoop tacked onto the last few minutes of the official build-up to the premiere. It'll be a sensation."

"No, Mel... Look. Talk to me first, okay? Don't make any hard decisions till I get back. And for goodness' sake — "

"Hey, honey, what's with all the girl-talk? We gotta cat waitin' ta meet ya, y'know."

Izzy's standing over us, grinning.

Mel beams up at him, overawed by this wrinkly remnant of rock royalty. "Wow — Izzy Bash in person. I can hardly believe it. This is a real honor."

"Mel, please listen to me." I step between them. "I mean it. Do be discreet. You've no idea who you're dealing with —"

Mel snorts. "Oh don't I? He's been lurking in the shadows all week, barking orders, pulling strings. I know a power-mad psycho when I see one and that asshole badly needs a lesson. Bye, now. You have a great time."

She blows me a kiss and sashays off through the crowd, leaving a trail of onlookers gawping after her.

I watch her go with a sinking heart. But now I've got problems of my own.

Izzy turns to me with a grin. "Mornin', ma'am. Izaak Bashnikov at your service. I'm here to escort you to your chariot."

Wrinkly Bad Men of Rock aren't really my thing, but I manage a chilly smile. I'm instantly taken aback by his shrewd, penetrating look.

"Hey, kid, you're kinda white. Ya nervous?" His blue eyes crinkle with real concern.

His kindness is so sudden and so unexpected I swallow. "It's just… I wasn't expecting to be auctioned at all. It's still a bit of a shock."

Just then fans of all ages, from seasoned film hands to junior kitchen staff, appear from nowhere and mob him for autographs. Eventually they're shooed away by two of the Babes.

It's another twenty minutes or so before we finally emerge into the sunshine and reach the car. Two more Babes are in front, one driving and the other riding shotgun.

As we settle into the long back seat, his hand accidentally touches mine and he clasps it briefly. "Hey, you're real cold, honey. Don't be scared." His lopsided grin vanishes and his wrinkled face twists into a mask of genuine worry. His faded blue eyes look intelligent and kind.

All at once I feel my eyes sting.

As the car pulls smoothly away, he reaches across and pats my shoulder. "Hey, honey, take it easy. Wassup?"

"It's just... I've got a bit of a thing about the Panther. Not in a good way," I add quickly, as his grin threatens to break out again.

To his credit, he stays solemn. "Honey, you'll be fine. The hoods an' whips an' stuff? S'all showbiz. Underneath he's a real nice guy."

"You know him, then?"

"Sure I know him. Known him since he was a kid. I know everybody. I bin around long enough. An' believe you me, he's one of the best. You'll see. Hey, we're here."

The car draws to a halt and I peer out at the private jet looming over us. It bears the Panther's logo, etched in black silhouette on the tail fin and along the side — a rampant black leopard under the curve of a long, elegantly penned whip.

Three crew members dressed in black are lined up to greet me at the foot of the steps.

"Las' chance, honey. You wanna go back?" He looks genuinely worried now.

I attempt a brave smile. "I'm fine. I'd better go through with this. He's paid an awful lot of money. And it's a good cause."

His smile flickers briefly but I hurry on, keen to get away. I want this over with. "Thanks, Izzy. You've been really kind. You know, for a Bad Man of Rock, you're surprisingly nice."

His face creases into his trademark grin. "Aw, shucks, honey, for a chick scared of cats ya gotta lotta guts." He leans toward me with a sly wink. "An' go easy on the *nice*. I gotta look bad for the fans, if you get my meanin'."

The car pulls silently away while I shake hands with the crew and at last I start the long climb up the short flight of steps. And as I climb, a strange thing happens, considering how nervous I've been up to now. I feel a spike of hot anger.

Indignation slowly burns away my fear as I'm gripped by one all-consuming thought. *This was all a trick.*

And if I ever get to see him again, Cade Fitzlean's got some tough explaining to do.

I step into the cabin. It's dim inside after the glare of the sunlit tarmac and full of quiet hush after the roar of the engines out in the open air.

For a few seconds I sense pale, padded luxury around me. Light streams in through the cabin windows and I glimpse the tower and the turrets of Beat Hall.

How far away the fairy tale seems now.

As my eyes adjust, I see a dark figure waiting in the shadows.

Little hairs rise all over my body as I make out first the glitter of his eyes, then the dark shape of the hood and the darker patches where the beard and the thick braids fall in coils over his shoulders and his chest.

He walks slowly toward me. In this confined space, he seems huge. I stand very still.

It's the figure from my dream, just as I remember him and just like I saw him that night over a year ago. And now I have a new, fleeting image of him—letting fly with the bullwhip on poor little Eileen only days before.

And the sheer, feline power and grace in the way he moved...

"I thought you'd never get here." His voice is deep and rich. It seeps through me like honey.

It's the voice from my dreams...

He reaches up with one hand to peel off his hood and it comes away with the beard and the braids still attached. *It's a costume.*

"Well? I'm waiting for you to throw up."

I stare up at him, my eyes full of joy and my heart full of rage. All at once I'm in his arms, pummeling his chest, while Cade crushes me to him, laughing, and covers my face with kisses.

* * * *

As the jet takes off, I lean across him for one last glimpse of Beat Hall, its towers and pinnacles rising over the trees, the colored pennants still fluttering in the sunshine. He keeps his arm firmly around my shoulders, unwilling to let me go.

Soon a smiling flight attendant brings us flutes of champagne on a silver tray.

"Lunch in twenty minutes, Mr. Fitzlean." She introduces herself as Lisa, gives me a friendly nod then retires to prepare our meal.

He turns to me and raises his glass. "*Salut.*"

I sip gratefully. As the tiny bubbles hit my tongue, I lean on his shoulder. "So would you mind telling me what all that was about? Letting me think I was being sold off to a complete stranger? Were you being deliberately cruel or was it your idea of a joke?"

He sits up with an expression of disbelief. "*Cruel*? I take you for an intelligent woman. Our arrangement's a secret. How else am I supposed to spirit you away for a whole week? If I'd bought you openly at the auction, we might as well have fucked all week by the pool and invited the world's press to watch."

He takes a swig of his drink, eyeing me over the rim. "I'm beginning to wish we had. It would have been a damn sight easier."

He looks away with a sigh, suddenly serious. "If you must know, I dreaded you finding out who I was. After the auction I waited till the last possible moment in case you freaked out. I was surprised you were so cool about it—enough to let Izzy bring you out here, anyway. He said you seemed scared to death but you behaved like a princess. I figured if you really freaked, I'd just about have enough time to throw you off the plane before we got airborne."

"And if I throw up now?" I ask, sweetly.

He grins. "I'll probably throw you off anyway. You've cost me enough."

I start to pummel again but he captures my wrists with one hand, laughing softy. "Anyway, our session with the quirt gave me hope."

This surprises me. "Why?"

He runs a finger down my throat, making me arch my neck, and lowers his voice to a soft purr. "Because it's as scary as the bullwhip. Stock whips are more for effect than contact. And you took it surprisingly well."

I glare at him. "Well, you can keep it for the bulls."

He kisses the tip of my nose. "They're a lot less fun. Anyway, after a whole week together, did you seriously think I was going to let another man get his hands on you?"

Lunch is served on a small table laid with formal white linen, crystal and silver. Lisa brings us a tasty smoked salmon starter, followed by chicken with prosciutto, green beans and a crisp white wine. Over coffee we toy with a bowl of cherries.

Cade watches me throughout, his gaze thoughtful and disturbing. "Did you enjoy the auction? I thought it was an interesting way to end the week."

I'd planned a protest but now I melt. He makes me face my fears — first heights, now this. I give in gracefully, a cherry part way to my lips. "Do all your surprises give people heart attacks?"

"Has to be worth it if we've fooled the world's media into thinking we're six thousand miles apart. For all they know I'm in LA and you're being ravaged by a wild beast in some underground cavern."

I sip some wine and dangle another cherry. "Izzy's nice. He's nothing like I expected. He produced your record, didn't he? He says he knows you really well."

"He does. After my mother went, he helped to bring us up. We owe him a lot." He eyes me over the rim of his glass and lowers his voice. "He was my mother's lover."

"The maniac?"

"What would you call him? He organized the first rock concert at Beat Hall. When my father took it on, the place it was a wreck. Izzy turned up, put together an entertainment program and together they turned the place round. That was how he and my mother met. By the time my father found out about them, Izzy was raking in so much money, Dad decided to play dumb."

"What was she like, your mother?"

He shrugs. "Beautiful, creative. Wild child."

"*Wild*?"

"She'd get everyone out of bed at two in the morning to look at the moon — that kind of wild."

I smile. "She sounds sweet."

His lip curls at the corner. "You try it three times a week. It soon palls. Not too popular with wealthy backers, either. To be fair, my father stood it as long as he could."

"Do you still see him?"

"When I'm in Europe. Maybe you've heard of him. Sir Gerald Fitzlean?"

His tone stays light but I sense tension. "*The diplomat?*"

This is news. I have heard of him — and of the wild parties with too many blondes.

"That's him. We'll see him later this week. He wants to meet you."

I stare. "*Me?*"

"Sure. I'm not the only man in the world who thinks you're beautiful." He pushes away his chair and takes my hand, drawing me close.

"But... How does he know about me?"

He kisses me gently on the cheek. "He's seen you on TV. Plus, I've told him about you. So has Izzy. And if you'll stop pestering me with questions, we're going to do something I've been wanting to do for a while."

He folds his arms round me and holds me close, his eyes dark and needy, and captures my mouth, his tongue and his lips soft at first then fierce, sending electricity sparking through me. I press against him, thrilling to the feel of him curving over me, the heat from his hips burning into my lower belly, a clear sign of his hunger and as urgent as mine.

But Mel's news is still burning into my brain. So I've got one more question.

"So you're the Panther? And that was you that night? You were there — professionally?"

His smile fades abruptly. "Is this the reporter's friend asking?"

My heart sinks. "I'm just curious. And over lunch it's called conversation, Cade," I add gently.

Why's he so edgy about this? It can only mean that Mel's on to something. But maybe now's not the time to ask. We've got a whole week. I'll try later.

"You call this *conversation*?" His eyebrow arches a fraction and all at once the blue of his eyes deepens to midnight. His hand lingers on the small of my back, his fingers playing a warm, soft rhythm of their own as his intention gleams on his eyes. "I'd call it something quite different. Darker. And definitely dirtier. Bring the cherries."

The plane has a bedroom, all pale, sleek and low-slung. It has flowers in bowls, soft lighting and all around us the hum of the engines make a soothing lullaby. He flicks a remote and I hear the strains of a Tchaikovsky love duet that always melts my soul.

He pulls me to him and kisses me with light, soft kisses while he runs his hands over me, tearing at my clothes and searching deep between my breasts. "Mm, you taste good. Better than lunch."

I smile against his kiss and run my hand lightly along his face, still tingling with relief and joy at the thought that we're together now for *a whole week*.

He throws himself down onto the bed and sprawls out with his hands behind his head. "Now the Panther wants to play. Strip."

Chapter Twenty-Two

"A corset *and* black stockings? The Panther's a lucky beast. Well, not quite as lucky as me, maybe, but close." Cade is reclining on the pillows, intent and watchful. The heat in his eyes fires my soul.

As the music swells over the deep bass undertone of the engines, I slowly strip for him, moving to the music, my hips swaying as the shocks of the past twelve hours melt away one by one. My moves are more for me than for him, the movement soothing me in the way that only dance can.

But the gleam in his eyes is catching. It fires a glow that burns deep and slow and heats with the music, flaring each time his eyes narrow or his breath quickens.

His expression darkens as I slowly unfasten the corset, taking my time with the tight lacing. I let it slide to the floor then peel off the stockings. As I fling away the second one, he rises to his feet and looms over me.

"Now lie on the bed, face up. I want to look at you."

He kneels next to me, his expression remote. "Spread your legs and put your arms up over your head."

I shiver. "Why? What are you going to do?"

He glances at me, his eyes opaque. "Do you ever stop asking questions? Why do you think? I want to examine you. For the whole of this week you're mine, twenty-four seven. That means there's a lot we could do, but we may have to go easy. We've been pretty intense so far. I don't want to overdo things."

He leans over and drops a kiss right on my navel, his lips moist and hot. His voice lowers to a deep, velvety purr. "But first I want some dessert."

For dessert he wants cherries and me. I lie very still while he deposits them in some surprising places then teases them out and eats them, occasionally leaning over me to place one in my mouth with his teeth and follow it with a deep, searching kiss. When they're all consumed, he follows with his lips in all the same places till I'm twitching with arousal then he swings me up onto his chest and lets me tease him back.

Now the examination resumes and it drives me wild.

He runs his hands over me—pressing, feeling, squeezing. He lingers on my breasts, checking carefully, squeezing my nipples until I cry out then squeezing again, raising them to hard points and checking my expression for signs of stress. "Tell me if anything hurts. I have to know."

"Is that why you wanted me this week? Just to whip?" The thought is chilling, but this is something *I* have to know.

He frowns. "I wanted you for this particular week because I'm over here to see my family. At this time of year I usually I fit in some visits. I thought it might be fun to take you along."

He wants me to meet *his family*? How exciting. But from the heat in his eyes, I can see that his mind's on other things—*me*.

I'll have wait to find out more.

I empty my mind and focus on his fingers, now moving south toward my clenched navel. I smile at his close, intimate inspection, thrilling to his touch as his strong, gentle hands caress me and search me. Apart from my wrists, still pink from the cuffs, I feel fine. "I love it when you do that. It's like electricity."

He pauses, a new glint in his eyes. "I can tell. When I touch you like this, your skin ripples. Now turn over. I'll check your back."

This time his touch is even more sensuous. As he examines the swell of my bottom and eases between my curves, I moan softly.

"You've a mark here. Does it hurt?" His voice is low but his tone is worried, almost fearful.

I moan again as wetness pools between my legs. In seconds he discovers this. Instantly I feel his breath on the back of my neck. "Is this *arousing*? Tell me."

I clench my teeth. "You *think*? Do I pass the inspection...Sir?"

He rolls me over onto my side and pulls my hips tight against his, nipping my earlobe with his teeth. "Yep, you pass. For the rest of the week, we'll have some fun. No dungeon, so we'll have to get creative. But your defiant response during inspection suggests to me that you're already in need of some discipline. Put your feet on the floor and your head on the bed."

Heat flares. I grin over my shoulder. "What, *here*? But...suppose the crew hears us?"

He reaches under the bed for a moment and leans up again with a smile. He dangles a scary-looking contraption in front of my face, all black leather and studs. I shrink back as a jutting, fearsome object halfway along jolts at me. "*What's that?*"

He pushes me off the edge of the bed and taps the back of my legs with his hand to get me into position, pushing my feet wide apart with his shoe. "It's a gag, with a dildo instead of a ball. Very effective in small spaces. Open wide."

He slides the obscene thing into my mouth and I feel the strap being fastened at the back of my head. After the loose ball I'm used to, it feels horrible. It fills my mouth, reaching almost to the back of my throat.

It's humiliating and to my shame, it's also *hot*. Now I'm securely trapped. And with my legs splayed wide and my bottom high in the air, I'm also very exposed.

"And for some extra spice, maybe we'll try some nipple clamps this time. These are light, perfect for a beginner. Try them for size."

He teases and pinches my nipples to raise them and snaps the clamps into place.

They sting and pinch as I breathe, my chest heaving with surprise and emotion then the feeling wears off as my swollen nipples slowly grow numb.

My head spins. Why this sudden need to *punish* me? Or *is* it punishment? I want this too...badly. Maybe punishment's the wrong word for it.

So what *can* I call it? I'm confused. All I know is I'm burning, and eager — and scared.

"Now push your head right down onto the bed. Hands behind your back."

He hardly waits for me to reach the position before the first slap lands. It takes me by surprise and it stings. I yelp against the gag, but the sound dies in my throat.

Noise is pointless. Curiously, the thought makes me relax.

I can hardly move. I can make no sound. I can only endure, sucking on the dildo like it's a pacifier.

It's deeply humiliating, wildly arousing. Strangely soothing.

The blows keep coming—just the flat of his hand, slap after slap. Soon I'm glowing and hot. The impact jolts through me, hauling at my clamped nipples, jerking repeatedly along my wet, swollen slit.

I'm used and invaded at one end, on fire at the other.

At last he pauses and curves over me, his fly rasping on my fiery bottom. "I'm going to fuck you until you're close then pull off the clamps. Ready?"

I nod. I'm already pulsing for him, craving his entry. I close my eyes as I hear the rip of foil then buck as he launches into me, his length filling me in a long, slick thrust that sends a loud, ecstatic cry into the unyielding leather tool filling my mouth, so frustratingly unlike his living, pulsing erection.

I feel his breath hot on my neck as he leans over me, his hands gripping my breasts. My nipples are numb now, the initial ache a mere echo though my jutting, swollen aureoles.

He growls against my neck like his panther namesake. "Grip me. Pull me in. Haul me deeper."

I tense my muscles, arch my feet and flex my thighs, straining to match the power of his thrusts. I fight to maintain position, pinned and bound with the awful gag and the clamps, held in place by his will.

He caresses my belly, his fingers sliding round to ease between my legs and deep into my dripping slit, pressing and circling in time with his thrusts.

It's everything I need. As my climax builds, I scream against the gag.

He hears me and slows, holding me at my peak for what seems like endless seconds then he jerks away the clamps with a single tug on the chain looping them together. A rush of feeling shoots back to my trapped nipples with an explosion of mingled pain and pleasure, mega pins and needles, fire and ice.

It fires my climax in a violent eruption that propels me forward onto the bed. He lands on top of me, pumping into me as I writhe beneath him, trapped, helpless and gorgeously filled.

* * * *

The Mile High club's a long way up—but afterward it's a long way down.

As we lie together, glowing and content, I recall Mel's sudden, startling announcement. *Should I tell him?*

Last time I kept her plans a secret, she and Ben were planning that awful raid and nearly got us all the sack. And that was just one night. Goodness knows what they'll get up to in a week. This time I'd better warn him.

"Mel thinks there's no footage of you from the club that night."

I'm lying across him as he strokes my hair. Now I feel him stiffen. To my dismay, the temperature seems to plummet several degrees.

Why did I have to open my mouth?

"She does?" His tone could cut glass.

I bite my lip and force myself on. I've learned my lesson. Last time was a fiasco. Maybe this time he can do something about it before they make trouble.

"She thinks there was somebody else in charge that night. That's all." I falter as I speak. It sounds so trivial, but I can tell he's irritated. The rigid muscles below me warn me he's angry.

Why?

He leans up on one elbow, his face serious. "There's not much we can do. We'll have to leave them to it.

Look, Tunis. This project's nearly complete. All I want from you now is assurance that you'll do a voiceover on the finished report, you'll fit in a statement somewhere to the effect that the Panther is a nicer guy than you thought and you'll turn up to the premiere. Will you do that?"

"Landing in approximately thirty minutes, Mr. Fitzlean." The voice from the cockpit murmurs around the cabin, blending with the dying notes of Tchaikovsky's ballet. With an angry gesture, he flicks the remote to switch it off.

"Well?" He's still glaring at me.

I take a deep breath and nod. "Okay. I can do all that."

We dress at opposite sides of the bed without speaking, the hum of the engines menacing and low.

* * * *

"Here we are. Millin Island."

Cade nods toward the view and I gaze out of the windows as we come in to land. The rocky island below us looks wild and rugged, the sea stretching away in a wide, wrinkly expanse of dark blue, little wavelets sparkling along the edge of the cliffs in the slanting afternoon sun.

There are very few trees here, just rolling hills and deep valleys, patchy with colored heather. Low stone buildings lie in clusters along thin, spidery roads. Along one of them a Jeep so tiny it looks like a toy is heading for the little patchwork airfield.

As we emerge from the jet, Cade shakes hands with Lisa and the crew then leads me quickly over the tarmac to the shelter of a low stone building. The air up here is sharp and cold after the soft Devon heatwave. I shiver in the wind, wishing I'd brought something thicker than a thin linen jacket.

As we reach the building, he hurries me inside. "This is our visitors' center. It's also a store for the residents."

Across the airfield, the tiny Jeep's waiting, now magically full size. The doors are flung open, and I can see the driver waving.

Cade waves back and turns to me with a grin. "There's our transport, but he'll have to wait. First we're going shopping."

"Sending Nera a postcard?"

He grins. "I might. Show her there's no hard feelings."

"Lucky her." I color slightly. My rear's on fire and everywhere down south is still aglow with my orgasm. Walking gracefully is a real effort.

He gives my bottom a cheeky pat. "Lively down there? Good. What clothes did you bring?"

I stare at him. "Linen crops, swimming costume, heels and sandals. Nera lent me some costumes. Why?"

"No stormproof? Thought not. We'll get you something here. You can't watch seals in heels."

I flash him a grateful look. This wind will finish me off.

I ransack the rail of anoraks and refuse the offer of a fitting room from the flustered assistant. Cade pays at the till and soon we're out in the wind again and heading for the Jeep.

"Mr. Fitzlean? Welcome back, sir." A rugged individual with a sandy beard and very blue eyes grins a greeting and takes the driver's seat as we clamber in.

I look around eagerly as Cade chats to the driver, asking him about his family and how the weather's shaping up.

Soon we pull into the entrance of a long, low stone building. A man and a woman come out to greet us, both wearing jeans. The man has a long beard and an earring, the woman tiny braids holding back her long blonde hair. She's serene and rather beautiful in trainers, jeans, a woolly poncho and several strings of heavy wooden beads.

"Hi, Cade. Treat to see you. So this is Tunis? Wow." They lead us through the low, rambling rooms, and I gather this is where we'll stay.

The interior's a strange mixture of polished granite, clean modern lines and outrageous pop kitsch. In the largest room, a vast area with a wide stone fireplace and long, low sofas in white leather, I see an original Lichtenstein, the giant comic book face, teardrop and speech bubble a dramatic note in the calm, peaceful room. On the opposite wall stand a couple of garish jukeboxes.

Cades murmurs close to my ear. "Maybe I don't need to tell you — the décor may have done that already — but this is Izzy's place. We're staying here for a couple of nights before we fly south to visit my father." He turns to the woman with one eyebrow arched. "My usual room?"

"Sure. It's all ready. You're still in the Walrus suite. We thought you'd like that. Supper at nine?"

Cade eyes me with the ghost of a wink. "Perfect. I guess we'll be tied up till then."

* * * *

Food has been thoughtfully placed in our rooms. After a beer and a sandwich, I'm keen to explore. The rooms all have low ceilings, sleek leather furniture and fabulous views over the low, rocky landscape leading down to the sea. Everywhere there's a clean, crisp smell of pine and polish.

"Has Izzy always lived here?"

"On and off. The island comes with the Beat Hall estate. It was the holiday retreat of the family who lived there. My mother loved it. She used to come here when she wanted time on her own. Later she brought her hippy friends with her. They founded a commune here and started the craft workshops. When she met Izzy, he used it as a base when he was touring Europe. After she died, he stayed on. Now he manages the workshops and the music studios."

"A lot goes on here, then? It seems so peaceful."

He grins. "You'd be surprised. It may have a sleepy feel to it, but this place is a positive powerhouse. We'll look round tomorrow. Just now I've got other plans. Shower first."

He undresses me slowly, deliberately fondling my tender bottom, his eyes gleaming when I wince. "We'll go easy on those for a while. Now the shower. Let's see if I can make up for the indignities of mile-high discipline."

Once again he soothes and teases with the gel, arouses and torments with the jet until I ache from laughing. When I've taken my own revenge with the jet, surprising him with some unusual flicks of the douche, he wraps me in a towel and pulls me into his arms. "Now I want to see you come."

He lays me down on the bed like a precious object, strips the towel away and spreads my legs wide. "Lean back and grip the bed head. Don't let go till I tell you."

Slowly, deliberately, he begins to caress the insides of my thighs, leaving a trail of kisses with tiny touches of his lips. He works his way slowly up my body, lingering on my tender nipples, sucking hard then nipping them with his teeth, laughing against my breasts as I cry out.

"Now for a bit more discipline." He grins at my outraged expression and his voice lowers to a murmur. "Relax. Good for you."

From his case he pulls out an object I've never seen in real life, but I know what it is and I feel myself go tense. *A butt plug.*

He grins at my horrified expression. "I mean to claim all of you, even your delicious ass. But first we have to prepare it. And it'll take a while, so we'll start now." He produces a canister of lube. "We'll need plenty of this, but first you can salute it with a polite kiss. Take it in your mouth."

"Must I?"

I catch a glint of anger.

"Yes, you must." His voice is low. "It's okay. It's clean and new, and it's the smallest size. Perfect for a beginner. Open."

I shudder at the thought of the enormity he's planning. The sheer *wickedness* of it sends a flare of arousal through me. He slides it deep into my mouth, his gaze locked on mine, his expression intent. "Now suck. Keep it in."

He fondles me as I suckle, his look full of heat, his hand easing into me, pushing deep and making my muscles ripple and haul at his fingers. He warms a handful of lube and smears it around my tight little opening, smiling as I clench. "Hey, relax. It's going in whether you like it or not."

His eyes gleam as he slides the plug out of my mouth and pushes the smooth, tapered end of it into me inch by inch.

I whimper as it fills me, part ashamed, part excited. At last it's in place and the wide base presses snugly against me. I'm filled, invaded and desperately aroused.

Within minutes his fingers are busy again as he gazes deep into my eyes. As my climax builds, he leans over me, his eyes dark and watchful. "You're so beautiful, especially like this. Now look at me. I want to watch."

He moves gently over me, his erection, huge and hard, pressing against his fly and jutting against me. His gaze burns into me, sending tremors through me while his fingers probe and tease. The weight of his hips forces me hard against the unforgiving plug.

Helpless in his grasp, imprisoned by his amused gaze and at the mercy of the unfamiliar pressures down below, I soon peak, tip and cascade into an abyss of pleasure as he captures my mouth, his tongue invading and controlling, filling me with honey and spice all his own.

Chapter Twenty-Three

When we finally make it to supper, the room is crowded and the jukeboxes are busy. Low tables are set out with dishes of food — mostly vegetarian, some with chicken. It smells heavenly. There's a large tureen of soup, a basket heaped with sourdough breads and piles of clean pottery platters, bowls and spoons.

No knives, I notice, and no formalities like napkins. On another table is an assortment of beer and homemade wine. Life here is casual and relaxed.

"Are you a musician too, Tunis?" "You known Cade long?" Their curious, quiet voices and their slow drawl remind me of Izzy.

The women wear no cosmetics and homespun clothes. All the men have beards. Both men and women wear their hair long, tied back with Indian-style bands or Celtic braids. Their calm air is misleading — their eyes are sharp and their comments witty. After about twenty minutes I'm surprised at how well informed they are about life in the wider world.

Cade mentions I'm on TV. I see no screens here but they exchange looks and the conversation is quietly steered toward what interests me. One of the women knows someone from my time with the ballet. One of the men recently saw Jake's photographs in an exhibition on a rare trip to the capital.

Cade keeps close, letting me talk but saying little himself.

It's clear he knows them well.

"Hey, Cade, you taking Tunis on the tour? She ought to see what we do." The rugged six-footer with a ginger beard who drove us from the airfield is introduced as Barney. He's delighted to see us again. "I'm free till noon tomorrow. Got a shipment to take to the airfield after that."

There are murmurs from the others. A regal blonde with wispy golden braids and a bright patchwork skirt lays a thin hand on Cade's arm. "You must show her round the workshops. We're just finishing off an order for Italy."

She's very attractive. In her late forties, I'd guess. Her voice is low and musical.

Cade gives her a warm smile and I felt a tiny spike of jealousy. I hide it with an unnecessary sip of nettle wine. I've had plenty, more than I should. Truth to tell, I'm nervous.

After a while, it tastes delicious.

"Thanks, Aria. We might do just that. The jewelry was partly why I brought her here. She loves the harness." He turns to me with a casual smile. "Tell them how it feels."

Whoa—way too personal. But I smile round at the group. "It's very…stimulating."

Aria raises an eyebrow. "You're telling me. It's shaping up to be our biggest seller. There's quite a waiting list." She tips her head toward Cade and shakes her head with a smile. "He's a bad boy…with a wicked imagination." She moves away, sweeping me with a knowing look. "See you tomorrow then. Maybe we'll fix you up with some more."

At the other side of the room someone is idly picking out a tune on a guitar. A singer joins in and soon a group gathers to listen. I feel Cade's hand on my arm and his warm breath on my hair.

"Nearly midnight. Seal time."

Back in our room, he throws me a sweater. I shrug it on over my skimpy top and jeans while he leans on the doorframe, his look sending tremors through me.

"How's the plug?"

I pause in the act of tying up my hair. I'd almost forgotten it. Now I blush. What can I say? "Okay, I think."

He cups my tight, jean-clad rear with his hand, his clasp intimate and fond. "Good. We'll leave it in a little while longer. And wear some trainers. The path can be rough."

* * * *

"Cade, they're beautiful. I've never seen seals swimming before." I give a deep, contented sigh as I gaze out over the moonlit sea. Far below us, at the foot of the cliff, glossy, bobbing heads are playing in the water.

It's late now, the night calm. The cliff edge is only feet away but I'm tightly clasped in Cade's arms. To my surprise, even though we're so high up, I feel almost safe.

Moonlight etches his jaw in silver and glitters in his eyes, turning him into some pagan god, timeless and cruel. He seems to fit in with this strange, primitive place.

"Do you trust me, Tunis?"

He's lured me up here, knowing I relish a challenge, once more forcing me to face the unknown and reach a new limit. Tethered in a dungeon, it might bring startling new pleasures. Out here it means I must confront yet another fear.

But I understand instinctively that he'll never knowingly hurt me.

I do trust him.

As the seals splash again, I shiver. He leans close, his lips moving against my ear. "Chilly? We'll go back now."

At the sound of our voices, the seals dart away and we walk back hand-in-hand. He talks about the people I've met and the workshops they run. It seems they're all expert craftsmen, specialists in their field. Even bearded Barney is an engineer. He works on the planes.

"And Aria? She knows you well?" What I really mean is *how well do you know her?* She's very attractive and she designs his bondage jewelry?

Jealousy prickles.

He glances at me, his look opaque. "Most of the people here know me well."

"She seems a bit…familiar, that's all."

"She's always measuring people up for jewelry. She's one of our best designers."

"That's not what I meant. You try out *all* your ideas on her?" My tone's sharp for good reason. I've worn some of it. I know exactly what it does.

He gives my hand a squeeze. "Hey, relax. I know what you're thinking, but she's Izzy's girl."

Chastened and relieved, I squeeze him back as we reach the foot of the steep rise up to the house. From here we can just see the croft and its outline of low, rambling roofs. The soft light from the candles in its windows is easily outshone by the brilliance of the moonlight, flooding us with silver.

I hesitate, pulling on his hand as he moves toward the steps. He turns back with a smile. "What? You want to stay out here a while longer?"

"Cade, where were you that night? Why does Mel think it's such a big deal?"

His jaw stiffens and all at once his look turns to ice. "Why?"

I frown. "That's no answer. It's a simple question."

In the shadow his eyes glitter. "Sure it is. Questions are always simple for rookie presenters with nosey friends. Shall we go in?"

I stare at him, taken aback at his tone. Why can't he give me a straight answer?

He lets go of my hand and takes the steps at a bound, leaving me to climb up after him. From inside the croft at the top of the steep climb, music and laughter filter out into the night, mingling with the soft murmur of the sea and the cries of the gulls.

At the top he's waiting for me to catch up, his expression grim.

What have I said? And why does this matter so much? A tiny part of me salutes Mel's unerring instinct for a story. She's clearly on to something.

Another part of me wishes she'd back off.

In our room he closes the door softly behind me as I walk in. "I'm not sure you get what this week is about." He pulls off his jacket, slings it over a chair and reaches over to the side table for a beer.

I shake my head as he offers one to me. He takes a long swig of his own.

"You're mine for the week. That was the arrangement. You stay with me at all times, and you strive to please me at all times. Even when you're away from the Hall, you're bound by your agreements and your contracts. You must understand that I'm taking you into the heart of my family and for the next few days, you'll be in a position of absolute trust. Is that clear?"

I stare at him. "Of course it's clear. What do you take me for? I've signed everything, I've accepted all your crazy terms." I also recall the vast sum of money he paid for me. "I'm all yours, if that's what you want."

His mouth is set into a grim line. "It *is* what I want. Take off your jeans."

I reach for my zipper but with an impatient gleam, he pushes my hands away and peels my jeans down my thighs. "Bend over."

"*Again*? Cade, I'm still—"

He fondles me briefly. "Tender? I know." He kisses me softly on my right flank. "The plug's coming out." He eases it out, drops it in the sink and washes his hands. "I'll show you how to clean it later."

He folds me in his arms, tilts up my chin and kisses me full on the mouth, his kiss long and deep. When he pulls away, he strokes the wind-blown hair out of my eyes and smiles. "They like you. Don't be fooled by all the hippy talk and the woollies. They love meeting celebs. Now we've got things to do."

They keep us busy for quite a while.

* * * *

The following morning I wake to the sight of sunlight glowing through a glass of orange juice and the feel of his arms pinning me down as he sits on the bed. "You look beautiful this morning, like you do every morning. Kiss me."

For the next few moments the room spins away as he invades my mouth. I stretch out lazily beneath him, but soon he pulls away.

"Up you get. We're touring the workshops this morning with Barney. But first, there's something I have to do."

Lazy and warm I ease myself out of the covers and stand before him, still flushed with sleep. He sweeps me with a look, the heat in his eyes sending a shimmer though me.

"Delicious. Put your arms out straight, legs spread wide." He walks around me, running his hands over me, lingering on my breasts and the curves of my bottom. "Bend over."

I bend low as he caresses me slowly, his fingers lingering near my tiny opening. I whimper as he eases inside a little way.

"Relax. Feel good?"

What a question. I gasp. But as his hand lingers, my outrage dies away and I lean into his touch. It feels weird but oddly disturbing and now I start to pulse gently. I smile up at him, coloring a little.

He gives me a knowing smile and pats me on the rump. "I told you it might be fun. Now for something new. Stay where you are."

I hear him wash his hands then he takes something out of a drawer.

I tense. "What are you doing?"

When he comes back, he's holding up a long coil of soft, thick rope. The gleam in his eyes warns me once more I'm in unknown territory.

"We're going to try out some rope bondage."

He's an expert at this, like at so much else. I watch spellbound in the mirror as the rope passes back and forth over my body, around my ribcage, between my legs, forcing open the cheeks of my bottom, thrusting my breasts forward, and hauling at either side of my pulsing center.

As the cruel cobweb takes shape, he glances up from time to time with a grin. "Surprising how useful a youth spent in boats and climbing rocks can be for someone with my tastes. I became an expert at knots very early on. Now for the money shot."

With a few flicks of his long fingers, he fashions a large, elaborate knot and positions it precisely between my legs, finishing off the tie with a flourish at the back of my waist.

I'm tightly trussed, the ropes spaced apart so they make the shape of a swimsuit, but with my every intimate place fully displayed. As I flex, my legs the final knot tightens at the very peak of my slit, making me throb.

He eyes me with a gleam. He can hardly keep his hands off me. "One day we might try some suspension. Here a few simple knots will have to do. Move around the room. Tell me if anything hurts or chafes."

I move about, bending and stretching then do a couple of arabesques. "It feels tight," I report, being honest but selective. I feel a whole lot of things about this, most of them confusing, all of them hot. "It's very controlling. Oddly, it feels *safe*." I stare at him, bewildered. "Is it supposed to?"

It's also extremely arousing, but I keep that part to myself. *He probably knows.*

His voice drops to a silky murmur. "Get dressed. Let's hope your jeans stretch over the ropes. If not, try a skirt. No underwear. A sexy top would be nice. Better cover up with the sweater. When we take it off we'll see how far the wind can raise your nipples."

* * * *

I follow him into the breakfast area feeling tightly trussed and acutely self-conscious, but under Cade's borrowed sweater, nothing much shows. Soon the rope corset feels normal.

The only snag is the persistent, maddening pressure between my legs. It's vividly arousing. I hope our walk will be short.

We eat alone. The others are already at work. Afterward he fondles my rear with a knowing grin and we go outside.

Barney, bluff and hearty this morning, drives us back along the rough track I saw from the plane. He and Cade talk about orders and shipments and after a while, we come to a collection of outbuildings. Each one is a separate workshop and surprisingly busy. Last night's laid-back hippies are hard at work and clearly skilled craftsmen. Everyone seems glad to see us, and they talk willingly about what they're doing.

Barney shows us round the smithy where the jewelry is forged then a workroom with a precision lathe where the pieces are finished. We wave to Aria, who is sitting at a vast drawing board set up at one end of the long room, poring over an elaborate design for a new piece.

After the clatter of the metalworkers, we find quieter rooms full of weavers, women knitting traditional fishermen's sweaters and even lace-makers.

Past the workshops is a collection of music studios where last night's band is busy working on a song. I learn Izzy's hoping for a new hit.

I should find all this really exciting. Mel wanted me to take notes. We never waste a chance of a good story.

But the rope's too distracting.

Cade glances at me from time to time, a faint smile playing at the corners of his lips. "Hard to concentrate? Good. Let's walk along the beach."

He turns to Barney. "We'll walk back. See you later."

"Sure." Barney eyes us with a grin. He sees us out and calls after us. "Izzy's flying in after lunch."

* * * *

The beach is deserted. We splash and run about, chasing each other and throwing skipping stones like children. It's glorious.

Every so often Cade pulls me into his arms as the surf froths around our knees and sand hisses between our toes. He leads me along the foot of the cliffs a little way until he comes to a deep gash in the rocks. As he draws me inside, I peer round.

After the chill wind along the shore, the heat in the cavern is a shock. The rocky overhang makes it as sheltered as a cave, but it's really a cleft in the cliff face. Sunlight streams in from the west.

The surf roars just a few feet away but inside here the rocks are dry and the sand is hot and soft. The sun has been shining here all morning and the rocks are hot to the touch. Light flickers over the sheer cliff face, reflected from the sun-splashed wavelets thundering up the beach. Set into the rock I see two rusty metal rings at about head height.

"This is an old fisherman's cave. They store boats in here in the winter." Gently he turns me round to face him and lifts my trainers, strung together by their laces, away from my neck where I'd taken them off to paddle.

"We'll lose these. Strip."

I unfasten my jeans and slowly peel away my top. He walks around me, caressing my tightly trussed body.

Pressure from the ropes already has me tingling with arousal after our walk as the money-knot works its magic. Now his touch almost sends me over the edge.

"Beautiful. I've been waiting to get a good look at you all morning." He pushes me back against the warm rock. "Now grab hold of those rings. You're going to keep hold of them till I tell you to let go. Keep still."

Wonderingly I reach up and grasp them while he pushes my feet wide apart. Hot sand spills over my toes. His eyes darken as he looks me over, his expression remote and absorbed then he starts to kiss me.

As the sun beats down and the waves whisper softly farther down the beach, his lips touch me with tiny kisses all down one side of my body then all down the other, lingering on my splayed thighs, my tightly bound breasts and my tight, erect nipples.

It's like worship, disturbing and intensely moving. It's increasingly hard to keep still.

As he leans up again, he places his hands on the rock on either side of me, his look strangely intense. "You look like Ariadne chained to the rocks, waiting for the monster." He kisses me on the forehead. "And you think I am a monster, don't you, Tunis?" He kisses me again. "I hoped you'd never find out I was the Panther. Ever since that night, I've longed to see you like this, but I dreaded you knowing. And now I hate myself." He closes his eyes and leans his forehead against mine. His breathing is ragged, his face anguished.

What? I stand very still, alarmed now. "What's wrong?

"Help me, Tunis. I don't want to be a monster. But the more I do this with you, the more I—" He breaks off, like he daren't finish his thought.

Slowly I let go of the rings and reach up my arms. "Look, Cade, no hands. I'm not chained up. I'm free."

To prove it, I wind my arms around his neck and lay my cheek close to his, my low murmur echoing off the hot, silent rocks. "I'm here because I want to be here. I'm here of my own free will. If you're a monster, then so am I."

His mouth fastens on mine, his kiss deep and long. At last he pulls away. "You mean that? Really?"

I drop a light, reverent kiss on his breastbone and lay my forehead against his chest. "Yes, I mean it. Really."

I breathe again as a smile dawns in his face like sunrise and the anguish fades.

He gives my nipple a friendly tweak. "Better get dressed now. Time to go back."

Chapter Twenty-Four

Tonight Izzy's expected back for supper and all the workers and craftsmen will be coming over to party. Until then we have the afternoon to ourselves. Without really meaning to, we spend most of it in our room.

Something between us has changed. Maybe not for long, but it affects us both. Our lunch lies neglected on a table at the side. We have eyes only for each other.

With sunlight slanting through the windows, Cade finally unwinds my rope during long, slow sex that sends me to the brink time and again. Finally I find release at the precise point that he finds his own and afterward we lie together, limp and content, him thoughtful, me sleepy and sated with pleasure.

After a while he insists I play table for his late lunch. When he teases me with morsels of food in hidden places that he seeks and captures with his tongue, I giggle and writhe. Then I take my revenge by spreading chocolate mousse all over his erection, topping it with a cherry and licking it off very slowly, savoring every mouthful. "Now, for dessert."

He eyes the wreck of our meal with a sardonic flicker. "You just had it."

"I'm still hungry," I say softly. I lean over him, kissing along his breastbone, licking his sharp little nipples with long, lustful sweeps of my tongue. Slowly I head south over his abdomen toward his strong, muscular thighs. There I find his erection, still wet and a little sticky with traces of missed dessert and now swollen to a hard, silky purple from all my attention. It twitches as it lies along his stomach.

"You're breaking one of the first rules." His soft murmur makes me smile, but his expression is stern.

I feel a twinge of dismay. "You're kidding, right?"

I touch the head of his bulging erection with the softest brush of my lips. He tastes delicious…

"You take charge only when I tell you." He's eyeing me steadily, a soft gleam in his eyes.

It's a warning. Will I never learn?

I grin playfully and decide to ignore it. "Not this time."

His eyes glitter dangerously and he lowers his voice. "*Every* time."

Boldly I lean up to kiss his beautiful mouth. "Wait till I'm done. Maybe you'll want it too."

I return to my task and kiss him again, licking gently along his twitching shaft until I reach the root, deep between his legs, all hot hair and soft, crumpled skin, growing smooth where his balls swell into hard mounds. He tastes of salt and earth, his hairy skin rough on my tongue.

I work my way back to the tip, letting my soft under-lip glide along his skin, thrilling as his shaft bucks against my teeth. Far away, past his chest, I see the tendons flex in his neck.

I take the head in my mouth and suck hard, making him gasp then draw myself up onto my hands and knees and smile down into his intent, watchful eyes. "How am I doing?"

His lips stretch in a faint, answering smile, his eyes dark as midnight. "You'll get fifteen strokes."

My smile freezes on my lips. "You're *serious*?"

"I warned you, I don't play at this."

His voice is calm and low, his eyes watchful.

He means it.

His expression is stern but his erection jolts against my leg, urging me to my task. It's all the permission I need. And now I discover a startling new fact. I simply want him, both in my mouth and out of it. And I want him so badly that *I want his punishment too.*

And so does he.

Fully aware of what I'm bringing on myself, I kneel between his splayed knees and begin to fellate him eagerly, pausing to lick him and fondle his root, teasing his balls with soft fingertips, massaging deep beyond and teasing his opening, making him groan. The thought of what might happen spices the act with danger and a hint of wickedness that sends flames of arousal shooting through me.

As he arches and tenses below me, I lean up, curious. "When?"

He gasps as I break off my rhythm, his voice husky. "When what?"

"The fifteen strokes? When do I get them?"

His mouth curves into a long, sardonic smile and I feel him twitch again. "I'll tell you when I've decided."

Now I'm part amused, part scared. Once more I take him fully in my mouth then down my throat as far as I can, sheathing my teeth and speeding up until he gives a low, deep growl.

He's close. Instinctively I pull away and take him, hot and glossy with my saliva, between my breasts, plumping them out so they bulge around him as I move. In moments, he begins to pump, the soft milk gushing out in precious drops, covering my breasts with his fluid.

I glance up daringly. "Is that what they used to call a necklace of pearls?"

He smiles, stroking my face with his hand, infinitely tender, his breathing still ragged. "If they did, they were mean, short-sighted tightwads. That's what I'd call one heck of a blow job."

I lean up to kiss him gently on the lips then curl up in the crook of his shoulder. "So what's the verdict?"

"You're astonishing. But you'll still get fifteen strokes."

I grin and kiss the edge of his jaw. "You mean you didn't enjoy it, *Sir*?"

He smiles and touches his lips to my hair, his voice deep and soft. "Because I did enjoy it, very much. That's how it works."

* * * *

As tonight is a special occasion, I'd hoped to dress up, but city satin seems out of place here. Luckily I have the perfect solution. In one of the workshops I'd lingered to watch an elderly woman knitting lace. Her fingers flickered over the needles as a whisper-soft cobweb of filigree lace grew across her lap.

Aria explained that she's an islander. She applies her traditional skills to imported raw silk yarns. Her work is beautiful and unique. The commune sells it on to the big fashion houses to be made up into wedding dresses and peignoirs.

I touched it gently. "How beautiful. It feels like air."

The woman looked up, pleased. Her piercing blue eyes twinkled as I turned away. At the door Aria called me back. "Aileen wants to know if you'd like some to wear."

I smiled at her, surprised.

"Ye're with young Cade, are ye not? Then if you like, ye might try yon gown. As a gift. Only if ye want it, mind."

Near her on a dress dummy was a delicate gown just finished, clearly a showpiece. It was a vibrant, sunshine yellow — the natural color of raw unbleached silk. It swirled to the ground, light as flower petals.

With a smile, Aria looked me over. "Would you like to try it? All our garments are bias-cut, so it'll stretch when it's on. The color should suit you. Honey-colored skin looks good in golds."

I blushed and thanked Aileen, who turned back to her work with a calm smile.

The gown was waiting for me when we got back, neatly wrapped in white tissue. Now I shake it out and slip it over my head. It's so light I can hardly feel it. It loops from one shoulder, clings all the way down my body so the close patterns close up to spare my blushes then it swirls free of my legs and feet, letting the light shine through so it seems to sparkle.

Cade eyes me appreciatively as I pirouette before him.

"Can I wear it? Would it be suitable?" I'm anxious not to appear too dressy.

He tilts up my chin and kisses me on the mouth. "It's perfect. You look almost as beautiful in it as you will when you're out of it."

* * * *

When we join the others I'm surprised to see almost everyone's dressed up. It seems Izzy likes holding court. Aria stays close to him and from time to time he gives her a fond look or absently touches her hair.

Food, wine and beer are all laid out in another room and many couples are already dancing. Aileen glances up with a delighted smile as I walk in.

"Ah niver get to see them on," she murmurs sadly, as I twirl before her to show it off. "They all go abroad, ye ken. You look lovely."

While I'm talking to Aileen, I see Aria glance across at me and whisper to Cade.

I feel uneasy. It occurs to me she might be making some snide remark about the fit of the jewelry. As he smiles back at her, I'm convinced of it, but when she comes over, she surprises me.

"I just checked with Cade, and he says I can ask. Would you dance for us, Tunis?"

He gives me an encouraging smile. I wait serenely while Aria makes some kind of announcement and clears the floor.

After a brief whispered discussion about music, she surprises me again, and Barney walks over with a grin and waves some panpipes.

"Allow me."

Impromptu dance is always tricky, but dancers are sensitive to atmosphere, and I've soaked up enough here to fill me with ideas for months. As the candles flicker round the edges of the room and the guests all sink onto cushions and lean against the walls to watch, Barney's panpipes send out fluting ripples of harmony and I start to move.

This place is beautiful and wild so some of my movement is, too. Sometimes it sparkles or grows dark, so I show that as well. As I dance, I think of our walk along the beach and the endless swell and beat of the sea. I think of surges and beats of my own. I think of love and despair.

And somehow all these thoughts fuse into movement. And at last I sink slowly to the floor in a full dancer's pose, my legs in the splits and my body curved low over my outstretched arms, and my hands flutter gently to a halt at Cade's feet.

The room explodes into applause and I smile round, a little bewildered and only now aware how quiet it was before.

The heat in Cade's smile is really all the applause I need.

* * * *

As it grows late, we relax together over wine and beer and the candles burn low. The sea whispers in the distance while Izzy talks about the old times — the groups, the hits and the gossip. He's funny and well informed, his easy drawl soothing and hypnotic.

Cade draws me onto his lap and holds me tight. I feel almost more intimate with him here, in front of his extended family of hippies, than I do when we're alone.

Much later, when we finally are alone, he takes me in his arms. "You were a sensation. Now we'll give some of the jewelry a workout."

He fastens sturdy silver-mounted leather cuffs on my wrists and ankles then holds up a glittering pair of nipple clamps, shaped like flowers and linked by a diamond-studded chain. "These should make life interesting."

With an impatient sweep, he strips the quilt off the mattress and signals I should stand between the carved wooden posts at the end. He clips my wrists and ankles to the top and bottom of the posts, spreading my legs wider than usual until our hips are roughly in line then he produces a newer version of the whisker gag and smiles as he slips the soft silver ball behind my teeth and fixes the clasp. "It'll be dawn soon. No need to wake everybody."

I'm languid from all the sea air but still hyper from my dance. This is just what I need. Arousal starts to pulse, its drumbeat calling all my nerve-endings into urgent service.

He cups my breasts in his hands, teasing my nipples into hard points then slips on the clamps. Once more the clamps are screws, so he tightens them slowly until I gasp then kisses me on the hair. "Ready?"

Leaning down, he fastens his mouth between my legs and I feel the glorious sweep of his tongue. The pleasure is so intense I almost sob but manage only to mewl against the merciless gag.

He ignores me as he feasts. But just as I think I'll explode with pleasure, his hot, thrusting tongue abandons me and he stands slowly upright, his look drinking in my navel, my belly and my glittering, clamped breasts. As he towers over me, he flicks the chain linking my imprisoned nipples and at the same moment flicks his fingers deep between my legs.

My orgasm explodes in a blast of silent heat, flaring through me in a surge of power. I buck and jerk in my bonds as he holds me close. And at last he stands fully upright and I hear the blissful rip of foil. After a moment he fastens both his arms around me and in seconds he slides into me. He takes me in long, deep thrusts, his wide, fond smile filling me with joy until he comes, too.

* * * *

Out on the airfield the following morning, Barney, Izzy and Aria come out to see us off. While Cade and Izzy clap each other in the back, hearty and male, Aria kisses me on the cheek. "You must come back soon." She leans forward to whisper. "And that dance was the sexiest thing I've ever seen. You must teach me."

This time the jet flies due south. I watch the towns and fields roll away beneath us as we head into the sun. When I ask where we're going and why, Cade is vague. He says only that we're headed for Southern Europe and we refuel at Heathrow.

After Heathrow, I learn that his father vacations in style.

We come in to land over another sparkling sea, just as blue as the waters around Millin Island. But the helipad on the vast, gleaming yacht and the blast of warm air as we step out of the air-conditioned bubble of the plane welcome us to a very different world.

In the summer the resorts around the Black Sea teem with tourists but this vast, solitary yacht, anchored a little way off the coast, teems with a population of its own, all designer beachwear and glossy suntans.

We're a long way from Millin's easy-going hippies. This is a very exclusive place.

Cade leads me down to the bridge, where uniformed crewmembers murmur to each other in Russian and English. A handsome, suntanned man with wavy white hair and the smooth air of an American politician is talking with the Captain. He turns and hails us with a polished smile.

He's immaculately dressed in blazer, white trousers and a cravat. He gives Cade a brief nod then bows low over my hand.

Cade grins as he introduces me. His manner seems casual but I sense a hint of reserve. He's not like this with Izzy.

"Tunis Vale, sir. She's a TV presenter and arts expert. Also a former dancer. Tunis, this is Sir Gerald Fitzlean, DSO and Bar and fuck knows what else. He's also my dad."

Sir Gerald beams at me, holding onto my hand just a fraction too long. "My dear, we're honored. Leonardo, Pavlova — and Tunis. You are one of the few people in the world known to millions just by the one name — a rare feat for one so young."

"Cut the crap, Dad. You'll scare her to death. Anyway, pop stars do it all the time. Is Emmeline with you this year?"

The older man's face softens. "Yes, she's around somewhere. Not that I've had much of a chance to talk to her. How's Izaak? Still stuck in the eighties?"

He goes on quickly before Cade can answer. "We've got a full ship this week — four film stars, three producers, eight ambassadors and several members of the Politburo and their assorted molls, so you won't be bored."

Cade snorts. "With that little lot? I wouldn't bank on it. Usual cabin?"

His father rolls his eyes at me in a proud 'What would you do with him?' kind of way. "No, son. Emmeline upgraded you to the Gorky suite in honor of your fair companion."

Cade grins. "Fine. So you won't mind if we go freshen up?"

I hang back as Cade walks toward the stairs for a few words with the crew. "I'm delighted to meet you, Sir Gerald. Cade's told me about you, but very little about everybody else. He's very secretive."

He smiles, his look, like his handshake earlier, just a little too warm. "Ah. Well he has a great deal on his mind just now. But I understand you were a dancer? How interesting."

We talk for a few moments about my former career while he lists some of the guests on board who are apparently looking forward to meeting me. At last I turn away and a respectful attendant leads me to our quarters.

As I walk into the spacious cabin, Cade's on the phone, looking out over the deck to the sea.

"So when's their deadline? You're sure about that? Fine. I'll deal with it."

He seems unaware that I'm here. As I watch, he runs his hand through his hair, exasperated. "Fran, I don't know how. I said I'll deal with it, okay?"

At that moment he catches sight of me. He ends the call and slips the phone in his pocket and for a few seconds he looks at me like I'm a complete stranger.

"How long have you been listening?"

I feel a chill steal through me. Something's happened, something serious. "I just got here. I was talking to your father. Why? Is something wrong?"

He looks away, his tone remote. "That rather depends. Let's go meet some of the others."

Now what?

Chapter Twenty-Five

I have to freshen up after the flight. When I peek out of the shower, he's already gone, so I take my time to change and fix my hair. When I wander up on deck, the sun is setting in a haze of opal and rose, the sea mirror-calm, as reflective as oil.

I weave my way through the elegant guests and finally spot Cade leaning against the rail, lonely as a classical statue, his perfect profile etched against the brilliance of the sky.

I feel a rush of longing so acute my heart races. All at once the rift between us seems urgent and dangerous, but I've still no idea what it is.

As I draw near, he glances at me, his look still cold and turns away to gaze out over the sea. "What exactly did Macallan say the morning we left?"

My stomach gives a jolt. "I can't do anything about it now."

His look sweeps over me with a chill. "But what did she say?"

"Just that Jake's seen security footage from the club. He says it proves you weren't there. Mel thinks you're covering for someone else."

Slowly he turns to me, his face cold. "And you? What do you think?"

It's obvious to me by now that Mel must be right. Surely he knows this.

But I don't want a fight. I know there's some mystery here, but I'm starting to wonder if the pain it's causing him is worth the effort of solving it.

I lean up and kiss him lightly on the jaw. "Well the Panther was there. We all saw him. So for my money, he was in charge that night. But nobody must ever know that was you, right? So you *were* there in one sense. Just *not* there in another. Anyway, I don't really care."

He stands very still, his face like stone. After a second a muscle moves in his cheek. "I wish I could believe that."

But as we join the others, I frown. Mel said the Panther *got there after we did*. He came up behind me. He was out in the rain.

So if Cade — aka the Panther — arrived late, who *was* in charge that night? Who was it made that girl pass out? *And why won't he simply tell me?*

She's definitely on to something. There must be a cover-up.

* * * *

Sir Gerald's yacht is the height of luxury. Staff are everywhere, milling among the guests, silently refilling glasses, slipping out of sight as we pass, slipping into our rooms when we leave to smooth beds, tidy stray clothes, freshen flowers and leave chocolates on pillows.

It's a far cry from the easy hippy-dom of Millin Island. To add to my dismay, Cade seems edgy here. He ignores the small talk around him as the guests mingle, chattering idly about golf and business, or parties and business, or property and business, teasing out common ground as they network.

Some laze by the pool, others are busy at cards and baccarat or watching movies in the elegant salons leading off the deck.

Sir Gerald strolls about like a benign monarch and at last we meet Emmeline, his mistress. She is slim, beautifully groomed and to me she has the hard, wary look of a professional.

Cade fends off her attempts to be friendly, his manner icy. She turns to me with a polite smile and a hint of relief. "And you're a dancer, Gerald tells me? How wonderful. I love the ballet. We go often."

As we talk, I warm to her. Her interest in dance seems real, and I'm flattered she takes the trouble.

We're treated like royalty. Gradually, from scraps of conversation I catch from the sun loungers and around the card tables, I find out why. This is a family affair. The yacht's chartered from one of Izzy's Russian contacts now in government and Cade foots the bill.

So he's still in control, even here.

It explains why everyone's so polite, but not why he's so edgy. I start to feel edgy too.

What's wrong? It's since that call. Business? Something personal?

On chilly Millin Island he was warm, passionate even. Here in the sunshine, he blows hot and cold. It's sudden and it's terrifying.

The simplest thing would be to sit him down and ask him. But while I do my best to socialize, chatting with one group after another, he simply slips away and paces alone on the upper decks, phone in hand.

* * * *

After what seems a very long evening, I'm heading for our stateroom. I've met more millionaires than I can count. I really should feel pleased with myself. I've never spoken before to so many people at one time who are real fans. I've had suggestions for further programs and two invitations to visit and film — one from a collector of Chinese jade and another from an Italian art curator.

Mel and Ben would be over the moon. Even Janice would be proud. I only wish she was here to see it. Maybe she'd think me less of a failure — once I'd explained to her what Chinese jade is.

But I long for night when I'll have him to myself and maybe find out what's troubling him. All day I've tingled all over, aching for him, still hyper from our delicious afternoon flight and our heady sessions on Millin Island.

Laid out on a lounger at the side of the pool, I fantasized all afternoon about the night ahead.

Fifteen strokes.

I see myself peeling off an elegant satin gown, sashaying up to him naked, maybe bending gracefully over his knees — or holding out my wrists to be handcuffed...

This is really getting to me. A great Russian dance teacher once said that ballet's like a drug. You constantly try to overcome yourself to achieve.

And so is this...

However far he takes me, I want more. Even if I'm scared. *Especially* if I'm scared.

Like he says, fear makes it fun.

But the reality, like all reality, is different. When I reach our room, still flushed with success and preening from so much interest in my work, he's standing in the middle of the room, waiting. As the door closes softly behind me, I hear once again his low, quiet command and heat courses through me.

"Kneel."

From now on I should stay silent, but I have to speak. "Are you angry about what the team is doing?" His unease must be something to do with Mel's warning. Back at Beat Hall I might have sorted this in minutes, but I've been out of touch for days…

"What do you think?"

So I'm right. "Look, I'd like to help, but I've lost contact. I seem to have lost my cell phone." It's a terrible admission. It makes me sound so inept.

I've looked everywhere, and there's been no hope of buying a prepaid.

Holding my gaze, he takes something out of his pocket and holds it up.

I gasp in dismay. "*You've* got it? Can I have it back?"

"No." He slips it back in his pocket and looks at me coldly.

I try to stay calm. *Don't lose your temper with this man. It never works.*

"Then…how is this my fault if I can't contact my team?"

"Did I say it was your fault?"

"But you're so cold. What's wrong, Cade? Can I help?"

He sighs, his expression opaque. "It's a bit late for that. The only way you can help now is to stay as close to me and as far away from your team as possible. How much do you know about what Simmons says he found?"

"The film footage of you? Nothing. Just that Mel wants to look into it. If I can't contact her, then how can I find out anything?"

My voice is rising now, along with my temper. Once again I'm being accused of something other people are planning…

I watch him warily, all my happy anticipation forgotten, as he moves purposefully about the room, taking off his jacket, loosening his tie, snapping open his case.

I'm still kneeling. My dress is caught up under my knees. It'll crease badly if I stay down here much longer. And what's he doing in his case? He never wears pajamas…

Wait. He keeps his equipment in his case…

Among his clothes I've noticed the occasional strand of leather, the braided end of a crop.

Fear sends a throb of excitement straight through me. But something else occurs to me. "Something's changed. It was okay before. Why's it different now?"

He turns to me, his face stony. "Don't play games with me. Naturally I expected trouble, Macallan's a gifted reporter. I planned to stay one step ahead. I took the risk when I hired all of you and so far, it's paid off. If everything goes to plan, the risk will have been worth it. Your colleagues might be good at their job, but I've got more money, better technology and good lawyers. And this week, I've got something even better than that."

His strange, cold smile sends a chill through me. "I've got *you*. You're the key to all this. As long as you're with me, they can't do much damage. Now to business.

You've forgotten your training already, so we'd better recap. What happens when you kneel?"

I swallow, thrown off course by this sudden change of tempo. "I stay silent. *Sir*," I add quickly.

"You stay silent. And how many strokes did you earn yesterday?"

His voice has lowered to a menacing whisper and instantly we're back in our deeply private world where nothing else matters.

Heat burns deep inside and with it comes a new thought. *Maybe this is how I reach him.*

"Fifteen, Sir."

He looks thoughtful. "We'll add on five for speaking out of turn. So how many?"

Indignation turns to hunger. I'm supposed to feel shame but instead all I feel is fire. Sometimes this ritual is fun. "Twenty, Sir."

But his spankings are relentless and efficient. How much more can I take?

His next words send a chill through me.

"You're math's more reliable than your word. I'm going to whip your breasts. First you strip then you shower and use the bathroom, then you come back here and kneel facing me. Got that?"

My breasts? Heaven help me... The heat flares into flame. "Yes, Sir. Thank you, Sir."

I rise gracefully to my feet, avoiding his eye, and begin to unfasten my gown. So here it is, the scenario I've longed for and dreaded. And to my intense shame, though it sounds terrifying, I'm deeply, wildly excited.

* * * *

For the breast whipping, I'm to be cuffed to the bedposts at the end of the bed by my wrists and ankles.

He wants me leaning forward in a long curve, so my breasts thrust forward and all my limbs are stretched and rigid.

"The usual way is to strap you into a chair and bind your breasts so they grow hard then flog them. But I like a little movement. And I like to see you posed. Makes it more fun."

Now his tone's light, almost cheerful. He might have been discussing the finer points of golf.

As he checks my cuffs and the fastenings that suspend me from the posts, his manner subtly changes and he becomes silent, withdrawn. When I'm fixed into position, he runs a hand over me, making me shiver.

"A ball gag would be sensible, with other people so close, but I might need your mouth. Can I trust you not to make too much noise?"

I nod, wide-eyed. *How can I answer that?*

He lowers his voice to a murmur. "Maybe I'll blindfold you instead. Make it more intense."

He slips a sleep mask over my eyes and instantly everything's dark. Now I'm suspended in air, my legs splayed wide, my breasts thrust out—a puppet on a string, a toy for his pleasure.

He takes a long time to prepare. Objects land on surfaces, doors open and close, something pops, something clinks, something whispers. At one point I catch the soft beat and the languid melody of a slow jazz number. It rises and falls in the background over a low, rhythmic beat.

And all at once something slides over my skin, the unmistakable slither of leather as the soft, cruel fingers of some long, many-stranded whip lands on my back like some giant creature coming in to land then snakes around my waist. It travels slowly up between my breasts and around my neck, claiming its prey, marking out territory.

I take a long, juddering breath and it starts. Stroke after stroke lands softly then eases over me, like a giant, questing hand. Just as I start to relax into its rhythm, it whistles through the air and lands with a sharp, multiple snap as each separate strand makes contact across my breasts.

"One."

Quivering, I wait for more, but nothing happens. After a long pause, something hard touches my nipple and I cry out in surprise. It's wet, and in seconds, my confused nerve endings tell me it's cold.

Ice. It slides slowly all around one breast then all around the other as I shiver and gasp. Finally it circles my nipples, making them numb and — as it bounces off them — hard. Just when I think they've lost all feeling, the whip lands again, stinging and merciless, the lashes zinging around my waist and snapping into my curves.

"Two."

Then something soft, so soft it might be a real animal. *Fur.* I shiver as it creeps slowly up the inside of one tight, quivering thigh, along my groin then down the inside of my other leg. I'm wondering where it's headed next when something soft, warm and deliciously wet circles one of my taut, pebble-like nipples — *his tongue.*

He takes my breast into his mouth, sucking hard then he pulls away and the air over my moistened skin is suddenly cold as the whip lands again. This time it makes me jump.

"Three."

And so it goes on, seemingly for hours. I lose track of time. It's impossible to tell hot from cold as sensation follows sensation. At one point his lips find mine as he kisses a dribble of fizzing champagne into my mouth.

Heavenly.

Another time his mouth, full of fizzing bubbles, fastens eagerly over my wide, gaping slit, probing and guzzling greedily with his tongue while the bubbles sparkle and tease around my tight, throbbing little center.

It's delicious, terrifying torment. The low sound of the jazz clarinet, the long leather lashes, now harsh, now fond, and the trails of fur, ice, tongue and fingers all come together in perfect, synchronized rhythm. Everything blends into a symphony of teasing, endless pleasure.

Is it twenty? It seems more, yet it's never enough. By the time he's finished, I've lost count. Sensation after sensation tingles through me. My bewildered nerve endings struggle to keep up, trying to tell hot from cold, sharp from soft, pain from pleasure.

Finally each new blow feels the same.

I give up trying to work it out and simply endure and enjoy, treating each new caress whether it stings or soothes as an act of love, a precious link between us, a contact only he can give.

At last I'm too tearful for any more and he releases me and carries me, trembling all over, to the bed.

And somehow, when the pleasure finally comes, after he's slowly made love, murmuring into my ear, kissing my neck, touching me softly all over my breasts that are still aflame from his whip, my climax is so intense I dissolve into sobs, crying into his shoulder like a lost soul.

This has been deeply, achingly intense. I curl up in his arms for the rest of the night, whimpering whenever he moves. And more than once when I wake suddenly, I catch him gazing at me, his eyes glittering in the darkness as if he can't get enough of the sight of my face.

* * * *

Next morning he's nowhere to be seen. Sunlight streams into our rooms but I'm alone in the bed. I shower quickly, slip into pale linen crop pants and a silky top and sandals and go on deck.

Early swimmers are already gathering around the pool and bulky business types are ordering breakfast. At last Cade joins me and we eat on deck out in the sunshine.

Guests come and go, greeting us and talking about themselves with the cheerful ease of people on holiday. We get no chance to talk.

At one point Sir Gerald sits with us, and I decide to pry while Cade is talking to out of earshot with a group of politicians.

"Cade's told me very little about himself, Sir Gerald. What was he like when he was young?"

The older man beams at me, his blue eyes crinkling at the corners, rather like his son's. "We all had a rough time after my wife went. Then came the terrible teens… He was quite a handful there for a while. They both were. Mind you, I was out of the country on diplomatic business for most of the time. Izaak looked after them then."

He talks easily, like he tells this story often. He looks at me in mock despair. "He was welcome to them."

I stare at him, appalled that he's so blasé at missing his son's youth. "So you saw very little of him while he was growing up?"

I try to keep my voice neutral but it's an effort.

He gives me a small, superior smile then waves his hand round at the crowded decks. "My career had to come first, naturally. Diplomacy is very demanding."

I glance round at the millionaires lazing on the sun loungers. "Yes, I can see." I'm careful to keep a straight face.

He gives me a sharp look. "Then there was all that trouble with Fran." He shakes his head sadly.

Fran again. Now I'm getting somewhere. "There were problems?"

He rolls his eyes. "She went to pieces, just like her mother before her. All that time in clinics. Rehab, you'd call it. Cade pulled her round eventually. When he sets his mind to something, he always succeeds." He glances at me with a hint of real pride. "Chip off the old block there. Ah, here's the Ambassador. Angelo, allow me to present Tunis, a former dancer. She's here with my son."

* * * *

Now Cade's slipped away again. At last I find him pacing the upper deck, phone in hand. When he sees me his eyes gleam as he draws me into his arms. "Did I ever tell you how beautiful you look in the morning?"

I smile into his neck and press against him, drinking in his delicious aroma of costly aftershave laced with a hint of male animal. "How would you know? You never wake up with me."

He kisses me gently. "I like to watch you sleep. But this morning I had business."

His phone buzzes again. He answers it with his arm still firmly around my waist.

I feel his arm stiffen.

Something's wrong.

After a few seconds the call ends abruptly. He turns to me with a strange expression. "That was Nera. I have to leave. Something's come up. You must stay here."

Nera again. I stare at him, horrified. "No. *No.* You can't do that. I'm yours for the week, remember?"

I've known him ten days. It feels like ten lifetimes. And soon we'll part, maybe forever. I scan his face, panic rising. "We can't lose our last few days together. I don't care what's happened."

He puts his arms around me and holds me tight. "Trust me, Tunis. It's better this way. You'll be safe."

I can hardly hear what he's saying. I can only see the pain in his eyes, mingled with something else — *fear.* It sears my heart. "I'm safe with you. I'm coming with you. You need me."

His face contracts, and he closes his eyes for a moment. I've never seen him like this. It's terrifying.

When he speaks again, his voice is husky. "You're right. I do need you. That's the trouble. That's why you'll be safer here." He swallows, like he's coming to a decision. "Okay. You can come too. Don't say I didn't warn you."

Chapter Twenty-Six

On the flight back, Cade is moody. He refuses to tell me what's wrong.

Lisa, our hapless attendant, hovers with coffee and drinks, but he waves her away with an impatient twitch of his fingers.

She gives me pitying looks. She thinks we've had a fight.

The minute she leaves us, we do fight.

He takes my phone out of his pocket. "Still missing this?"

Startled, I stare at him. "Yes. Can I have it back?"

"No."

I feel a sudden chill. "Why not?"

"Let's check your texts."

I stare in shocked, silent outrage as he scrolls through the list.

He starts reading them aloud, his voice calm. *"Just landed at Tenerife. Janice getting a suntan... Dad.* Here's another. *Call me. Call me. Call me... Mel."*

He glances at me, his expression blank. "All hers say much the same..." He scrolls farther down the list, his jaw rigid. "Here's two more. *Jake's dying to tell you. We're going to blow the Fitzlean empire sky-high.*" He pauses, his face expressionless, then resumes. "*This is urgent – we can't do this without you. Please call... M.*"

He looks at me, thoughtful as a broody poet, his eyes burning into mine. "Anything to say?"

My heart sinks. "Would it? Blow you sky-high, I mean? If it came out you weren't there that night?"

"Why do you ask?" His voice is soft – too soft.

I frown. "Well... *Would it?*" I wait for him to explain, dismiss my fears with a wisecrack and a grin. Nothing happens. His expression stays blank.

"See what I mean?" He slips my phone back in his pocket. "The inner reporter never sleeps."

* * * *

At Beat Hall preparations are now under way for the coming festival. As we come in to land, we can see the grounds already teeming with activity. Staging is being erected and cabling laid. Recording vans and container trucks are gathering on a remote field, out of sight of the main house.

On the short drive through the grounds, Cade relaxes a little as he talks about the festival.

For two weeks each year, Beat Hall becomes Izzy's domain as he spins the magic that brings in the crowds. The grounds here will be flooded with a sea of people, the night sky bright with dazzling color, the ancient house transformed into a living backdrop for acts from all around the world.

It will delight thousands of fans, launch careers – and make a staggering amount of money.

On the drive, Izzy's waiting to greet us. "Hi, you guys. See the ol' man?"

He and Cade exchange a few terse remarks about Sir Gerald and his circle. When Izzy offers to show us round, Cade shakes his head. "I've got to find Nera. Catch up with you later."

I'm happy to stay and bask in Izzy's lazy Southern drawl. First he leads me over to meet a group of technicians and as we walk around, I marvel at the scale of the event taking shape here. Catering, toilets, amusements and emergency tent cover will be provided for thousands of people. It sounds like a logistical nightmare, but he makes it all sound like an afternoon picnic.

At last we come back onto the drive and he looks me over, his blue gaze shrewd. "How's tricks, anyway? Aria sends her best. She says you gotta come again real soon. She wants dance lessons." He breaks off with a frown. "Hey, honey, you okay? You look kinda peaky. Mr. Big Cat not treatin' you so good?"

I sigh. "I'm fine. Well, I would be without Nera pulling his strings. What is it about her, Izzy? What's her hold over him?"

He scratches his head. "Hey, babe, this is heavy. Cade oughta tell you all this hisself. Tell ya what... Ya seen that photo in his office? The one by that hotshot newsman, the one with the kids?"

"The Nathan Gemmell?" I frown, puzzled.

"Yep, that one. Take a good look at it, honey. Says it all."

* * * *

In the main house I learn that Cade and Nera are downstairs. I feel an instant pulse of heat. *Downstairs* means the cellars, and to me that means just one thing — the dungeon.

As the service elevator speeds downward, I feel the old thrill pulse through me. Maybe there's still time for another session, before the end of our time together…

As the doors slide open, the dungeon is gloomy, the only light a soft glow from a room at the far end. It slants over the walls, gleaming on the rails of whips and floggers, glinting off the metal hooks and chains.

Ignoring a distinct pulse from somewhere down below, I hurry past them. I pull up short as I make out angry voices and catch my name.

Cade and Nera are arguing — about me.

"It's the best place. You want her out of reach, and I want a display. It's a no-brainer. And in two days their deadline's past. Look, I've got a lot riding on this, Cade. What's your problem? She's trained now, isn't she?" Nera sounds exasperated.

Cade's deep tone is barely audible. I strain to catch the words.

"Not in the sense you mean."

"You had her in the dungeon two hours a night. What were you doing? Embroidery?"

"It's complicated. She's delicate. "

"*Delicate*? She's a dancer, for fuck's sake. She's strong as an ox. You should have left her to me. I'm used to vanillas."

He's saying something else. Slowly his voice gets louder. "I can't do this. Not with her. You don't understand. She's too intense. I might lose it." He adds something else, too low for me to hear.

Whatever it is, it's a game-changer. It stops Nera in her tracks.

After a long pause, her voice comes again. She sounds flat, defeated. "*Shit*. So that's it. Then we're screwed."

What's he saying about me?

I push open the door and step into the room. They stare, their faces twin masks of shock.

"What's all this? Why are you screwed?"

Nera gives an angry snort. "You tell her. If you don't, I will."

Ice clutches at my stomach. "Tell me what? That you're lovers?"

For a second Cade looks bemused. "*What?* No, nothing like that. Nera's her professional name. This is Fran, my sister."

His sister? My startled brain races to assemble scattered fragments of conversation. *All that time in clinics. Rehab, you'd call it...*

She went to pieces after her mother's crash and Cade and Izzy put her back together. No wonder Nera's so weird.

Poor girl.

Sympathy mingled with deep relief floods through me. "*Fran?* I'd no idea. I'm so pleased to meet you."

Nera scowls. "It's a secret, for fuck's sake. Don't tell anybody. We keep our professional lives separate." She glances at Cade. "I'll tell her the rest. He wasn't in charge of the club that night. I was. It was my first night, and I overdid things. The girl threatened to sue. Cade took the rap to protect me."

She fixes me with a look of venom. "And your so-called friends are trying to expose him. If they do, we're both finished—maybe you too. They're looking for you. They want to slot their exposé into the end of the film you're making so it airs too late for us to stop it. But your contract states you've got to give the okay or they can't go ahead. Cade wants you kept out of the way."

"Why?"

Cade looks stony. "You're too loyal. You'll give in. It's simpler to keep you out of reach."

I glare at him. "It's simpler to trust me, surely?"

His cynical glance warns me that aspect of our relationship still needs some work.

Nera's impatient now. "I've offered to hide you here for a couple of days until after the deadline, but he refuses to do it."

I frown. "Why?"

They exchange a look. Cade speaks directly to me, his voice low. "She's set up a dun-cam."

"A *what*?"

Nera gives an impatient wave of her hand. "A live feed on the Internet. Mine's called 'The Lair of the Panther'." She breaks off and her brow wrinkles in a worried frown. The sultry crimson lips droop a little. "Cade's booked for the opening set but our professional sub's off sick, and he won't use you."

My heart skips a beat. "Why not?"

Nera snorts. "He's in love with you."

For a moment we're suspended in space and time as I stare at him and wait for him to deny it.

Nothing happens. "You are?"

His face is like stone. "Yes."

"And you won't do this?"

"Not with you."

I gaze at him, my heart full. "Why not?"

He pauses, his eyes full of pain. "Because I want it too much. That's why."

I touch my cheek to his. "Then I want it too."

"You don't understand, Tunis. It's a bullwhip. It's—"

"A stock whip. You told me." I kiss him on the jaw. "More for effect than contact." I kiss him again. "With you at one end and me at the other. What's wrong with that?"

He looks down at me in a daze. "Everything, damn it."

He loves me. I wind my arms around his neck and I feel his arms fold around me. As he pulls me close, everything sings.

I glance at Nera. "When do we start?"

She gasps then claps her hands. "Thanks, Tunis. You're a star."

With the decision made, Cade and his sister become brisk and professional. Their matter-of-fact instructions take my breath away and make me pulse with excitement. Part of the time I'll be chained at the wrists and ankles. At other times, I'll be free to dodge and move about.

In his presence I'm to be respectful and graceful at all times. If I make too much noise, I'll be gagged. Rest and comfort breaks will be frequent.

As we build up footage, earlier film will fill in when we're off set. At night I get a longer break.

I'll be masked, Cade in costume. Out of shot behind a glass screen, assistants will watch in case of emergency.

I sign a new contract, submit to a final medical and by evening, we're ready to start. Masked, oiled and wearing only wrist and ankle cuffs and a thin body harness, I pose center stage to await my first encounter with the Panther.

At Nera's signal, the lights dim, drums roll and he appears.

He looks absolutely terrifying.

It's the first time since that fateful night I've faced him in his own territory. I'm rooted to the spot. It's not just the costume. Something about him seems different — taller, more powerful, more menacing. Beneath the hood, his eyes glitter. They hold mine in a steady, unblinking gaze.

He's a stranger but also disturbingly, thrillingly familiar.

He takes up a stance with his legs apart, arms crossed. A fearsome whip is looped under one arm. It coils at his hip like a serpent.

He's naked to the waist, his body oiled and gleaming. His armlets, loincloth and thigh cuirasses are all in black leather. Power crackles around him like static, sending my senses into free-fall, robbing me of breath.

I'm used to theater. I know it's all fake. But oddly, now that we're in costume, the threat seems real.

This is dangerous.

"Kneel." His voice is deep and stirring.

I hold his gaze, my head high. "No."

My voice sounds loud in the sudden silence. There's a short pause.

Excited whispers come from beyond the glass. I ignore them.

"Kneel." His voice is louder and has a note of impatience. I see his hand twitch.

"No."

The whip lands with a terrifying crash near my toes, making me jump. I clench my jaw and raise my chin.

"*Kneel.*"

I'm not up to this? Who says? "Make me."

With a sudden twist of his body, the whip and his arm uncoil as one, fast and lethal as a snake. I feel a searing pain at the backs of my legs as the whip wraps around my hamstrings. He jerks his arm back, and I sink to my knees with a shriek.

In a split second, the whip is withdrawn and lands again, this time around my waist, the end snaking up between my breasts with a curling sting that makes me catch my breath.

At a burst of applause, he coils the whip and nods to the assistants, who race in to chain me into position for his display. I'm hauled up between the rings, arms splayed, feet pulled wide apart and the Panther begins in earnest.

I've no idea how long it goes on. All I know is the blows and the lithe, athletic being they flow from are one and the same. The sound is far worse than the sting. I guess he's using every ounce of his skill to spare me, the crash of the whip coming mainly from its contact with the walls and the floor.

Soon I'm released to move freely, and I dart and twist to avoid him. The onlookers love this. But the whip's flicking tail licks and snakes everywhere, even at the hands of an expert, and somehow each hissing stroke echoes in my groin and sets up an agonizing ache.

Soon I'm burning up with arousal. I crave each new blow, praying the jolt will grant me release.

I'm eternally denied.

At last he coils the whip, walks over and presents me with the phallic-shaped handle.

We've gone over this. At the end of each display, I'm supposed to kiss it in token respect.

I jerk my head away.

For a moment or two, the invisible onlookers hold their breath. Then he turns abruptly and strides off the stage to a chorus of shouts and applause.

There's no real audience, only passing technicians and assistants, but even they're impressed.

He's a star.

I slump forward in my chains, exhausted.

At that moment the lights dim to signal the start of a six-hour break. My bonds are unfastened, and I'm led away for a rest.

My first day is over.

* * * *

"What the hell do you think you're doing?" Cade, freshly showered and furious, is pacing our room. Even without the Panther costume, he's almost as fierce as the real thing.

I'm drenched in sweat and still shaky. I shrink into the chair and sigh. "They want a show, don't they? So we give them one."

He pauses by my chair, his face like thunder, his bathrobe a poor cover for his huge, twitching erection. *This affects him too.*

"You're supposed to submit at the end of a session. That's the convention. Subs don't answer back."

"Well, guess what? This one does." I glare up at him, my nerves a riot of strange, unexpected emotions. I'm angry too, and I'm aroused — possibly more than he is.

Maybe he knows. Maybe that's *why* he is.

Since we started doing this, I've been consumed with lust. It fires my will, gives me strength.

And now it wants satisfaction.

I glance down and lick my lip suggestively, rising slowly to bar his way. He stares at me as I press against him, thrilling to the feel of his powerful erection jutting between us. I sigh as his arms fold around me.

Right now he's got everything I need…

As I move in his arms, his eyes fill with heat and his lips part. When he speaks, his voice is deep and edged with menace. "I know what you want. So do I, but you'll have to wait. You chose to do this, but I make the rules. If you defy me in one way, I'll discipline you in another. No sex until afterward. Save your strength for show time. You're going to need it."

"*What?* You can't mean it?"

He takes my face in his hands and touches my face and neck with his lips—slow, tiny kisses soft as whispers while down below I'm burning up with rage and frustration.

He smiles, his eyes calm, his erection anything but— a cruel reminder who's in charge here. "I do mean it. And right now you need a shower."

It takes a while and it leaves both of us more aroused than ever, but he stands firm—in both senses.

Afterward he makes me eat a little. Later in bed he curls round me until I sleep.

* * * *

The following day our sessions start for real. This time there'll be only brief comfort breaks.

It's so intense that during massage, I sleep soundly. Even a few minutes are enough to refresh and revive me, help me face each new onslaught.

Sometimes he pauses to give me a rest, letting the whip slide over my skin in a teasing caress, firing my arousal even higher. I lean back in my chains—my eyes closed, my breath ragged—taking long juddering breaths while he comes close and whispers low to avoid the microphones. "Are you okay? Safeword if you have to."

I hiss back, my lips barely moving. "I'm fine. Don't stop."

Another time he moves in again, his eyes glittering behind his mask, his jaw rigid. "For fuck's sake, Tunis, this is not a contest. Submit, damn it."

But whenever he challenges me to kneel, I still refuse.

Nera reports our battle of wills is a big hit. Viewing figures soar.

She even shows me a grudging respect. "You've got more than guts, Tunis. You're a genius."

I vow to redouble my defiance.

Prove him wrong. I can do this.

Last year, an eternity ago, the Panther and all he stood for terrified me. Now something else terrifies me—my hunger for him. Whenever he appears, I quiver with need.

It flares the moment he arrives on stage, and it becomes my secret weapon. It fires my will and sustains me throughout his attack. During our breaks he tries to make me see sense—my defiance is dangerous—I'll overtire. I'll do myself lasting damage. It has to end.

But tonight I sense a new edge to his manner. I brace myself. As he pulls his arm from behind his back, I feel my stomach clench.

He's brought two whips.

I've no time to prepare as he unleashes both, unfurling a ferocious mass of hissing leather. One grips me around the ankle while the other snakes in hot, searing coils around my waist.

For a second, his body poses with athletic grace as the lashes slide harmlessly away then he draws them back and launches again.

His skill is dazzling. An excruciating display leaves me panting and running with sweat as applause erupts from beyond the glass. He turns and bows, his chest heaving while I brace myself for his next assault.

He signals to the assistants to chain me up again then he steps back and takes aim with both whips together, the ends curling in precise, agonizing symmetry, coiling first over my breasts in stinging spirals of fire then around my waist and thighs.

Between the double blows, he pauses just long enough for me to recover then lunges again, his body connecting so beautifully to the line of the snaking whips that I can only look on in wonder.

It's like the pain comes directly from somewhere deep inside him and the terrifying whips are just extensions of his will, jets of flame launched from his gut.

But now I realize where the blows are heading. I'm helpless in their path, hauled wide open by the taut, merciless chains as the ends of the lashes edge, infinitely slowly, up the insides of my legs.

With terrifying precision, the snaking tips curl at last into the apex of my thighs, slide away and surge again. Moments later, with a final, intimate flick, they meet in my cleft and my orgasm erupts like a volcano.

I buck and sob, my juices running in streams down my thighs. He coils the whips and calmly looks on, arms folded. Assistants race on to loosen the chains and I sink slowly to my knees. He moves up close and instead of the whip handles, he presents his erection, sheathed in unforgiving black leather.

Exhausted, limp, drained of resistance, I lean forward and kiss. The gleam of triumph in his eyes is the last thing I see before the room slides sideways.

Chapter Twenty-Seven

Cade is gazing down at me, his face gaunt with worry. "*Tunis.* You scared me half to death. Are you okay?"

"Of course she's okay. She just fainted. That's all. No surprise after all that. I've never seen anything like it." Nera appears over his shoulder. She sounds gruff, but she looks worried too.

Brother and sister exchange a look then Nera quietly ushers the masseuse out of the door. "We'll give you a moment."

I'm lying in the massage room, the small recovery room just off the dungeon. I gaze up at him, my heart full. Our display is over. Now I can rest.

He's peeled off the mask and his hair stands out in dark, sweat-soaked curls all round his head. The lighting in here is harsh after the soft, atmospheric glow in the dungeon. The sharp light etches hollows in his cheeks and gleams on his oiled, powerful shoulders.

"Was I okay?" I manage a shaky smile.

A flicker of emotion crosses his face, and he touches his lips to mine. "More than okay. You were sensational."

"You too." I sit up, clutching the sheet over my sweat-streaked body. It soaks through in dark patches.

His face contracts in alarm. "Hey, easy. How do you feel?"

"Like I've been under a steamroller."

He grins and touches his lips to my forehead. "Me too. Don't ever let me agree to another bullwhip session with you — not before I get a pacemaker fitted, anyway."

* * * *

Back in our rooms he runs a deep, scent-filled bath. I try to protest. I can walk perfectly well. But it's fun being spoiled.

We lie together in the water, weary but blissful, saying little. When we finally get out, he swathes me in towels, scoops me up and carries me into his room, laying me reverently on the quilt like some precious object.

His wet, glorious body looms over me like some ancient sculpture, perfect, honed — his erection jutting into me whenever he draws close.

"You've not eaten much today. I can order some food. Are you hungry?"

I bite my lip. *Yes, but not for food.*

His eyes gleam, like he knows. "Every time we met on stage, I wanted to eat you whole. Now I'll do just that."

He parts my legs and drops kisses along my thighs and across my belly, making me shiver. Soon his eager mouth fastens on my groin, and I lie back and groan as heat courses through me. Another climax, after such intense emotion and so many sensations, rockets through me in seconds. As my spasms die away, he flips me over and hauls me up by the hips. His erection juts, burning hot against my opening, still slick with juices and pulsing with need.

He pauses, letting its girth and its heat torment me, teasing me with small, impatient thrusts as my muscles haul at him, willing him to fill me.

Instead he leans over, his breath hot on my neck and takes firm hold of my heavy breasts, plumping them with his hands and squeezing my nipples until I whimper.

"A word of advice. Next time you face a Dom with a bullwhip, be very" — he plunges inside then slowly withdraws — "*very*" — he lunges again, harder this time, making me cry out in delight and shock — "careful what you say. And if he says *submit*" — he plunges harder, hauling my hips even higher so I moan aloud — "you do it. Or you might just find yourself being fucked like this."

With a few strokes more, he pauses then comes with a shout, filling my belly with honeyed heat. It seeps into my weary muscles and is instantly followed by wave upon wave of deep, contented sleep.

* * * *

"I once dated Brad Pitt." I smile up at the ceiling.

"In your dreams." Cade is lying next to me, his arm cradling my head. We're still panting, limbs laced together from our latest encounter.

It's nearly dawn. We've slept, made love and slept again. Now, in the small hours, we're lying together, contented and idle. We're playing a game.

"I once bought a hardware store."

I giggle, ludicrously happy. "Nonsense. And don't pretend you like DIY."

He grins briefly. "You're right. That's untrue. I fancied one of the assistants." He kisses my cheek. "And I bought the whole chain."

I kiss the edge of his armpit, thrilling to his warm, animal smell. "I once kissed a frog. But he never became a prince."

"No? You amaze me." He nuzzles my neck. "I wanted to whip your ass the second I met you. That was before I masterminded your career so I could."

I stare up at the ceiling as his words sink in. Slowly the smile fades from my face and with it, my tide of happiness. I sit up and peer at him in the dim light from our single bedside lamp. "You did *what*?"

He smiles lazily up at me. "You heard."

I stare down at him, numb with shock. "That's untrue, right?"

He shuffles up on the pillows, his long, naked body glowing and glorious. "No, it's true. Why? What's the matter?"

"You masterminded my *career*? How?" Ice seeps through me.

His smile twists into scorn at the corner of his mouth. "How do you think? I own the network. Audience figures can be massaged, producers told whom to hire and when. It was just a matter of time."

I spring off the bed and search through the rails for my clothes. I bring an armful back with me and start to dress with swift, angry movements.

"Tunis, what are you doing?" He leaps off the bed. "Are you going somewhere? At this hour?"

I don't trust myself to speak. I fasten my jeans, step into my trainers and shrug on my jacket. As I reach for my case, I snap it open and pile in the rest of my things, the gowns and underwear all jumbled together, the shoes stuffed in anyhow.

"I'm leaving. I'm horrified you did that."

Tears are close. I fight them off. "I've worked hard at my job. I thought I was good at it. I thought I was a success. I thought I was bringing you something— talent, ambition, success—whatever. I thought I was somebody. But Janice was right all along. I'm a nobody."

I glance back at him from the doorway. "Thanks for reminding me."

His face contorts with shock. "*What?* You *are* a success. They even watch you abroad."

"Yes, but you did it all. I'm just a...toy." I slam my case shut and haul it off the bed. "What is it with you, this mania for control?"

He bars my way. "What are you doing? You can't go anywhere now."

I glare at him. "No? Watch me. I can't stay here. I've got a job to do. I'm wanted in post-production. Next time, get yourself a blow-up doll. It should be easy enough to control that. And find one you can whip."

I blunder past him, snatching up my bag as I go.

"Wait." His eyes flash. Now he's angry too. "Take no notice of Janice. You're not a nobody. Don't *ever* say that about yourself. And here, you'll need this." He tosses something over to me.

By some miracle, I catch it.

It's my phone.

I slip out of the main door into an eerie gray world. It's nearly dawn. The park's shrouded in thick white mist full of weird echoes, muffled birdcalls and odd rustling noises. Treetops poke through like islands in a lake.

I trudge along the drive in the early chill. My mind's still blank, but I think vaguely that on the main road I might hitch a lift to a town. There I can pick up a taxi, train — whatever.

At that moment I hear the crunch of gravel as a large, darkened car draws up beside me.

Cade.

I try to hurry, but it's hopeless. My case is too heavy. "Miss Vale?"

I pause and turn as Mason, Cade's driver, calls after me. "I'm to drive you wherever you want to go, miss. Mr. Fitzlean insists. He's concerned for your safety."

I glare at him. "Is he in that car?"

"No, miss. Where are you headed?"

I hesitate. I'm miles from anywhere. It's probably the best option. "That's kind of you, Mason, but I'm going back to London. If you could drop me at the nearest railway station?"

"What address in London, miss?"

Impatiently I rattle off the address of Mel's flat in Hammersmith. He turns and opens the passenger door, his face impassive. "If you'd get in, miss."

* * * *

Mason's a fast, efficient driver. In just over two hours, we're blending effortlessly into the early traffic on the Chiswick Flyover and heading for central London. Without being told, Mason takes the north exit to make the right turn for Hammersmith and soon we're nosing into the alleyway outside Mel's tiny apartment.

A tousled Mel answers the door in pajamas, toothbrush in hand. "*Tunis.* Where have you been? We've been worried sick."

I turn and wave to Mason, still sitting in the car on the street below. Lifting a gloved hand, he slowly draws away.

Mel stares after him. "Who's that?"

"He gave me a lift. Sorry to barge in, Mel. I need somewhere to stay for a few days."

"Who is it?" In the tiny kitchen, Ben looks up from a sizzling pan full of bacon and eggs. "Hey, good timing. Take a pew."

"I don't want anything to eat. Just somewhere to sleep." I shake my head at his polite offer to share breakfast. I accept a small glass of juice.

"You look terrible." Mel scans my face. "Have you been with the Panther all this time? What's he done to you?"

I sigh. "Please, Mel, not now. I'm fine, just tired. That's all. So, can I stay?"

Mel throws an arm around me. "Sure you can. Take the spare room. You'll have to squeeze in with Ben's stuff. He's moving in later this week."

"You're together at last? I'm so glad for you. Mel, can I talk to you for a minute?"

Mel arches an eyebrow at Ben. "Girl-talk, Ben. Okay?"

When he's gone, Mel fixes me with a worried stare. "What?"

Rapidly I explain about Cade and his sister, and why he was covering for her. Mel's eyes glow. "Wow. That's terrific. His *sister*?"

I take a deep breath. "But he wants it kept quiet. Please don't use it. And don't tell anybody, not even Ben—as a favor to me."

She looks aghast. "For Pete's sake, why ever not?"

I want to tell her that I love him, and it's the last thing that will ever be in my power to give him, but I'm too shaky. "It's for Cade. It's just... I owe him. It's...complicated." I break off and my eyes fill with tears.

She's frowning. "You're *keen* on him?"

I nod. "Yes. Truly."

"As in—madly, deeply? The real deal?"

I nod again and bury my head in her neck.

She pats me on the cheek, hands me a tissue and gives me one of her tough, pale smiles. "Okay, done. We'll drop it."

* * * *

Two hours later, after a shower, a nap and a reviving cup of coffee, I hurry through the busy streets to the small cluster of warehouses and workshops housing our editing studio. Waving to the technicians, I pick my way past delivery crates and banks of recording equipment to the small, familiar group of people in a booth at the end of the building.

They're like family. It seems a long time since I saw them.

"Hi, stranger. Ready for the big finale?" For once Jake's relaxed and happy. "Sonja's worried about you."

"You're together?"

Ben claps him on the back. "Yep. I'm moving in with Mel and Sonja's moved in with Jake. Happy families all round. You?"

"Free as a bird." I avoid Mel's eye. How can I tell them I've got no plans, no prospects and never even had a career?

"So, the voiceover. Where do I start?"

* * * *

For the next few days I sit in a soundproofed booth in front of a small screen and a script and read aloud. Sometimes I falter when my narrative touches on times when I recall what Cade and I were doing in other parts of the Hall.

The hardest parts are when I see him on screen. Several times Ben's voice breaks into my headphones. "Cut, cut. Sorry, Tunis. We lost you there. Go again."

The work's tiring and slow, but it stops me thinking.

During breaks I chat to the engineers and peer over their shoulders at the screens. They're on a tight schedule. Post-production usually takes months but the team here's got just three weeks. It'll be a marathon. Most of it's on computer, but some of Jake's footage is old-style film and takes even longer. Discarded pieces roll about on the floor in curls like carpenter's shavings.

Idly I pick them up and hold them to the light. One shows the roofs and turrets of Beat Hall, another shows blurred close-ups of Garth Delaney leering at Mel. There's even a strip of interior shots of Cade's office. I peer more closely and Izzy's lazy drawl drifts through my mind.

That photo in his office? Take a good look at it, honey. Says it all.

I hold the strip up to the light and there it is—the Gemmell photo of the two children.

So what's it saying?

Jake walks over, curious. "Thought I'd get a print off that strip. It's the only way I'll ever get my own copy if Mr. Megabuck's bought up all the rights."

I frown at the picture, trying to see what it was that had caught the photographer's eye.

A boy and a girl sitting on a bank... The boy is reaching out to the little girl in a simple, protective gesture. In the space between them is a blur of shapes — an overturned car, police, maybe an ambulance.

It makes a graceful, striking composition. But that's all I see.

It must be something here. "Jake, can we enhance this?"

Ten minutes later I'm staring at an enlarged, clarified section of the picture on his computer screen. I flip the image so it shows the car upright. Inside a figure slumps at the wheel. The car bonnet's badly crumpled, the marque unrecognizable, the number plate indistinct. It's short, distinctive. OPL? OPI?

I look again and something clicks into place. *It has to be…*

"Jake? Look at the number plate. It says GF1. That must be Sir Gerald's car. This is a picture of Cade and his sister at the scene of the crash that killed their mother."

Is this the final piece of the puzzle?

His mother's life was out of control, like the car that killed her.

Control… He always has to be in control, and this is why. It's the only way he feels safe.

* * * *

Somehow I survive as one day follows another, but the pain stays the same.

Other people break up. Other people survive.

Now it's my turn.

Our report's done. We deliver on time and it airs to instant acclaim. Public interest in the movie and the launch spikes. Our viewing figures hit the roof.

I even manage to say how much of a pussycat the Panther is, without saying who he is and without breaking down.

Now for the premiere.

With my voiceover finished, I go home. Janice is back now, rested and pleased to see me. There's no mention of clinics.

On the second morning, I'm sitting in the kitchen, my head in my hands, unable to face breakfast. Janice gives me a hug.

"You must eat, Tunis. Being miserable won't bring him back."

"Why should I want him back?"

I've told her nothing, but she's a good guesser.

Janice sits down next to me. "Because he's nice. He cares for the people he loves. And you love him, don't you?"

She's right. I do.

"And he'll be at the premiere, right?"

She kisses me on the cheek. "Then you're going too. Leave this to me."

* * * *

Janice may know nothing about Chinese jade, but as a former dancer herself, she knows plenty about premieres. She does me proud. On the evening of the premiere, I step onto the red carpet looking—and feeling—like a queen. The roar of the crowd and the flashing cameras tell me my stunning Millin lace gown, my matching heels and my piled hair look perfect, as does Cade's beautiful necklace with the little key—the key to his heart.

Sadly a key's not much use without the lock it fits.

I smile brightly as I mingle with the stars. I've seen so many of them *in extremis* or under a whip that it's hard to feel shy with anyone here.

Nera greets me with a tight smile. "You look ravishing, Tunis. And your report was terrific. We're all really pleased. "

She leans closer and lowers her voice to a fierce hiss. "And if we were alone, I'd slap your face. What the fuck have you *done* to him?"

She strides off before I can ask her what she means — or where he is.

Now I'm worried. What does Nera mean? *Is he ill*? I start to panic. If he's not here, I may never see him again.

Soon I'm swept upstairs by the press of stars making their way to the circle balcony overlooking the auditorium. As I walk through the curtains, the crowd thins out at either side to reveal the deep cavern of the theater yawning below.

I'm suspended in space over a sea of faces. The audience clap and roar approval as the stars line up along the rail, me included.

Just then I see him.

He's standing a little apart, somewhere on the other side. He looks stunningly handsome in formal dress. Our eyes lock. The scene around me starts to sway then he's gone.

Oh no. He's avoiding me. I should never have come.

But I had to. I promised.

With a supreme effort, I smile down at the upturned faces. I'm just one in a bevy of stars here. My part in all this is very small. In this sea of celebrities, I don't count for very much. But the rail's swaying toward me now and the edges of my vision are starting to blot out...

"*Tunis.* Come away from the rail."

Strong arms slide around me and haul me to safety. A warm, powerful presence covers my back and a deep, familiar voice growls in my ear.

He's here.

I spin round to see him looking down at me, his eyes filled with heat.

"Where have you been? Please, please don't do this. I can't stand it. I can't stand being without you."

Eager starlets push forward to fill our places at the rail. No one's looking at us.

We stand close together, completely unnoticed in the crowd as people flow past to get to their seats before the movie starts.

He ignores them, his eyes locked on mine. "Do you really want to see this thing?"

I gaze up at him, my throat almost too tight to speak. "No."

His eyes narrow and I see the hint of a smile at the corners of his beautiful, sculpted lips. "Hungry?"

I lean up and kiss him gently on the jaw. "What do you think? It's been weeks."

His jaw line tenses. "I've got a car waiting. Your hotel or mine?"

I can hardly speak for joy. I simply stare at him. "Which is closest?"

"Does that mean…you're coming back?" His voice is husky with emotion, full of pain.

Of course I'm coming back. He's my life now. He's everything I need, everything I've ever wanted or ever will want.

But even I have limits, and he's crossed one.

I suppose, given all the things I've let him do up to now, it's a fine point. But manipulating my career is a step too far. However much I love him, he has to know I'm not a puppet.

I smile serenely and lay my cheek against his. "I'll tell you tomorrow."

As the houselights dim for the movie to start, we're already heading for the exit, hand in hand. The gleam in his eyes tells me we've a long and glorious night ahead. Maybe a lifetime — who knows?

If he asks, I'll tell him that tomorrow, too.

About the Author

Flora is married with two children and lives in the UK. She loves reading, writing, good reviews, cold, crunchy ice cream and hot, smooth movies. And especially connecting with readers — a real thrill!

Flora loves to hear from readers. You can find her contact information, website and author biography at
http://www.totallybound.com.

Home of Erotic Romance